"You could pose as my girlfriend."

Dru centered him in the crosshairs of her iciest glare. Strong men—Marines, protection agents, and some of the best pistol shooters on the planet—had wilted under that glare.

Gray didn't. In fact, since their conversation had begun, his demeanor toward her had been frank and unflinching.

"Don't you have a girlfriend currently?" Dru asked.

"I'm in between."

"Wouldn't any girlfriend of yours have a job? I can't imagine that she'd be free to trail after you five afternoons a week."

Two of the team's coaches nodded to Gray in parting as they moved toward the door. Gray lifted his chin in response. "Maybe my new girlfriend is a preschool teacher who only works in the mornings."

Dru had never—not even in elementary school when she'd done a unit called What Do You Want to Be When You Grow Up?—hoped to become anyone's preschool-teaching girlfriend. "I could be a journalist working on a story about you."

He raised an eyebrow with an air of smugness. "For days and days on end? No one would believe that, sweetheart."

"Don't call me sweetheart."

Praise for *Her One and Only*

"Dru, being the youngest Porter, is headstrong and sympathetic, and when she matches wits with Gray, their connection is as electric as their budding romance is sweet. A delightful read."—*RT Book Reviews*

"Inspirational-fiction fans can jump into the Porter world at any point and enjoy Wade's tales of heart and spirit."
—*Booklist*

"Romance readers will find this a satisfying conclusion to the PORTER FAMILY series."—*Christian Retailers + Resources*

Praise for Becky Wade

"Becky Wade creates characters readers will love."
—**Lisa Wingate**, national bestselling author of *Blue Moon Bay* and *Dandelion Summer*

"I love finding new authors, and Becky Wade is definitely one to watch. Her debut novel offers romance, laughter, and poignancy. The perfect combination for a night out with you and your book."—**Deeanne Gist**, bestselling author of *A Bride Most Begrudging* and *Love on the Line*

Books by Becky Wade

My Stubborn Heart

THE PORTER FAMILY NOVELS

Undeniably Yours
Meant to Be Mine
A Love Like Ours
Her One and Only

A BRADFORD SISTERS ROMANCE

True to You

HER ONE
AND ONLY

BECKY
WADE

BETHANYHOUSE
a division of Baker Publishing Group
Minneapolis, Minnesota

© 2016 by Rebecca Wade

Published by Bethany House Publishers
11400 Hampshire Avenue South
Bloomington, Minnesota 55438
www.bethanyhouse.com

Bethany House Publishers is a division of
Baker Publishing Group, Grand Rapids, Michigan

Printed in the United States of America

ISBN 978-0-7642-3088-2

Library of Congress Cataloging-in-Publication Data for the original edi-
tion is on file at the Library of Congress, Washington, DC.

This is a work of fiction. Names, characters, incidents, and dialogues
are products of the author's imagination and are not to be construed
as real. Any resemblance to actual events or persons, living or dead, is
entirely coincidental.

Cover design by Jennifer Parker
Cover photography by Mike Habermann Photography, LLC

17   18   19   20   21   22   23   7   6   5   4   3   2   1

For editor extraordinaire, Charlene Patterson

Thank you so much for the effort and belief
you dedicated to my novels. Your intelligence
and experience were matched only by
your kindness and enthusiasm. Your input
strengthened each story in important ways
and I'm wholeheartedly grateful to you.

PROLOGUE

Dru lifted her handgun, leveling it on Gray's stalker as she rushed forward through the crowd. The realization that she'd been outsmarted washed over her with sickening certainty. Gray was unprotected. The stalker had pistols in both hands, both barrels aimed at Gray. Had she been next to Gray, she'd have shoved him down, been able to dodge in front of him to keep him safe. But she was much too far away for that. Despair arced through her mind and heart. She was too far. He was unprotected.

"Lower your weapons," she demanded, shouldering past bystanders.

The stalker's face turned sharply in her direction, giving her a direct line of sight into facial features that were drawn and blank. Viciously cold.

The attacker kept one of the guns trained on Gray. The other pistol moved, with chilling deliberation, until its barrel aimed squarely at Dru.

"No!" Gray yelled.

The stalker's attention returned to Gray, fingers whitening on the triggers.

Dru fired.

Her bullet met its mark.

But so did the stalker's. *So did the stalker's.*

Ammunition tore into tender flesh, destroying the muscle and bone and organs in its path. A screaming denial the color of red obliterated Dru's thoughts.

Furious, she fired again.

CHAPTER
ONE

Dru Angelica Porter was a former Marine, a black belt in jiu-jitsu, a national pistol-shooting champion, and an experienced executive protection agent for Dallas's most prestigious security company. She was also about to meet her new client. A new client who would, just like all her past clients, be too busy trying to process the fact that she was female to give a hoot about her qualifications.

When people heard the term *bodyguard*, they very predictably imagined big, muscle-bound guys in suits and sunglasses, with wires coiling up from their shirts into earpieces.

Dru wasn't big or muscle-bound. Today's "suit" consisted of a pewter-colored leather jacket, closely fitted, with several creatively placed zippers and a collar that turned up behind her neck. High-quality white shirt. Slim black trousers. Heels. Her sunglasses were stashed in her purse. No wire coiled into an earpiece.

She was an executive protection agent à la the new millennium.

She made her way down the hallway that led to the administrative offices for the NFL's Dallas Mustangs. The Mustangs' complex, which also housed the team's practice field, gym, and a physical therapy wing, had been decorated, without a great deal of creativity, in the Mustangs' colors. A carpet of light blue trimmed in hunter green and white absorbed her footfalls. The gleaming ivory walls sported horizontal green and blue stripes, as well as framed action shots of the team.

Go Mustangs! the decor seemed to shout. *Rah, rah, rah! Go, fight, win, team!*

She paused to peer at one of the photos. Confetti laced a brightly lit sky behind the team as they hoisted the Lombardi Trophy. The season before last, the Mustangs had won the Super Bowl. Dru frowned slightly at the image, which showed the players with sweaty hair and big grins and hastily donned hats and t-shirts pronouncing them the champs. No doubt she'd find all this team spirit more charming if she actually *liked* the Mustangs.

Like any good Texan, she was a born and bred Cowboys fan. She'd always viewed the Mustangs, a relatively new franchise team and the Cowboys' crosstown rivals, the way one might view an upstart in-law who arrived at a family reunion and ate all the sheet cake.

Her gaze traced across the photo before coming to a stop on the face of her new client. Gray Fowler, famed Mustangs' tight end, battle-hardened warrior, object of a million infatuations, was not the client she'd have chosen for her first executive protection assignment after the disaster in Mexico.

Celebrities who'd reached Gray Fowler's level of fame could be egotistical, bossy, and unmanageable. Athletes of his caliber were sometimes full of testosterone and stupid machismo. Add the two together and—no. They did not equal Dru's dream client. Any type of business-person, even the brash, hard-charging type who never set aside their smartphone, would have been preferable. A politician? Fine. The teenage daughter of a billionaire who needed to be taken to field hockey practice after school? Sure.

Since Mexico, for the past year and a half, she'd been riding a desk job at Sutton Security's downtown Dallas office. It had taken her longer than she'd expected to rehabilitate her body. To put her life back together. To earn back the complete trust of her boss, Anthony Sutton. The backward step on her career ladder had dealt a blow to both her professional aspirations and her pride. She'd been itching for, praying for, waiting for this chance to get back out in the field and prove her capability.

So she *would be* fulfilling her protective responsibilities toward Gray Fowler expertly, doggedly, and exactly by the book. She drew in a slow, determined breath and straightened her posture. Gray Fowler had decimated the baddest defensive players the NFL could serve up. But he'd yet to meet the likes of her. Woe to him if he got in her way.

She knocked on the door of the team's GM at exactly two o'clock. An administrative assistant ushered her into a spacious office filled with at least twelve people and five conversations.

One group of executives thronged the centrally positioned desk. Another had gathered on the room's left. On

the right, she caught sight of Big Mack, her co-worker
at Sutton. An African-American man in his early forties, Mack looked every inch the bodyguard stereotype.
Unless one knew him, one would never guess that his
two tween daughters had gotten their gentle giant of a
father hooked on the Disney Channel and the musical
stylings of 5 Seconds of Summer.

Big Mack smiled at her and motioned her forward
with a large paw of a hand. "Afternoon, Dru. How you
been?"

"Afternoon, Mack. I've been well. You?"

"Can't complain." He stepped to the side, giving Dru
her first glimpse of Gray Fowler. Their agency's newest
client was sitting on a small sofa, leaning back, one hand
tucked casually behind his head. He'd focused his attention up and to the side and was in conversation with a
fellow player who stood at the sofa's end.

Fowler had the profile of a gladiator, no prettiness
to it whatsoever. His corded neck gave way to the hard,
clean line of his jaw. His skin was lightly tanned, his lean
cheeks marked with a five-o'clock shadow. He kept his
dark brown hair short on the sides, slightly longer on top.

Dru had done her best to study him, both through
the information provided by her agency and through
her own private research. Very few details existed about
his childhood. She'd been able to learn only that he had
a younger brother and sister and that he'd overcome a
mysteriously rocky start in small-town Mullins, Texas.
He'd then parlayed his athletic ability into a star turn
at Texas A&M before being drafted in the early rounds
by the Mustangs.

He was not a man who'd stumbled or bought or

lucked his way into success. He'd earned his success one tackle, catch, block, and injury at a time. His toughness, speed, and steely concentration had lifted him to his current status as one of the Mustangs' most popular players. He had a reputation with journalists as a straight talker and a reputation with entertainment reporters as a ladies' man. He'd been selected to the Pro Bowl eight times in his ten-year career, was one of the architects of the Mustangs' Super Bowl victory, and in general, broke football records as easily as other people ate cereal.

The player Gray had been talking to moved off, and Gray's face turned toward Dru. He looked squarely at her, holding himself still, his eyes glinting an unusual pale green.

He's trouble. Of all the words in the English language, those were the two that slid into her mind.

This particular client might prove even *more* difficult than the garden-variety celebrity athlete she'd been steeling herself for. Grayson Robert Fowler looked to her like a load of dark, headstrong, dangerous trouble.

He rose smoothly to his feet without breaking eye contact. She'd known before entering the room that he stood at six feet, four inches and weighed two fifty. Even so, the physical reality of his size took her back.

It wasn't common, in everyday life, to come across a person as big as he was. Beneath the Mustangs hooded sweatshirt and track pants he wore, his body was huge, his muscles ropy and hard.

Not for the first time, she wished she'd grown to a height of six feet, eight inches, like some of the WNBA stars. Instead, her three-inch heels boosted her up to five-eleven, not a quarter inch more.

"Gray," Mack said, "this is Dru Porter. She's with Sutton Security. She'll be your protective agent for the 2:00 p.m. to 10:00 p.m. shift five days a week, starting today."

Gray's face remained unmoving, as if he was waiting for someone to shout, *Just kidding, dude!* and fist bump him. Exactly as expected, he was busy trying to process the fact that she was female.

"This is Gray Fowler," Mack said to Dru, "our new client."

"Nice to meet you." She extended her hand, and Gray shook it, his grip strong and slightly calloused.

"Likewise." He had blunt cheekbones. Faint creases marked the skin at the edges of his eyes and across his forehead.

Mack edged toward the GM's desk. "I'll just go and let Mr. Morris know that Dru's arrived."

Gray stuck his hands into either side of the rectangular front pocket on his sweatshirt and took his time studying her. "You're my new bodyguard," he stated slowly.

"Executive protective agent."

"You're my new executive protective agent."

"I'm one of them, yes."

"You."

"Yes. Me." She brought her long, straight, dark hair forward over one shoulder.

"I was expecting all of the agents from Sutton Security to look like Mack."

"*All* of our clients expect the agents to look like Mack."

"You don't look like Mack."

"No."

"How old are you?"

"Twenty-six."

He scratched the side of his head, returned his hand to the pocket. "Why would Sutton Security send a woman younger than I am and half my size to protect me?"

On the one hand, his skepticism irritated her like stinging nettles. She'd faced this same sort of skepticism all her life from her three older brothers. On the other hand, his directness meant that she could address him with equal directness. She wouldn't have to waste her time on political correctness and fake politeness. "Sutton sent me because I'm qualified. I'm a former Marine, and before I became an agent I had to undergo rigorous training at Sutton Security—"

"Which included?"

"Study of armed combat, threat assessment, first aid, and lots more. On top of all that, I've been licensed by the state of Texas to do this job."

He still looked doubtful.

"Executive protection mostly requires me to use my brain," she stated, "rarely my body or my gun."

"What was your name again?"

"Dru Porter. What was yours again?"

His expression filled with a mix of humor and disbelief. "Gray Fowler."

"Ah." She gave him a small smile. "That's right."

"How do you spell your name?"

"D. R. U."

"Huh." He sized her up. "Just between you and me, Dru Porter, I'm not worried about my safety." Gray's team had hired Sutton's services, not Gray himself. "I didn't ask for protection in the first place, so if Sutton wants me to hang out with someone who looks like a model, I'm fine with it."

"I don't look like a model."

"You look exactly like a model."

"Also, I won't be *hanging out* with you. I'll be working."

"Here's my issue with you." He continued as if she hadn't spoken. "I can't have everyone knowing that a hot-looking, twenty-something girl—"

"—woman—"

"Is my bodyguard—"

"Executive protection agent."

"I'll never hear the end of it in the locker room."

Chauvinism was still alive and well. She crossed her arms and narrowed her eyes. "Your safety is my top priority, not your locker-room reputation."

"My reputation's important to me, though. And if it's important to me, it'll be important to him." He angled a shoulder toward Brian Morris, the general manager.

She wanted to tell Gray to shove his concerns about his reputation. In fact, she wished she could bark out all sorts of orders that her clients would be compelled to follow. As it was, her clients were entitled to a pesky thing called free will. She could advise them, but she couldn't force.

Compromise stunk.

"No one has to know that I'm assigned to you other than the people you decide to tell," Dru said, her voice level. "But if you want us to go that route, then you'll lose the deterring effect that agents can have. If your assailant sees that you're accompanied by agents, he or she will be less likely to attack."

"I don't care about the deterring effect."

Figured. "In that case, I can provide low-profile protection that won't give people any reason to think I'm an agent."

"You could pose as my girlfriend."

Dru centered him in the crosshairs of her iciest glare. Strong men—Marines, protection agents, and some of the best pistol shooters on the planet—had wilted under that glare.

Gray didn't. In fact, since their conversation had begun, his demeanor toward her had been frank and unflinching.

"Don't you have a girlfriend currently?" Dru asked.

"I'm in between."

"Wouldn't any girlfriend of yours have a job? I can't imagine that she'd be free to trail after you five afternoons a week."

Two of the team's coaches nodded to Gray in parting as they moved toward the door. Gray lifted his chin in response. "Maybe my new girlfriend is a preschool teacher who only works in the mornings."

She uncrossed her arms, somewhat incredulous. "Does anything about me read preschool teacher?"

"Nothing. But there's always an exception that proves the rule. You can pretend to be my unorthodox, preschool-teaching girlfriend."

Dru had never—not even in elementary school when she'd done a unit called What Do You Want to Be When You Grow Up?—hoped to become anyone's preschool-teaching girlfriend. "I think it makes far more sense for me to pose as your administrative assistant."

"I don't need an administrative assistant. I have a

housekeeper named Ashley who handles my house and my schedule for me. All the players know her."

"I could be a journalist working on a story about you."

He raised an eyebrow with an air of smugness. "For days and days on end? No one would believe that, sweetheart."

"Don't call me sweetheart."

Brian Morris stood and politely requested that everyone not a part of his scheduled 2:15 meeting clear out of the office.

The room emptied. Mack introduced Dru to Morris, then Dru settled into one of the leather chairs facing the desk. Mack opted to stand near her elbow. Gray took the remaining chair, crossing an ankle over a knee. His big athletic shoes looked brand new, as if he'd put them on for the first time an hour ago. Maybe that came with the territory for a professional football player. Women. Glory. New Nikes.

Mr. Morris's rimless glasses looked as expensive as the designer business shirt he wore. He appeared to be in his fifties, fit, with tidy auburn hair that had begun to gray and thin.

Except for more of the blue, green, and ivory carpeting, Morris's office didn't continue the *Rah! Rah!* chant. The furniture was serviceable. The lighting, fluorescent. The desk supported neat stacks of paper and three family photos. On this second Friday of November, the bright and cloudless sky beyond the windows behind Morris's desk camouflaged a cold day that wouldn't reach fifty degrees.

"Weston Kinney will be coming by later today to introduce himself," Dru told Morris. "He'll be working the 10:00 p.m. to 6:00 a.m. shift on the days that Mack and I will be working. Other agents will rotate in for us on our days off."

"Good." Morris centered a notepad in front of him, picked up a pen, then leaned back in his chair to take Dru and Mack's measure. "I wanted this chance to meet you so that we can get communication going between us. I'd like a lot of back and forth on this."

"Yes, sir," Mack agreed.

"Have you both read through the threatening letters Gray's received?" Morris asked.

"We have," Dru answered. Black 18-point Arial font printed by an inkjet printer onto plain white paper. The letters were always mailed in ordinary business envelopes that could be purchased at any Walmart. So far the fingerprints the police had salvaged from the envelopes all traced back to employees of the U.S. Postal Service. Both the mailing address and the return address were always printed onto labels in black 11-point Arial font.

"Gray, remind me how long it's been," Morris said, "since you started receiving the letters."

"More than a year." Gray appeared slightly bored, like he had a pressing game of golf to get to now that practice had wrapped up for the day.

Irritation with him simmered beneath Dru's cool facade. *Sweetheart? Really?* "I heard that you threw out the first several letters."

"Yeah. I've been getting mail from people who don't like me since college. If letters are really nasty, I hand them off to team security. If they're just ordinarily nasty, I throw them out."

"When you first started receiving letters from this individual . . ." Mack prompted.

"They were just ordinarily nasty," Gray answered. "I tossed them."

"What types of things did those early letters say?" Mack asked.

"I hate you, you're worthless." The expression Gray turned on Dru seemed to say, *What'd you think? That this job was all roses? You're not that naïve.* "They were short, just like all the letters have been. A few sentences."

Morris leaned forward, settling his forearms on his desktop. "Here at the Mustangs, we differentiate between critical comments and actual specific threats toward our players."

As did the law, Dru knew.

"Recently, the letters from this individual have turned into threats," Morris continued. "We've seen the situation escalate in other ways, too. For example, Gray used to receive the letters only at home. Lately the person who's sending the letters mails some here. Some to Gray's lake house, some to his cabin in Colorado. Even to his mother's house in Mullins."

"Do the letters arrive at the locations when you're there?" Dru asked Gray.

"Yes."

"Which is why we've come to the conclusion that this individual is stalking Gray," Morris stated. "How often did the letters come at the beginning, Gray?"

"Over the first eight or nine months, the letters came every month or two. Then it was every few weeks. Since our first preseason game, I've been receiving a letter at least once a week, sometimes more."

"Anthony Sutton told us that the letters are mailed from a variety of locations," Dru said. Anthony, the owner of their agency, had a background in special ops and wasn't the kind of person you'd want to attempt to rob in a dark alley.

"Yes," Morris answered. "Since the time Gray told us about the letters, we've been keeping record of the postmark on each envelope, as well as scanning the letters themselves before turning them over to the police. The letters have come from places as far as a four-hour drive from here in every direction. The return address is always that of the stadium where we play."

"Who have you been working with in the Dallas PD?" Mack asked.

"Detective Carlyle," Morris answered. "He's good, but he doesn't have any leads yet." He tapped his pen twice against his notepad. "Which is why we brought in Sutton Security. Until this thing is resolved, we'll all feel better knowing that Gray has protection."

Except Gray himself, according to what he'd already told her. Gray met her eyes. A trace of cynicism lit the green depths.

"Anthony Sutton mentioned that you've noticed an older-model maroon truck following you," Dru said to him.

"I haven't seen it following me, exactly. I've seen it parked on a street near where I live. Then outside the stadium, and then at a restaurant I was leaving the night before last."

"Did you get its license plate number?" Dru asked.

Gray nodded. "When I saw the truck outside the restaurant, I wrote down the license plate number and gave it to the police. Apparently, the truck's registered to a little old lady who lives in Bonham, Texas."

"Make of the truck?" Dru asked.

"Ford." He smiled, looking genuinely entertained for the first time. "Do you think a little old lady is my stalker?"

"It could be," Dru answered.

"I think it's more likely that it's a coincidence that I happened to notice a couple of maroon trucks around."

In real life, coincidences happened. But in Dru's line of work, coincidences were taken seriously and with a heaping dose of investigation. She addressed Morris. "We'll look into the maroon truck, and we'll work out threat assessments on anyone known to have animosity toward Gray."

"The entire fan base of the Cowboys?" Gray asked dryly under his breath.

She forged ahead. "We'll surveil the environment when we're with Gray, and we'll also run a fair amount of counter-surveillance. In other words, we'll hide ourselves and observe Gray and the places he visits from a distance in an effort to catch the person who's following him while they're in the process of doing just that."

"Good," Morris said. Two more pen taps. "Thank you."

"If Detective Carlyle comes up with any information we need to know," Mack said, "please contact us with it."

"We'll contact you," Morris assured them. "This is a group effort. Our security team here at the Mustangs can provide you with badges, passes, clearance, whatever you need. The safety of our players is our highest priority."

Excluding when those players were out on the field.

Then they could thrash each other bloody. It's what made football so entertaining.

"I'm hoping that we'll find Gray's stalker in short order." Morris gave Gray a subdued smile. "Gray's important to this team."

An understatement. In the multi-billion-dollar business of the NFL, Gray was as close to priceless to the Mustangs organization as a player could be. They wanted to protect their asset in the same way the Metropolitan Museum of Art would want to protect their Rembrandt. The Mustangs weren't about to let their Rembrandt get damaged.

Dru had always liked puzzle-solving. The more challenging and dangerous the puzzle, the better. Gray Fowler, with his thickheaded chauvinism, would surely prove to be a pain. But finding his stalker was going to be a pleasure.

She moved to rise from her seat—

"Dru and I were just talking," Gray said to his GM. She resettled herself.

"I told her that I'd like for the bodyguards to stay low-key. I might tell one or two of my close friends about them, but other than that, I don't want anyone knowing about them or the letters." He held steady eye contact with Morris. Clearly, he'd been around the negotiating table a few times.

"All right." Morris looked questioningly at Mack and Dru. "What do you think?"

"Sure, sure," said Mack, who was naturally easygoing and friendly. Dru wondered how often anyone in Gray's life piped up and said no to him. Rarely, she'd guess. He probably hadn't received a tenth of the reprimanding he deserved.

Gray moved his weight forward in his seat. "This is going to be the story, in case anybody asks. Mack is my new chauffeur. Is that good with you, Mack?"

"Yeah, man. That'll give me a reason to buy a chauffeur's hat. Very cool."

"Dru is my new girlfriend," Gray continued. "If anyone wonders why a woman her age is free several afternoons a week, she and I decided we'd tell them it's because she teaches preschool."

She and I decided? The nerve! Dru straightened as if she had a metal rod for a spine. All the scathing things she wanted to say piled up on her tongue.

"How old's Weston, the guy that'll be working the night shift?" Gray asked Mack.

"Around thirty," Mack answered.

"When Weston's with me at dinner or clubs or whatever, I'll just introduce him as a buddy of mine."

A stretch of silence descended. Gray made eye contact with each of them, self-assured and forceful.

Dru longed to tell him how much she loathed his plan. However, she hadn't known her new client for even an hour yet. It might be wise to attempt a full hour in Gray's company before opposing him in public. If she gave either Gray or Morris a reason to call Anthony Sutton and ask to have her replaced, she'd instantly be replaced.

This case was the chance she'd been waiting for, the chance she needed. *Remember, Dru? Compromise. Plus a few Advil.*

"Sounds good, Gray," Mack said admiringly. Mack

was a Mustangs fan and couldn't be trusted to view Gray objectively. "We'll do our best to accommodate your ideas."

He didn't particularly like his new bodyguard.

She was about as warm as January.

Gray had squeezed a lot of living and too many girl-friends to count into his thirty-two years, so he knew what he liked. He liked sweet women who laughed at all his jokes. If he had to pick between a rich girl with a lot of education and a friendly girl with no education, he'd go with the friendly girl every time. He liked curves and easy smiles and cheerful, agreeable personalities. If he said, *Want to go to a nightclub?* his ideal woman would say, *Sure!*

Want to wear my jersey and cheer for me at the next home game?

I'd love to!

Would you mind serving my buddies and me drinks while we watch Monday Night Football?

Happy to!

Crazy guess, but he didn't think his new bodyguard would answer any of those questions the way his ideal woman would. He slanted a look across the restaurant, to where Dru sat alone at a table for two.

An hour ago, they'd arrived at this modern Japanese restaurant near his Dallas neighborhood so he could at-tend a dinner meeting with a few of the board members of Grace Street. Grace Street was a nonprofit that offered outreach programs for abused women and children. He supported a handful of charities, but Grace Street had become his favorite.

Dru, who didn't shy away from offering her opinion, had told him that she saw no need for him to insert his new fake girlfriend into his dinner plans. She'd informed him that she'd go her separate way as soon as they entered the restaurant. Which was how things had gone down.

The board members were talking amongst themselves, trying to figure out some of the details that had come up regarding his participation in their Winter Family Fun Day event, scheduled for early February.

He looked down at his small plate. It contained small pieces of sushi, a small lump of ginger, and a small lump of wasabi. Why was everything in Japanese restaurants so small? Did this place have any idea how much he ate?

Board members still talking. He returned his gaze to Dru.

She ate politely, one hand in her lap, her attention taking in their surroundings.

After the meeting with Morris, he'd driven to Sutton Security's Dallas office. She'd followed him on her motorcycle. She drove a *motorcycle*. He had a few bikes himself, but his were big. They were the kind of machines you could drive and have a beer afterward and not be made fun of by anyone in the bar. Her motorcycle was an older-model Kawasaki Z750, all black, made for agility and speed.

At Sutton Security, Dru and Anthony Sutton had questioned him for hours about the idiotic letters, what his blood type was, who his friends and employees were, and about all the people he'd ever come across in his life who hated him. He'd also had to give them addresses, phone numbers, the locations of the places he usually visited in a week, a list of places he'd be going this week in particular, and on and on.

When Anthony Sutton had excused himself, he'd been alone with Dru, who'd taken the opportunity to lecture him. She'd outlined the dangers he was facing, rattled off statistics about all the ways he could be killed, and tried to convince him to follow her rules exactly in order to improve his likelihood of seeing his thirty-third birthday. He waited for her to finish.

"Has that little speech scared your other clients into obeying you?"

"Only the smart ones."

"It's not going to come close to working on me."

She scowled in that threatening way she had, and he almost laughed.

"I've got a lot on my plate right now," he continued. "The only thing I want to care about or have time to care about is winning football games." So far this season, his team had a seven and two record. "All my energy is focused on one goal. Another Super Bowl title."

"It'll be hard to win the Super Bowl if you're a corpse."

"I told Morris he could hire you guys because it's in my best interest to get along with the Mustangs admin. But I don't want to be inconvenienced by you or your security measures. So go ahead and do what you need to do, but I'm going to continue living my life. I'm not afraid of my stalker."

"You might take him or her more seriously once—"

"I'm a corpse? I'd rather be a corpse than bend over

backward to do whatever crazy thing it is you want me to do."

She reminded him of those lady detectives on cop shows set in New York. She was tough. No nonsense. Intense. He'd only seen her smile once all day, in Morris's office when she'd pretended to have forgotten his name.

So far, there were only two things he liked about her.

One, she was beautiful. When he'd first seen her, he'd had a hard time adjusting to it, her beauty. Her eyes were the color of the light blue water that ran up onto the beaches of the Caribbean island he visited every spring. She was both taller and slimmer than the average woman. She had long brown hair, so dark it was almost black. Her perfect creamy skin didn't show a single freckle or wrinkle. She looked like an icy European princess.

Two, he found it sort of . . . entertaining to rile her. She was easy to stir up. And every time he stirred her up, she got all offended and defensive. Her eyes would snap white sparks, her mouth would purse, and she'd look like she was dying to cuss him out, and would have, if she'd been allowed to. He might enjoy hearing her let him have it with both barrels sometime. He'd cornered her into pretending to be his girlfriend mostly because he could tell the idea made her mad, which, in turn, amused him.

With a face like hers—the cheekbones, the narrow nose, the sculpted chin—she could have been a model or the kind of actress who starred as the babe in action movies. She'd have made a fortune doing either. Instead she was here in this Japanese restaurant tonight, supposedly guarding him.

A fresh sense of disbelief washed over him. Part of him was still waiting for the crew of a show like *Punk'd* to jump out of the bushes with their cameras, laughing, and admit that they'd played an elaborate joke on him.

The small woman protecting the big football player? It insulted him some, the fact that anyone would think him so defenseless that he'd need *her* as a bodyguard. What could she possibly do for him that he couldn't do for himself?

As a young kid, he'd been too adult for his age, responsible, a rule-follower. Then the dirt bag had come into his life.

He remembered sitting in the back of a closet with Colton, who'd been a kindergartner at the time.

"You idiot, Gray! What a sorry excuse for a human being. You're an embarrassment."

Gray had put his hand gently over Colton's mouth and held a finger up to his own lips to tell Colton to be silent. His little brother's eyes got big and round. Gray drew his knees up and tried to make both of them as small as he could in the closet's corner. Clothes brushed against his head. His heart beat like fast-running feet.

"Where are you, boy? Worthless kid!" The door to the closet ripped back, and light fell over them. The dirt bag's body filled the opening, his face screwed tight by anger. The man had gripped Gray by the upper arm and yanked him out.

After . . .

After that, Gray had ditched all the sucking up he'd done when he'd been younger. The polite rule-following hadn't served him well.

By ninth grade, he'd finally started to grow into his size. At first, he'd been gangly. His hands and feet and nose had gotten big before the rest of him could catch up.

He'd begun wailing on a punching bag in his basement. Midway through that year, his freshman year, a kid had picked a fight with him. He'd finally had a chance to use his size and his new skills. He'd beaten up the kid so badly that he'd knocked him unconscious.

That fight had given Gray a taste of something he'd never had before.

Power.

After that, he'd searched out more fights. He'd started drinking and smoking, started stealing money from his mom's purse and driving her car. He'd gotten in and out of trouble with the police and school administrators. His grades had tanked because he'd avoided school as much as he'd attended.

Month after month, he grew. In height, in weight, in strength.

By rights, he should have ended up in prison. He probably would have if his algebra teacher, who'd also been the school's assistant football coach, hadn't seen potential in him. When his teacher had first challenged Gray to try out for the football team before the start of his sophomore year, Gray had flipped the guy the bird. He'd had no interest in making an idiot of himself on a football field.

Gray had always told himself he hated organized sports, mainly because he'd never had the kind of mom who could be counted on to sign him up or pay for uniforms or take him to games or practices.

His algebra teacher had kept after him until Gray had finally agreed to show up for the first day of tryouts. Nothing more.

On that day, he'd been introduced to the great love of his life.

A game.

A game in which aggression was an asset. A game that had brought him fame and glory and money and thousands upon thousands of fans who idolized him because of how he played it. He was a Pro Bowl tight end in the NFL. He was a warhorse. He could protect himself without the help of a woman.

At last, Dru glanced in his direction, caught him staring, and gave him a subtle shake of her head. She didn't want him staring because, if his stalker was watching, she didn't want his interest in her to link them.

He gave her a "who cares?" expression and kept on staring.

CHAPTER TWO

Pregnancy was a miracle. A strange, awe-inspiring miracle that took your regular body from you and exchanged it for something totally different and foreign: your pregnant body.

Meg Porter rested her hand on her pregnant tummy and felt, both from the sensory details of her hand on the outside and the sensory details on the inside, a distinct jab from a tiny body part. Maybe an elbow? A foot? There it came again.

Bo, who was sitting next to her in the grandstands at Lone Star Park racetrack, glanced at her.

Gently smiling, she took his hand and placed it on her belly. Her very tight, firm belly. She was only in the second trimester, but thanks to the fact that they were expecting boy/girl twins, her belly had already grown to what felt to her like huge proportions. Hard to imagine that her tummy still had at least three and a half months of growing to do.

The baby moved again, bumping Bo's palm. Good

baby. Sometimes when she held Bo's hand to her belly so he could feel what she was feeling, the babies would decide to nod off to sleep, and Bo would be left waiting patiently for a kick that didn't come.

Another thump.

Miracle babies, Meg thought, emotion and gratitude lifting her heart.

Bo regarded her with amazement, as if she'd shown him a flower that could talk or a butterfly wearing a dress. "Incredible," he whispered.

"Incredible," she agreed.

His hand was big and exceptionally masculine against the fabric of her coat. His was the hand of a man who worked with horses, who'd once served his country as a Marine, who was her very best friend in all the world, her husband, the father of her unborn babies.

She and Bo had four nieces and nephews, all thanks to Bo's brother Ty and his wife, Celia. You'd think, being such an experienced aunt and uncle, that the two of them would have become accustomed to pregnancy and baby-dom. However, this pregnancy of theirs was a whole new, hushed, mysterious, and remarkable experience. The two of them were goofy over it. Every tiny event— each sonogram, each doctor's visit, each purchase for the nursery, every miniature outfit they received—struck them both with awe and excitement.

They'd been married now for eight years. The first year had been all-out bliss. The past seven had been tempered by infertility and the crushing sadness of two miscarriages. The journey that had brought them to this place had been a long and sometimes brutal test of faith.

Meg was an only child. She'd inherited a fortune from

her father upon his death, then turned right around and set up the Cole Foundation so that she could dedicate herself to the task of giving away her father's money. She took immense joy in paying medical expenses, education costs, debts, and more for the single-parent families who came to live at her Whispering Creek Ranch while they were getting back on their feet.

She'd been giving away terrific amounts of money for years and still hadn't made a dent in her accounts. The money from her father's oil company continued to flow to her like the Mississippi River.

Meg was very aware that God had given her much. When He'd failed to answer her longtime prayer for a baby, she'd sometimes wondered if He was letting her know that she was off-base to ask for anything extra.

Except, she and Bo had continued to feel year after year that God had a baby for them, that a family was still a part of His plan. Meg had gone the traditional medical route and done hormone studies, taken medications, received shots. They'd tried IVF several times. No go.

She'd also gone the holistic route. Healthy eating regimens. Sleep. Vitamins. Supplements. Acupressure, even. No go.

A few years into their struggles with infertility, they'd researched adoption. Many times since, they'd revisited the possibility. As much as they loved the idea of adoption, though, they'd never heard God call them to it in a personal way.

Twelve months ago, Meg had come to a place of utter exhaustion with it all. She'd been unable to forge ahead with the stress and hope and disappointment. She'd worried that her preoccupation with having a baby had drained her ability to experience complete contentment with the things God *had* given her. So, she'd gone off all the treatments. She'd stopped counting the days of her cycle, and she'd quit beseeching God for a baby. Instead, she'd focused simply on thanking Him for and embracing the life she did have.

A few months later, she'd become pregnant. Without charts and doctors and technology. Pregnant, the old-school way.

She was now thirty-six, and Bo was forty.

They'd been astonished and painfully hopeful when they'd discovered the pregnancy. It was terrifying to want something as much as Meg and Bo wanted a healthy pregnancy and baby. As thrilled as they'd both been at the news that they were expecting, they'd both also been heavily aware that neither of Meg's two prior pregnancies had made it out of the first trimester.

There had been times, between the day they'd learned of this pregnancy and this day, when anxiety had riddled her. She'd sought to squash it and trust God fully, but she hadn't always succeeded. Even now, at twenty-three weeks along and with nothing but glowing reports from her OB, she still didn't feel fully confident and assured that all would be well with her twins.

The movement went quiet, the baby having apparently settled into a spot that pleased him or her. Bo took hold of Meg's hand and drew it over the little stadium-seating armrest so that he could set their interlaced hands on his leg. As always, a sense of security and strength coursed into Meg through Bo.

"You good?" he asked. "Do you need me to get you anything?"

"I'm good." Her husband had grown more handsome over time, in that annoying way men had of improving with age. He still wore his dark hair shaved close to his head, just like he had the day she'd met him. His gray eyes still had the power to make her go swoony with attraction. "I've been looking forward to this day for months," Meg murmured, taking in the wide scene spreading before them. "Now that it's here, I can hardly believe it."

"Believe it, Countess."

A large section of the racetrack's grandstand had been cordoned off especially for them and their friends and family. Today marked the final day of the fall quarter-horse racing season. Racing wouldn't begin again at Lone Star until the Thoroughbred racing season opened in April. To celebrate their closing day, Lone Star Park had planned several festivities, including the unveiling of a statue to honor one of the greatest Thoroughbreds ever to grace the dirt of Lone Star's oval.

A dapple-grey Thoroughbred stallion named Silver Leaf.

The horse's phenomenal success had been a family affair. Meg had the great pleasure of owning Silver Leaf. Bo managed Whispering Creek Horses, the horse farm on their north Texas ranch where Silver Leaf had been bred and raised. Jake, Bo's younger brother, and Jake's wife, Lyndie, had trained Silver Leaf.

Meg looked immediately to her left, where Jake and Lyndie sat. They had their heads bent toward each other and were talking quietly.

Jake resembled Bo, except he wore his dark hair longer, and his face bore a scar caused by an IED explosion during his time overseas with the Marines. The explosion had ended Jake's military career and marked the years that followed with post-traumatic stress disorder. Though there was no cure for the condition, Jake had greatly improved since falling in love with Lyndie.

Jake pressed a kiss near Lyndie's temple, and Meg hid a smile at the sight. Muscular and dark, Jake was the perfect foil for his wife's petite fairness and wavy blond hair.

For this special occasion, all the men in the family had worn suits, the women dresses and coats. Meg had purchased a blue maternity dress and an A-line double-breasted gray wool coat. When pregnant, one needed cute jewelry or a fabulous scarf or a hat or *something* in order to attempt to look dashing. If not dashing, Meg trusted that her gray felt fedora with its black leather band looked, at least, stylish. The lady at Neiman Marcus had told her it did.

Then again, the lady at Neiman Marcus could have been motivated by nothing more than commission.

A race went off, and many of those in attendance either jumped to their feet or started calling out encouragement to their favorite horses. The voice of the track announcer poured over them.

Meg hadn't once worried that the weather might not cooperate for Silver Leaf's big day. Silver Leaf had always radiated a kingly demeanor. With every win he'd amassed, his bearing had become even more esteemed and dignified. Frankly, the weather wouldn't have dared to insult him.

The horses raced under an early-afternoon robin's-egg-blue sky, dotted here and there with cheerful cotton-ball clouds. Trees spiced with autumn's yellow and orange leaves ringed the track at a distance.

A baby's squeal brought Meg's attention to the right, where Bo's other brother, Ty, sat. In his charcoal suit, with his bronze hair and aviator sunglasses, Ty looked far more like a movie star dressed for a premiere than like a father of four.

Ty and his wife, Celia, had brought all their children. Addie, age ten. Hudson, four. Connor, two. And little Ellerie, six months. The squeal had come from Ellerie. She was laughing at her father, who was holding her facing him. Every few moments, Ty blew at her tuft of hair and elicited more giggles.

"I think she wants me to take over," Bo said to Ty, reaching for the baby.

"No way, dude. She has daddy love. She likes me best." Ty blew on her forehead again. Another baby chortle. "All my kids are under the impression that I'm awesome, which is probably why I like having them so much."

"Hand over the baby," Bo said.

"Fine." Ty shot Meg a crooked smile as he passed the little girl into Bo's hands. Bo renewed the game, and Ellerie laughed with amusement.

The horses pounded past their seats on their way to the wire. Dru, the youngest Porter sibling, sat on the far side of Ty and Celia's crew, holding Connor in her lap. She helped the toddler clap for the horses, then showed him how to hoot and holler once they'd crossed the wire. The boy, usually a bundle of relentless energy, watched Dru with fascination and did his best to mimic her actions.

Dru had that effect on the kids. They were all dazed with adoration of her. If Dru asked them to line up like the Von Trapp kids at the sound of a whistle, they'd all rush to do exactly that.

"In fact," Ty said, "I like having kids so much that I'm going to try to talk Celia into one more." He winked at Meg, because they both knew what was coming.

Celia Porter snapped to attention at Ty's statement. "No way, showboat." She had the fine and graceful features of a fairy. Her curly auburn hair fell in artful layers down to her shoulders. She didn't look like someone spunky enough to hold her own against the strong-willed Ty. But she was. "Thank goodness you're taking over the baby baton from us, Meg and Bo. Because we're done. Completely and totally done. As my husband very well knows."

"But look at our kids, love," Ty said. "They're perfect little specimens. We'd be robbing the world of something important if we don't have any more."

"You'll be robbing me of something important if we do have more. My sanity."

"You've got more sanity than all the rest of us in the family put together, sweet one."

Celia murmured something about that being God's honest truth as she bent to re-tie Hudson's shoe.

Bo turned Ellerie toward the track and set her on his lap so that she was leaning back against him as if he were her recliner.

The three youngest of Celia and Ty's children had all been born while Meg and Bo had been struggling with infertility. Each of those pregnancies and births had brought joy to everyone in the Porter family, including Meg and Bo. Each of those pregnancies and births had also carved into Meg's heart like a knife. Ty and Celia were younger than she and Bo. Their oldest child had been a complete surprise. The other three had come to them with extreme ease.

Meg hadn't wanted to feel jealous, especially not of Celia, whom she loved. The fact that she hadn't wanted to feel jealous, and had known it was wrong to feel that way even, had made the jealousy she'd grappled with all the more wretched. She'd pleaded with God to take it from her, but since He hadn't, she'd just gone ahead and been the very best sister-in-law and aunt that she could possibly be.

Now she could watch Bo interacting with Ty and Celia's kids and experience within herself nothing but tenderness. What was it about the sight of a masculine man holding a baby that carried with it such slaying power?

She wanted, dearly, to see Bo holding their own babies. That sight would surely be one of the deepest joys of her whole life.

Another race went off, and Meg consulted the schedule. Silver Leaf's honorary glory lap around the track was listed next on the itinerary. Then they'd all move to the area in front of the clubhouse where the statue would be revealed. Meg's anticipation, mixed with a dose of nervousness, heightened. "Ready?" she asked Bo. "Silver Leaf is up next."

"I'm ready if you are." They looked at each other, and a wealth of communication passed between them.

"I love you," Bo said. He spoke the words with transparent honesty, spoke them as a man who'd backed up those three words with actions for years upon years. He was steadfast. Honorable. He'd told her on the day of their first kiss that he'd love her every hour of every day for the rest of his life, and he'd been doing just that ever since.

"I love you, too," she answered. In her early twenties, Meg had gone through a very brief, very heartbreaking marriage to a dishonorable man. She hadn't, and wouldn't, forget how much a man's integrity meant.

Bo handed Ellerie back to her parents as Meg swiveled to take in all the friends and family members assembled behind them in the stands. Bo's father and mother, John and Nancy. Her uncle on her father's side and her aunts on her mother's. Numerous cousins and their numerous children.

Stretching up row after grandstand row were many of the families that had come to live at one time or another at Whispering Creek Ranch's main house, thanks to the Cole Foundation. The main house, the one her father had built, was huge and not at all to Meg's taste and filled with an overabundance of memories from her childhood. So when she and Bo had married, they'd built their own house on another section of the ranch's property, and she'd turned the main house into a place that functioned as both the Cole Foundation's headquarters and a dwelling for the people it helped.

All the faces looking back at her now came with stories and fondness attached. They'd filled her father's house with new memories. These families were a testament to hope and to God's ability to grant new beginnings.

She turned back toward the track and leaned her shoulder into Bo.

Suddenly, dramatic music rushed from the speaker system, and the big screens began showing a montage of clips featuring many of Silver Leaf's races. The crowd whistled and cheered.

Silver Leaf did not belong just to her. Horse-racing fans loved him. He was *theirs*.

The announcer began detailing some of Silver Leaf's accomplishments. "Winner of the Texas Classic. Winner of the Mesquite Tree Stakes. Winner of the Southwestern Invitational Handicap. Two-time winner of the Breeders' Cup Classic. Ladies and gentlemen, please give a warm Lone Star welcome to Silver Leaf, returning once more to his home track!"

The packed stands erupted, everyone pushing to their feet for a standing ovation.

Silver Leaf burst onto the track, a stunning sight. Moisture gathered in Meg's eyes. She was, admittedly, a bit sentimental. Happy moments like this one never failed to make her tearful. The tall grey stallion galloped with his famously coordinated stride, his snow-white mane and tail floating in the air.

The announcer continued while majestic music played as backdrop. "Silver Leaf is ridden by his jockey, Elizabeth Alvarez. Elizabeth told me that Silver Leaf never once let her down. She traveled to be with us today because she couldn't consider letting Silver Leaf down on his big day."

Elizabeth wore the pale blue and brown silks of Whispering Creek Horses, the same jockey's uniform she'd worn all the times she'd raced Silver Leaf to victory. Elizabeth had been a mid-level jockey when she'd been paired with Silver Leaf. Nowadays, because of the respect she'd gained riding Silver Leaf, she'd become a top-tier jockey with mounts in all of racing's biggest events. She wasn't just one of the best female jockeys. She'd proven herself to be one of the best. Period.

The cameras followed Elizabeth and Silver Leaf as they sailed along the back side of the track.

"Silver Leaf was bred," the announcer said, "at Whispering Creek Horses in Holley, Texas. He's owned by Meg and Bo Porter." The screens cut to a live shot of Meg and Bo. Though she'd known what was coming, Meg still started at the sight of the two of them in such enormous proportions. Her nose alone had to be six feet tall. They both smiled and waved.

"Silver Leaf was trained by Lyndie and Jake Porter." The cameras cut to Lyndie and Jake. Jake made a move as if tipping his Stetson, even though he wasn't wearing one. Lyndie laughed and lifted a hand to thank the audience for their support.

Silver made the turn to the homestretch, moving with gorgeous fluidity. The screens once again followed his progress. The crowd went wild. It felt like delight, pure delight, to watch Silver Leaf and Elizabeth galloping together, just like the old days, this one last time.

Once he'd found his form, Silver Leaf had competed for three seasons. He'd taken Meg and the other Porters on an amazing journey straight to the top of American Thoroughbred racing. He was the kind of horse an owner or trainer would be supremely lucky to come across just once in a lifetime. Meg had no expectation of ever owning another like him.

They'd retired Silver Leaf a year ago, not because he was losing his form, but because he'd worked hard and accomplished far more than enough. He was a relatively old stallion. There'd been no reason to risk injuring him by continuing to race him. Thus, Silver Leaf had gone where all fortunate great stallions go: back to their home farm to eat and rest and stand at stud.

Once they crossed the wire, Elizabeth turned Silver Leaf and trotted him back along the grandstands. The Thoroughbred pranced, and his jockey waved and beamed.

Track employees came and escorted Meg and the rest of their group to the pretty paved area in front of the clubhouse. The hulking statue waited there, covered by white fabric, a wide circle of colorful flowers ringing its base.

Zoe, Silver Leaf's longtime groom, led the horse to a place of honor beside the statue. Track dignitaries, then Bo and Meg, then Lyndie and Jake, then Elizabeth stepped to the podium to say a few words.

Meg couldn't quit smiling. Though Silver Leaf had traveled to races from coast to coast, the people of Texas and of Lone Star Park were very, very proud to call him their native son.

At last, one of the track's administrators swept away the fabric and revealed the statue. Photographers clicked pictures.

A life-sized likeness of Silver Leaf gleamed like mercury in the sun. The sculptor had captured him perfectly. The real Silver Leaf stood next to his replica, both of them striking the exact same pose. All four feet planted squarely and straight, neck arched at an elegant angle, face slanted toward the onlookers. *This is quite what I deserve*, Silver Leaf communicated to the assembled crowd. *I've earned this statue and will accept your acclaim and adoration.*

Sometime later, Meg spotted Bo's sister in the midst of the throng and made her way over to give Dru a hug. "Thank you for coming."

"I wouldn't have missed it. How are you and the babies doing?"

"Really well."

Dru's wintry blue eyes softened.

Dru had been a teenager when Meg had first been introduced to the Porters. Back then, Dru had been headstrong and defiant. Bo and the rest of the family had spent Dru's high school years rescuing her from one ill-destined scheme after another.

In those days, Meg hadn't known how to take Dru. They were ten years apart in age and completely different in personality. Over time, though, she'd come to appreciate and admire her sister-in-law. Dru had matured. Instead of pursuing danger, she now protected others from it. Also, she was one of the most genuine people Meg knew. She was, very simply, exactly who she was. Formidable. Like a female Old West sheriff come to life in this modern day. Girl power personified.

"Bo told me that you have a new client," Meg said.

"I do. Gray Fowler. He's a football player."

"What?" Ty approached, sunlight sparking along the upper rim of his movie star sunglasses. "Your agency is protecting Gray Fowler?"

"Yes."

"And you've been assigned to him?"

"Yes, but that information is for our family's ears only."

"But . . . Fowler plays for the Mustangs." Ty said *the Mustangs* the way a person might say *the Nazis*.

"I'm aware of that," Dru said dryly.

"Why does Gray Fowler need protecting?" Meg asked.

"He has a stalker."

"Probably an angry ex-girlfriend," Ty said.

"It's possible," Dru answered.

Ty summoned Bo and Jake with a beckoning hand motion.

Dru's pencil skirt, high heels, and tailored suit jacket accentuated her slender frame and sleek hair. At this point in her pregnancy, Meg didn't think she'd be able to get so much as one thigh into that pencil skirt. Since she wasn't pregnant in her thighs, she didn't understand why they'd turned traitor on her.

"Dru's been assigned to Gray Fowler," Ty announced to his brothers. "She's protecting him from a crazed stalker."

Bo made the kind of face people make when they smell something awful. "Fowler plays for the Mustangs."

Meg laughed.

"Next time the Mustangs come up against the Cowboys, what do you think about the idea of sabotaging Gray?" Ty asked Dru. "You could rub itching cream into his uniform or unplug his alarm clock so that he sleeps through the game. That sort of thing?"

Bo and Jake nodded in support of the plan.

Dru pretended to think it over even though Meg knew she'd never sabotage a client. "Worth considering."

"Women love him, you know." A trace of suspicion filtered into Ty's face. "Some of the ladies who come into the coffee shop have Mustangs-watching parties just so they can *ooh* and *ahh* over him and Corbin Stewart. Rita Marcus came in last week carrying a Mustangs wall calendar. She showed Celia and me the picture of Fowler. I was worried for a minute there that she might faint over it."

Jake's face, already intimidating because of his scar, darkened until it resembled a thundercloud. "Don't even *think* about falling for Fowler, Dru."

Meg relished it when Dru's brothers gave their sister grief because Dru was so deliciously good at standing up to them. The youngest Porter had had a lifetime of practice.

"Fall for him?" Dru repeated with insulted dignity. "He plays for the Mustangs. And he's my client. I'm not allowed to date clients."

"I don't think you have the right to look so scandalized by our concern," Ty said to her. "As I recall, you got pretty emotionally invested in your last client. It could happen again."

"No. It couldn't. I've changed since then." Dru planted her fists on her hips and regarded Ty with so much loathing that her expression would have been considered too melodramatic for a WrestleMania event. "I just met Gray yesterday. I only know him well enough to know that he's intolerable."

"Which days of the week will you be working?" Bo asked.

"Thursday through Monday."

"You took on Gray's case yesterday and you're already taking a day off to come here?"

"Are you kidding, Bo? Of course I'm here. I asked for today off weeks ago."

"So . . . you're definitely not going to fall for him?"

Jake clarified, refusing to release either the line of questioning or his resemblance to a thundercloud.

"Just so you guys know, I don't fall for men." Dru set her chin and made eye contact with each brother in turn. "I prefer to let them fall for me."

Meg whistled under her breath.

"We don't want Gray Fowler in the family, Dru," Ty stated.

"As aforementioned, I don't even find him tolerable!"

"Good," Bo said. "Then hurry up and find his stalker so you can move on to the next client."

"Planning to," Dru replied.

Meg interlinked her fingers with Bo's, lightness filling her. It was a sparkling day in November. The Porters were bantering. And she liked her new fedora.

It seemed possible, very possible, that things might turn out just fine for her and Bo and their babies. She hoped. Was it possible? Yes, it was. Everything was going to turn out beautifully.

CHAPTER
THREE

So, Gray lived in a mansion.

It was Sunday, the day after Silver's Leaf's ceremony. The Mustangs had played a noon game at their home stadium. Due to the strength of the team's security on road trips and at home games, the Mustangs had informed Sutton Security that they wouldn't need agents guarding Gray while he was under the team's watch.

Thus, Dru had fallen in behind Gray's black Denali when he'd left the stadium's property. The route from the stadium to his home had taken them to Preston Hollow, a classy Dallas neighborhood filled with big homes on even bigger lots. No sidewalks here, which gave Preston Hollow a bit of a country air. The grass ebbed into the street like water lapping a beach.

As Gray turned off the road, a wooden gate set into a stone fence opened to admit them. His driveway invited Dru deep onto a huge parcel of rolling land dotted with trees.

Dru had watched the Mustangs' game on the TV in

her office at Sutton's headquarters. The Mustangs had won, but the Dolphins defense had been vicious, and Gray had taken numerous hits. One particular hit had knocked him flat. He'd lain on the turf for long seconds before he'd finally rolled onto his side. It wasn't until he'd made it to his feet and walked off the field that Dru had noticed that she'd scooted all the way to the front edge of her chair. And that she'd been scowling.

She'd been sort of . . . worried about him . . . for a second. Which confounded her. Gray would be easier to guard if he was injured and confined to his bed.

Dru had never before spent an entire football game watching just one player. On the downs when he hadn't caught passes, Gray had used his body to throw blocks. From the first quarter through the end of the fourth, he'd executed the team's strategy with concentrated ferocity.

A wooden garage door tucked into the side of his house creaked upward. Gray slid the Denali inside next to two sports cars.

Dru brought her Kawasaki to a stop alongside the Honda CR-V parked on the far side of his driveway. She'd just finished removing her helmet when Gray walked out to meet her.

He'd showered and changed after the game. If he'd worn a full suit earlier, then his jacket and tie had already been ditched. He'd turned the cuffs of his business shirt up a few times and pulled one button loose at the throat of his white shirt. The moody gray of the near-dusk sky caused his incongruously light green eyes to shine like gems.

Some big men looked strange in formal clothing, the garments always too large or too small. Not Gray. His business shirt and suit pants had been tailored to fit him perfectly. "Hi, bodyguard," he said.

"That's *executive protection agent* to you." She shook back her hair and ran her fingertips through the mass to comb it into place. "You're limping." He was both moving slowly and limping a little.

"Did you watch the game?"

She motioned her chin in the affirmative.

"That's why I'm limping."

"Ah. I was thinking maybe you'd acquired a hopscotch injury."

He lifted a dark brow and crossed his muscled arms over his chest. "Is hopscotch that game little girls play? With the chalk and the squares?"

"Yes."

"Just wanted to make sure I understood your insult." He gave her a tough guy's smile, the smile of a 1920s gangster.

"How badly are you hurt?" she asked.

"It's a hip flexor strain. Nothing that a shot of naproxen won't help."

She gave him a skeptical look.

"It just needs rest. Sweet of you to care, though."

She met his regard head-on. "It's not that I care. It's that I need to know how badly you're hurt so that I can adjust my methods of protecting you accordingly."

"I think you care," he said.

"Wrong."

His eyes flared with subdued laughter. "C'mon. I'll show you around." He led her toward the backyard. As they walked, he explained how he'd found the property and why he'd decided on it.

The whole place had a Spanish flair, in the most modern, tasteful, and expensive way. The backyard's covered patio had dark overhead beams, two wall-mounted flat screens, a built-in barbecue, and a stone fireplace. The outdoor furniture positioned around the pool looked like pieces most people would love to have on the *inside* of their homes, not like the kind of thing that should be left outside to be speckled by rain.

Two people from Sutton Security had already conducted a thorough search and evaluation of Gray's house. She'd read their report, which had rated his onsite electronic security system as top notch.

He held open the back door for her. She passed through into a spacious, high-tech kitchen smelling of pot roast. A blond woman around the same age as Dru stood on the far side of the kitchen's granite-topped island. This must be the owner of the CR-V.

"Welcome home," the woman said to Gray. Both her voice and smile were sweeter than Splenda. "I watched the game." She shook her head as if she couldn't get over her pleasure and amazement. "Great playing."

"Thanks, Ash."

"Really great playing," she continued. "So good."

"Dru"—Gray made his way to the appetizer platter set out on the island—"this is Ashley Huey, my housekeeper. Ash, this is Dru Montana."

Dru squelched the urge to knee him in the groin. During their long meeting at Sutton's headquarters, she'd asked Gray to introduce her using a fake last name. She'd campaigned for Smith. He'd campaigned for Montana— as in Joe. She'd thought she'd made it clear that she had *no* interest in Montana as a surname.

"Nice to meet you!" Ashley said to her. "Any friend of Gray's is a friend of mine."

"Dru's my girlfriend," Gray stated.

"Oh? How nice." Ashley's smile didn't budge. It stuck there, like a sticker to a kid's shirt, even as some of the life drained out of it. How cotton-pickin' predictable. Gray's housekeeper had a thing for him and wasn't delighted to be introduced to the newest of Gray's long parade of girlfriends. "How did you two meet?" Ashley asked.

"I'll let you tell the story," Dru said, giving Gray a direct look full of challenge. He's the one who'd insisted she pose as his girlfriend.

Idly, she picked up a tomato mozzarella basil skewer. Ashley had put together a seriously impressive tray of appetizers. In addition to the skewers, she'd set out veggies, dip, cheese, and rosemary-flecked nuts.

"Dru teaches preschool," Gray told Ashley. "We met when I went by her school for this . . . thing the Mustangs were doing." He angled a small handful of nuts into his mouth.

"And?" Ashley prompted, clearly full of curiosity.

Gray finished chewing. "And Dru's a saint. She lives to teach ABCs and how to use a potty."

"I live for the potty training, especially," Dru said to him, deadpan.

"Awww!" Ashley gushed kindness. It spilled out from her words, eyes, posture. She was of average height, with a body that didn't look like it had ever met a weight-lifting machine. All slim softness. No muscle tone. Her fine, pale hair stood out from her head about an inch in every direction before curling to a stop near her jawline. Blandly pretty face. Fair skin. She'd tied a floral-printed apron over her knit sweater dress and leggings. "Tell me more," she encouraged.

"When I first saw Dru," Gray said, "she had five kids hanging off of her and she was wearing a Thanksgiving sweatshirt and one of those little"—he made a motion above his head—"headbands that has, you know, holiday stuff sticking up out of it?"

"Sure!" Ashley said.

Dru pursed her lips.

Gray slid her a look that said, *Beware of laying a challenge in front of me, sweetheart. Because if you do, I'll nail it.*

She'd had a few clients in the past who'd asked for low-profile surveillance, so this wasn't the first time she'd operated under a cover story. She didn't blame him for answering Ashley's questions in a way that maintained the cover story. But she did blame him for taking so much enjoyment in it at her expense, and for overdoing what could otherwise have been straightforward answers.

"Her headband had a turkey and leaves and a pumpkin on it," Gray said.

"I just love holiday headbands!" Ashley replied. "That's something we have in common, Dru."

Um . . . "Yep."

"I knew right then and there that I wanted to ask her out," Gray continued.

"I wasn't interested," Dru said flatly. "I'd never heard of him before in my life."

Ashley set both palms on the island and leaned forward. "What?! You'd never heard of Gray Fowler?"

"No. I'm guessing there are a lot of people who've never heard of him. Thousands." She tugged the final mozzarella ball off the skewer and into her mouth. "Millions."

"But, see, I liked that about you, babycakes—the fact that you weren't swayed by my celebrity." Gray leaned his hip against the counter.

Dru narrowed her eyes. *Babycakes* was going too far.

"It usually takes me half a minute to win a woman over," Gray continued. "With you, it took me five whole minutes."

"To the contrary. I'm still not won over. We preschool teachers attract men like flies, so we have the freedom to be very choosy."

Ashley giggled, then cut the sound off. She looked between Dru and Gray, uncertain.

"Cracker and cheese, honey?" Gray extended a cracker toward Dru's mouth.

She intercepted it before he could feed it to her and took a bite. Delicious black-pepper-flavored crunch. Creamy soft cheese. The food here sure beat taquitos from 7-11.

"I've made pot roast, potatoes, bread, and fresh green beans for dinner," Ashley announced. "Sound okay?"

"Sounds great," Gray answered. "Thanks, Ash."

She dimpled. "Everything's ready when you are."

"We'll be ready in about thirty minutes." Gray picked up the platter of appetizers and made a head motion for Dru to follow him.

A head motion. As if she were his collie.

"Dru and I will probably be doing some pretty serious kissing." Gray strode from the kitchen. "So hold my calls."

Ashley tittered and blushed.

Dru followed him into a room off the front foyer that turned out to be his office. The luxurious space showcased leather furniture, walls of books, and a Persian rug in shades of cinnamon and beige.

"I'm going to need a tour of the entire floor plan," Dru said.

"Later. Would you mind shutting the door? So we can get to the serious kissing?"

"You can shut your own door," Dru shot back, standing in the middle of the room. "The only thing I'd like to do with you in a serious manner is bash in your head. Potty training? Holiday headbands?"

"What? You don't enjoy potty training and holiday headbands?"

"Next time, just stick to the basics of my cover story. Don't embellish."

He set the platter on his desk, shut the door, and faced her. "I'd like to see you try to bash in my head. C'mon." He made a beckoning motion with his hands. His lips tilted up at the edges. "Let's see what you got."

She was actually tempted. She'd love to flip him onto his back and plant her boot on his sternum. Against the average man, she liked her chances. But Gray wasn't average. If she tried her jiu-jitsu on him and failed, it might prove suicidal to her pride.

Also, she was being paid to keep him whole and healthy, not to try her best to maim him.

"Well?" he asked.

"You have a bad hip."

"Even with the bad hip, I'm pretty sure I can protect myself from you."

"Another day."

He shrugged. "Fine. Steal all my fun." He lowered into the chair behind his desk, swabbed a carrot stick into the bowl of dip, and held it out to her. "Here."

She hesitated, then took it. She was almost always hungry. The dip tasted homemade. Spicy and smooth. "Where did you find Ashley? 1954?"

"For your information, there are a lot of women out there who still enjoy homemaking." He leaned back in his chair and, with a soft grunt of pain, crossed his feet on his desk's corner.

"What exactly is her role here?"

"She keeps my house in order. She goes to the cleaners, the grocery store, runs errands, cooks. Plus, she handles my calendar and correspondence. Wait until you taste how good her pot roast is." He shook more nuts into his mouth.

"She sounds like a wife."

"She's better than a wife. I tell her what to do, she does it, and she never nags."

"Charming. I suppose you throw coins in her direction every now and then as compensation."

"I pay Ash very well. She's been working for me for three years. She loves me."

"I think she might. Love you, that is."

"She's harmless."

"She seems a little crazy to me."

"No, Dru." He gave her a crooked, very male grin. "That's how nice people act. You're probably not familiar with the species."

"As a protection agent, I may not be familiar with nice, but I'm plenty familiar with crazy." She turned on her heel and crossed the room. The laptop that Sutton

Security had left onsite for their agents awaited her on a low coffee table near a picture window framing a view of the front yard and the darkening sky.

Dru made her way through the laptop's password protection and pulled up the background check Sutton had run on Ashley Huey. Attacks were often pulled off with the help of insiders. It was possible that Gray's stalker was Ashley, was working with Ashley, or was pumping information about Gray from Ashley, possibly without her even realizing it.

Ashley's background check was squeaky clean. Gray's assistant had never even had a speeding ticket. *Not even one speeding ticket?* Dru thought with a flair of disgust. Between the two of them, Ashley was clearly the one who ought to have become the preschool teacher.

Next, Dru read through the entries made in the log by the agents who'd guarded Gray since her last shift.

She glanced at Gray. He'd flicked on a TV positioned flush into a bookcase and tuned it to football.

"You received another letter from your stalker yesterday," she said.

"Yeah." He didn't take his focus from the game.

The other agents had noted the reception of the most recent letter in the log. Sutton had set up protocol. The agents went through Gray's mail each day wearing plastic gloves. Letters suspected to be from the stalker were opened by the agents. Both the envelope and the letter were scanned onto a computer file, then the file was forwarded to team security. Finally, the agents delivered the letters and envelopes to the police.

Dru studied the scanned image of the envelope that had arrived yesterday. It looked exactly like all the others.

The addresses had been printed onto labels and stuck onto a standard business-sized envelope. This one bore the postmark of Wichita Falls, Texas.

She opened a separate document containing a map on which each of the letters' postmark locations had been noted. Wichita Falls was north and west of Dallas. A slight majority of the postmarks had come from towns to the north, as far up as Tulsa, Oklahoma. It might be that the stalker lived to the north. Or it might be that he or she preferred to drive north to mail the letters.

She clicked to the scanned image of the letter.

> You think you're someone but you're not. You're nothing and I'm going to kill you. I think about killing you day and night. I think about how I'll do it and when. I plan.
> I plan to succeed.

She reread it a few times. Most of the letters were around the same length as this one. Sometimes the stalker mentioned places Gray had been. Sitting back in her chair, she repositioned herself to face Gray fully. He was still reclining, a forearm resting across his abs.

"One of my brothers suggested that your stalker might be an angry ex-girlfriend," she said.

In response to her comment, Gray rolled his head in her direction. "As I told you and Anthony Sutton, I have a long list of ex-girlfriends but hardly any angry ones."

"Usually ex-girlfriends are angry by definition."

He stretched for another cracker and piled it with cheese. "It's different with me because none of my girlfriends have been serious. I keep things light. Short-term. No commitments."

"No talk of undying love?"

"No talk of love at all."

"Ever?"

"No." He ate the cracker, then dusted the crumbs from his hands. "I'm not cut out for that kind of a relationship."

Why? Dru wondered, her curiosity sharpening. What had happened to him that would make him think himself incapable of a relationship with a woman that might last past two months and include the *L* word?

Dru and Anthony Sutton had asked him questions about his childhood during his time at Sutton Security's headquarters. He'd told them as little as possible. His mother had been twenty years old and unmarried when she'd had him. Gray didn't know his father's identity. His mom had married three times, each time for three years or less. She'd had a son with husband one and a daughter with husband two. After husband three, it seemed she'd thrown in the towel on love and marriage. She worked at a hair salon in Gray's hometown.

The fact that Gray wouldn't divulge more than that was damning. So was the fact that his half brother was in jail for grand theft auto and his half sister had been busted on marijuana charges, arrested twice for DWI, and given birth to two kids by two different fathers—all before hitting twenty.

It couldn't have been easy to be raised in a home where stepfathers came in one door and left out the other, where marriages that began in hope ended in ashes. Dru had snooped into the court records and police records covering the years Gray had lived under his mother's roof. The records had been silent. If anything unlawful had happened during Gray's childhood, it had happened without the notification of authorities.

"Let's talk about Kayla Bell," Dru said. "According to what you told Anthony Sutton and me, she's your only angry ex."

He motioned his head toward the TV. "Look. Fourth and inches."

"How come Kayla didn't leave her relationship with you smiling, like all the others did?"

The offense converted their fourth down into a touchdown, and Gray moved his attention back to her. "Almost all my girlfriends were nice. Kayla was more like you. A little on the . . . forceful side."

Dru glared. "You're comparing me to Kayla Bell?"

"I dated Kayla for a few months two years ago. She wasn't satisfied with the flattery and the gifts and the friendship I offered her at the end. She wanted me."

"But she couldn't have you, so several weeks later she told you she was pregnant."

"Right. She was pregnant. But I knew the baby wasn't mine, and the prenatal paternity test agreed. Ever since then, though, she's said the test was wrong."

"How often does she contact you?"

He hefted one big shoulder. "Every few months. She calls me or texts me when she's drunk or mad at me or in love with me."

"Has she shown up here?"

"Yeah. She can't get in the gate so she parks her car on the street."

"Do you talk to her in those situations?"

"Sure. She's some kid's mom. I don't want her sitting outside my house in her car all night."

"Has she become so angry in the past that she's tried to physically assault you?"

"A couple of times." He gave her a droll look. "So what? You threatened to assault me five minutes ago."

"But I showed heroic restraint and didn't actually come after you."

"Needless to say," Gray went on, "the few times Kayla came after me, she didn't succeed."

"Do you have reason to think Kayla knows how to use a gun?" The stalker's letters occasionally mentioned plans to shoot Gray.

"Kayla grew up hunting with her dad." He picked up a tomato mozzarella skewer. "Don't give me that sharp, interested look, Dru. There's no reason for you to waste your time on Kayla. She's not my stalker."

"Someone has to be your stalker."

"It's not Kayla. So . . . is it time to start in on the kissing yet?"

"Have you ever heard of something called sexual harassment in the workplace?"

"Have you ever heard of a sense of humor?"

"You may not need to worry about your stalker, Gray. It might be me—"

"My bodyguard?"

"—your *executive protection agent*—that you'd be wise to fear the most."

"Is this when you take your computer into another room and make yourself scarce like the other bodyguards do? I like to watch football in peace."

She unplugged the laptop from the power cord and carried it toward the door. "This is exactly when I make myself scarce. And, let me add, I do so with pleasure."

CHAPTER
FOUR

If anyone with nefarious intentions ever targeted Dru for a middle-of-the-night home invasion, they would not, no sir, find her wearing a pair of flannel pajamas.

She slept in workout clothes. And she kept her gun in the top drawer of her bedside table.

On this particular morning, two days after her first visit to Gray's house, she planned to put the workout clothes to good use after breakfast. She didn't, however, have need of the gun. Nothing more dangerous than watery morning light infiltrated her bedroom.

She tossed aside her sheets and blankets, causing her golden retriever to grunt from her spot at the foot of the bed. Slipping her feet into a pair of Adidas flip-flops, Dru made her way to the window, where rain ran in slow, mournful stripes down the panes.

Four years had passed since she'd returned to her hometown after completing her term of service with the Marines. Holley, set in rolling land northeast of Dallas, had been built in the era of cattle drives and six-shooters and horsepower that meant exactly that.

Almost as soon as she'd been hired by Sutton Security, Dru had started looking for a home to call her own. She'd known herself well enough to know that she wasn't a city dweller, nor a suburbs kind of girl, nor suited to Holley's beautiful, but very feminine, Victorians.

She'd decided to search for a tiny, modern house set outside of town on acreage. The acreage had been a necessity because, like most of her family, she required land around her. Tiny, because of her budget. Modern, because she'd been enamored with the idea of sleek concrete, minimalism, and walls of glass.

She'd ended up with just one out of three. She'd purchased acreage. Her house wasn't especially tiny, however. And there was definitely nothing modern about it.

The first time she'd driven out to see the abandoned log cabin in the woods, the entire structure had been leaning to one side. No one had been more stunned than Dru herself when she'd fallen in love with the place at first sight.

She'd managed to swing the purchase financially because country land north of Holley was reasonably priced, because the house was one step away from tumbling over beneath the force of the next stiff wind, and because she'd saved the lion's share of her income from the Marines.

It had taken a year to restore the place with the help of her family and the workmen she'd hired with the money her grandfather had left her in his will. Slowly, all twelve hundred square feet—living areas on the bottom floor, one bathroom and two bedrooms with sharply pitched ceilings on the second floor—had been transformed.

Though she'd been living in the cabin for almost three

years now, there were still moments like this one when her affection for her house felt like a physical thing. An inner softening.

Fi, her golden retriever, gave a soft *woof* and wiggled to the edge of the mattress.

"It's ridiculous to demand to be lifted down and up from the bed," Dru grumbled good-naturedly. "You realize this, right? You're getting older, but you're not so old that you can't jump down and hop up on your own power."

Fi peered at Dru with patient pleading.

"Fi in the sky with diamonds," Dru muttered. Since *Fi* rhymed with *sky*, the silly nickname had stuck. She hoisted her dog from her nest of blankets. Not easy. Fi weighed sixty unwieldy pounds. Carefully, she set the dog on her paws, and the two of them made their way downstairs.

Horizontal logs, interrupted only by the smooth, white chinking between them, marked the home's downstairs interior walls. The tawny, burnished colors of the logs complemented the same tones in the thick-plank wood floor. The scarred textures of both told stories to Dru of residents long gone.

Dru got coffee going in her kitchen, then slid a Pop-Tart into the toaster. The walls and floors of the kitchen were as ancient as everything else, but the cream-colored cabinetry, limestone countertops, and stainless steel appliances were wonderfully new, new, new.

Dru freed a dog treat from its canister and flicked it to Fi, who caught it midair. Dru was finishing her final bite of Pop-Tart when her cell phone chimed to signal an incoming text. She slanted the phone in her direction. From her boss, Anthony Sutton.

Detective Carlyle just got back to me with the details on the maroon truck whose license plate number Gray took down. It's an '88 Ford Ranger. It belongs to Mildred Osbourne, age 86. She lives in Bonham.

Dru swallowed, tasting strawberry and pastry crust. Just because Mildred owned the truck didn't mean she was the one driving it. In fact, an '88 Ranger didn't exactly seem like the car of choice for an eighty-six-year-old female.

I'll take a trip to Bonham to talk with Mildred the next time Gray travels to an away game, Dru typed back.

Gray. In all honesty, and perhaps even regrettably, Dru didn't need text messages from Anthony to keep her new client at the front of her thoughts. He was already there. This was her first case in the field in a long time, and she was dead-set on not just meeting but exceeding her responsibilities, which had to explain why she was extra-consumed with the big, famous gladiator and the confusing mystery of his stalker.

Today was Tuesday, however, the first of her two days off per week. Gray had no business being in her head today. *Think about other things, Dru. Things you actually like.* She could think, for instance, about taking a trip to the practice range to dust off some of her rarely used guns. Might be fun to shoot the .44 Magnum Colt Anaconda.

Dru drained the last of her coffee and the last of her glass of water. Near the cabin's back door, all her running gear waited. Different thicknesses of shirts and jackets on pegs. Caps. Headbands. New Balance shoes.

She donned what she needed, then opened the back door and gave Fi a chance to take in the wet weather.

"You're not going to come this morning, are you? Too wet for the royal princess?"

Fi hesitated, then plopped onto her belly. The retriever gave Dru a look that said, *I draw the line at mushy moisture. Thanks, but I'll be staying put right here where it's dry and cozy.*

"That's what I thought." Except when it was rainy, Fi, the wuss, came along on Dru's daily morning runs.

She set out, her stride even. Moisture tickled her face and fell, cool and weightless, against her chest, shoulders, hands. Autumn leaves mashed beneath her running shoes. Air that smelled like wind and dew enveloped her, both close and vast.

In order to uncover the identity of Gray's stalker, she'd need to investigate any lead, no matter how small or unlikely. So she'd do exactly as she'd told Anthony. She'd drive to Bonham and check out the maroon truck. The fact that Gray had noticed what he thought was the same truck more than once and then gone to the trouble of jotting down its license plate number indicated that the vehicle had tripped his intuition. Dru had a heck of a lot of respect for intuition—

Think about other things!

Her New Balances pounded downhill toward Whispering Creek. Mist and a light crackling of frost coated the stream's pebbly bank. In every direction, she could see nothing but unbroken, hushed, and drizzly nature.

Her breath jutted in and out of her lungs in a rhythmic pattern. She ran because running felt like exertion and challenge and freedom. Since Mexico, it also felt like a way to chase down her own rehabilitation. Painstakingly, she'd built her injured leg and wrist back to full strength. On cold, damp days like today, however, they still ached. The leg especially. With every footfall, she could tell the difference between the shin bone in her right and her left leg. She pushed past the reminders and the discomfort, taking care not to favor either leg.

Look here, God. I'm gaining strength and stamina. I'm willing to put in the work not just spiritually, but physically. I'm not wasting your redemption of me.

Dru had been born restless and daring, two qualities that didn't exactly form the recipe for a happy life. From the age of fifteen on, she'd sought out and tried just about every dangerous stunt and wicked vice the world had to offer. The losses and griefs she'd encountered on her tours with the Marines had only added a dark and cynical edge to her self-destructive bent.

It wasn't until Mexico—she blew out a painful, uneven gust of breath—that God had hit her across the head with a divine baseball bat. At her lowest point, she'd put all her faith in Him. In answer, He'd rescued her. Changed her.

Fundamentally, He'd changed her. He had not, however, removed the restlessness or the daring from her DNA. The daring she'd been able to channel and temper. But she considered the restlessness her thorn. She had a home and a job and a family and faith. Why was there still this little corner of her heart that seethed for something more? That was not satisfied?

She jogged along a tree trunk that had fallen across the creek, forming a natural bridge. A memory of Gray, walking toward her from his garage wearing that crisp business shirt, rose to the fore of her mind.

He hadn't turned out to be as completely intolerable as she'd diagnosed him to be at first. He was stubborn and stupidly unwilling to do her bidding, even for the sake of his own safety, but he was also quick-witted and he had a sense of humor.

After becoming overly invested in her last client, it would be ideal if she and Gray could keep their rapport purely professional. But so far, Gray didn't appear interested in pure professionalism. He seemed to enjoy the whole fake girlfriend ruse.

Perhaps she could allow a careful, workplace-type friendship to develop between them. Certainly nothing more. Big Mack became fast friends with all his clients, despite the fact that Sutton frowned on personal relationships and outright forbid romantic ones between agents and clients. It was Sutton's stance that when confronted with a dangerous situation, personal relationships between clients and agents could muddy an agent's decision making.

Dru happened to agree. Her experience with her last client had only strengthened her resolve to avoid emotional entanglements with future clients. Some of Sutton's employees had come to doubt her now and watched her closely. Far more that that, though, on a personal level, she didn't want anything bad to happen on her watch to anyone else she cared about.

So, a tepid workplace friendship with Gray would be the most she could offer—

Think about other things!

What was wrong with her? Why couldn't she let go of her focus on Gray?

Remember the Colt Anaconda? Think on that.

"Let's talk about Kevin Lee," Dru said to Gray on Thursday evening, during her first shift back at work after two days off.

"Let's not. How about we relax and order appetizers and drinks?"

"I don't drink. And even if I did, I wouldn't drink on the job."

He gave her a skeptical look. "You don't drink at all?"

"At all. I gave it up a year and a half ago."

They sat in a luxurious round booth at an embarrassingly overpriced steakhouse. After practice today, Gray had spent extra time undergoing PT on his hip. They'd stopped at his home for a few hours before heading out for this pre-scheduled dinner with Mustangs' quarterback Corbin Stewart.

Dru had lobbied to eat alone at a separate table. Gray had refused. He didn't believe his stalker watched him all day, every day. However, his stalker did seem to watch him often enough and carefully enough to eventually notice the dark-haired woman who always sat alone at restaurant tables near Gray's table. "That'll raise his suspicions," Gray had said.

A new girlfriend sharing restaurant dinners with him and his buddies? "Noticeable," he'd said. "But not suspicious."

Dru had asked him if he planned to make Mack and Weston eat with him every time they accompanied him to restaurants. He'd explained that he didn't often eat out during the morning hours of Mack's shift or the late-night hours of Weston's shift. But if the situation arose, yes, he'd make them join him, too.

Dru didn't know whether to believe him.

And she sure didn't like sitting next to him in these romantic surroundings. Light hovered over the interior of the steakhouse like dusk. The miniature lantern on their table flickered. Servers swept by carrying trays that supported tall goblets of deep red and clear white wine. All the occupants of the restaurant snuck glances at Gray. Some shyly approached, like the father and teenage son currently making their way toward them.

This would be the third time since their arrival that fans had come over to Gray. They drew near him with dazzled smiles and a tinge of self-consciousness. Gray handled his admirers with ease. This was his tenth year in the NFL, and before that he'd been a college star. He and fame were not strangers.

Before the father and son could finish apologizing for interrupting, Gray rose and politely introduced Dru as if they were all at a cocktail party.

After he'd introduced her to the first group of fans who'd come to ask for his autograph, she'd asked him not to bother. Not only were introductions unnecessary, but she wanted to be known as Dru Montana to as few people as humanly possible. He'd kept on introducing her anyway.

The father praised Gray and reminisced about a few of the Mustangs' recent games and Gray's winning heroics in the Super Bowl. The son gawked with openmouthed awe.

Dru and the rest of the Porters had always enjoyed football—a lot. But they'd steered clear of idolizing it or its players. Even the Cowboys players. While Gray's talent at football was impressive, she had no trouble seeing him for what he was. A man. A man who could be killed by a stalker's bullet as easily as any other person could be.

Dru's attention slowly swept the diners, cataloging them. While on duty in a public environment, she'd made it her habit to know at all times which person in the vicinity represented the biggest threat. Each time new people arrived, she rescanned and updated her assessment.

Earlier today, she and Mack had typed up Gray's itinerary for the week, including an address and contact phone number for each stop. They'd also compiled information on the trauma centers and police stations nearest to the locations Gray was scheduled to visit, as well as maps with routes and alternate routes highlighted clearly and notations about which choke points to avoid. She'd sent the information to her smartphone, but she and Mack had also printed out paper copies. No expert in her profession placed all their trust in electronics.

While Gray had been at PT, Dru had visited this steakhouse and performed an advance. She'd observed the parking, the entrances and exits, and which space she could use as a safe room if necessary.

Gray's fans asked if they could get a picture with him. Gray smiled obligingly as the dad took a group selfie, then parted from the guys as if they were all old friends. He slid back into his place, bringing with him the faint smell of his soap, crisp and clean, like the sheets at an expensive hotel. He flagged their server, and ordered a drink and three different appetizers, all without consulting Dru.

"I'll be ordering and paying for myself tonight," she said.

"You're welcome to order for yourself," he answered smoothly. "Those appetizers are just to snack on."

"You ordered calamari, lobster, and stuffed mushrooms for a snack?"

"Have you seen the size of the Jets' defensive end I'll be blocking on Sunday? If it's okay with you, I'd rather not lose any weight between now and then. Besides, Corbin's coming. He'll be hungry."

A third place setting at their table waited for the yet-to-show Corbin.

Gray extended one of his powerful arms along the top of the booth, which brought the hand of that arm near Dru's head. "Tell me about yourself," he said.

"What would you like to know?"

"How did you get the name Dru? It's unusual."

"My mom named me after her favorite aunt Dru, who went everywhere barefoot and knitted us all winter caps."

"You don't seem to have turned out much like her."

"I'm nothing like her."

"Were you one of those little girls who did ballet and loved rainbows?" The glimmer in his green eyes assured her that he knew very well she hadn't been that kind of girl.

Dru flicked a discouraging look at his hand, still resting on the top of the booth seat. He didn't move it, and *she* couldn't very well move it with so many spectators. She pretended to readjust her seat, scooting back from him slightly. "How long has Kevin Lee been a fan of yours?" she asked, refocusing on the topic she'd been trying to raise earlier. Staff at Sutton Security's headquarters were busy digging up information on all the people, including Kevin Lee and Kayla Bell and others, who Gray had told them might have reason to wish him ill. In the meantime, though, she wanted more info from Gray himself.

"So no ballet, huh?" he said. "Tap dancing?"

She had no intention of answering questions about her childhood. Ever since they'd sat down, he'd been steering the conversation away from business and toward things that two people their age might discuss on a date. "How many years has Kevin been a fan?" she asked.

"Jazz dancing?"

"About Kevin—"

"Did you wear those, um, crowns little girls wear? What are those called?" His phone rang, and he pulled it from his pocket. Furrows grooved into his forehead as he read the display.

"Who is it?" Dru asked.

"My mother." He rejected the call and returned his attention to her. He wore a long-sleeved, white Under Armour shirt. The loose kind, not the kind that vacuum-sealed to your body. Jeans. He looked effortlessly comfortable in the clothes and seemed not to notice or care that they were technically too casual for this restaurant. Who was going to complain about the dress code to the idol? No one.

"Kevin Lee has been a fan of yours since . . . ?" Dru prompted, dogged.

"Are you always this intense?"

"Yes."

"How come this information on Kevin is so urgent? Do you think the bartender there"—he nodded in the direction of the darkly paneled bar—"is going to rip off a plastic face, reveal himself to be Kevin, then lift an Uzi?"

"At the moment I'm more concerned with the woman sitting at one o'clock. Of everyone here, her face looks the most plastic."

He chuckled. Their server slid a glass of Southern Comfort on the rocks in front of Gray.

He leaned back to take a slow sip. "Kevin Lee has been a fan of mine for something like four years."

"How old is he?"

"Forty or so."

"What is it about him that worries you?"

"Nothing about him worries me," he replied.

She gave an irritable sigh and rephrased. "What is it about him that motivated you to mention him to Anthony Sutton and me?"

"Most of my fans have a sense of boundaries. Like the father and son who just came by."

"But Kevin Lee doesn't have boundaries."

"No. He mails letters to my house. He mentions me on Twitter all the time. He phones the Mustangs. He sends several emails a day."

"What does he say?"

He studied her, looking a little sheepish. "How much he likes me, how glad he is that we're friends, how much he looks up to me. He asks me to give him jerseys or footballs or pictures or whatever and sign them."

"Have you ever given him any items?"

"I gave him a photo once, right at the beginning. Since then, no."

"Has he sent letters to your other homes? Or just your Dallas address?"

"Just Dallas."

The beautiful trio of steaming appetizers arrived.

"How often do you see Kevin in person?" Dru asked.

"Every time I pull into the practice facility or the stadium, he's at the fence. Every time." He picked up the plate of stuffed mushrooms and held it toward her. She took two. He slid a few onto his plate. "When he sees me coming, he waves and shouts stuff like, 'Go, Gray! You're the best! Good to see you, buddy!'"

"What's his interaction like with other players?"

"He'll wave and yell stuff to them when they're driving in or out, too. But he doesn't try to contact them."

"Is he all there—mentally, I mean?"

"No, I don't think so. How could he park at the fence waiting for me to drive in and out every day and still hold down a job? I'm guessing that Kevin still lives with his parents. He's strange, and he doesn't have boundaries, but you don't need to worry about him. He's not my stalker. I only mentioned his name and those other names because you and Anthony weren't going to let me leave until I gave you guys something to work with. Lobster?"

"Just a bite."

"Now that I've answered your questions about Kevin, you need to return the favor and answer some questions about yourself."

She set down her fork. "How come you keep trying to initiate get-to-know-you conversation with me, Gray? There's no need."

"Of course there's a need. You'll be going where I go five afternoons a week. I'd like to know something about you." He hadn't paused like she had. He continued eating, very relaxed, as if he'd just said that the calamari had a nice sauce.

"I was thinking the other day that we can perhaps have a tepid sort of business friendship." She spoke grudgingly. "That's my best offer. I'm your agent, not your buddy."

"What does tepid mean?"

"Lukewarm."

"A lukewarm business friendship. Wow. Generous. Hard to imagine turning that down."

"Feel free to turn it down," she groused.

"I'll take it. Now answer my questions. You were not a little girl who did ballet and wore a crown."

"No. Not that my mom didn't try. I'm the youngest and the only girl."

A lopsided smile broke across Gray's face. Speaking from a strictly scientific viewpoint, Dru could see why some women—not her—might find him attractive. "The youngest and the only girl," he said. "That explains a lot."

"My mom was always trying and failing to interest me in princess dresses and tea parties."

"What were you busy doing instead?"

"Trying to chase down Bo on horseback. Trying to shoot Ty with homemade bows and arrows. Trying to execute a standing leg sweep on Jake."

"You have three older brothers."

"Three much older brothers."

"And you've been wanting to prove yourself equal to them since birth," he concluded.

His observation struck home. "Nope," she lied. How

could this stranger have guessed that after so few questions?

Dru caught sight of Corbin Stewart making his way in their direction. Excitement rolled through the already-stirred-up diners like a tsunami swell as they recognized the Mustangs' most famous player.

Corbin was a workingman's quarterback. Much more Brett Favre's ilk than Tom Brady's, he'd grown up tall and brawny, fast, with unmatched arm strength.

Corbin had not posted staggering numbers in college. Thus, he'd been selected as a backup quarterback by the Mustangs eight years ago in a late round of the draft amid lackluster hopes. What the scouts hadn't been able to anticipate? How much Corbin would continue to improve and how astonishingly good he'd be under pressure. Whenever the game was close and the situation critical, Corbin Stewart's bravery honed, his nerves steadied, and he delivered the football with flawless precision.

Gray performed introductions once Corbin had taken a seat. The quarterback wore flat-front pants and a simply cut, expensive-looking, coffee-colored sweater.

"I'm glad to know that Gray has you for a bodyguard," Corbin told her.

Corbin knew the truth about her, thank God. She wouldn't have to pretend to be Gray's girlfriend with him.

"Gray needs someone," Corbin continued, "to protect him from himself."

"I'm a protection agent," Dru answered, "not a miracle worker."

The two men grinned. "Do you know what Dru here

just offered me?" Gray asked Corbin. "A tepid business friendship. Do you know what tepid means?"

"Lukewarm," Corbin answered.

Gray's eyebrows rose. "You two are made for each other."

Corbin winked at Dru. "A guy can hope."

Gray frowned.

More Mustangs fans approached.

Dru, Gray, and Corbin ordered entrees.

Corbin's hair wasn't dark brown or auburn, but a shade in between. He had a face that a woman could look at for a long, long time. An interesting, intelligent face. Square-jawed and brown-eyed.

If Gray were the gladiator willing to charge first into a fight carrying a sword, Corbin was the Roman general, studying field maps and strategizing.

The two men and teammates shared a laid-back camaraderie born of a long friendship. Dru joined in their conversation when she wished or when they asked her questions. Mostly, though, she watched the room and listened and secretly gloried in her meal. Amazingly tender and topped with a melting dollop of chive butter, her steak all but dissolved on her tongue.

A few minutes before ten, Weston Kinney entered the restaurant. With his lean physique, white-blond hair, and hip clothing, her replacement resembled the bodyguard stereotype almost as little as Dru herself.

Weston's line of sight made a glancing cross with hers before he took a seat at the bar.

"My shift's over," she announced.

Both men turned say-it-isn't-so faces on her. "What?" Gray asked. "We haven't even ordered dessert."

"Be that as it may, my shift is over."

"Stay," Gray said.

Most women, presented with two handsome bachelor NFL players and an invitation to stay through dessert at a ritzy steakhouse, would jump at the chance. Just one more reminder of how unlike most women Dru was.

"Good night." She nodded at Corbin, whom she actually somewhat liked.

"Good night. It was nice to meet you."

"G'night, bodyguard," Gray said.

"I'm not even going to dignify that with a response."

"You just did," he pointed out.

Dru slid her purse over her shoulder and strode toward the door, leaving the click of her stilettos in her wake.

"I can't believe you have a bodyguard who looks like that," Corbin said to Gray. "You *lucky* jerk."

"I've always told you that it's better to be lucky than good."

"I've suddenly decided that I need my own bodyguard."

"Fine. But you can't have mine."

"I want yours."

"You can't have her."

Corbin looked in the direction Dru had gone. "She's . . . how should I say it? Bigger than life?"

"I know. She's more like a comic book superhero than a regular human woman."

"She needs a superhero name." Corbin bent his fingers in a signal that brought their waitress rushing to their table. They both ordered what Gray knew would be their final drink of the night. It was sort of like when you were a kid and you weren't allowed to stay up late on school nights. Gray and Corbin didn't let themselves drink much on practice nights.

"Motorcycle Girl?" Gray suggested when their waitress had gone. "Dru drives a motorcycle."

"Of course she does," Corbin said in an affectionate way that irritated Gray. "Motorcycle Girl is too plain for her, though. And the *girl* part is too young. Protector Woman?"

"Huh. Dark Siren?"

"Blue-Eyed Avenger?"

"Avenger's sort of good," Gray said. "How about Revengeress?"

They both let the name settle for a moment as their drinks were served. "I like it," Corbin said.

Gray nodded. "Done, then. Revengeress it is." They clicked their glasses together.

"I want to go out with her," Corbin stated.

Gray's stomach wrenched, and it took effort to calmly swallow his Southern Comfort. "You just met her."

"I shared an entire dinner with her, which is more time than I usually spend with a woman before asking her out."

The idea of Corbin going out with Dru hit Gray all wrong. Gut-level wrong. He wanted to tell Corbin that Dru was *his* and shove the younger man off his territory, exactly as he'd just done when he'd told Corbin that Dru was his bodyguard and not up for grabs.

The difference was that he'd had a right to defend his place in Dru's professional life. He had no right and no reason to defend his place in Dru's personal life. He had no place in Dru's personal life.

Corbin was a good guy. He'd treat Dru well. And it wasn't as if he himself wanted to date Dru. Geez, she was so . . . "Don't you think Dru's a little too . . . hard?"

"Who cares? She's gorgeous. Did you see those eyes?"

"She's one of those women who's always trying to compete with men and impress everybody with how capable she is." He liked women who were content being women. "It's tiring."

"She's welcome to compete with me all she wants. Bring it on."

Gray scowled.

"She likes me." Corbin leaned back as far as the booth allowed and crossed a foot over his opposite knee. "She likes me better than you."

Gray didn't understand where this lame sense of possessiveness had come from. Even so, it stuck with him as two thirty-something women approached their table and asked for autographs.

He almost never felt possessive of women. He and Corbin had gone after the same woman a few times in the past. It had been fun—more of a sporting contest than anything. His feelings hadn't been involved. A few other times he and Corbin had dated each other's ex-girlfriends. He'd never cared.

Maybe he was drunk. He'd go to sleep tonight and wake up tomorrow and feel completely different about all this. He'd laugh at himself for getting worked up over the thought of Corbin dating Dru. Of course Corbin could date Dru. He was welcome to her. He should be saying *good luck with that, man*, patting his teammate on the back and teasing Corbin with warnings about Dru instead of sitting here with his mouth shut.

Football required his complete focus. Outside of football, all he wanted was peace and pretty, easygoing women. Dru had a mouth on her that wouldn't quit. She was too feisty to get along with for half a minute.

The thirty-somethings left. In the silence after their departure, the background noise of other people's conversations seemed to increase. As did the scent of filets cooking.

"Care to make a wager?" Corbin asked.

He and Corbin wagered often. They golfed together during the off-season and placed bets on every single hole. They wagered on the backgammon games they played while traveling. On how many pounds Corbin could bench press. On whether it would rain.

"What do you have in mind?" Gray asked.

"I'm willing to bet that I can get Dru to kiss me before you can," Corbin said. "It doesn't count for you or me to kiss her. That's too easy. Kisses can be stolen. I'm talking about a kiss that *she* initiates."

Gray set his jaw. "I don't think Dru's allowed to date me because she's been hired to protect me. That fact puts me at a disadvantage."

"But you're with her for several hours each week. Which puts me at a disadvantage. Our disadvantages weigh out. We're even."

"What are you offering me if I win?" Gray asked.

"The new flat screen in my living room."

Corbin was speaking Gray's language, and Corbin knew it. Corbin's flat screen was brand new and sweet. Sixty-five inches, 4K HD. Gray had grown up with one lousy little television that he and his brother and sister and mom had shared. He had a weakness for televisions.

He already had four of them in his Dallas house, a house that he lived in alone. But to win one off Corbin? And then have the right to brag about it to everyone who came in the door for years to come? That was rare and worth way more to him than the TV itself.

"What will you give me if I win?" Corbin asked.

"Which you won't."

"I think I will. What're you going to give me?"

Gray thought for a minute, then pulled back his left sleeve. His new Rolex GMT Master steel watch caught the light.

Corbin smiled. "I like."

But did Gray? Was he seriously considering going through with this? As Corbin had said, Dru was gorgeous. From a physical-attraction standpoint, kissing her would be no problem. It was the personality thing that was the hurdle.

Dru was difficult but—he groped for something optimistic to grab on to—he didn't think she was *mean*, exactly. He wasn't a hundred percent sure of that, but he didn't think so. She made him laugh, a good quality. He was used to feeling as though his brain was processing information more quickly than the people around him, but he didn't feel that way around her. She shot comebacks at him with blazing speed. So, there was that.

"Well?"

"I'm trying to decide whether I want to take your bet or not."

"If she's too much of a challenge for you, then I recommend you let me have her and keep your Rolex, old man. How old are you now, anyway? Forty-five? Pushing retirement for sure."

Gray was only twenty months older than Corbin. "I've got two more seasons after this one on my contract, rookie. Which is something you should be thanking God for every night." So long as his body held up, Gray was committed to playing through the end of his contract. By then, he'd be thirty-five. The average length of an NFL career was three and a half years. The average age of retirement, below thirty.

NFL contracts went to those who performed. It was as simple as that. He got it. The idea of spending his final years in the league trying to produce at his past level, begging other teams to give him a chance, taking less pay, and playing third string and special teams turned him cold. He'd rather push hard these final seasons and finish strong.

Once he retired, he planned to expand the summer camp he already offered into a year-round program. He'd also toyed with the idea of coaching. College coaching especially appealed to him.

"Do we have a deal?" Corbin asked. "About Dru?"

Gray had game when it came to women. Dru, though. Dru would be tough to win over, and Corbin would be hard to beat. Women always liked quarterbacks best.

Corbin rubbed his thumb on the lip of his glass while he waited for Gray's decision. "Gray?"

"Shut up and let me think." As he considered the angles and judged his odds, his familiar competitive streak began to take over. He and Corbin both liked challenges and they both loved to win, two traits that were useful in life and sports but that could be foolish in situations like this. Think reasonably—

He was thinking. He was thinking he could win. It

was going to take strategy and smarts, but he could get Dru to kiss him. Before Corbin could. He had a head start with her. She didn't actually like him. But he had a head start. And, as Corbin had mentioned, lots of hours with her every week. He liked his chances.

More than that, he couldn't bring himself to hand Dru over to Corbin without opposition. "We have a deal," Gray said.

"Good. You want to go ahead and hand over the Rolex now? You know, for the sake of convenience?"

"Nah. But when you get home tonight you can go ahead and start unbolting your flat screen from the wall."

Corbin released a bark of laughter.

"You're going down," Gray assured him.

CHAPTER FIVE

Gray's courtship of Dru did not get off to a good start.

The day after he struck the bet with Corbin, Gray drove toward the exit gate of the Mustangs' facility after a long, brutal practice.

"Gray!" called Kevin Lee, waving excitedly. Kevin had dressed his overweight body in a puffy green-and-white Mustangs jacket. "I'm here for you, buddy! Way to go. You're the best there is!"

Gray rolled down his window. "Thanks, Kevin."

"Sure, man! Go Mustangs! I'm cheering for you, Gray!" Kevin trotted next to the Ferrari, panting a little, his mostly bald head shining. "Can you give me a jersey? I really want a jersey. A jersey . . ."

Kevin's voice grew faint as distance separated them. Gray closed his window and, a few turns later, pulled onto the tollway toward home. He slid his Ferrari into the fast lane.

His hip was still screwed up, and pain had dogged him during practice. He'd dumped a lot of time into the hip lately. Trainer's tables. MRIs. Massages. Ice baths. The team doctors had decided to shoot the strained muscles with cortisone tomorrow.

Injuries annoyed him. Royally. A lot of his success in the NFL had come because his body was rugged. Through luck or genetics or a combination of the two, he'd been given a body that could withstand a beating. His muscles and tendons and bones were up to the task of professional football. After hits, he didn't need a stretcher. After hits, he got up and walked off the field.

He'd played his position for every down and executed every exercise today. But it had hurt, so he hadn't played as well as he could and should. He couldn't stand it when he performed below his potential.

He let his car race forward, fueled by frustration. The speedometer climbed to one hundred. Then above. Adrenaline began to overpower his bad mood.

He glanced into his rearview mirror and saw a motorcycle pull into the lane behind him. A few seconds later, he cut his vision to his rearview mirror again. The motorcycle had neared—

Recognition bolted like ice through his veins. Black motorcycle. Black helmet and leather jacket. A rider with a slim build.

He nearly had a heart attack. His first instinct was to slam on the brakes. He didn't go that route because doing so would send her straight into the back bumper of his Ferrari. Instead, he slowed his speed gradually. Very gradually.

Dru. She must have been trailing him since . . . since he'd left the facility? That was her usual procedure. His attention had been on Kevin when he'd pulled through the exit. Since then, he'd been wrapped up in his own thoughts. He'd forgotten about his protective detail, and he'd only looked in his rearview mirrors out of blind habit.

He couldn't believe she'd been stupid enough to stay on his tail at that speed.

His heart was thundering, his hands shaking where they gripped the wheel. He'd almost gotten her smeared across a section of highway because he'd been doing 110 and she'd been crazy enough to follow him. If anything had gone wrong just now, it would have been partly his fault. The idea of that, of her involved in an accident because of him, made him sick to his stomach.

Shooting glances at her again and again, he pulled over carefully and took the next exit, which happened to be the one he always took home. At the end of the off-ramp, he turned into a church parking lot, Dru behind him.

He parked, threw open his door, and stalked toward her bike, his hip throbbing with every step.

Dru was already off her Kawasaki and pulling free her helmet. "Are you an idiot?" she demanded, almost yelling.

"Are you?" He matched her volume, his hands fisting at his sides.

"You're going to get yourself killed, driving like that." Her cheeks were pink with anger.

"Me? I was the one driving a car. You were following me at that speed with nothing but two wheels between you and the road."

"It's my job to follow you." She stood tall in a pair of Dr. Marten boots, holding her helmet against her thigh with a white-knuckled hand.

"I forgot you were behind me. Anyone with sense would have backed off and simply caught up with me at my house."

"How was I supposed to know for sure that you were going to your house? Sometimes you make unplanned stops."

"You could have called me," he growled. The scare she'd given him had rattled him, which, in turn, had made him mad. "Why did you stay with me?"

"One, I have confidence in my ability to ride my bike fast. Two, I've been charged with the responsibility of keeping you safe. Protection is my profession, do you understand that? It's my livelihood. If Sutton is going to pay my bills, then I'm more than going to earn what I'm paid." Her words came out clipped with impatience. "I wouldn't have been protecting you if I'd let you drive off to goodness-knows-where at that speed. Your stalker could be waiting for you at your destination. Or you could have crashed your Ferrari into some poor defensive driver who was just trying to get out of your way."

He stepped close to her. Maybe a foot, a foot and a half between them now. She did not retreat, just like he'd known she wouldn't. Features both classically beautiful and sharply stubborn tilted up so that she could look him full in the face. Never before had he met a woman who evenly matched him in will. His was iron. But so was hers.

He wanted to strangle her or lecture her. The last thing he wanted was to . . .

Admire her.

But standing there, looking into her fierce expression and combative posture, admiration expanded within him. It would have been easier for him if he could control Dru with a look or a word. But he couldn't.

Dru was strong and brave. So much so that it made him feel unsteady, like the ground beneath his feet was shifting.

Her breath lifted her chest beneath the leather of her jacket. Cool air whispered between them while a group of blackbirds took to the sky at the parking lot's edge. Orange leaves rattled to the ground in the birds' wake. And surprising need for her tugged at Gray, hot and deep.

He wanted her.

Gray held himself in check, betrayed by the surprising response of his body. He'd bet Corbin his Rolex that he could convince Dru to kiss him. He'd known it wouldn't be a chore. At the same time, he'd expected to stay fully in charge of himself the whole time. He didn't lose it over women. "Dru," he said, doing an imitation of a reasonable human being, "I don't expect you to risk your safety in exchange for mine."

"You might not expect it, but I can assure you that my boss, Anthony Sutton, does. And your boss, Brian Morris, does."

"It's ridiculous, Dru." He wasn't worth her wellbeing, and his situation wasn't worth the fuss the agents were making over his supposed stalker. "If I screw up and drive that fast again, just let me go."

She tilted her head to the side. "Would you give that same order to me if I were a man?"

See? Like he'd told Corbin, the woman felt a need to compete with her male counterparts. "Sure." Though the actual answer was no. If it had been one of his male agents behind him on the tollway just now, he'd simply have driven home and said *sorry about that* to the guy when they'd gotten there.

Dru wouldn't thank him for the truth. And he couldn't explain to her that the desire to protect women had been branded into him through the events of his childhood.

There was nothing she could do to change it. And he refused to apologize for it.

He assessed her furious almond-shaped eyes surrounded with sooty dark lashes. Delicate mouth.

Geez. That mouth.

He turned for his car. "I'm not used to having agents babysitting me."

"You'll get used to it."

At no point on the route to Gray's house did he drive even five whole miles above the speed limit. He crawled along the asphalt in his Ferrari, hands at ten and two.

In order to stay in control of things with Dru, he needed a plan. He needed action. Otherwise, he was in danger of getting stirred up by emotion and desire again, the way he had just now.

How did a man get a woman like Dru to kiss him?

Not through a straightforward romantic approach, he didn't think. Dru would shove advances and compliments back in his face. Friendship was his best bet. He'd build on that. He'd make her laugh. He'd listen to her and show her that he was a decent person.

That's what it would take. That, and a whole lot of patience.

A lady with jet-black hair fashioned into a Marilyn Monroe style answered Dru's knock. The cut might have suited a retro-type person in her early twenties. But the face attached to the hair looked to be over eighty.

"Mildred Osbourne?" Dru asked.

"Yes?" Mildred, owner of the maroon Ford truck, lived in the country. Her tidy, white clapboard house with green shutters stood on a two-lane road in the middle of nowhere.

"I'm Dru Porter. I work for Sutton Security in Dallas and drove out to ask you a few questions about your truck." Two cars occupied Mildred's carport. Neither was the truck.

Mildred's blue eyes, lined with cat's-eye liquid liner, rounded. "Has something happened to the truck?"

"No."

"Would you like to buy it? 'Cause I'd be happy to sell that old thing."

"No, I'm not here to buy it." Dru offered the little lady her business card.

Mildred took a drag on her cigarette while she studied the card. Just five feet tall, Mildred had dressed in a yellow cotton sweatshirt and matching yellow sweatpants, the kind that gathered in at the ankle. "A security company, eh? Are you here to sell us one of those alarm systems for our house? Because we don't use an electronic alarm. We have a dog and a shotgun." She laughed a smoker's laugh, her pink lips smiling the way broads smiled in 1930s movies.

"I'm not here to sell you an alarm system. I'd just like to talk with you about your truck."

Mildred beckoned to her. "Then come on in, doll. Walt and I are driving up to the casino in Durant to play the slots today. But not for another hour or two." She led Dru into a house choked with cigarette smoke.

Gray and the rest of the team were flying to New York on this Saturday afternoon for tomorrow's game. He'd told Dru what it was like to travel by air with the Mustangs. No sitting with seatbacks up and tray tables secure. The players moved around the cabin at will, confident in their belief that a plane carrying an NFL team would never, ever crash. Right at this moment, Gray was probably reclining in 12A while flight attendants buzzed around him, hoping for a chance to slip him their number.

Gray had been strangely charming since yesterday morning's Ferrari-racing incident. He'd been driving everywhere carefully. On a few occasions he'd—shocker—actually done something she'd asked of him. He'd been smiling a lot, asking her questions, and teasing her. All of which made her wary. It couldn't possibly be, could it, that she had him trained already? No. That was too much to hope.

When she'd watched him board the team bus to the airport earlier today, a stab of regret had pierced her. She may have been a tiny bit sorry to see him go. She had no idea why. Just because he'd been acting like a satisfactory human being didn't mean she ought to give a rip about whether he was at home or away. She should be glad he was away so she could pour her full concentration into his case.

Mildred showed Dru to a seat at a round kitchen table with a fake-wood laminate top. A mini rectangular container bristling with Sweet'N Low packets stood guard next to a napkin holder and an ashtray containing butts sporting pink lipstick marks.

"Can I offer you something to drink?" Mildred asked. "Iced tea?"

"Thanks, but I'm fine."

"Cookie, then?" Mildred opened a Ziploc and set an oatmeal raisin cookie on a napkin for Dru. "Everyone loves my cookies."

"No one's liked those cookies for twenty years!" an old man's voice called from an unseen room.

"Keep your opinion to yourself, Walt!" Mildred hollered.

The cookie didn't look like much, and since oatmeal raisin had always been among Dru's least-favorite type of cookie—who really liked raisins?—Dru felt inclined to side with Walt. Nonetheless, she took a bite of cookie and gave Mildred a pleasant expression while chewing.

The cookie was . . . astonishingly tasty. Dru was no expert. She mostly ate either fast food or prepackaged food. But these were amazing. Soft, melt-in-your mouth oatmeal with just the right amount of cinnamon and salt to make them addictive.

"Delicious?" Mildred asked.

"Very."

"She loves my cookies!" Mildred shouted to Walt. Using her molars, she bit off a section of the cookie she'd selected.

"No, she doesn't," Walt called back. "She's just being nice."

"Keep your opinion to yourself, Walt!" Mildred winked at Dru. "Good men like their women to have some sass."

"About your Ford Ranger . . ." Dru said.

"Yes?" Mildred held her cigarette aloft between two fingers. Dru could feel her lung tissue shriveling in the cancerous air.

"One of our clients is Gray Fowler. Does that name ring a bell?"

"Is he a football player?" Mildred asked.

"He is."

The older lady nodded. "For the Mustangs."

"Right. Have you ever had any personal interaction with Gray Fowler?"

"Me? Goodness, no. I keep up with football because Walt and the boys have it on a fair bit. But I've never been to a game."

"Gray has been receiving some threats."

"Oh?" Mildred cocked her head forward like a bird.

"It's my job to protect him."

"Well, good for you for protecting him, doll. That's swell." She bounced a skinny fist with peach oval nails into the air. "I am woman, hear me roar!"

"Gray's seen a maroon truck around town a few times. Enough times that he started to wonder if the driver of the truck was following him, so he took down its license plate number. You, Mildred, came up as the owner."

Mildred's forehead turned even more wrinkly. "That's strange."

"I didn't see the truck parked in the carport. Do you still drive it?"

"I haven't driven it in fifteen or twenty years. It was sitting around here rusting. Walt wouldn't let me sell it"—she raised her voice—"because he kept saying he might need the truck to carry something."

"I might need that truck to carry firewood next week!" Walt thundered.

"No, he won't," Mildred told Dru. Her inky black hair really was a marvel. How did a woman her age manage to keep her hair that dark and shiny? "To transport firewood," Mildred said, "Walt would actually have to lift up a piece of wood. Too much effort."

"Where is the truck?" Dru asked.

"A few years back, I told my son to take it so I wouldn't have to look at it anymore. I believe he drives it now and again when he has something to haul."

"And your son's name is?"

"Rich Osbourne."

Dru made a note of it.

Mildred nipped off another chunk of cookie. "I'm afraid you're barking up the wrong tree, doll. We sure haven't been following anybody around. My best guess is that our truck looks like the one your football player saw those other times."

"That could certainly be the case. Does Rich live here in Bonham?"

"He does. He's a trucker. Hardworking man."

"I'd like to give him a call."

"Of course." Mildred rattled off her son's number.

Dru added it to her notes, then stood. "Thank you for talking with me. I appreciate it."

"You're welcome."

Dru moved to the doorway of the adjacent room, the one Walt's voice had emanated from. Before she left, she wanted a visual on Walt. "Goodbye."

A wizened old man who resembled Yoda from Star Wars saluted from where he sat with newspapers on his lap and a game show on TV. He gave her a conspiratorial smile, as if he was glad Dru had been privy to the running good-man/sassy-lady routine he and Mildred had going.

Dru did not suspect either Mildred or Walt to be Gray's stalker. Rich Osbourne, however? A possibility.

She drove a few miles down the road, then pulled onto the shoulder to dial her cell.

Rich answered after the second ring. "Yep?"

Dru introduced herself and her agency the same way she had with Mildred. "We ran the plate, and the maroon truck that Gray Fowler saw is the one that you're driving."

A pause. Based on his mother's age, Rich would likely be in his late fifties or early sixties. His deep, slightly raspy voice with its thick Texas accent gave Dru a mental image of a heavyset man. "You think I'm the one following Gray Fowler?"

"No, not necessarily. I'm just trying to tie up loose ends."

"It's not me."

"Okay."

"When and where was our truck spotted?"

She told him.

Another pause. "I took my wife to dinner that night in Dallas."

"Do you often drive the truck when you and your wife go out?" She kept the question very mild, no accusation in her tone. Nonetheless, a decades-old, rusty truck seemed like a strange choice for date night.

"Sometimes. When the cars are low on gas or we're trying not to put too many miles on our lease car."

"I'm in Bonham today," Dru said. "If you're at home, I'd like to swing by and ask you a few more questions." Face-to-face interaction always guaranteed Dru the best read on a person.

"I'm on I-40 heading west an hour out of Amarillo. Go ahead and ask your questions now."

Dru asked him if he'd ever met Gray, if anyone in his family had ever met Gray. Rich answered with a string of no's. When she asked him what he used the truck for, other than the occasional date night, he said he most often used it when he needed to carry a load.

Once they'd disconnected, Dru called Sutton's headquarters. She asked Sutton's tech support guru, Julie, if she could unearth an address for Rich Osbourne of Bonham, Texas. In under a minute, Julie texted the address to Dru's phone.

Rich lived on a shady lot near Lake Bonham, in a house that looked like it had been built in the eighties, with alternating patches of beige paint and dark wood shingles. Before Dru came to a complete stop, she spotted the maroon truck parked on the far side of the closed garage.

She knocked on the front door. Rang the bell. Waited. When no one answered, she made her way to the truck. It was locked. She took her time studying the car's body, squinting into its interior, snapping pictures.

For an old vehicle, it had been kept up reasonably well. The tires were inflated, and it looked to have been washed in the past few weeks. It hadn't earned a place inside the garage, which indicated that it might be just what Mildred and Rich had said—an extra vehicle used from time to time.

When she arrived back at Sutton's Dallas office, Dru asked Julie to see what info she could dredge up on Rich. Neither her phone conversation with Mildred's son, nor his house, nor her examination of the truck had given her the rush of adrenaline and rightness she sometimes experienced when she latched onto a viable clue.

At this point, Rich and his mother's maroon truck could logically be categorized as slightly suspicious. Just suspicious enough to merit a little more digging.

Meg woke from a nap Monday afternoon bleary-eyed
and fuzzy-headed. Her health had been slightly off all
weekend, but as today had dragged on, she'd begun to
feel worse. Run-down, faintly nauseous, headachy. She'd
wrapped up the most urgent matters at the Cole Foundation and driven home, thinking a nap would help.

Gingerly, she levered her pregnant body to sitting and
slid her feet over the side of her bed. A wave of sickness
bowled into her.

Meg typically tried to talk herself out of coming
down with things when the symptoms first made themselves known. *You're fine, Meg. You're well!* Sometimes
it worked.

But this time, there could be no more denial. She was
sick. Her heart sank at the thought, dull pain pulsing
within her skull.

The sandy browns and creamy whites of their master bedroom surrounded her. Golden afternoon light
slanted through the numerous windows, highlighting
the autumn wreath she'd hung on the stone fireplace—

Her vision blurred.

Panic dove down through the center of her. The twins.

Something was very wrong. She blinked and blinked
again, willing her vision back to normal. It stayed blurry.
Then began to go foggy.

She'd left her phone on her nightstand. She groped
for it. With shaking fingers, she dialed Bo. *Breathe in
and out, Meg. Smoothly, slowly. In and out.* She closed
her eyes so she wouldn't have to see a warbled view of
her familiar bedroom. As the phone rang, she placed a

hand to her stomach and nudged the babies gently. *Kick me*, she asked them. *Move and show me that you're fine.*

No movement.

"Hi, Countess." At the sound of Bo's reassuring voice, Meg almost sobbed with relief.

"Something's wrong," she said, reaching for calm. "My vision. It's blurry. I almost feel like I'm going to pass out."

"Where are you?"

"Home."

"I'm on my way."

"Okay." Her voice broke.

"I'm here at the farm. It'll only take me a minute to get there." The horse farm where he worked was located nearby on the property of Whispering Creek Ranch.

"Don't hang up," he said. "Stay on with me."

"I will." She clasped the phone like a lifeline and continued to place her palm around her stomach, praying fervently to feel her babies' motion. Still nothing.

She'd battled panic attacks in the past. Anxiety, her old enemy, was coming for her again now. Coming for her like a freight train. Her chest had already begun to tighten. Her throat constricted. Her breathing grew shallow despite her efforts to lengthen it. What if . . . what if something terrible had happened to her babies?

"I'm still here," Bo said. "Talk to me." Bo's words warred against the terror, calling her away from the edge of it and back to him.

"I'm here, too," she said.

"Tell me what you've been feeling all day. Start with this morning."

She spoke. Having to use her brain to remember

meant it couldn't be used fully for fear, which kept her from hyperventilating. Her voice, though. Her voice sounded hollow and thin. Bo didn't need to ask her if she was afraid. She knew that Bo already understood, based on her voice alone, exactly how afraid she was.

She opened her eyes and tested her vision. Everything looked normal. Relief trickled into her. All right. Everything looked fine—

The bedroom turned blurry again, as if she was looking through a camera lens that someone had taken out of focus. *No.* What was happening? This was all wrong.

Bo arrived, immediately gathering her onto his lap and into his arms. He felt like strength. Like home. He hugged her, then held her face in front of his. "It's going to be fine."

She could see him perfectly. The masculine features, the dark hair shaved short, the steel-gray eyes she loved. Thank God for the blessing of being able to see him clearly. He'd paled. And his chest was pumping more quickly than usual, probably because he'd rushed to get to her. But those eyes she loved communicated steadfast confidence.

"The babies," she said.

"They're all right," he insisted.

There was no possible way that he could be sure of that. Nevertheless, his apparent certainty gave her courage.

"Can you walk to the car?" he asked.

"With your help."

"Let's go, then. I'm taking you to the hospital."

CHAPTER SIX

Several miles to the south and west, Dru was about to enter one of the few male bastions she'd yet to breach. This would be the first time she'd ever set foot within a men's dressing room.

After another Mustangs win, Gray had returned from New York during Weston's shift late last night. Mack had texted her thirty minutes ago to tell her that Gray was shopping at Nordstrom at Dallas's fancy and long-established NorthPark mall. He'd explained that they'd taken Gray to a dressing room separate from the ordinary public one, unavailable to mere mortals and ruled by men who made their livings as personal shoppers.

Her watch read 2:00 p.m. She was now officially on duty, and since Mack had assured her that everyone inside the dressing room was decent, she let herself in.

She found Gray, his back to her, standing on a carpeted dais two steps up. Vertical mirrors reflected the front side of his body back at her from three different angles. He was shirtless, clothed only in a pair of tuxedo pants that were being pinned by a tailor hunkering near his feet.

She stopped, crossed her arms, and met Gray's gaze in the mirror.

His mouth moved into a grin at the sight of her.

Gray's personal shopper, a dapper fellow in a three-piece suit, fell into an instant state of fluster. "Excuse me, ma'am, this is a private—"

"She's with me," Gray said.

The dapper fellow pinched his lips together. He wouldn't contradict Gray.

"Hello, Dru," Gray said.

"Hello, Gray."

"I've got this charity thing to go to in a few nights. I needed something to wear."

"Don't let me stop you." Now that she was taking in the details of the space, she was finding it somewhat underwhelming. It looked just like the plush women's dressing rooms she'd visited in her life.

The sight of Gray's bare chest, however? Somewhat overwhelming.

Big slabs of muscle melded one into the next with undeniable athletic splendor. Gray's muscles weren't just for show. They were muscles with purpose, conditioned and trained to do the job of the professional football player. He wasn't lean. At the same time, he didn't carry fat. His body was both ferociously fit and brawny. Beautiful in its way, yes. Perfect, no. A wide bruise flared across his ribs. A few old, white scars marked his skin. And a tattoo began at one pec and continued over that shoulder to band around the top of his upper arm. She could see no other tattoos, just the one. It was all bold linear lines and graphic, Mayan-inspired shapes. The tattoo struck her as unapologetic, like him.

"How've you been, honey?" Gray asked.

Just like that, her warm feelings toward him popped like a soap bubble.

"I haven't seen her since I left for New York on Saturday," Gray told the dapper fellow. "Being away from her for two days felt like forever."

"Mmm," the personal shopper murmured.

Big Mack, standing at the room's edge, looked back and forth between her and Gray with amused interest.

"I don't know," Dru said lightly. "The weekend passed pretty quickly for me."

"For me, every hour dragged." He was laying it on way too thick. "Every minute dragged."

The tailor finished his work. The moment the man sat back on his haunches, Gray made his way to her. Dru quashed her gut reaction, which was to give him a roundhouse to the face or clock him in the esophagus. She let him wrap her in his arms.

He'd put his back between her and their audience, so the others couldn't see her peering up at him mutinously. He chuckled and hugged her even more closely.

His body was deliciously warm. His powerful arms held her with just the right amount of strength and a surprising, juxtaposing gentleness. The clean scent of him that probably came from some stupidly expensive soap wound through her senses. Shoot, he smelled amazing.

He bent his head near her ear. "You planning to loosen up a bit? Or are you going to continue standing there like a flagpole?"

"Flagpole."

"C'mon. For the witnesses."

"I'm not getting paid enough to perform for witnesses."

"I'll pay you more."

"You're not my employer."

He released her, but not before taking hold of her hand. "Dru's trying to convince me," he told the others, "to take her to the private changing area over there so she can greet me properly, if you know what I mean." He had the nerve to wink. "But I convinced her to wait for later."

"He's kidding," Dru informed them. "I said no such thing."

"'Course you did, honey. But you know me. I'm a stickler for propriety."

"I'd like to stick you with something," Dru muttered under her breath.

While Gray changed, Mack and Dru spoke briefly outside the dressing room. Dru was waiting alone for Gray, carefully cataloging the activity on the store's floor, when he emerged. He had on an old pair of jeans, a weathered ball cap, and a long-sleeved gray cotton shirt, pushed up at the wrists.

"Did you get the bruise on your ribs yesterday?" she asked. "When you caught that pass thrown down the middle and got creamed?" Sunday was a work day for her, so she'd once again watched the game from her desk at Sutton Security. In between plays, she'd compiled contact information, routes, and alternate routes for Gray's schedule this upcoming week.

His lips curved. "Were you looking at my ribs just now?"

"I'm trained to notice details." They began walking down one of the store's glistening tile aisles. Alertly, Dru took in every aspect of their environment. Who posed the greatest threat? "Is the bruise from that play?"

"It is."

"What about your injured hip?"

"Still jacked up."

"But yesterday's game didn't worsen it?"

"No."

"Am I or am I not going to need to push you out of here in a wheelchair?"

He didn't answer because he was already distracted, his vision following the line of her hair. He reached up as if intending to take hold of a lock—

She sideswiped his hand away. What did he think he was doing, reaching for her hair like that?

He appeared entertained, which, in turn, annoyed her. She didn't want to entertain him. She wanted to intimidate him into submission the way she did most people.

"I'm surprised to hear that you watched my game, Dru. I thought you were a Cowboys fan."

"I am. If I slit my arm open, it'll bleed blue and silver."

"Huh." They walked in silence for a few yards. "Has Corbin contacted you since dinner the other night? He mentioned something on the trip. . . ."

"He's called me twice."

"And?"

"And what? He's handsome and easy to talk to and a quarterback. He's more than welcome to call me. I like him." It was a physical impossibility for any woman not to like Corbin. Went against the laws of nature.

Gray stopped, so she stopped. She scanned the area behind them. Now who posed the greatest threat?

"Like him as a friend like him?" he qualified. "Or like him as a boyfriend like him?"

She stiffened. "What business is that of yours?"

"I'm the one who introduced you to Corbin."

"That doesn't give you a right to pry."

He considered her, consternation stitching his brow. "Corbin's one of my best friends. But I don't think you should date him, Dru. He's not good boyfriend material."

"Funny. He said the exact same thing to me about you."

"He did?"

"Yes. But I informed him that whether or not you're boyfriend material isn't my concern. You're my client. See how admirably I stayed out of *your* business?"

"Corbin has ugly feet."

She smiled. He was pointing out his friend's flaws in an effort to dissuade her. "Ah."

"And he's a terrible singer."

"I'll keep that in mind."

"I have good feet, and I can sing."

"Whether or not you have good feet and can sing isn't my concern. You're my client."

He was looking her square in the eyes, unflinching.

He was big and bad and a man who'd lived up to his hype when he'd transitioned from college to pro ball. Hardworking, forceful, blunt, he went through women the way Fi plowed through doggie kibble. His eyes glowed a slaying shade of pale green. And, unfortunately for her, she now knew what he looked like shirtless. All of which was muddling her head a little.

Tension thickened between them. Awareness.

He turned and resumed walking. She fell into step beside him, catching a cluster of three store employees watching them. One had been pointing at Gray but quickly lowered her hand when Dru frowned.

"Want to shop for something for you?" Gray asked.

"No."

"Too bad. You have to follow where I lead, right?"

"Unless I taser you. Then you'll have to go where I drag you."

"We're going to the women's section." Moments later, he entered the department that carried the most expensive clothing in the building. Dru waited on the walkway.

She did most of her shopping online. She'd never enjoyed the act of walking around with bags on her arm, looking at things, and trying on clothes. She'd certainly never set foot in the most expensive section of any store. She liked quality, but if she had the kind of money these clothes required, she'd use it to winterize her cabin.

She worked at turning her attention toward surveying the people around them. Ruefully, though, her brain was having a hard time focusing. It kept wanting to analyze the moment that had passed between her and Gray just now. They'd been staring at each other, and for a small space in time she'd been painfully aware of him as a man. Not as a football player or the recipient of death threats or someone she was responsible for. Just as a man. Her temperature had shot up about ten degrees; her skin had flushed.

She'd given herself permission to have a tepid friendship with him. Just then, her body had been interested in more.

"How about this one?" Gray held up an awful pale blue chiffon dress with rhinestones sprinkled over the bust. He was kidding.

"You jest."

"Not hardcore enough for you, Revengeress?"

"Revengeress?"

"Corbin and I think that you could be the star of your own comic book series."

"That's the most sensible thing to ever come out of your mouth." That he thought her comic book–worthy pleased her more than it should have. "I *would* make a good comic book character."

"Preaching to the choir," he said as he moved off. "By the way, it was me who came up with the name Revengeress. Not Corbin. He's not very creative."

He returned with a rocking black dress. Hard-edged gold studs ran along the top of both shoulders.

"How about this one?" he asked. She'd kept an eye on him and knew for a fact that he hadn't so much as looked at the dress's price tag.

"No, thank you."

"What size are you?"

"The size that likes to buy her own clothes."

He went to the counter and handed the dress to the saleswoman. Dru rolled her eyes. If he didn't have enough sense not to spend hundreds of dollars on a dress she wasn't going to wear, then he didn't deserve to keep ahold of his money.

Her phone vibrated silently with an incoming text or call. Ordinarily she'd have ignored it until she was on a break. But this particular buzz sent foreboding snaking down her spine. She checked her phone and saw that she'd received a text from Bo. Her heart grew small and cold with worry as she read it. Stashing her phone, she instinctively started praying.

"What's the matter?" Gray approached, carrying a hanger and the bag-covered dress.

"My brother has taken my sister-in-law, Meg, to the hospital. She's pregnant with twins, but she's not due for months. Something's gone wrong."

"Is the hospital close by?"

"About thirty minutes."

"Then let's go."

She hesitated. "Protection agents shadow their clients' activities, Gray. Not the other way around."

"Yeah, but this situation isn't an everyday thing. Your sister-in-law is in the hospital. So we both need to go and make sure she's okay because you can't go without me. Right?"

"Right."

"I'm not so much of a jerk that I'd expect you to ignore something like this, Dru. Let's go."

"You have appointments this afternoon."

"Not for a while. We can take my car."

Meg lay on the bed in the emergency room while a nurse prepared the baby heart rate monitor. The woman chatted pleasantly. Meg did her best to answer, but it was difficult—inwardly her pulse was pounding and fear was flailing like a caged animal.

Bo stood next to her, holding her hand.

The nurse pressed the monitor to Meg's belly. No

sound. She moved the monitor to a different area, searching.

Over the many weeks of her pregnancy, Meg had
grown familiar with the beautiful whooshing sound of
her babies' hearts. She swallowed convulsively, willing
herself to hold it together. *God . . .* she prayed, unable
to think further than His name.

Over the years of infertility, she'd become very, very
well acquainted with pregnancy heartbreak. *I can't bear
another heartbreak, Lord.* Her mind and soul rebelled
at the possibility. The miscarriages had been crushing,
but they'd come in the first trimester. She hadn't been
nearly this far along.

They . . . they'd already started working on the twins'
nursery. The walls of that room, and the length of her
arms, and a big place in Bo's heart were all awaiting
these babies.

Shush shush shush shush. The rapid, rhythmic sound
of a fetal heartbeat flowed, at last, from the monitor. Meg
hadn't realized that she'd been holding her breath, but
now it rushed from her. Relief heavied her tense muscles.
The nurse moved the monitor, and the one heartbeat
mingled with the sound of a second.

Bo squeezed her hand, and she gave him a wobbly
smile. *Thank you, God. Thank you for Your mercy.*

Her vision had returned to normal, and their babies'
heartbeats sounded strong. Yet, something wasn't right.
The certainty of that had woven its way into her psyche.
There was a reason her eyesight had faded, of that she
was sure.

Her personal obstetrician had been summoned and
would want to run more tests.

A group of kids rushed to greet Dru when she and Gray entered the waiting room on Meg's hospital floor. Gray watched a girl and boy wrap their arms around Dru's legs. The smallest one, a boy who couldn't have been more than two, took a running jump into her arms.

Dru caught the boy, pressing his head against her upper chest and kissing his hair. He wrapped a chubby hand around her neck.

"Your hands are sticky, Connor," Dru said. "What have you been eating?"

"Daddy brought lollipops for us," the girl answered. She looked like a third or fourth grader. She had dark blond hair and glasses. "He puts lollipops in his pocket when he takes us places so he can give them to the boys when they start to get fussy. If he gives them to the boys, then he has to give one to me, too, even though I'm never fussy."

"Lollipops, huh?" Dru unhooked Connor's hand from her neck. "Where's mine?" She pretended to give his palm a lick.

All three kids giggled. Gray pulled his head back, felt his brows lift. He'd labeled Dru as cold and unemotional. But it looked like she wasn't that way with everyone. Some people, she loved. Seeing the evidence of it was like believing the moon was square only to realize all of a sudden that it was round.

"What flavor were your lollipops?" Dru asked the kids.

"Mine was cherry!" the bigger of the boys answered.

"Really? Let me see your tongues."

The kids obeyed. "Okay, yep," Dru said. "Yours looks

like cherry, Hudson. Yours looks like green apple, Addie. And you had to have . . . um, whatever fruit is blue, Connor. Blueberries?"

"Blue!" the little one said.

Dru glanced at Gray. "These are my nephews and my niece. I have another niece, too, who's a baby, but it doesn't look like her dad brought her today."

"He didn't," the girl stated.

"Everyone, put your tongues back in your mouths," Dru said. "This is Mr. Fowler."

The kids blinked at him with shy interest.

"Hey," Gray said.

The children nodded, then started telling Dru about how their pony, Whitey, had the flu. Dru listened intently.

Why had he been so quick to label Dru? He categorized people often, he knew.

She's cold.

He's trustworthy.

She's harmless.

He's a jerk.

It was a defensive technique left over from childhood, from a time when keeping himself emotionally and physically safe had been up to him and meant the difference between life and death. He still did it, without meaning to. He judged a person and then put them in that box. The boxes gave him distance and protection.

Despite himself, he'd come to like and respect Dru. She wasn't staying in the box he'd tried to fit her into. Which made him edgy. He wouldn't hate it if she looked at him or listened to him the way she did her niece and nephews. That made him edgy, too.

For one small woman, Dru had begun to take up a lot

of space in his thoughts. In fact, since her shift had started this afternoon, he'd been so focused on her that the pain in his hip and ribs had faded into the background.

He needed to be careful. To convince Dru that she wanted to kiss him, while at the same time keeping himself from getting too wrapped up in her, was going to be like walking a tightrope.

An older man and woman approached, followed by two men around Gray's age. Dru introduced the older couple, Nancy and John, as her parents and the men as her brothers, Ty and Jake. They all shook Gray's hand.

Nancy treated him with the most warmth. John, who'd dressed in the western wear of a true cowboy, had the good manners of so many of the men Gray had known growing up in small-town Texas. Ty and Jake both seemed to be sizing him up. Neither appeared to like him. The kids, Dru explained, were three of Ty's four children.

The family didn't know anything about Meg's condition yet, other than that she and the babies were stable. They expected Bo to come at any moment and give them an update.

As the Porter family members talked to one another in serious tones, Gray looked between them, trying to find resemblances. Jake and Dru had the same dark hair and precise features, but Jake had a jagged scar across one side of his face. Ty and Dru both had light blue eyes. Dru seemed to have inherited her slimness from her father. It hadn't come from her mom, who was of medium height and big-boned. Nancy's short, dark hair had a wide gray stripe in the front. She'd tied a scarf or bandana around it like a headband. The scarf, together with the short hairstyle—which looked like a style a woman would have if she were trying to grow her hair back in—made him wonder if she was a recovering cancer patient.

Gray noticed that Dru had edged around the group so that her back faced the wall—in order to get a better view, he assumed. Even now, she was keeping a careful eye on their surroundings.

Still trying to protect him? Here? If his stalker rushed into this waiting room with an automatic weapon, he'd step in front of Dru. Not behind.

A man with shaved dark hair rounded the corner. This must be Bo, Dru's oldest brother and Meg's husband. Looking tired but calm, he hugged his family members, introduced himself to Gray, then stepped back, sliding his hands into the front pockets of his jeans.

His parents, brothers, and sister waited in taut silence.

"Meg and the babies are doing okay," he reassured them. "But Meg has something called preeclampsia."

"What's that?" Ty asked.

"It's a condition that causes high blood pressure." Tension was clear on Bo's face. "It can be serious. When I looked up information about it online, it mentioned complications like stroke, water in the lungs, and heart issues."

"Everything was going so well," Nancy said. "Do they know what caused it?"

"The doctor told us preeclampsia is the result of a placenta that's not working properly. Why the placenta stopped working properly is less clear. It may have something to do with blood flow or how the blood vessels formed in the placenta. They don't know. Apparently it's more common in twin pregnancies."

Nancy nodded slowly. "Are you and Meg holding up all right?"

"At this point, we're just trying to get our heads around the fact that Meg was fine a few days ago and now we're dealing with this."

"What can be done about it?" Dru asked, her arms crossed in what Gray had come to think of as a typical position for her, especially when confronting something she had to steel herself against. Of course it would be Dru who'd ask what could be done, to want to go to war against a pregnancy complication she could do nothing about. Revengeress.

"They can treat it to some degree with medicine." Bo frowned. "But the only cure is delivery."

On the drive over, Dru had told Gray about Meg and Bo's history. He knew that Meg still had three and a half months to go before the babies were due.

He shifted his weight. This conversation had turned far too personal. He was an outsider. Not a family member. He met Dru's eyes. She must have guessed that he wanted to slip off because she gave a small shake of her head.

"The doctors will have to weigh their options," Bo said. "The babies need more time to grow. On the other hand, I won't let them put Meg at risk."

Jake, the one with the scar, stood half a step back from the others. He looked as grim as death and said nothing. With that glare, he'd have done well on the line of scrimmage in the NFL.

"Will Meg be staying?" Dru's mom asked.

"They're going to keep Meg here for a few days to monitor her and the twins. After that, we'll see."

"Can we say hi to her?" Ty asked. "I'm sure you're both tired, so we'll keep it short."

"Sure." Bo led them down the hall. Jake walked alongside Bo, the two talking quietly. Ty swung the littlest boy over his shoulders so that the kid's legs dangled on either side of his neck. Nancy and John took hold of the other kids' hands. Dru and Gray fell in last.

Gray resettled his ball cap, tugging its brim lower. "I'm going to skip the meet and greet. I'll go downstairs and get us some coffee. Are you hungry for anything?"

"If you go downstairs, then I'll have to go downstairs."

"My stalker isn't here at the hospital with us, Dru."

She skimmed a look at him out of the corners of her stunning eyes. "Does your stalker inform you of his or her whereabouts?" The question had no sting to it. She'd asked it almost kindly.

"I'll wait in the hall, then."

The family began to file into one of the rooms. "Nope." She took hold of his sleeve and tugged him in.

Warning bells rang in Gray's head. He shouldn't be part of these private moments. He kept his relationships with women light. Easy. He had no desire to get pulled into Dru's family's drama.

Yet here he stood, looking at a pregnant blond woman on a hospital bed and hoping—really hoping—that everything would turn out fine for her and her children. Even in a hospital gown, probably feeling poorly and with worries on her mind, he could see kindness in Meg's face as she interacted with her relatives.

Meg was releasing one of the kids from a hug when her attention caught on him and held.

"Meg," Dru said, "this is Gray Fowler."

Meg's expression showed recognition. "Oh, yes. I know exactly who you are, Gray. Thanks for bringing Dru. I'm glad you both could come."

"You're welcome." Glad he'd come? She couldn't want a two-hundred-and-fifty-pound stranger lurking in the back of her hospital room on what had to be a very bad day for her.

The family stayed with Meg and Bo for less than ten minutes.

As Gray and Dru walked through the hospital's central lobby on their way to the parking garage, Gray was stopped twice and asked for autographs. Both times by his favorite type of fan: kids who themselves had football dreams. They always came toward him with nervous excitement and started the conversation the same way: *Are you . . . Gray Fowler?*

Dru stood beside him as he chatted with the kids. She was pretending to be a normal person and not a bodyguard, but Gray could sense her watchfulness.

Instead of taking him through the main exit doors, she guided him down a hallway to a side exit, then left him inside while she went to get his Denali. When his agents had first been assigned to him, they'd explained that a high number of attacks took place at entrances and exits. They approached those areas with extra care and, by this point, he was used to the drill.

Whenever one of his cars was left unsupervised in a public place, the agents ran an inspection on it before starting the engine. Dru had never said, *I'm looking for a bomb because I don't want someone to blow you up.* But as far as he could tell, that's exactly why they checked over his cars.

She pulled the Denali to a stop, he climbed in, and she steered them from the hospital campus.

"I want to drive," he said.

"No."

"I don't think you're allowed to tell me no, seeing as how I'm your client. And this is my car."

After a long stretch of silence, she finally pulled over. They exchanged positions. Gray moved the driver's seat back to accommodate his much larger frame, and they were on their way again. "It goes against my beliefs to let a woman drive me around."

She released an offended huff.

"Everybody knows women are bad drivers."

Her eyes flashed with so much anger that he laughed. "I'm just kidding, Dru."

"I can see I'm going to have to have *the talk* with you."

"The one where you go through all the dangers I'm facing and tell me tragic stories that support the idea that I have a better chance of getting through this alive if I do exactly what you tell me to do?"

"Yes. That talk."

"You gave it to me on our first day together. Remember?" He could feel her irritation radiating in his direction, which, as usual, brought him perverse pleasure. He cut a look at her. She was sitting at an angle that pulled her jacket tight against her side. Above her waist, he could see the angular outline of what had to be a gun. She always wore either fitted blazers or jackets, just like his male agents did. "Do you carry your pistol in a shoulder holster?" he asked.

"What pistol?"

"Take off your jacket. I'd like to see what you have going on under it."

"And I'm sure you'd be interested in seeing my gun, too."

He grinned. The mental image of her wearing a gun in a shoulder holster struck him as incredibly sexy. "So? Shoulder holster?"

"I plead the fifth."

"Did you become familiar with guns in the Marines?" Growing up, he and all his buddies had gone hunting. He wasn't too bad with a gun himself.

She half faced him, the seatbelt cutting across her diagonally. "My dad taught me how to shoot when I was a kid, long before the Marines."

"Were you good at it right from the start?"

"Yes."

"You're like . . . who was that famous woman shooter?"

"Annie Oakley."

"You're like a modern-day Annie Oakley."

"No, I'm Revengeress. Remember?" Humor laced her voice.

"I'm looking forward to seeing Revengeress in the black dress I just bought for her."

"No problem."

"Seriously?"

"Just hire a cartoonist, show him the dress, and I'm sure he'd be glad to oblige you with a comic strip."

He kept the speedometer on the speed limit, which meant the Denali was grounded to the slow lane. Everyone else shot past them in the direction of Dallas.

He'd still be able to make his scheduled interview at a local sports radio station.

Dru glanced out the back windshield, no doubt checking to see whether someone was tailing them.

"Is your mom a cancer survivor?" he asked. Drizzle from the low, pale gray clouds began to dot his windshield.

"Did her hair give it away?"

"Yeah." He rubbed the sides of his thumbs into the steering wheel.

"She had breast cancer, but luckily, they caught it early. My mom never thought the cancer would take her down, and it didn't. The surgery and chemo and radiation were successful. She finished treatments nine months ago, and all the follow-up tests say she's cancer-free."

"I'm glad."

"Me, too. Has your mom ever been seriously sick?"

"Often."

"With what?"

He focused on the road before him, doors slamming shut inside himself. Part of him wanted to believe that he could trust Dru just a little. And that might be, in part, what was causing the doors to slam. He needed to be *very* careful.

"Gray?" she prompted.

"I'll just say this. There are thousands of kids who have good parents. There are thousands who don't. I didn't."

The air inside the car turned so thick that he punched on the radio. Bob Marley's "Three Little Birds" flowed from the speakers. It played while they exited and came to a stop at the light.

"Reggae?" Dru asked.

"I like it." In fact, he kept Sirius tuned to it. "Makes me feel like I'm on a beach somewhere."

"I'm more of a mountains girl."

"Figures." He nodded his head to the beat. How could she not at least tap her toe in time to this song? He faced her and lip-synced, *Don't worry about a thing because every little thing is gonna be all right.*

"I'll feel more certain of that," she said over the music, "when we confirm that the Cherokee behind us isn't following us."

He quit singing and looked into the rearview mirror. A seven- or eight-year-old beige Jeep Cherokee came to a stop two cars back. "How long has he been behind us?"

"Since a few miles after we got onto the freeway."

The light rain and the distance made it hard to see. The driver appeared to be wearing a hat and sunglasses. Male?

"Have you ever seen this particular car before?" she asked. "Does anyone you know drive a car like that?"

"No. Do you want me to continue to the radio station?" He checked the map on his phone. They were close.

"How much time do we have before you need to arrive at the station?"

"Twenty minutes."

"Then let's take a short detour. Go right. At the stop sign there, take a left."

The light turned green, and he did as she'd asked. The Cherokee followed, though it never neared.

"Maybe I was wrong about the maroon truck," Gray said.

"We don't know that yet. I'm still checking into it."

"I don't see a license plate on the front of the Chero-kee."

"No. There's not one even though it's against the law to drive without one in Texas." She took a picture of the vehicle with her phone. "Go right again. Then left again. Then right." She spoke without emotion, but with a bucket-load of professional authority. "We'll drive in a stair-step pattern that no other car would naturally take."

After the third turn off the highway, the Cherokee disappeared. Gray pulled to the curb in the industrial district and waited. No Cherokee. "What do you think? Was it a coincidence that the Cherokee took a similar route to ours?"

"Maybe." She didn't sound convinced. She continued to watch the road behind them.

Whoever had been sending him the letters had been hunting him for a long time now. That person may have just made a mistake by stepping out, revealing himself, and giving them a chance to hunt him in return. "Or do you think that was my stalker?" He hoped so. He was more than ready to confront his stalker.

"Maybe," she said, meeting his gaze.

CHAPTER SEVEN

The next morning, Dru's running shoes crunched over pebbles and twigs as she ran toward the home of her nearest neighbor, Augustine Jones. Fi had deigned to come with her today because, though the weather was overcast, no rain had fallen. Fi's face had whitened with age and she had to be lifted onto and off of Dru's bed like a queen on a litter, but she could still run.

Dru slowed her pace, cooling down by walking the last hundred yards to her neighbor's. Augustine lived a mile from Dru. They'd met shortly after Dru had purchased her cabin because they shared a stretch of road before the fork that split in one direction to Augustine's and the other to Dru's. The two women had their road, their Christianity, and their love of motorcycles in common. That's where the similarities ended.

Augustine was a seventy-year-old African American who looked to be about one hundred and two. She lived alone in the sort of boring brick house that should have had a residential development surrounding it, but didn't.

At least once a week, Dru stopped by Augustine's on her morning run to check on her. And every Wednesday night, she drove Augustine to a biker church service at Holley's motorcycle dealership.

Stopping on Augustine's front walkway, Dru stretched her quads, hamstrings, and calves while her breathing settled into a quieter rhythm. Fi dropped onto her tummy, legs splayed out, nose on the cement path, panting. The retriever eyed Dru with eyebrows twitching.

"C'mon in, child!" Augustine left her door wide, then turned and retreated into the house.

"Hello to you, too," Dru called.

Augustine's delighted cackle floated to her.

Shortly after they'd met, Dru had invited Augustine to a Porter family Sunday lunch. Augustine had brought English pea salad. Dru could only very vaguely remember (a) enjoying it and (b) telling Augustine so. Augustine had been making the salad for Dru relentlessly ever since.

Dru no longer liked English pea salad.

Whenever she arrived at Augustine's, she said a brief prayer, asking God to spare her from the pea salad.

"Stay," she told Fi. Probably unnecessary. Fi knew that Augustine didn't allow pets with muddy paws inside her home.

"You're in luck," her neighbor said as Dru entered. With some effort, she set a glass bowl on her kitchen table. "I just made that pea salad you love."

"Mmm." Dru rested a hand on her stomach in the universal sign for *I'm stuffed*. "As it happens, I just ate. Would it be okay if I took some of that yummy salad home in a Tupperware container?" *Where I can introduce it to my garbage disposal?*

"Of course." Augustine waved a bent and knotty hand in her direction. "I'll just spoon you out a little now. So you don't have to wait." Rheumatoid arthritis had come for Augustine way ahead of schedule. Because of it, she shuffled more than walked, and her back bent forward at a forty-five-degree angle.

Dru opened the under-sink cabinet and pulled the full trash bag from its container.

"You don't have to do that," Augustine said. Dru always emptied Augustine's trash, and Augustine always told her she didn't have to.

"I know I don't have to," Dru replied, carrying the bag outdoors to the trash cans.

Augustine had married at twenty and remained married for twenty-five years, until the day her husband had abruptly informed her that he no longer loved her. On that day, he'd packed a suitcase and walked out of her life. He'd never been seen again by either Augustine or her sons.

At the time of her husband's departure, Augustine's three boys had already left home. Newly single and an empty nester, Augustine had set about doing all the things her husband had discouraged her from doing. She quit her teaching job. She cut her hair extremely short. She bought a motorcycle and joined the local Riders Burning Up the Road for God chapter. She became a guide for an adventure tour company. She began collecting Precious Moments figurines.

Dru returned to the kitchen, picked up the dish of salad Augustine had prepared for her, and passed numerous figurines as she followed her neighbor into the den. A Precious Moments boy and girl clasping each other's hands sat on a windowsill. An angel stood on a book-shelf. A mother sticking a Band-Aid on her daughter's knee, plus about twelve other mini statues, covered the top of the dresser.

"I sold that one this morning for forty-two dollars!" Augustine gestured to the mother with the Band-Aid.

"You're a pusher, Augustine. A Precious Moments pusher."

Augustine laughed. "I love eBay. Have you changed your mind about taking a few of the figurines and start-ing your own collection? I'll give you a great deal."

"I haven't changed my mind." Dru had disappointed herself with her wimpiness regarding the English pea salad, but she drew the line at Precious Moments por-celain.

Augustine backed up against her huge mechanical chair, which was currently splayed almost fully upright. At the command of her remote control, the chair whirred lower, bringing its occupant into a reclining position. "What're you going to do today on your day off?" the older woman asked.

Think about Gray. Dru shook her head, scattering the ridiculous notion. "I'm going to the grocery store be-cause I'm making pumpkin pie for my family's Thanks-giving dinner the day after tomorrow. After that, I'll swing by the hospital and visit Meg." She filled Augustine in on Meg's condition.

"You can be sure that I'll be talking to the good Lord about Meg and those twins."

"Thank you. I'm pretty convinced you have a direct line."

"That's because I still use a landline."

They shared quiet smiles weighted by the seriousness of Meg's condition. "What are your Thanksgiving
plans?" Dru asked.

"I'm going to my son Marvin's. Listen, did you say
you were making pumpkin pie? I have a recipe for pumpkin—"

"Don't even start with me, Augustine. I always make
the recipe on the back of the Libby's can."

Her neighbor looked scandalized.

"My family likes the simple version," Dru said.

"But you need more nutmeg and—"

"Don't even start." Dru chewed peas.

"How's the football player?" Augustine's gentle eyes
and bow-shaped mouth were recessed in a soft, doughy,
and beautifully mocha-colored face. Her neck looked
less like a column and more like three small, squishy
spare tires. She always wore nondescript black cotton
clothing, big flashy earrings, bifocals, and old-person
shoes with thick soles.

When Dru had told Augustine about Gray last week,
Augustine had been instantly fascinated. Her ex-husband
Roy had been an avid NFL fan. So avid that he'd started
amassing player autographs and football memorabilia
when he'd been a boy and never given up the hobby. His
admiration for the sport had rubbed off on Augustine.

"The football player is frustrating," Dru replied. Yesterday, she'd texted the photos she'd taken of the beige
Cherokee to Julie at Sutton's headquarters. She didn't
expect the photos to generate useful information. The
rain, the separation between the vehicles, and the lack
of a license plate would all make identifying details difficult. Still. An agent could hope.

"Have I told you that I dated an ex–football player back when we were both in our forties? Edward Clark, Jr. *Mm-hmm!* We rode down the side of the Grand Canyon one time on mules."

"Wow." Dru had a lot of respect for Augustine's daring spirit. Even so, she didn't believe that all of Augustine's tales of adventure had *actually* happened.

"Then we rafted along the Colorado River," Augustine continued, "and slept in tents before helicoptering out."

"Edward was cool with the mules and the tents and all?"

"Oh, yes. Mmm! I love football players. If that Gray Fowler is ever around here, you be sure to bring him by to see me, all right?"

"All right." Chew, chewing away. She believed— hoped?—she'd eaten enough salad. She set the bowl on the coffee table next to a Precious Moments depiction of the first Thanksgiving.

Augustine's expression turned wistful. "I've never hang-glided off the Grand Canyon, but I sure would like to. I'm going to see if I can get a group together." The older woman pulled a blue crocheted throw blanket over herself.

Hang-gliding off the lip of the Grand Canyon was not going to happen for Augustine. Ever since Dru had known her, it had been all Augustine could do simply to hobble around her house. It physically pained Dru to watch Augustine move.

There were those who would say that Dru had a hard heart. But actually, it felt frighteningly soft toward some things. Her nieces and nephews. Her mother's cancer diagnosis. Her brother Jake because of his post-traumatic stress disorder. Augustine. Fi.

Despite Augustine's body's deterioration, the older woman still had a strong, very human need to be relevant. She still had a need to dream. Dru respected those needs, deeply. Visiting with Augustine always heightened Dru's awareness of the shortness of her own life. God hadn't promised her that she'd get to keep the healthy body she had. Nor had He guaranteed her opportunities for new adventures. She only had the present.

"Anyhow"—Augustine set her hands atop the blanket—"I think we're getting closer to finding Roy."

A year ago, Augustine had suddenly decided she wanted one last face-to-face with her ex-husband. Like the character Inigo Montoya from *The Princess Bride*, Augustine had prepared a speech that she dearly wanted to deliver to her life's villain. She and her sons had been trying to find him.

"Closer, huh?"

"Child, I *better* be getting closer to a phone number and address for that no-good sack of bones. Marvin thinks Roy's somewhere in the state."

"Let me know if I can help."

"I will."

Dru might not be able to make hang-gliding a reality for Augustine, but if she could, she'd help make the scolding-of-the-ex-husband thing happen.

Twenty minutes later, Dru was running through the woods on her way home with a Tupperware container of pea salad in one hand, dog beside her.

Twenty minutes after that, Dru flopped onto her living room sofa and pulled up her email on her laptop.

Julie had sent her a file of information on Rich Osbourne, driver of the maroon Ford truck. Dru scanned through Rich's history. Nothing very concerning or out of the ordinary. He'd spent his whole career in trucking after a failed early bid as a country singer/songwriter. He'd been married for decades to a woman named Mona. One son named Kyle and a daughter named Nicole. He had a few driving and parking tickets and one drunk-and-disorderly charge from when he'd been in his early twenties. That was it. No trace of anyone filing a restraining order against him or accusing him of stalking.

Dru scrolled through the handful of pictures included in the report, most of which were grainy shots from Bonham newsletters and church communications. Rich was ruddy, tall, and on the burly side, though most of what would have been called burly on a thirty-year-old just looked like excess padding and an aspiring potbelly on the sixty-year-old Rich.

Dru's brain stretched and reached, trying to find an inconsistency between what Mildred and Rich had told her and the information presented. Nothing surfaced. The maroon truck lead was still hitting an ambivalent note within her.

Yet, there *was* something—a small, niggling something—about Rich or Mildred that wasn't lying right. She couldn't put her finger on what it was, and the fact that she couldn't gave her a faint sense of uneasiness, sort of like when you heard something disturbing, then turned your attention to other things, but still felt a buzz of underlying upset.

She glanced at the clock on the upper right side of her computer screen. At this time of day, Gray would still be at the Mustangs' facility, either on the field, watching film, or in meetings.

Fi jumped onto the sofa and rested her head on Dru's thigh. Dru kept on flicking through her email.

The agent working the present shift in Gray's protection detail had sent her and the other agents a scanned copy of a letter that had arrived for Gray in today's mail.

> I hate you and I'm going to kill you. Maybe I'll kill your new girlfriend first, and then you. So you can watch.
> I saw you together at Circle M Steakhouse and I saw you arguing in a church parking lot. Do you have a temper problem, Gray?
> I do.

Dru's breath left her in a slow exhale.

Gray's stalker knew about her.

Setting a hand on Fi's warm body, she turned her focus to the autumn trees beyond her windows. The scene looked peaceful and harmless, very much in contrast to the words of the letter. Turned out it wasn't all that enjoyable to receive a death threat from a crazed stalker. The letter sobered her the way a strong cup of coffee might have.

They'd known that Gray's stalker watched him carefully, so Dru had somewhat expected the stalker to see her with Gray at some point. Not just her, but his other bodyguards, too. She hadn't expected, however, that the stalker would feel quite so violently toward her specifically.

She reread the letter. Actually, it sounded more like the stalker was interested in killing her only because it might cause Gray pain to watch it.

Clearly, the stalker didn't know that she was Gray's bodyguard and not his girlfriend. Maybe she ought to take another look at Kayla Bell, Gray's angry ex. To want to kill a new girlfriend in front of a man sounded like something a vengeful ex-girlfriend might want to do.

That the stalker had seen them at the steakhouse didn't strike Dru as highly unusual. The steakhouse had been filled with people who might have been using social media to announce Gray's presence there. The bar had been bustling. The restaurant's exterior windows would have allowed the stalker a visual of them, even if he or she hadn't entered the establishment.

I saw you arguing in a church parking lot was a whole different story.

Dru placed Fi's head on a throw pillow and went to the kitchen to open a bag of Cool Ranch Doritos. She placed the sole of one foot against the calf of her other leg and ate chips, thinking.

Prior to their argument in the church parking lot, Gray's car had been parked in a secure lot at the Mustangs' practice facility. The stalker would not have been able to place a tracking device on the Ferrari while it had been parked there. She and Gray had traveled from the practice facility to the church at very high speeds on the tollway. It wasn't logical to assume that the stalker had kept up with them. If he or she had, Dru would have noticed a car screaming down the tollway behind them.

How, then, had the stalker come upon them in the church parking lot?

The freeway exit Gray had taken that day had been his usual exit. Either the stalker had been waiting near the church for Gray to return home via his usual route, or when Gray and Dru had accelerated on the freeway, the stalker had followed at a slower pace, taken the exit that led to Gray's house, and come upon them arguing in the parking lot.

She popped another chip into her mouth. It might be worthwhile to do some counter-surveillance in the area around the church. To stalk the stalker.

Gray stood in his office later that day, holding the stalker's most recent letter. They'd slipped it into a Ziploc like they always did.

As the letter's message penetrated through to Gray's brain, rage began to heat to a boil within him. This person who'd been tracking him and spilling his hate in letter after letter had threatened Dru.

Dru.

Anger beat against his temples so strongly that he found it hard to remain still against the force of it.

He'd put up with the irritation of the letters, his general manager's concern, the inconvenience of having to adjust to 24/7 bodyguard protection. But this right here?

This upset him.

The male agent who took Dru's shifts on her days off had handed him the letter, then moved to the far side of Gray's home office to tap the keys of the Sutton Security laptop.

Ashley slipped in carrying a protein smoothie in one hand and a plate of homemade snacks in the other. "Welcome home, Gray. Something to eat?"

"Sure." He felt sick to his stomach but knew from

experience that it was better to accept Ash's food and not eat it than to turn it down. The latter hurt her feelings.

She set the things on his desk. "If this is a good time, I'd like to chat with you about some of the invitations you've received and how I can help you around the house this week—"

"This isn't . . . a good time."

Her cheerful smile slipped on one side.

"Can you give me thirty minutes?" he asked. "Then we'll talk about it."

"Of course." She responded sweetly and immediately, leaving him in peace.

He crossed the room and handed the letter back to the agent. "Can you excuse me?"

The agent left, too, shutting the door behind him. It sure was gratifying to have a few employees who actually did what they were asked. Unlike Dru Porter. He pulled out his cell and hit Dru's number.

Instead of saying hello like a normal person, she answered the phone with, "It's my day off, you realize."

Instead of leading with *How are you?* like a normal person, he countered with, "Did you see the letter that arrived today?"

She didn't answer for a moment. He could hear faint background noises. She was out somewhere in public. Not at home.

"I saw it," she said.

"And?" he demanded.

"And?"

"He wants to kill you now and make me watch."

"I know. Your stalker's a real barrel of laughs."

Gray set his back teeth together hard. "Today's letter has *seriously* irritated me."

"As much as a Green Bay linebacker?"

"Worse. It was one thing when he was threatening me, but now that he's threatening you, I'm not taking it very kindly. I've dated plenty—"

"You can say that again—"

"—since I started receiving the letters, but this is the first time he's threatened any of the women I've been out with in public."

"This must be just one more example of the escalation we've noticed in recent weeks."

He wrapped a hand around the back of his neck and looked at the floor. He did not want her hurt. And definitely not because of him. "I want to find this guy, Dru."

"So do I."

"Like, now."

"It's my day off, you realize," she repeated. "It'll be a little difficult for me to bring down your stalker at the moment, seeing as how I'm at the grocery store."

He filled his lungs with air, making himself settle down. She was fine. His stalker didn't know her identity. Whenever he'd introduced her to people, he'd introduced her as Dru Montana, never Porter. So even if the stalker got ahold of the name Dru Montana, he wouldn't be able to locate her home address. And whenever Dru left him, he knew she took measures to ensure she wasn't followed.

"Still there?" she asked.

"Yes." He neared his bookcase and frowned at the titles of the books without truly seeing any of them.

"Do you know a Rich, Mona, Kyle, or Nicole Osbourne?" she asked.

"Why?"

"These are the names of the people connected to the maroon truck. Do you know any of them?"

"Never heard of them."

"Sure?"

"Yeah."

"On to the next topic, then."

"Shoot."

"Last week you told me you weren't planning to go out of town for Thanksgiving."

"I'm still not."

"You're not planning a trip to Mullins to spend the day with family?"

"No."

"Have you decided where you *are* going to spend the day? Sutton will want to perform an advance tomorrow and start compiling information about the people you'll be with."

"I think I'm going to stay home." He'd received dozens of invitations to join friends for Thanksgiving. Though holidays depressed him, he usually took someone up on their offer and drove to their decorated house to eat a fancy dinner with a big, happy group of their relatives. The men would wear sweaters or ties. The women would wear pearls. There'd be a fire in the fireplace. Expensive silverware. Tricked-up pumpkin pie and the kind of whipped cream that didn't come in a Cool Whip container.

Everyone would be incredibly nice to him, slap him on the back with friendship, and bend over backward to please him. And they'd do their best to present their family as the perfect American family. A family in which no one would ever think of beating up their kids. Most of the time, he believed the perfect American family picture they presented. Which only depressed him more.

"You ungrateful idiot, Gray!" He remembered a fist swinging into the side of his face, then the floor spinning up to meet him. He felt a boot, kicking into his side, his thigh.

No, he didn't have the energy for the perfect American Thanksgiving this year. He'd rather keep his stalker away from his friends' families. He'd rather eat whatever Ashley left in the fridge and watch football and Netflix.

"Stay home?" Dru asked. "Do you mean that you're going to host Thanksgiving dinner at your place?"

"No, I mean that I'm going to sit the whole thing out this year."

He could all but *hear* her disapproval.

He missed her. Two days a week off was too many. Especially because he traveled to away games so often this time of year. On the weeks when he traveled, he was apart from her both then and on her days off.

She was scheduled to come back to work on Thursday, Thanksgiving Day. They could eat Ash's cooking and she could insult him while they watched football and Netflix together. He wanted that. Selfishly, he did.

At the same time, he didn't expect her to miss her family's Thanksgiving because of him. "Why don't you take Thursday off, Dru? Spend it with the rest of the Porters, opening a can of martial arts on the world's archvillains or shooting bull's-eyes from a mile away, or racing around on horseback, or whatever else it is you people do."

"You forgot to mention flying around in our invisible jet plane."

"How could I forget?"

"Gray?"

"Yes?"

"I'm not taking Thursday off."

He shouldn't feel relieved. But he did. He'd have her with him on Thanksgiving. "What're you shopping for?"

"Pumpkin pie stuff."

He lowered onto the sofa, his hip grinding painfully. Carefully extending his legs onto the ottoman, he stuck a hand behind his head. He wondered if she was a bad cook. She was probably bad.

"Our family usually eats around two-thirty," she said. "My mom and my sisters-in-law decided to move our meal to eleven this year so that I wouldn't have to miss it. But since you're insisting on being antisocial, not to mention anti-American, by ignoring Thanksgiving—"

"I'm a football player. How much more American can I get?"

"—I'm now thinking that my family can move our meal back to two-thirty because you can just come with me."

"I'd rather turn in my Super Bowl ring than attend your family's Thanksgiving."

"Surly." It sounded like she'd stopped the forward motion of her cart and found a deserted section of the store.

"I'm pretty sure your brothers hate me," he stated.

"You're completely wrong. They only strongly dislike you."

"I have a stalker," he reminded her. "It wouldn't be safe to bring me around your family."

"You're not allowed to tell anyone where you'll be going for Thanksgiving. And you won't be able to tell anyone where you spent the holiday after the fact, either. By *no one* I mean no one, not even the suspiciously optimistic Ashley—"

"She made pulled pork sandwiches last night for dinner. They were delicious."

"Is Ashley heavily dosed on antidepressants? She's not normal."

"She's heavily dosed on friendliness."

"I'll make positively certain that we aren't followed to my family's get-together. You'll be the safest during Thanksgiving dinner that you've been in months."

"It's still your day off, you realize," Dru grumbled to herself the next afternoon.

Fi, the only other passenger in the car, cocked her head from her spot on the passenger's seat.

Dru drove her motorcycle most of the time. Exceptions: bad weather, situations in which she needed to transport something, and outings on which she wanted to take her dog. Today she'd opted to drive her ten-year-old black Yukon because she'd be a really bad dog mom if she left her pet alone for hours on her days off.

Ever since she'd read the latest letter from Gray's stalker, the words had been itching at her like a tag on the inside of a shirt. She'd decided to drive to the church where Gray's stalker had spotted her and Gray having their parking-lot argument. She'd pulled her SUV into a spot on the road that lined the far side of the lot.

For the past twenty minutes, she'd sat hunched down

in her seat, watching cars exit the freeway. She'd also been scanning the lot itself, adjacent streets, parked cars, pedestrians, alleys. She was looking for someone else who'd be doing what she was doing, watching and wait-ing. Even better if that someone happened to be driving a maroon truck or a beige Cherokee.

So far, she'd seen nothing out of the ordinary.

Gray should be coming this way any minute on his way home from practice. Gray, whom she'd invited to her family's Thanksgiving. She hadn't intended to in-vite him. But he'd performed a one-two punch on her defenses when he'd told her he'd be staying home alone for Thanksgiving and followed that up by very decently offering her the day off.

It had felt one hundred percent right to her in that moment to inform him that he'd be coming to the Porter family gathering with her. Since their conversation, she'd had time to think through the reality of it. Gray's pres-ence at Thanksgiving would ruffle her brothers' feathers. Plus, she herself wouldn't be able to enjoy a relaxed meal, not while on duty and not with the green-eyed football player nearby.

Her choice to invite him still felt mostly right to her. Just no longer one hundred percent right.

She tore open a package of peanut butter crackers, broke off a piece, and flicked it to Fi, who snapped it up midair. "How are you liking counter-surveillance?" Dru adjusted her sunglasses while chewing. "Glamorous, isn't it? Really exciting. Why would I ever need to drink caffeine when I have this?"

Fi eyed the crackers in Dru's hand without blinking.

Her body had stilled in peanut butter cracker–induced concentration.

"You're a cutie. I'll give you that." Dru tossed her another bite just as she spotted Gray's Denali. It eased off the freeway before catching a green light at the intersection. A few cars turned in the same direction he had. One of them would be the car driven by the agent on duty.

She held still, scouring the scene. Thirty seconds passed. She started her car and made her way toward his house.

When she pulled up outside the gate of Gray's property, she caught a glimpse of his garage door closing. The agent had already exited his vehicle and gone inside.

She stacked her palms on top of the steering wheel and scowled. "Shoot."

She'd noticed nothing suspicious.

Across town, Meg peered up at Dr. Peterson, her obstetrician. Meg was reclining, hands gently stacked on the crease where her belly met her rib cage, in the same hospital bed she'd been reclining in for three days.

Dr. Peterson stood near the foot of the mattress, looking over Meg's chart.

Meg chewed the inside of her cheek.

"I'm going to discharge you today." Dr. Peterson lowered the chart and smiled at Meg.

Reluctance—part fear, part weird instinctive negativity—rose in Meg. "Oh?"

"Just in time for Thanksgiving tomorrow. I'm sure you're eager to get back home and sleep in your own bed."

No. Not so much. Meg loved her home. Absolutely loved it. But she felt safer here, with a team of doctors and nurses monitoring her babies. They'd run blood tests, urine tests, ultrasounds, biophysical profiles of the twins. Here, they were completely on top of her medications and her response to them. If she went home, she'd be leaving this island of relative protection. At home there were no machines to reassure her. Her mind would scrabble with worry every time her babies stopped moving. She could have another episode of impaired vision and find herself, once again, miles from help.

"It'll be nice to sleep in my own bed again, yes," she said carefully. "But my primary concern is for the babies' welfare. What confidence do I have that they'll do as well at home as they've done here?"

Dr. Peterson set aside the chart and sat on the end of the bed.

Meg had a great deal of fondness for her obstetrician, who'd been with her through the years of infertility. A stout redhead in her late forties, Dr. Peterson loved camping and hiking, wore an Ironman watch, and had teenage sons. Her REI-style clothing was unpretentious, as was her mostly makeup-free face and the simple tortoiseshell clip she used to catch back her wavy shoulder-length hair. A stethoscope peeked out from the chest pocket of her white doctor's coat.

Meg had always had the sense that Dr. Peterson genuinely cared about her. She was a great listener and never seemed rushed. As a rule, she didn't spout off fast sentences that sounded like, *The immunoglobulinology is elevated and so we'll increase the level of niatoxitocitinphlanx, which will help your thyrodociashechmodia if*

you follow a baccarinal protocol. Okay? To which one
felt obligated to nod.

"We've done a pretty good job of stabilizing your
blood pressure and improving your kidney function,"
Dr. Peterson told Meg. "I'll be keeping you on the same
medications once you go home that you've been on here,
so there's every reason to believe you'll do just as well
at home."

Bo had been with Meg at the hospital almost nonstop
since she'd been admitted. Just thirty minutes ago, he'd
run home to shower, catch up on a few things, and bring
her back the items she'd requested. Part of her wished he
were here. If he had been, he might have told the doctor
that he wanted Meg to stay—

No. He wouldn't tell the doctor anything of the kind.
He'd be relieved at her improvement and glad for the
chance to bring her home. Everyone was always glad to
leave hospitals and return to their comfortable, familiar
homes. The same would be true of Bo.

But he wasn't the pregnant one responsible for the
wellbeing of two tiny lives. Calm, strong Bo had not
been, she didn't think, as shaken by the episode at the
house and the ensuing preeclampsia diagnosis as she
had been.

"How will I know, once I'm home, that the babies are
continuing to thrive?" Meg asked.

"I'll send a blood pressure cuff with you and explain
how to use it and how often to check your blood pressure.
Plus, I'll want to see you in my office for appointments
more often than we'd initially scheduled. And, of course,
if you experience anything that you're worried about,
you can call me to talk about it."

Meg inhaled shakily.

"Look, Meg. I know pregnancy complications can be scary. But I wouldn't send you home if I didn't think that's what's best at this point."

"All right," she said, mostly as a pep talk to herself.

"The best course right now is to give the twins more time in utero to grow. As of right now, they only weigh about one and a half pounds each."

Meg longed for the ability to fast forward time. *Just twelve or thirteen weeks, God?* Then—*whoosh*—the angst would be behind her and she'd have fully formed babies ready for the world.

Instead, the idea of getting through each hour of those twelve or thirteen weeks the old-fashioned way, the sixty-minutes-per-hour way, seemed like a Herculean feat. "Do you want me on bedrest when I get home?" She'd been on modified bedrest while at the hospital.

"There was a time when we prescribed bedrest for preeclampsia. But research isn't definitive on the benefit, so you don't need to stay in bed all day long. Take it very easy, but go about your life."

My life has become these babies.

Had that thought really leapt right to the front of her mind? Her whole life wasn't these babies. She had a full life that was composed of many elements. Yet, from this hospital bed, it felt as if everything in her world—her past, her future, her marriage, her sanity—had distilled down to the safe delivery of these twins.

How could she go on if she lost them? Just the thought of losing them caused cold iron to knot in the core of her. "I just . . . I really, really want for these babies to be okay." She needed to articulate that, to be positively sure that Dr. Peterson knew how important this was to her.

Sympathy settled into the wise wrinkles around Dr. Peterson's eyes. She extended her hand to Meg, and Meg, always comfortable with affection, clasped her hand in response. "I know," the doctor said. "They will be."

Her warmhearted doctor could not guarantee that absolutely. Heartbreaking things happened to unborn babies sometimes.

Meg glanced around the now-familiar hospital room. Cutting-edge medical technology and medicines and a highly trained staff couldn't positively assure her of a happy outcome, either.

Whether here or at home, she knew—in her brain she really did know—that God and God alone held the fate of her twins in His hands. He'd been faithful to her in the past, and she could trust Him. Her head understood this. But her heart was quailing. It frightened her to trust Him with something that meant *this* much, that she'd waited for *this* long.

Meg's instinct was to rush in and try to *do* something to force the result she wanted. In this situation, though, everything that could be done was being done.

They were sending her home.

To wait, to hope, and to let the babies grow.

CHAPTER
EIGHT

Gray spent the ride to the Thanksgiving celebration quizzing Dru about her family so that he'd have a shot at knowing their names and understanding who belonged to whom when they arrived for the meal. The moment the door opened and they were greeted by a mass of people and dogs, however, he realized he didn't have a shot. The Porter family was big.

"Happy Thanksgiving, everyone," Dru called.

Her family responded enthusiastically. Some called out greetings from the living room; some waved from the kitchen.

Since he was the one carrying the pies, Dru closed the door behind them. The scent of baking turkey hung thick in the air. There were other scents, too. The earthy smell of cooking potatoes. Cinnamon. Bread dough baking.

A few of the women were smiling at him so cheerfully that, if this were any other family, he'd say they were tipsy. But Dru had made it clear that the Porters were a Christian group. They probably didn't toss back alcohol on holidays.

In contrast to the smiling women, Dru's brothers were looking at him like they didn't trust him. The one with the scar on his face, Jake, was staring at him like he was measuring him for a coffin.

Happy Thanksgiving to him.

According to Dru, she'd told her family she'd be bringing a guest but not that she'd be bringing *him* in particular. She hadn't wanted to announce him until she'd had a chance to lay down ground rules.

"For those of you who haven't met him already, this is Gray Fowler." Dru spoke in a loud voice that commanded the attention of everyone in the house. "He plays tight end for the Mustangs, and he's a client of mine. He didn't want our family to change our usual Thanksgiving routine on his account, so I brought him with me because—"

She was interrupted by the charging arrival of Hudson. Dru caught the blond boy and swung him onto her slim hip with ease.

Gray felt stupid, standing in the entryway of an unfamiliar house, holding Dru's two pumpkin pies covered in tinfoil, while two brown, black, and white dogs pawed his legs and someone else's family eyeballed him. He should have been a jerk and insisted Dru stay at his place with him and watch Netflix.

"Here." Dru's mom bustled over, her hands extended. "Let me take those."

He passed over the pies. So now he just had the dogs, panting up at him. He patted their heads awkwardly.

"I was saying," Dru continued, "that I brought Gray

with me today because I know I can trust you not to take any photos of him and not to say anything about his presence here on social media. Not that you'd want to, since he plays for the Mustangs."

Everyone chuckled.

"It's not too late to kick me out," he told the group. "Cowboys fans don't usually share their cooking with me."

"Kick him out!" Dru's brother Ty called, grinning.

The curly-haired brunette standing next to Ty elbowed him.

"He's staying," Dru pronounced.

The group responded as if a general had just issued an order. Dru might be the youngest sibling, but she was very . . . convincing.

"Also," Dru said, "I'd appreciate it if, when we all leave here and go our separate ways, you wouldn't mention Gray being here at all. Not to anyone. Not even in a conversation with a friend. Again, can't imagine why you'd want to . . . ." Her beautiful mouth curved as she glanced at him.

He felt something hitch in his chest when their eyes met. Emotion. "Since I play for the Mustangs," he finished.

Her family called out assurances that they had no interest in taking a photo with him or telling others about his presence. "Then that concludes my announcements." Dru motioned with her hands. "Ya'll can go back to talking amongst yourselves." She turned to the boy, still sitting on her hip. "Please don't tweet out a picture of Gray with the hashtag *NFL*," she said in a softer voice. "Cool?"

Hudson played with a piece of her dark hair. "What's has-taa?"

The emotion that had broken free within Gray just now for Dru remained, a warm heat that he hated. It made him feel vulnerable.

Chemistry existed between him and Dru now. He'd accepted that, up to a point. Any man would be drawn to her physically. Today she had on a burgundy suit jacket, a silky white tank top, black leather pants, and high heels. What chance did he have against black leather pants?

Chemistry he could deal with. He had experience with it and a fair amount of faith in his ability to control it.

But emotion? He didn't have experience with it or control over it. Didn't want it.

He'd left home for college a long time ago. Ever since, he'd been committed to his own pleasure. He liked being single and unattached, with only his football goals to focus on. He had his life organized exactly how he wanted it.

Yet he hadn't come here today for his own pleasure. He'd come for Dru's sake. Which left him feeling like he'd bought a ticket for one destination and ended up somewhere else, even though he hadn't given the chauffeur permission.

A short, slim blonde, very pretty, with long, wavy hair approached them. "I'm glad you could join us for Thanksgiving, Gray."

"Thank you."

"This is Lyndie," Dru said. "Jake's wife."

Poor thing.

"This building used to be Holley's Candy Shoppe." Dru set Hudson down, and the boy ran off. "When Lyndie first moved to Holley, the building was broken into two apartments, and she lived upstairs."

"Yep," Lyndie said. "See the woman over there in the red sweater?" She gestured to a dark-haired woman sitting on the arm of a chair occupied by a square-jawed man holding a toddler. "That's my friend Amber. Back when I moved in upstairs, she lived here on the downstairs floor. When she got married to Will—the guy sitting next to her—she moved out. Will's holding their eighteen-month-old son, Logan. Isn't Logan cute, Dru?"

"Very. When Amber moved out," Dru explained to Gray, "Jake surprised Lyndie by buying this entire building." Dru made the kind of face you'd give a child who'd eaten three cookies and asked very nicely for a fourth. "I haven't told you this about my brothers yet, but they're all crazy about their wives. It's embarrassing. They do things like that, like give their wives houses."

"Just FYI"—Lyndie's brown eyes sparkled—"the Porter brothers' wives are crazy about their husbands, too."

"To make a long story short," Dru said, "Jake and Lyndie renovated this building and also added a new addition over there that goes out into the backyard. Now the house forms an *L* shape."

"You did a great job." Gray had watched renovation shows on TV about people who took old buildings like schools and barns and converted them into modern homes. He'd always liked the idea. He could feel the history in the hardwood floors and the beams stretching across the ceiling of the open-concept den/kitchen/dining room.

"Meg and Bo usually host family holidays at their house," Dru said to him as they separated from Lyndie and made their way toward a group of her relatives. "But because of Meg's pregnancy, Lyndie and Jake offered to host Thanksgiving months ago. As it turns out, we're lucky that Meg and Bo are here at all."

Gray met Lyndie's parents and grandfather. Dru had told him on the ride over that Lyndie's younger sister Mollie, who'd had cerebral palsy, had died three years prior. He could see in Lyndie's parents' faces the weathering that came from loss. But he also saw warmth and kindness. Lyndie's dad and grandfather, both sports fans, chatted with him and Dru about the Mustangs.

Next, he met Celia, Ty's wife. She was wry and friendly and couldn't talk to him long because her younger son ran by holding a pair of scissors and laughing. Celia rushed after him.

Gray shook hands with Celia's uncle Danny, then Danny's girlfriend, Oksana, who had on so much makeup that she looked like a Russian grandmother about to go on stage to sing opera.

Danny was in the middle of a story about his recent mountain biking trip when Dru's parents began gathering everyone in preparation for the meal. Were they forming a circle? He hoped not. They didn't stand in a circle and pray or anything like that, did they?

They did.

"I'm not part of this family," he murmured to Dru while the kids were being rounded up. "This might be a good time for me to check my phone in one of the bedrooms."

"The big football player's afraid of sharing what he's thankful for?"

He groaned inwardly. "That's what we're doing? We're

going to stand in a circle and share what we're thankful for?"

She nodded slowly at him, looking like she was about to burst out laughing.

"I haven't been asked to share what I'm thankful for at Thanksgiving since I was in Mrs. Ensign's first-grade class," he said.

"Then you're overdue."

"I really do have some things on my phone that I need to—"

"There will be no escape."

"You're enjoying this."

"Of course I am."

The Porter family began reaching out to hold hands. At the last second, Dru tried to stick a kid in between them so she wouldn't have to hold his hand, but he was fast. He might be inducted into the Football Hall of Fame one day because he was *very* fast. He snagged her hand and leaned near her ear. Her shampoo smelled as clean as winter. "If you wanted to hold my hand, Dru, all you had to do was ask."

"Later," she whispered, "I might shoot you clean through with a .22-caliber bullet."

Ty and Celia's oldest daughter stood on his other side. He had to look down about five feet to meet her eyes.

She pushed up her blue glasses and solemnly offered him her hand. He took it just as John Porter, Dru's dad, started talking about how glad he was that everyone had come.

Gray stood there holding hands with Dru and Dru's niece, listening to each person say what they were thankful for. Luckily, the Porters kept things light. They were a family who liked to laugh.

Just like the other times he'd spent holidays with families that weren't his own, Gray felt alone and out of place. But he was more comfortable here than he had been at those other places because the Porters weren't a plastic kind of perfect. Nancy and John Porter were small-town, country people like him. Their kids had gone on to impressive careers but had been raised in a small town, too. And some of these people were downright strange. Like Danny and his Russian girlfriend. Some weren't very friendly. Like Jake.

This group was real. They'd use Cool Whip from a plastic container on top of their pumpkin pie.

"What are you thankful for, Hudson?" Celia prompted when it came to the boy.

"Um . . . T-Rexes."

It was Ty's turn. He held a baby girl in front of him. "Ellerie's thankful for squash baby food. I'm thankful for my family. For all of you. But, to be honest, especially Celia." He smiled a crooked smile at his wife before turning his attention to the toddler holding his other hand, the one who'd been running with the scissors earlier.

The boy froze.

Ty squeezed his hand.

"Da da," the boy said.

"Well said, buddy. Of course you're thankful for daddy. Rightly so. I think Connor might be a genius, Celia."

"Or well coached," she said. "What about *mama*, Connor?"

"Mama!"

"Quite right."

Meg and Bo took the next turns. Then Jake and Lyndie.

A short, white-haired old lady listed about ten things, including Meg and Bo's twins, her Lord and Savior, and her husband who'd died in the war in Korea. Then she circled back and finished with Meg and Bo's twins.

"I'm thankful for books," the girl—Addie—standing next to him announced. Then she tilted her head up to him. Her straight blond hair fell back from her sweet face.

"I'm thankful for football," he said truthfully. The sport he loved had given him an opportunity to make something of himself. Without it he'd still be nothing and no one.

Several of the Porters responded to his statement with agreement. One said, "Here, here!" Another whistled like a cheering fan, and John Porter called football the best game on earth.

"I'm thankful for my house and my dog," Dru told them all.

"I'm grateful," Danny's girlfriend said in heavily accented English, "for Lancôme's new mascara."

At last John prayed. When he finished, everyone murmured, "Amen."

Nancy called out, *Bon appetit!* though Gray had no idea why. "Let's eat!" Nancy continued. "Everyone find your name card, grab your plate, and form a line, okay?"

Gray located his name at the kitchen table, written in a child's handwriting on a white card. Addie must have filled it in after he'd arrived.

Carefully, he picked up the china plate. Then he and

Dru took places in line. "When it was your turn, you said you were thankful for your house and your dog," he said.

"This surprises you because . . . ?"

She didn't seem to him like an animal lover. "I thought you'd live in a castle somewhere," he said. "You know, with the other comic book superheroes?"

She stared a him for half a second, then laughed. "No, no. Too many of the comic book superheroes are male, which gets tiresome. I have to put up with more than my share of testosterone as it is, being around you."

They reached the front of the line. Gray waved Dru ahead of him, then helped himself to turkey, dressing, mashed potatoes, sweet potato casserole with crunchy brown nuts on top, green beans, gravy, cranberry salad, and bread. He came to a platter filled with roasted vegetables like tomatoes and zucchini. Catching Dru's eye, he gestured to it with his elbow.

"Ratatouille. My mom's crazy about all things French."

Meg and Bo were seated at the kitchen table with them, as well as Lyndie's grandfather and the white-haired lady who had been so grateful for Meg and Bo's twins.

"Gray, I'd like you to meet Sadie Jo Greene." Meg indicated the older woman. "She was my nanny when I was young and, well, basically raised me herself."

"Aren't you handsome!" Sadie Jo said to him. "How tall are you? My goodness, you must be seven feet tall."

"I'm six-four."

"You remind me of Jack LaLanne in his prime, with all those muscles."

Was she talking about the guy who had worn the tight shirts and gymnasts' pants?

"I had difficulty hearing what Dru was saying when you walked in." Sadie Jo extended her soft, wrinkled face in his direction. A pair of glasses sat on her nose, slightly askew. "Do you ride mustangs? Is that right?"

He'd been about to take his first bite of the Thanksgiving meal, but he rested his fork back on his plate. "No, ma'am, I play for the Mustangs. We're a football team."

"Who?"

"The Mustangs."

"I've never heard of them."

First the gymnastic tights. Now this.

"Football," Lyndie's grandpa barked from the other end of the table. "In other words, ah, the Mustangs are an NFL team," he informed Sadie Jo loudly. "They won the Super Bowl recently."

"Oh, then I'm sure you're very, very good," Sadie Jo hurried to say, staring at Gray with deep affection.

"Actually," Dru said, "he's just okay." She shot him a cocky, you-can-thank-me-later expression.

"You need to eat, dear." Sadie Jo squeezed his forearm as if he were her own grandson. "Don't let me keep you. You need to eat all that and go back for seconds. That can't be enough food for you. And, Meg, you're definitely going to need more turkey and dressing."

"You might be right," Meg said mildly, clearly used to dealing with Sadie Jo.

He'd seen Meg in the hospital, and then again here. She'd carefully styled her long, thick blond hair. Beneath her perfect makeup, her skin looked pale, and he could see strain in the set of her lips and around her eyes. She was doing her part to talk and smile and celebrate the day, but Gray could see it there. Strain.

It made him worry, then call himself a fool for worrying. He and Meg were practically strangers. He had no reason to get dragged into concern about her babies.

"Connor spilled!" Addie called from the kids' table. "It's getting all over the turkey centerpieces we made!" A few of the adults sitting nearer the kids' table jumped up to help.

"The coach's right to challenge," Lyndie's grandpa stated out of nowhere.

"What's that?" Bo asked the old man kindly.

"The coaches in the NFL these days have the right to throw the, ah, red flag and challenge what's happening in the game."

"They do," Gray answered.

"A red flag?" Sadie Jo asked. "Like the Soviet Union?"

And that's pretty much how the conversation around Dru's family's Thanksgiving table went. However, the food was outstanding. And Dru was beside him in those leather pants.

When Gray finally made it to where they had the pecan and pumpkin pies laid out on a side table, what did he see?

A plastic container of Cool Whip.

Dru knew without having to turn around that it was Jake who'd entered the upper-story guest bedroom of the house they all still called the Candy Shoppe. She could tell by the sound of his steps.

This was her third trip upstairs since arriving at Lyndie

and Jake's for Thanksgiving. From this particular window, she had a clear view of the street in both directions. "Jake," she said by way of greeting.

He leaned a shoulder into the wall on the far side of where the windowpanes ended. Crossing his arms, he studied her. He was comfortable with silence, Jake.

Fine. She was in no rush herself to talk about what he'd come to talk to her about. She slanted her gaze in the direction of Holley's old town square. Nothing out of the ordinary or suspicious. Golden light fell over trees still half covered in burnished red, dark orange, and tempered yellow. Fallen leaves tumbled down the road before coming to rest on curbs and front yards like shallow, crackling ocean waves of autumn. A few houses down, a family was playing basketball in their driveway. She could hear the muted sound of the bouncing basketball and shouts of "I'm open!" and "Good shot."

She peeked the other way along the street.

Jake was the sibling closest to her in age. But that *closest in age* thing was perhaps a moot point because she was a full ten years distant from all of them. It was almost as if the boys had been part of Version One of the Porter family and she'd been part of Version Two. In the second version, she'd been an only child. Except not, because even though they were much older, her brothers' influence over her life had been powerful.

For as long as she could remember—*from her very first memory onward*—she'd wanted to catch up with the three of them. Wanted to, and never succeeded.

Bo, Ty, and Jake were their own little pack. Of the same generation. All male. The Porter boys. When they were little, they'd wrestled and made paper airplanes and laughed in dark bedrooms when they were supposed to be going to sleep. They'd learned to ride and swim and shoot at the same time. They'd believed in Santa and had wiggly teeth and been scolded by their parents and discovered the simple joy of playing in the mud together.

All before she'd even been born. She, who was so far behind them, hadn't had a chance to experience any of those things with them because they were all well past early childhood when she'd come along.

Some kids like her, surprise babies born late, probably gloried in all the parental attention. They likely enjoyed the pampering and their unchallenged "baby" status. But her personality didn't bend that way. God had wired a sense of justice into her, as well as a healthy, or unhealthy, dose of competitiveness. She'd been a feisty kid with scrapes on her arms and a rifle slung across her back. That kid had longed to earn the right to be included by her brothers. The disadvantage of her age and size and gender had always infuriated her.

As she'd grown, the fact that she *wanted* to be included in the first place had infuriated her, too. What did she care whether she was a part of their little trio? She was who she was. She loved them. They were her brothers. But she wasn't like them and didn't need to be like them.

Yet, a small, painful splinter caused by the loneliness of her isolation from them had lodged in her heart. She was an adult now. Perfectly independent. *Ferociously* independent. She wasn't the indignant little girl she'd been. Nor was she the wild teenager who'd dared one crazy stunt after another, thanks in part to the vein of restlessness within her and in part to her desire to gain the attention of her brothers.

Nowadays, she didn't need anyone to be hers, nor did she *want* to need anyone to be hers. Not even Bo, Ty, and Jake. Even so . . .

The splinter remained.

She stepped away from the window and, mimicking Jake's posture, met his hazel eyes.

Dru and all three of her brothers had served in the Marines. For Bo, Ty, and herself the experience had matured and toughened them. Service instilled confidence, honed bravery, and reinforced character. She and Bo and Ty were all stronger for it. They'd all come away unscarred.

Jake's history with the Marines was longer and more complex. His experiences had scored deep scars into his body and psyche.

Dru had been a freshman in high school when Jake's Humvee had been struck by an IED in Iraq. The other three men in the vehicle had died. Jake had sustained a punctured lung and lacerations to his face, thigh, and side. He'd returned to Texas and the Porters with a body that was healing, but a soul that was shattered. The brother she'd once known had become a closed-off, bitter, anxious man. The diagnosis? PTSD.

For the first eight years after the IED, Jake had worked as a horse trainer, shown up at family gatherings when required, fished Dru out of trouble when needed. He'd functioned. But he hadn't *lived*. Because of his mental state, Jake had caused Dru more worry than her other brothers put together.

Then, four years ago, Lyndie had come into his dark life. It had been a miracle, to watch how God had used

Jake's powerful, unstoppable love for Lyndie to rescue and redeem Jake. Her brother had come back to life.

Jake smiled at times now, especially at his wife. He'd become comfortable in his own skin again. His eyes had lost their haunted cast. He'd found peace.

When he wanted to be, though, Jake could still be as intimidating as all get out. He didn't have a personable veneer spread over the top of him. He didn't fake anything for the sake of manners.

If she found herself down to her last bag of Cool Ranch Doritos, Bo was the brother she could trust to guard her Doritos for her faithfully, even at large cost to himself. Ty was the brother who'd eat most of the bag but smile and tease her so skillfully when he handed the bag back that she'd end up thanking him for eating her food. And Jake was the brother who'd spend a long, scorching moment scowling at everyone who had intentions of stealing her Doritos and, in doing so, scare them all off.

"I know what you're going to say," Dru said.

"What am I going to say?"

"You're going to say that you don't like the fact that I brought Gray with me today."

He straightened to his full height. "You're right. I thought Gray Fowler was being stalked by someone who's potentially lethal."

"He is. But I made absolutely certain that we weren't followed when we came here."

"What about tracked by electronics?"

"No. The only way that the person who's threatening Gray could have followed us here is by airplane."

"Then why are you looking both ways out my window?"

Touché. "Because I'm on the clock, and Sutton pays me to be overly vigilant."

His lips tightened. "Lyndie lives here, Dru."

"I'm aware of that."

"I don't want danger anywhere near Lyndie." He was deadly serious. Jake's wife's safety was sacred ground for him. Non-negotiable. Some people might take up arms over the right to free speech. Jake's cause was Lyndie. He'd take up arms for her in a split second.

"I don't want danger near anyone in this family," Dru said.

"Then why'd you bring Gray Fowler?"

"He didn't have anywhere else to go."

His brow furrowed.

"Things are broken between him and his own family for some reason."

"And one of the most famous men in Dallas/Fort Worth didn't have a single invitation to Thanksgiving dinner?"

"I think he had plenty of invitations, but he decided to turn them down. I didn't want him to sit home alone on Thanksgiving."

A brief pause. "You're not . . . softening toward him, are you?"

"No." Perhaps she *was* softening—a little. But whatever softening might be occurring was wholly unauthorized by her brain. "He's my client."

Jake didn't look as though her answer put him at ease. "This will be your client's first and last visit to my house. Agreed?"

"Agreed."

"And I really hope you don't have a thing for him, Dru.

He plays for the Mustangs. Remember the touchdown pass he caught against us in September?" The controversial fourth-quarter play had given the Mustangs the win over the Cowboys.

They began descending the staircase. "I remember. But can we really hold a grudge? Gray plays for the team who signs his checks."

"Can I hold a grudge?" Jake gave a soft snort. "Yes. I can definitely hold a grudge."

They went in separate directions when they reached the main floor. Some of the family sat around the dining room table, nursing coffee. Dru found Gray in the living area with the rest of the family. He was sitting on the sofa, watching Lyndie's mom trying to act out something in a game of charades. Baby Ellerie sat in his lap, facing him. The infant stared up at Gray with a look of lovesick interest while gnawing on the cuff of his sweater—a charcoal-colored sweater that was probably wildly pricey.

Was she softening toward Gray? Why, yes. Yes, she was. It was unauthorized, to be sure. She liked him. She appreciated his work ethic, his directness, his confidence, his sense of humor. Gray was a man with a messed-up family life and the strength to pick up the coffee table sitting in front of him and snap it over his knee. And yet, he was holding a baby on his lap and playing charades.

"Wind?" he called out in response to Lyndie's mom's terrible pantomiming.

Karen shook her head and continued.

"Storm!" Addie yelled. She was sitting next to Gray, leaning forward.

Nope. The guesses kept coming, increasing in urgency.

"T-Rex!" Hudson jumped up and down. "It's T-Rex!"

"A surfer being churned under a wave?" Uncle Danny guessed.

"A French can-can girl!" From Dru's mom.

More head shaking from Lyndie's mom. Poor woman.

"T-Rex!!!"

"A lady looking for the false eyelashes she dropped?" from Danny's Russian girlfriend.

"It's clearly a squall," Ty said. He stood behind the sofa with a coffee cup in his hand. "Moving over Cooper Lake on a springtime evening."

"T-Rex!"

"Eleanor Roosevelt?" Sadie Jo offered, with a big dose of confusion.

Dru watched Gray laugh. It gave her strange pleasure to see him here, in her town, surrounded by her people. To be here *with him*. Tenderness expanded through her—

She stiffened against the sensation. Her tenderness toward Gray was a terrible echo and a sobering reminder of how she'd felt for her last client.

She absolutely couldn't date Gray. It was strictly against the rules. It couldn't happen. So since nothing would come of it, was it awful of her to enjoy the sight of a handsome man playing charades with her family?

It wasn't awful. But it wasn't advisable, either.

It's hurricane, *Gray.* She leveled her attention at his head. *That's the word Lyndie's mom is acting out.*

Gray turned to her as if she'd spoken. For an instant, he met her eyes with a small, chagrined twist of a smile. Dru felt their eye contact pulse through her body like heat.

He'd been caught by her, playing charades and holding a baby who was gumming his clothing. He faced forward again. "Hurricane."

"Yes!" Lyndie's mom laughed with the thrill of success. She punched her fists into the air, exhilarated. "Thank you, Gray!"

Had Gray just read Dru's mind?

Perhaps the two of them had already grown closer than she'd realized.

Shoot. He wasn't just *in* trouble due to the threats that had been leveled against him. Gray himself *was* trouble.

Her first impression of him, formed the moment they'd met, was proving itself accurate.

He was trouble. Dark, headstrong, dangerous trouble.

CHAPTER
NINE

How are things going between you and your bodyguard?" Corbin asked Gray three days later.

"Big Mack and I get along great," Gray answered,
deliberately misunderstanding his friend's question. He
didn't want to talk about Dru with Corbin. For one
thing, the topic was guaranteed to cause him irritation
toward his friend. For another, he wanted to concentrate
on football. He and Corbin were sitting on side-by-side
tables in the trainer's room at their practice facility, getting stretched out and taped up before hitting the field.

Corbin smiled. "I'm not all that interested in how
things are going between you and Mack. I'm interested
in how things are going between you and your bodyguard
who's hot-looking and female and named Dru."

"Things are going well."

"You're taking a slow-and-steady approach with her,
aren't you?"

"There's no way I'm going to show you my hand."
Sure enough, irritation was already needling him. Gray's

trainer bent, then lengthened his leg, to warm up the muscles in his injured hip.

"I'll show you my hand," Corbin said easily. "I feel like it's only fair to let you know that I'm not taking the slow-and-steady approach. I've talked with her on the phone every day this past week. Last night, she finally let me take her out for a late dinner after her shift ended."

Everything inside Gray went still. "Oh yeah?" Dru had left her shift with him for a date with Corbin? An unsettling emotion, part jealousy and part pure male possessiveness, darkened his heart and mind.

"I'm off to the races," Corbin said. "If you don't make a move soon, it'll be like the tortoise and the hare."

"The tortoise beats the hare. Remember?"

Corbin laughed. "Oh, that's right. Okay, then . . . it'll be like Jeff Gordon racing against a kid on a Big Wheel." Corbin's trainer finished taping one of the quarterback's ankles and moved to the other.

"You haven't asked me for my Rolex yet. So she must not have kissed you," Gray said. That didn't mean, though, that *Corbin* hadn't already kissed *her*. Geez, just the thought made his stomach tighten. "Have you kissed her?"

"I wish. Revengeress is going to take more effort than phone calls and one dinner. But you already know that."

Gray held his silence because he was afraid of what he'd say if he opened his mouth. Corbin's use of *Revengeress*, which he'd come to think of as his personal nickname for Dru, only added to his frustration.

Stretching complete, Gray sat on the edge of the table and watched the trainer go to work with expert speed, taping his ankle. His heart was thudding with anger and envy and the worry that Corbin would succeed.

Corbin had guessed correctly about the approach Gray had decided to take with Dru. He'd been taking things slow and steady, building their friendship first. Corbin might very well beat him to her.

He'd invited her to tomorrow's Monday night game. She'd said no to the invitation the first ten times, but eventually he'd worn her down and she'd agreed. He'd viewed it as a victory because, ever since he'd been in high school, inviting women to his games had been a surefire way to soften them toward him.

But Corbin would be playing in front of Dru tomorrow night, too. And while Gray's position on the offense was critical, it was a lot less flashy than Corbin's position. He'd wanted her at the game for him, but her presence there might end up benefitting Corbin.

Why had he entered into this stupid bet?

He regretted that he had, and at the same time, he knew exactly why he'd done it. He hadn't wanted to give her over to Corbin without a fight.

He still didn't. At this point, it had become an over-my-dead-body type of thing.

Dru—*his* Dru—couldn't really be falling for Corbin. But immediately he had to wonder why she wouldn't be. Corbin wasn't just rich and famous. He was a good person, a generous person. His past wasn't as screwed up as Gray's. He was more open to relationships and would probably make a better boyfriend.

Corbin hopped off his table. "My wrist is ready for your Rolex."

"My wall is ready for your flat screen."

Corbin clapped him on the shoulder, eyes creasing with humor, then walked toward the exit. "You're just the tight end," he teased. "I'm the quarterback. Women love the quarterback best." His laughter seemed to hang in the room long after he'd left it.

Well, Dru thought later that day while peering through binoculars, *it looks as though I'm going to have the questionable pleasure of meeting Gray's angry ex-girlfriend.* Kayla Bell.

"How much longer you going to leave her sitting out there?" Gray asked.

"Not much longer. I just wanted to observe her for a while."

She'd taken over from Big Mack an hour and a half ago. Twenty minutes ago, Kayla had hit the intercom button mounted in front of the entrance gate to Gray's property and asked if she could come in. Dru had declined. There was no way she was allowing either Kayla inside to talk to Gray or Gray outside to talk to Kayla. Five minutes ago, Dru had entered the upstairs media room, where Gray was currently playing Xbox, so that she could watch Kayla through the media-room windows. She'd already tested out the view from two other rooms. These windows gave the best vantage.

Kayla had parked on the road in front of his house. Appearing ready to wait Gray out, Kayla had been sitting behind the wheel of her silver Lexus SUV, alternately staring out the front window and using her index finger to swipe through the content on her phone. She didn't appear agitated. Dru couldn't see a weapon, nor was

Kayla wearing oversized clothing that would allow her to conceal a gun.

Dru switched out the binoculars for the camera the agents kept onsite. She zoomed in on Kayla, took shots of both her and her vehicle, then turned toward Gray.

He was reclining on the leather sofa, wearing a white t-shirt, track pants, and a ball cap on backward. When she'd arrived for her shift, Rashid and Duayne, two of the Mustangs running backs, had been here with him, and they'd all been trash-talking and laughing as they'd taken turns battling each other at Madden NFL. After his buddies had gone, Gray must have switched to a road-racing game because a 1970s Dodge Charger was zooming across the screen. A screen that was approximately the size of the *Titanic*.

She and Gray would be leaving soon so that he could check into the hotel where the Mustangs stayed the night before home games. Playing Xbox was part of his pre-hotel stay and pre-travel ritual. She'd observed his habit herself, and read about it in the log that all the agents contributed to. She could only guess that he used Xbox to occupy his hands and focus his mind.

She headed for the door.

"Finally going to talk to her?" Gray asked. The noise and motion of his game paused.

"Yep."

"Have fun." He smiled at her the way a ticket seller might smile while wishing you fun on a haunted house ride.

"Talking to your ex-girlfriend will be a great deal of fun for me, Gray. This is exactly what I dreamt of when I pursued this line of work. Can't wait."

"If I had any reason to think Kayla's dangerous, I'd go with you. But she's not my stalker, and she's not dangerous."

"She might be your stalker."

"Nope. She's just a little bit crazy. She's not the kind of crazy that needs to be admitted to a psychiatric hospital."

"Mm-hmm."

"Also, I don't know if you've heard, but I'm going to be playing Monday Night Football for the only time all season tomorrow."

"Really? You don't say."

"And, just between you and me, we're in contention for the playoffs."

"What?!"

"So I'm happy to skip Kayla's drama today." He straightened his thumb toward the screen. "I'm very busy racing in Switzerland." He winked and resumed the game.

"I'm happy to skip Kayla's drama today." Yep, and she'd be willing to bet that whenever he'd been confronted with drama in past relationships, he'd opted out those times, too.

She and Anthony Sutton had asked him lots of questions about past relationships that first day at the headquarters. His longest relationship had been back when he'd been at A&M. For ten months, he'd dated a very pretty, smiling blonde—they'd done their homework at Sutton and dug up pictures—named Raelynn. Raelynn had been raised in a small town in Oklahoma and now lived in Austin with her wealthy husband and their two very pretty, smiling, blond children.

Gray's string of short romances seemed to have been

based mostly on sex and friendship. Which made Dru suspect that he wasn't willing to put in the real work that real relationships required. Which, in turn, made her wonder why. Why wasn't he willing?

She gripped the door handle.

"When you come back," Gray said, "race against me. I want to slaughter you on the advanced hill course."

"Can you try for a minute to set aside your chauvinism? I'm female, but that doesn't mean I'm bad at Xbox. I'd be the one slaughtering you, which wouldn't be good for your delicate self-confidence the day before taking the field against the Eagles." She closed the door behind her.

Three days had passed since Thanksgiving. In that time, Gray had received one handwritten letter from creepy super-fan Kevin Lee, ranting about his adoration of Gray and asking for a laundry list of signed items. Gray had also received another letter from his stalker. Once again, the stalker had mentioned Dru.

Yesterday, Dru had gone back over the information she'd typed up from her time in Bonham investigating Mildred Osbourne and her son Rich. How was a person supposed to find something they hadn't seen in the first place? It couldn't be done, yet the unsettled sense that she'd overlooked a detail continued to niggle at her.

Worse, Gray had begun to look more handsome to her with every passing day. Whenever their eyes met, her pulse picked up speed. And she'd developed a sort of sixth sense about him. No matter where they went during her shifts, she could almost *feel* his presence. If they were at his home, for example, and she was working online at the kitchen counter, she was keenly aware the entire time of Gray in his office. If he moved to a different room, she hardly needed sound to know it.

Frankly, the distraction of his attractiveness was of absolutely no benefit to anyone. Some people received actual, useful benefits at their jobs—like dental coverage.

She'd have preferred dental coverage.

Before leaving Gray's property, she double-checked her weapon and texted Sutton Security to let them know that Kayla Bell had arrived onsite and that she was going to interview the subject.

As soon as she exited Gray's gate, she used her phone to snap a photo of Kayla's license plate. It wouldn't hurt to make sure Kayla was driving the car the DMV said she was driving. Dru switched her phone to record, then pocketed it.

When she'd drawn within ten yards of the Lexus, the driver's-side window rolled down. "Hello?" Kayla asked.

"Hello." Dru came even with the driver's-side door, adjusting to the close-up reality of someone she'd heretofore only seen in pictures or from a distance.

Kayla regarded her, assessing, doubtful, ever so slightly disdainful. Her features had a faint exotic cast and were covered in Jennifer Lopez–style makeup. She'd either flat-ironed her long brunette hair or come straight over from one of those shops that offered professional blow-outs.

"I'm Dru, Gray's friend." The calm, cool weather hovered motionless, as if holding its breath. "Sorry, but he's still busy. He's not going to come out."

"Really."

Dru's vision caught on the outline of a small girl sleeping in a car seat in the SUV's back row. The rear windows were tinted, which explained why she'd been unable to see the child from the house. Two tiny pigtails sprouted from the sides of the little girl's head. Her face tilted up and to the side, mouth slightly open.

Kayla slid out of the car. The sound of a Katy Perry song, volume low, followed. "Are you Gray's friend or Gray's girlfriend?" She leaned against the SUV and stuck the tips of her fingers into the front pockets of her snug pants.

"His girlfriend." Her faux girlfriend status might actually prove useful in this situation. If it stirred Kayla's anger, then Dru might get a more accurate glimpse into the other woman's psyche.

"How long have you been dating him?" Kayla asked.

"A few weeks."

Kayla's eye narrowed. "Did he tell you about me?"

"Yes."

"What did he say? That I'm crazy?" Tension stretched thin her tone.

"His exact words were that you're 'a little bit crazy.'"

Insult flashed in her expression. "I'm not crazy. I *love* him. But since he doesn't know what love is, he can't tell the difference. Gray wouldn't know love if it hit him in the face." She met Dru's eyes challengingly. Clearly, Kayla was no stranger to confrontation. She might even be the type of person who enjoyed it. "It won't last between you," Kayla assured her.

"Okay."

"I was the best thing that ever happened to him. We were great together. Perfect."

Kayla's confidence was Herculean enough to be just one door north of delusional.

"He pushed me away when I got too close," Kayla continued. "If you manage to get close to him, he'll do the same to you. Just warning you. He will."

They faced each other. Two women standing tall in their high heels, evenly matched in height, both dark-haired.

There were similarities between them outwardly. But Dru had no interest in becoming anything like Kayla inwardly. Kayla was piteously, doggedly pursuing a man who didn't want her. Kayla's determination might serve her well in other areas of life, but it was wasted on Gray Fowler.

"Are you sure he's not going to come out?" Kayla asked tightly.

"I'm positive."

Kayla released a frustrated breath and reached into her car. She brought out two packages of Trident gum, spearmint flavored. "I came today because I know he'll be driving to the hotel soon. On game day tomorrow, he'll stretch out and jog onto the field and take a few cuts to test out his cleats. Then right before he runs from the tunnel, he'll chew two pieces of spearmint Trident. I brought these for him for good luck." She cocked her head. "Did you know about the Trident?"

"No."

She extended the two small packages on her palm, looking smug. "Will you give these to Gray for me?"

Not a chance in the world. Nowhere in the Sutton Security handbook did it recommend giving a client theoretically tainted gum from a suspect. Dru dropped the packets into her jacket pocket. "How long were you and Gray together?" she asked.

"Two and a half months."

"And when did your relationship end?"

"More than two years ago."

"Then why are you still calling him and texting him and coming by here to see him?" Dru asked levelly. "He's moved on."

Bitterness overtook Kayla's face, leaching away the beauty in her carefully powdered features. She didn't answer.

"Do you ever send him letters?" Dru asked.

"Why would I? I have his phone number."

She watched Kayla's body language. No obvious evidence of lying. "It's time to let him go." Dru didn't break eye contact with Kayla, even for a second. Kayla Bell might be combative, but Dru had seen *actual* combat. Kayla didn't scare her.

"I have a daughter with Gray."

"No." Gray had a public persona. But that didn't mean he deserved to be stalked and threatened and badgered into being someone's baby daddy. "The paternity test proved that he's not your child's father. No amount of wishing or waiting can change that."

They stared at each other, the air humming. *Do you seriously want to throw down with me while your daughter's asleep in the back of your car, Kayla? If so, it won't go well for you.*

Kayla retreated into her car, shutting the door with more force than necessary.

Dru stood on the street—a pistol strapped to her body beneath her jacket, two packages of gum in her pocket—and watched Kayla go.

Dru had acquired a football fan's healthy admiration for Monday Night Football. Until now, however, she'd never attended a Monday night game live because she'd never achieved the level of financial insanity necessary to lay out cash for tickets.

In the case of tonight's game, Gray had supplied her with her ticket. Her seat's location was both excellent and also awkward. Awkward because she was surrounded by the friends and family of Mustangs players. She wasn't part of Gray's circle of friends and family. She wasn't even *supposed* to be a Mustangs fan.

Unlike those around her, Dru hadn't decked herself out in a Mustangs jersey, Mustangs merchandise, or Mustangs colors. For tonight's crisp, cold weather she'd donned her Dr. Martens boots, her silver ski jacket, and a black cable-knit cap. Impartial clothing. Yet when Gray's offense took the field, she didn't feel very impartial. She felt invested. And hopeful that he'd crush the Eagles' defense. And worried about him getting his head ripped off. And . . .

Proud of him.

His on-field presence was concentrated and quietly intense. He gripped the shoulders of rookies whenever he looked down at them, helmet to helmet, to instruct or congratulate or correct. He moved through some plays with athletic grace, confident and sure. Other times, he collided with defenders in an explosion of ferocity. He was a blocker, a receiver, a menace.

He was football poetry. He was lethal effectiveness.

As the third quarter ebbed away, Dru took to her feet

with the other fans to watch the end of a long touch-down drive. On third and goal, Gray ran a button-hook route. Corbin threw a bullet at him. Gray caught it and pounded his way through defenders like a cement truck. When he crossed into the end zone, he did so dragging the Eagles' safety and a cornerback. The stadium erupted in a mighty roar of approval.

Dru grinned and accepted a jubilant hug from the woman sitting next to her, the mother of the Mustangs' nose guard. The woman was wearing one of those huge round pins that featured a photo of her son.

The Mustangs scored the extra point, and the offense jogged off the field. Dru had made a concerted effort not to stare at Gray when he was on the sidelines below her seat. She wasn't responsible for his protection dur-ing this game, so she didn't need to stare at him. Plus, it was ludicrous to come to a Monday night game and not watch every second of the action. *Plus*, earlier he'd searched the stands until he'd found her. She didn't want him looking up again and catching her ogling him as if entranced and starstruck like the other seventy thousand people in the stadium. He had plenty of people in his life who were entranced and starstruck.

He needed her to be smart and cool-headed and pro-fessional.

She wouldn't stare. She'd just slant one quick glance downward—

Her gaze collided with his. He was standing near a bench, holding his helmet in one hand. In the way of macho football players, his arms were bare despite—or to spite?—the temperature. One sleeve had bunched up enough so that she could see his tattoo's markings snaking out from underneath. Sweat drenched his hair. Ruddy color marked his cheeks. Scuff marks, including a reddish one that might be blood, marred his jersey and pants. He was standing in the midst of swarming activity, looking right at her with a questioning smile.

Longing for him that went much deeper than mere physical attraction clenched within her. She gave Gray a slight nod and a look that said, *You did well.* Then she returned her focus to the game.

Her thoughts went into a riot.

No, she didn't feel very impartial at all toward him. It was galling. Astounding! Embarrassing. Memories of her last client drifted through her brain, mocking her. Exactly what she'd been so determined *not* to let happen—the establishment of an emotional connection between her and Gray—had happened, nonetheless. At least on her side.

What was she going to do?

You're going to do what you've always done, Dru. You're going to get ahold of yourself. She refused to be one of those women who was ruled by feelings. To feel romantically toward Gray would be incredibly stupid career-wise and colossally dumb on a personal level.

Kayla's words came back to her. *"He pushed me away when I got too close. If you manage to get close to him, he'll do the same to you."* Dru had no interest in becoming just one more of Gray's casual, short-term girlfriends. It seemed to her that Kayla was right. Gray had no problem pushing girlfriends away. Nor did he seem to have any problem landing new girlfriends.

There were literally thousands of women in this stadium who would date him and thousands more around

Dallas/Fort Worth and the rest of the country. He certainly didn't need a girlfriend to cook his meals or dote on him or take care of his house. He didn't need one to organize his calendar or his charitable commitments. He didn't need one to dress in his jersey and cheer him on from the friends-and-family section.

What he needed was someone to keep him safe and find his stalker. And that was what Dru was uniquely qualified to do. It would be best to take a step back from him in her mind and her emotions. She was his protection agent.

That was her only role where Gray Fowler was concerned.

CHAPTER
TEN

Gray watched their server set a plate of red velvet cake onto their table. An unlit candle had been stuck into the top of it, and someone had written "Happy Birthday!" in cursive chocolate on the plate's rim. Ash would love it.

"Oh." The server hesitated, extending his arm back toward the dessert. "Did I miss her? Should I wait and bring the cake back?"

"Nah, it's fine," Gray told him. "She's in the restroom. She'll be out in a second."

"Okay. As soon as I see her, I'll hurry back over to light the candle." The server moved off.

Ash's birthday was tomorrow and so, like he did every year, Gray had taken her out to dinner at the restaurant of her choice to celebrate. Luckily for him, Ash wasn't the only female on this dinner date.

Dru sat across the table from him, candlelight playing along her neck and the line of her jaw. Whenever they were out together, she spent most of her time focusing on their surroundings. But tonight it seemed like she was deliberately avoiding looking at him. He'd been staring at her more than usual, and she'd been staring more than usual at anything *but* him.

Ash had chosen a restaurant named Urban Country in an artsy, renovated area called the Bishop Arts District. The place specialized in fancy Southern food, which seemed strange to him. The Southern food he'd eaten growing up hadn't been fancy at all.

They were surrounded by modern furniture, but old decorations. Big wooden racks hung on the walls, holding antique red and white plates. The drapes looked like they'd been made from a 1950s fabric. Were those cherries on the pattern, in between the blue diamonds? They'd reached the early days of December, so the restaurant had placed a rustic-looking tree in the foyer near the bar and greenery above each window.

Not really his type of place. Too girly.

"You watch," he said to Dru. "When Ash gets back, she'll close her eyes and take a while to make a wish before she blows out her birthday candle."

She glanced at him. "A wasted wish, because I'm certain that she'll squander her big moment by wishing to become your girlfriend."

"She doesn't want to become my girlfriend. She's happy being my assistant."

"How wrong you are." She moved her attention toward the front of the restaurant. "You should consider dating her, Gray. She's inhumanly nice and her pot roast rocks."

"She's nice and her pot roast rocks, but I'm not interested in dating her."

"Suit yourself."

Once again, he was left with only her profile to look at. Frustrating. He wasn't used to being brushed off. He was much more used to wishing for less attention from people. Not more.

He'd wanted to see Dru after the team's win on Monday night, so he'd hurried through his shower afterward. He'd known she wouldn't work on Tuesday or Wednesday, and he'd been determined to say goodbye before her days off. Also . . . it had meant something to him, to have her sitting in the stands.

During the game, the collar of her silver jacket had framed her chin, and her black hat had been pulled low. Her dark, shiny hair had hung down both sides of her chest. Her cheeks and the tip of her nose had been pink.

He'd played hundreds of football games. But Dru's presence at Monday's game had brought something new to the table. It had made an already important game that much more important to him. It had pleased him, her being there. He'd been aware the whole time that she was watching, and that knowledge had motivated him.

When he'd rushed out into the players' parking area after the press conference, Dru had been gone. Weston Kinney had been waiting for him. His disappointment had put him in a dark mood that had stayed with him for the two boring, uninteresting days that had followed. Gray frowned at his Rolex as he adjusted it on his wrist.

It was Thursday, and she was back. He'd probably looked at this watch a dozen times this morning while he'd been attending meetings with his unit, watching film, practicing, lifting. When two o'clock had arrived, and Dru with it, he'd been able to tell right away that something had changed. Gone were the smiles and the sass and the swagger. Today, she was all business.

Turned out he wasn't handling her change of heart that well. "Are you mad at me?"

"What?" At last she looked directly at him and held eye contact.

"If you're mad at me, go ahead and tell me why. I can handle it."

"I'm not mad at you."

"Then why are you giving me the cold shoulder today?"

"I'm not. I'm simply doing my job."

"Yeah, but something's different. You're supposed to be posing as my girlfriend, but you've hardly looked in my direction since we got here."

"I'm more concerned with protecting you than posing as your girlfriend."

"Has the threat level against me increased recently?"

"No."

"Then relax. We're getting more attention from the people around us than we'd normally get because of the way you're *not* looking at me."

She wrinkled her forehead, skeptical.

"I was hoping that you'd have a crush on me after watching me play." He grinned. "I should be able to seduce you now."

Humor softened the clean angles of her features. At last! He felt like he'd waited a year to see her smile. "Do women usually make themselves available for seducing after a game?"

"Always. So what's the holdup? You're a football fan."

"I'm a *Cowboys* fan."

He leaned against his chair's back, hands on his thighs. "You are *stubborn*." He stretched stubborn into three syllables, which was fewer syllables than her brand of stubborn deserved.

"I'm not available for seduction. Not to you anyway. And also not without a ring on my finger."

A ring on her finger? Seriously? The only woman he knew who was anywhere close to that conservative was Ashley.

"Fun talk," she said. "Here comes Ashley."

Gray rose briefly as Ash took her seat at the table.

"What's this?" Ash asked, lacing her hands together near her throat.

"Dessert. You love red velvet, right?" Gray asked.

"Yes. Oh, this is so nice. So kind of you. Wow, it looks wonderful." She was going on as if she'd never seen a restaurant birthday dessert before. "Thank you, Gray."

"Do you want us to sing? Because I'm sure Dru would be glad to."

"No, no. This is perfect."

The server appeared, used a lighter to get the candle going, and left them to it.

"All righty," Ash said. "Time for me to make a wish."

Dru gave Ash a quick glance. "If I were you, I'd make it count, Ashley. Wish for something like a motorcycle."

His housekeeper laughed, round-eyed. "Oh, goodness no."

Ash was about as familiar with motorcycles as fish were with skateboards.

Dru eyed Gray with resignation.

Ash closed her eyes for a long moment, then blew out the flame. Pulling the candle from the dessert, she gestured to the three forks the server had left. "Help yourselves."

"You first," Gray said. He tried to catch Dru's eye again, without luck.

Dru always chose tables set near walls and always sat in whichever seat faced the center of the restaurant. He assumed she did this so that no one could sneak up on her and so that she could keep watch over the entire place, exactly as she was doing now.

Her dark gray leather biker jacket was just a few shades lighter than the black top she wore underneath. A long, silver necklace hung down over the center of her shirt, ending in a simple rectangular bar of silver. He'd been distracted all night by the sight of that necklace, lying against her shirt—

"This is absolutely delicious," Ash said. "Here, Gray. Have some."

He forked off a bite of cake. Not dry, like red velvet could go. The cream cheese frosting tasted rich and smooth.

Ash started talking about her birthday plans with her mom. Gray listened halfheartedly, his vision on Dru—

A muffled popping noise burst through the restaurant, followed by the ping of breaking glass.

Dru reacted instantly. She was out of her chair and immediately launching herself into his side. They both went over. Gray had just enough time to catch his fall with his hand before the rest of his weight landed on his shoulder and thigh. Dru came down on top of him. His chair crashed to the floor.

Had that been a gunshot? That popping sound could have been caused by something other than a gun. A car backfiring. A firecracker. Except those things wouldn't explain the breaking glass.

"Don't move." Dru untangled her legs from his and knelt behind him. She grabbed Ashley's wrist and dragged her down beneath the level of the table.

Another *ker-pow*. More glass raining down. Someone was firing into the restaurant. Because of him? These people—and Dru and Ash—were in danger because of . . . him? The possibility hit him like a punch to the gut. Was his stalker behind this? What kind of person would shoot into a full restaurant when it was him, specifically, that they hated?

Dru gripped his shoulder. "Are you hurt?"

"No. Are *you* hurt?"

"I'm fine. But are you sure *you're* fine? Take a second." He read concentration in her expression, but not the slightest bit of fear, as her gaze combed over him.

"I don't need a second," he said. "I'm sure."

The people in the restaurant were reacting with normal human speed, just now murmuring with confusion and fear.

"Get down, everyone!" Dru yelled. "Shots have been fired into the restaurant. Get below your tables. Call 911."

There was a mass of panicked movement as people did what she'd instructed.

"I'm going to move you to a safer location," Dru said to him.

He rose onto one knee. "And Ash."

His housekeeper's hair stuck up crazy on one side. Her already pale skin had turned white.

"Fine," Dru said. "You're going to run down that

hallway, there, Ashley. It leads to a utility room and the kitchen and the back door. Hunch over and keep your head and shoulders down as you run. Stop at the utility room. Gray, you'll follow right behind her. Good?"

"No. You follow Ash, and I'll be right behind you."

Her eyes blazed turquoise fire. "No," she hissed. She turned to Ash before he could argue further. *"Go!"*

Ash ran for the hallway. Gray followed, with Dru right behind, close, putting herself between him and the restaurant. Ash wasn't moving fast enough in her heels to suit him, so he picked her up in one arm and ran them into the hallway.

Dru pushed open the utility room's door. A light came on automatically, showing a medium-sized space full of cleaning supplies and shelves stocked with things like extra plates and tablecloths and flour. "Inside," Dru ordered.

Ashley went in, but Gray stood in the doorway, watching Dru walk to the end of the hallway in the direction of the exit. Drawing her gun, she opened the restaurant's back door. She kept flat against the wall, making herself a difficult target as she scanned the dark parking lot behind the building. It was all he could do not to go to her and yank her back.

She'd actually tackled him when that first shot had gone off. It had happened fast. In less time than it took him to snap his fingers, she'd tackled him.

Many people had told him how important he was to them. Fans. His team. His coaches. His agent. But this was the first time that he'd ever seen anyone put themselves between him and a threat. It was Dru's job to do so. But the fact that she'd actually done it, that she'd put action behind her words, caused something within him, something cold and closed, to crack.

Dru let the exit door swing shut and holstered her gun beneath her jacket as she strode down the hallway toward him.

He cared about her. He cared about her way more than was wise.

Gray wasn't inside the utility room like she'd ordered. Instead, he was standing mostly out in the hallway. Earlier today, she'd performed an advance on the restaurant and chosen the utility room as her safe room.

She wanted Gray *inside* the safe room.

However, he'd set his rugged face in harsh lines. His eyebrows were low, his pale green eyes seething. All of which told her he wasn't in an agreeable frame of mind. His hair looked disordered thanks to the tackle she'd aimed at him. One of the cuffs on his light blue business shirt was about to come unrolled, and wrinkles marred the fabric.

"Get inside," she barked. He was huge, but she wasn't above trying to shove him back into the utility room. "Gray. Get—"

He walked straight up to her and kissed her.

She struggled to overcome her shock. There was a shooter. . . . She hadn't expected . . . *What was he doing?*

He was kissing her.

His strength, standing up against her, staggered her. He kissed like an expert, all mastery and confidence. Without words he powerfully communicated his desire and his feelings. He communicated hunger. He communicated affection.

Her body responded. He smelled delicious and expensive—

He *was* expensive. Too expensive to her career and her ambitions and her independence.

She wrenched back from him.

He watched her, his chest expanding and deflating and expanding.

"What was that?" she demanded.

"A kiss."

It had probably only lasted four seconds, their kiss. But each of those seconds had spun out and had the impact of ten. She could have ended it after two seconds. That she hadn't, that she'd liked it as much as she had, shamed her. *Executive. Protection. Agent!*

"Get inside the utility room." She spoke slowly, each word heavy with warning.

Ashley peeked out, the door in one hand and the jamb in the other, her face hovering in between. Her mascara had smeared. With tears of fear? Ashley did her best to smile. With her rickety, half-grimacing lips and terrified eyes, she looked certifiably insane. Great.

She got both Gray and Ashley inside the room and locked them all in together. "We'll stay here for a few more minutes until the police arrive," she said. "Everything will be fine."

"Did we just get . . . shot at?" Ashley asked tremulously.

"Two shots were fired into the restaurant, yes."

Ashley rested a hand on her heart.

"Why do you think it's better to stay here than to exit out the back?" Gray asked.

It was hard to look at him without the sensory memory of that kiss flooding her. "I don't like the back exit. I checked it earlier today when I came by here and again just now. It empties into a parking lot. If we cross the lot, there's nothing to protect us. Nothing to hide behind. It's possible that the shooter was hoping to flush us out the back. I'm not going to give him a clear shot at you, Gray."

Ashley released a small squeak.

"We're fine here," Dru continued. "I haven't heard any more shots. Everything's settling down, and the police will arrive shortly."

"Do you think my stalker did this?" Gray asked.

"Yes. Any other scenario seems too coincidental to me at this point."

"What kind of . . . ?" Ashley swallowed convulsively. Back came that nutty smile. "What kind of preschool do you teach at, Dru?"

The naïve Pollyanna thing was getting on Dru's nerves. "I'm not a preschool teacher. That was just my cover story. I'm one of Gray's executive protection agents."

"An . . . an executive protection agent?"

"Yes. The Mustangs hired us to keep Gray safe because he's been receiving death threats from a stalker."

Ashley weaved on her feet. Gray wrapped an arm around Ashley's shoulders the way one might with a child and drew her against his side. "You're okay, Ash. We're all fine."

"Mm-hmm. I'm okay."

"I'm trained for exactly these kinds of situations," Dru assured her.

"You're not Gray's girlfriend?" Ashley asked.

"No. I'm not. But that *is* my cover story. So if anyone asks, I'd appreciate it if you'd support it."

"All right." Ashley cleared her throat. "Well. I'm glad we were able to get in our meal before the, um, gunfire." Ashley's words emerged high-pitched and sugary sweet. Completely out of place for their circumstance. If an earthquake were to strike, Ashley would stand among the falling rubble with dust in her hair, smiling and talking about how nice it was to be able to see the sky *through* the ceiling. "The food was lovely."

"You know what really chaps my hide?" Dru asked.

"Can't wait to hear," Gray said dryly.

"I never got a bite of the red velvet cake."

CHAPTER
ELEVEN

True to Dru's prediction, the police arrived shortly afterward. Dru, Gray, and Ashley gave their statements. Dru explained to the officers that Sutton Security had been working with Detective Carlyle from the Dallas Police Department on an open investigation into the threats against Gray.

The policemen attempted to care about what Dru was saying. They really did, but Dru could see their struggle. They were huge NFL fans, and all of them wanted pictures with Gray and autographs for their sons. One of them even produced a football for Gray to sign.

While they were revering her client, Dru looked over the evidence. One of the restaurant's shatterproof glass windows had two bullet holes through it, one about five inches lower than the other. The bullets had lodged into the interior's back wall several feet above where they'd been sitting. If the shooter had intended to hit Gray, then his aim stunk.

Sutton would be in touch with Detective Carlyle to get ballistics data on the ammunition that had been used in the shooting once the information became available. The bullets' entry point and their final resting place, taken together, gave Dru a fairly decent idea of the angle at which the shots had entered the restaurant. Which, in turn, provided her with a fair guess as to where the shooter had likely been positioned.

Ashley was sitting on a chair, clutching her sweater around her shoulders, and Gray was laughing about his Super Bowl win with the officers as Dru let herself out the front entrance of Urban Country. She stood on the sidewalk. Lots of foot traffic on this block. Old-fashioned streetlights. She walked to where she could see the window that had been struck, then imagined the trajectory the bullets would have taken to get there. The gunman had been shooting at a slight downward angle from a higher position.

Across the street, several storefronts that had been built in the days of the Old West stood in a neat row. All were occupied. Some of the structures were two stories, some one. She snapped several pictures with her phone, then made her way behind the row of buildings. An alley lined the rear, complete with hulking trash dumpsters. She clicked on her phone's flashlight app.

There was no easy access from the alley floor to the rooftops, but it wouldn't have been difficult to walk down the alley with an expandable ladder, climb onto the roof of a single-story building, then pull the ladder up after. That done, the shooter would have had all the time he or she wanted to look through the scope and watch them through the windows.

Dru would return here tomorrow when she had daylight to give the alley and rooftops a thorough search. If the shooter was Gray's stalker, which she suspected to be the case, she was pretty sure she'd find nothing. Gray's stalker wasn't sloppy. Even so, she'd return.

Dru stood in the alley, frowning at the back of the building she believed the shooter had used.

What had motivated the stalker to move from letter writing to the much dirtier and riskier work of lugging a weapon onto a rooftop and taking shots at Gray? Had something, a clarifying moment, tipped the scales and caused the stalker to take this new step?

Had the stalker's aim been half as deadly as Dru's own aim, she'd be at the morgue beside Gray, who'd have a tag around his toe.

The thought of that sent an icy shudder between her shoulder blades.

When she'd heard the sound of the first shot, fear for Gray had driven through her like a spike. She hadn't known, in those first split seconds after she'd knocked him to the ground, whether or not he'd been hit. She could deal with concern over her own safety. Dealing with her fear for Gray in that moment had been far harder.

Her first few years at Sutton, she'd felt only professionally protective of her clients. Which was appropriate. Then she'd been assigned to Mark. And now Gray. She'd become emotionally protective of both men. It was humbling and infuriating to have to struggle this hard for objectivity. And it was straight-up confounding to be kissed by a client.

That kiss . . .

She was glad for the muted quiet and solitude of the alley, for the breeze that cooled her cheeks. That kiss had been intense. He'd walked right up to her and kissed her. No slow incline or whispered words. He hadn't asked permission, and he certainly hadn't been intimidated by her the way most men were. Just . . . boom. He'd kissed her.

She still hadn't fully wrapped her mind around it. The only thing she knew for sure was that she'd be removed from Gray's detail if Anthony Sutton found out about that kiss.

She'd report it to Anthony and resign from the case herself if she believed that the relationship she'd formed with Gray impaired her ability to do her job.

But, in this situation, she didn't. Believe that.

Gray had surprised her with a brief kiss. Excitement had been running high. He'd survived danger. Whatever. It didn't mean anything. She'd ended it very quickly. Maybe not as quickly as she could have, but still . . . quickly.

She had no plans to kiss Gray again or wade into a romance with him. She liked him and was drawn to him, but those truths didn't have to hinder the quality of her work. They might even make her better.

You're rationalizing, Dru. Pieces of dark hair skated over one eye. She dashed them away. She'd hoped that she'd gotten past her tendency to rationalize her concerns into the background so that she could go ahead and do whatever it was she wanted to do. In this situation, however, her wants were going to win out because she *really* wanted to catch Gray's stalker. Single-mindedly, that was what she wanted.

She was a grown-up. She could resist temptation.

She snapped a few more photos, then headed back to the restaurant.

Since Dru had reason to suspect that Gray's stalker knew their whereabouts this evening, she also had reason to suspect he'd had access to their cars. She called Sutton and asked that a staffer drive over one of the firm's company cars. Then she escorted Ashley and Gray from the restaurant into the back of the new black Suburban with darkly tinted windows. Dru took the driver's seat, the Sutton staffer the passenger's seat.

"I don't usually sit in the backseat," Gray said as they pulled away from Urban Country. "I feel like I'm twelve."

Sure enough, his body looked humorously oversized in his captain's chair.

"Shh, big football player. Eat some of the snacks from your backpack and play on your Nintendo DS until we get where we're going."

Dru went through her usual measures to ensure they weren't being followed. After dropping the staffer at headquarters, she drove to Ashley's parents' home. Neither Dru nor Gray wanted Ashley alone at her apartment tonight. Better for her to be surrounded by family who could nurse her through her trauma and pamper her on her birthday tomorrow.

"Thanks for treating me to dinner, Gray." Ashley gave Gray a parting hug that seemed to last longer than necessary for an employer and his employee. Dru felt an unaccountable twist of jealousy.

When Ashley stepped away, she turned to Dru. "Thanks for saving my life."

Dru wanted to tell her that the thing that had saved her life was the fact that the bullets had been shot several feet too high. Instead she said, "Anytime."

Dru drove Gray north, darkness and charged silence blanketing the interior of the Suburban.

"I want to drive," Gray said.

"Nope."

"I'm the client."

"But this time, this isn't your car. Get over it."

The dashboard lights glowed. Occasional highway lights zipped by, sending illumination darting through the space, then vanishing. The memory of their kiss hovered between them, growing larger and larger with every mile.

When Dru passed the exit leading to his house, Gray looked at her.

"I'm taking you to my house," she said. "Just for tonight. Maybe tomorrow night."

Surprised quiet met her announcement. "An agent taking a client to their house doesn't sound like something from the bodyguard handbook."

"It's not. It's outside the box."

"Then why take me there?"

What had happened with Mark had made her overly protective. She hadn't fully understood *how* hyper careful it had made her until bullets had zinged through the air above Gray's head. So. There it was. "My house is remote. I can be sure you'll be safe there until we're certain things have calmed down and we have time to collect more information about tonight's shooting."

"We could just as easily go to a hotel."

Of course they could. But she had no desire to take him to an unfamiliar hotel. She wanted to take him to a place where she had the upper hand. She knew Holley, Texas, and her piece of property by heart, and knowledge was power. "There's no need for both of us to be removed from our residences. Weston can gather whatever you need and bring it to my place when his shift starts."

Gray thought for a moment, then said, "You're not planning to stick me on your sofa, are you? Sticking me on your sofa is a no-go."

His body recovered from the daily beating it took during sleep, she knew. Adequate rest was as necessary to an athlete as nutrition. "I have a spare bedroom. Any other grievances?"

"I don't think Weston needs to come. Not if your house is as remote and safe as you say it is."

"My house is remote, but it's still only relatively safe, not completely safe. And I'm off work at ten." It was already 9:20. "Weston and Mack are going to work their shifts like always."

"Weston's strange. Has anyone considered the possibility that *he* might be my stalker?"

"No."

He clicked his tongue. "Might be worth looking into. Just a tip."

Dru couldn't help but smile. True, Weston was a little strange. People who worked through the night had to be. She hit auto-dial for Weston's secure phone and flipped her cell to Gray. "Let him know what you need."

She listened to his voice as he spoke.

Driving a vehicle in which Gray was a passenger made her extraordinarily aware of how priceless he was. Which, in turn, made her aware of just how responsible she was for his safety. It was like driving the president around. Now that she thought about it, Gray might merit even more defensive driving than the president. People liked Gray better. If she crashed this Suburban with him in it, America would never forgive her.

He ended the call and shifted sideways in his seat,

resting a brawny shoulder against the side window. He watched her like he was trying his best to read her mind, one hand relaxed casually on the armrest between them.

He had a strong and interesting face. A no-nonsense mouth. A masculine chin. The planes of his features were as well balanced and uncompromising as any of the carvings on Mount Rushmore.

Gray wasn't young. And he wasn't soft. He was a man who'd grown up thanks to experience and effort and, if she had to guess, hardship.

"Did you mean what you said earlier," he asked, "about not being open to seduction without a ring on your finger?"

"I always say what I mean."

"You're not a virgin, are you?"

"No."

"Then what's your story?"

She weighed her options. She'd have liked to shut him out and maintain her privacy. However, he'd asked for the reason behind her "no sex before marriage" stance, and she couldn't, in good conscience, hide that reason under a rock. "From the time I was seventeen up until a year and a half ago, I tried every stupid, crazy thing there is to try. For a long time, I was daring and driven and edgy in all the wrong ways. Whatever you've done, I've done worse."

"No way."

"Yes, but I'm not proud of it. When it was time to work, I'd be there on time and I'd work hard, but as soon as I was off work, I'd chase whatever kind of rush I could find. I'm fortunate to have lived through it."

"And?"

"It was fun in some ways." There was a degree of pleasure and excitement to be found in being bad. If there wasn't, sin wouldn't be an issue. "Over time, though, I was doing wilder and wilder stunts to achieve the same level of adrenaline. And none of it was ever . . . fulfilling. I'm guessing you know something about that, right? About looking for fulfillment in stuff like achievement and wealth, only to find it empty?"

His expression sharpened with disbelief. "Dru, I have a job that almost every man in this country would kill to have. No one's more fulfilled than I am."

"Uh-huh." She smiled out the front windshield. Gray could say that all he wanted. But she'd gotten to know him, and she didn't believe his statement.

"I'm fulfilled," he insisted.

"Whatever you say."

"So . . . what happened a year and a half ago that changed you?"

The pain and grief had dulled over time. But they'd never disappeared. They still came for her in waves. "I was in Mexico on assignment, protecting an executive. He was kidnapped."

"Is this the right time to tell your current client that your previous client was kidnapped?"

"You asked." Her memory pulled up the scene from that hot and dusty day. The smells came rushing back to her. The sounds. The awful futility. "The kidnappers were highly professional. They clogged the route I'd asked our driver to take, then bottlenecked the street we took as an alternate. They ambushed us."

Gray waited for her to continue.

"The exec was named Mark Hanson," Dru said. "Sutton had assigned me to him a year before that particular trip."

"What happened in the ambush?"

Her lungs felt tight. "When the kidnappers rushed our car, the driver flung himself onto the floor. I pushed Mark down and engaged them in fire. I would have had a better chance at success if I'd had another agent with me or if they'd come at us from one direction. But I was alone, and they came from two directions. I took out a couple of them on one side of the car, then swung my gun to the other side and got off a few more shots. While my back was turned, they pulled open the door and yanked me out from behind. I fought them. But there were more of them. They disarmed me, and they took Mark."

"It sounds like you did all that you could. You were outnumbered." He was defending her. Gray was loyal enough to defend her even though the outcome of that day in Mexico made the fact of her failure indisputable. "Were you injured?" he asked.

"My arm was grazed by a bullet in the initial fire. In the fight outside the car, I moved to block a kick and the impact snapped my tibia. They chained me to a post, and I ended up breaking my own wrist to get free. But by then it was too late. They were gone."

He cursed. At least a mile went by beneath the Suburban's tires.

"Tell me about Mark," Gray said.

"He was sixty-five. He'd been happily married for forty years and had three kids and seven grandkids. He was a great guy. Extremely smart, but also extremely kind. Patient. A listen first, talk second kind of person. Unlike *some people*, he got along with me very well, and he did whatever I asked."

"You cared about him."

"I did. Like a dad or a favorite uncle."

"What kind of work did he do?"

"He was the CEO of a clean energy company."

"You keep saying *was* when you talk about him. I'm guessing the kidnapping didn't turn out well for Mark."

She shook her head. "They held him for ransom after they'd taken him. The price was outrageous, but his company and his family were willing to pay it. Before that could happen, though, things went bad between him and his kidnappers. We don't know the details. Mark may have tried to escape. All we know for sure is that he was shot in the back and died far from home and far from his family."

"I'm sorry," Gray said.

She pursed her lips. These things—this truth, these memories, this unhappy ending—were all miserable to live with. "I explained what had happened to Anthony Sutton in great detail. But the driver had his face against the floor mats the whole time. He couldn't corroborate my account. It didn't look good, that my client had been taken and that nonetheless I was still alive. Everyone at Sutton was suspicious of me for months afterward. I knew that I'd done my best for Mark, but it was little comfort because, even though I'd done my best, I'd still failed. Have you ever heard the term *come-to-Jesus moment*?"

"Yeah."

"That attack was my come-to-Jesus moment. It wasn't that I hadn't seen death before. I had, overseas with the Marines. I can handle death, to a point. But I couldn't handle the guilt that ate at me after the ambush. Or my anger over the whole thing. Or, worse, having to confront that, when it mattered most, I was helpless to save Mark. Before that day I'd always been cocky about my abilities. God used the kidnapping to bring me low. To bring me to Him."

"I never had you pegged as a church lady."

"I'm an unorthodox one. I attend biker church on Wednesday nights with my neighbor."

"And when you had your come-to-Jesus moment, you gave up sex and drinking and everything else?" he asked doubtfully.

"Well, I kept one motorcycle." She cut him a glance full of wry amusement. "But otherwise, yes, I kicked the rest of it out of my life. Once I got it through my head that I'd been forgiven, and how huge that was, it changed me. I started living like I'd been forgiven. What about you?"

"What about me?"

"You mow through women and throw back liquor. You're living like you're unforgiven."

"Suddenly you *are* starting to sound like a church lady."

She took the off-ramp that led to Holley.

"I pray with the other Christian guys before every game." He spoke in the tone of a schoolteacher trying to talk logically to a hotheaded student. One might be tempted to categorize all football players as temperamental. Not Gray. He saved his ferocity for the field, and even there he controlled it with laser accuracy. "I'm fair to people. I spend time supporting charities like Grace Street, and I give a lot of my money away. I went to church when I was a kid. But most of all, I'm from Texas." He gave her a lopsided smile. "Everybody who's from Mullins, Texas, is a Christian."

"I was raised in church, Gray. If you'd asked me during my wildest phases if I was a Christian, I'd have told you I was. But there was a disconnect there."

"You're judging me."

"No, I'm calling it like it is, unlike most of the people you know, who would all agree with you if you said the sky is red."

They reached one of Holley's few stoplights. She faced him.

"I like you, Dru," he said. No shyness or apology about it. "I want to go out with you."

Her skin rushed with sensitivity. Her blood heated. Her body! Her body was betraying her, despite that fancy little speech she'd just given him about God's rescue of her and her changed life because of it.

This was the thing about temptations. God didn't take them away. They were there—powerful and still needing to be dealt with. If you gave them an inch of leeway, they had the dark strength to take you under. "No."

"Please?"

"No."

A few seconds passed, and Dru had the worrisome feeling that her answer had goaded his natural competitive streak. The way a matador waving a red cape goaded a bull. He was a confident man who thrived in the face of challenges.

"The nicest thing I can say to you is that you're my client. It's against company policy for agents to date clients."

"So?"

"So, that matters to me."

Gray held her gaze steadily. "Would you date me if I wasn't your client?"

A pause. "Maybe. Then again, maybe not."

"Why 'maybe not'?"

"You're egotistical and chauvinistic and . . ." *You have fifty good qualities. I'm into you even though I wish I weren't.* ". . . you're disagreeable in general, and you're going to have to get yourself straight with God before I can take you seriously."

"I am straight with God!"

Was he? He'd accused her of judging him, and it was true. She had judged him by his behavior. His past behavior. It was possible that he was, at present, as Christian as he claimed, even though her instincts murmured otherwise.

"Who said you need to take me *seriously*, anyway?" Gray asked. "You don't have to be serious about me to go out on a date or two."

Doubt pricked her. She hadn't spent lots of time pondering the issues Gray was raising. She hadn't had cause. Since her come-to-Jesus moment, she'd been asked out on plenty of dates. She'd turned them all down due to lack of interest on her part.

Just how prove-ably "Christian" did a man need to be to be dateable? Was she cool with going out with someone a couple of times if she wasn't sure about his faith? A *no* answer seemed ridiculous. How was she supposed to be one hundred percent sure about someone else's faith? Moreover, unbelievers surrounded her at work, at the gun range, around town. She'd been one of them until recently. Refusing to go out to dinner with a suspected unbeliever seemed like a huge overcorrection. Christians were supposed to be out in the world—otherwise how would God increase His kingdom?

But dating is different, Dru. Unequally yoked and all that.

She had no answers. "I'm done having this conversation about whether I'd hypothetically date you if you weren't my client," she stated. "The reality is that you *are* my client."

"I'm going to take my time, Dru. And one of these days you're going to go out with me."

She flung out a hand. "You can date anyone you want, Gray. Go date one of the million women who'd jump at the chance."

"I don't want to date those women. I want to date you."

The car crackled with tension so fierce it made her throat go dry. It made her want to bunch the fabric of his pale blue shirt in her hands and tug him toward her.

"My goal," she said a bit hoarsely, "is to put more professional space between us, not less. There can't be any more kissing, like in the hallway tonight."

"You liked it."

"No. I didn't."

A beat of quiet while he absorbed her statement. "You're direct," Gray said.

"Yes."

"And you even pride yourself on that fact. Right?"

"Yes."

"When you stop telling the truth, that's no longer called being direct, Dru. That's called lying."

Irritated with him and with herself, she clenched her teeth. He was right. She'd lied when she'd said she hadn't liked the kiss. And he knew it. Her words from earlier—"*I always say what I mean*"—came back to haunt her.

He was giving her a headache. She needed some Cool Ranch Doritos.

A truck pulled up behind them and honked. She looked at the light. Bright green. No telling how long it'd been green while they'd been sitting at a standstill. She accelerated. "If you kiss me again, I'll have to inform Anthony Sutton, and I'll be taken off your case."

There. That sobered him.

Fifteen minutes later, the Suburban bumped down the dirt road to her cabin.

"You must be more reclusive than I realized," Gray said, "to live this far out in the woods."

They parked and made their way to the front door. She arrived home late every work night, so she always left the rustic light fixture next to the front door on, as well as one lamp in her living room.

"This isn't the kind of house I expected you to live in," Gray said. "You don't have enough room here for your superhero car."

She shouldn't be so delighted by his insistence on her superhero alter ego. Really, she shouldn't be. "I store the car in a top-secret underground cavern."

The sound of Fi's nails clicking against the hardwood reached them a moment before the retriever herself. Dru gave the dog a neck and under-ear scratch. "This is Fi."

"As in Semper Fi?"

"Yep."

The dog moved to Gray, who patted Fi while her tail wagged. "Your dog looks like he or she's about thirty."

"She's eleven. I adopted her from a shelter while I was recovering from my broken leg and wrist. It was part of my transformation into a reliable human being." She put out one hand, palm up. "Wild party person." She put out her other hand. "Dog owner."

It took about thirty seconds to walk him through her living room and kitchen. Her house wasn't dirty, but it was on the untidy side in a cozy sort of way. Throw blankets, books, an empty water glass, and mail lay here and there. She could see two pairs of her shoes on the floor—New Balances for running and L.K. Bennett heels for general awesomeness. Her laptop sat ajar at a haphazard angle on the sofa.

Upstairs, she motioned toward her bedroom and showed him the location of the bathroom. Then they paused in the doorway of the second bedroom. "Here you are."

Gray stepped into the tiny space, filling half of it. "Is this a closet?" He appeared on the verge of laughter.

"It's a very small bedroom. My nieces and nephews sleep here when they come over for slumber parties."

The twin bed, with its antique brass headboard and navy, red, and white quilt, occupied the wall opposite the window. A low bookcase containing kids' books and toys also functioned as a nightstand. A lone lamp stood atop it.

"Well, will you look at the time?" Dru peeked at her watch. "It's ten. I'm off duty, so I'm going to take my dog out, then shut myself in my room and hide from you. I feel like a teacher who had to bring one of her students home from school with her."

Mischief lit his eyes. "You want to play teacher?"

"You're hopeless."

G ray would have liked a chance to snoop around Dru's house. Check out the contents of her refrigerator and pantry. Leaf through her magazines. Click through her recorded TV shows so he'd know what she liked to watch.

But when he came downstairs the next morning after showering and dressing in the track pants and Dri-Fit shirt Weston had brought over last night, he found Big Mack sitting in the living room. Fun-spoiler. "Hey, Mack."

"Hey, Gray." Taylor Swift's "Blank Space" played quietly from his heavyset bodyguard's phone. Mack bobbed his head and pointed at Gray as he sang, "'I've got a blank space, baby, and I'll write your name.'"

"You need counseling." Gray turned toward Dru's kitchen.

Big Mack lumbered after him, bringing Taylor Swift along. "I heard you had an exciting dinner last night."

"I did." Gray motioned to Dru's coffeemaker. "What

are the chances that we can find the stuff we need to make coffee?"

"Eighty/twenty?" Mack switched back to singing, this time with some dance moves thrown in as he helped Gray look for coffee grounds, filters, and mugs. "'So it's gonna be forever,'" he crooned, "'or it's gonna go down in flames . . .'"

Gray got to do some snooping, after all. Dru didn't keep a very well-stocked kitchen. Nothing like the way Ash kept his. None of the food was organic or especially healthy.

Where was Dru, anyway? He wanted to see her before he had to leave for practice in thirty minutes.

Once the coffeemaker began brewing, Gray stood with his hands braced on the counter, looking out the window above the sink at the view of mostly bare early-December trees. He wasn't used to being surrounded by space or solitude. It felt strange. And welcome.

Her house reminded him of the sort of place that high-end resorts built for weekend guests in search of privacy. His media room had more square footage than this whole structure. That so-called room she'd assigned to him last night was smaller than his dining room table.

Even so, he'd slept well in the room's twin bed. Very well. Much better than someone accustomed to sleeping on a California king should have slept.

He and Mack were sitting at the round table in her kitchen, and Mack was telling him all the things he thought Gray should know about the Patriots defense before he left for Massachusetts tomorrow, when Dru and Fi entered the kitchen.

Gray went still, taking in the details of her. She wore

running shoes, black exercise pants, and a lightweight long-sleeved Nike shirt in bright blue. No makeup. Her shiny, very dark brown hair was pulled back in a ponytail.

To be staying here and seeing her like this felt like being let in on a secret. Until now, he'd never seen her in anything but her work clothes. He'd always liked how women looked in exercise clothes. Dru, though?

Man, she looked painfully gorgeous in hers.

"Good morning, gentlemen."

"Morning."

"It looks like you've figured out the coffee. Anyone hungry for breakfast?"

"Sure," Gray answered. "I'll have pancakes and bacon." He grinned and waited for her comeback.

"Your stereotypes about women are bottomless, aren't they, Gray?" Her blue shirt made her eyes appear even brighter than usual. "First, I don't cook. Second, even if I did, I don't have the ingredients for pancakes. You're not waking up with June Cleaver in your kitchen, like at your house."

Mack cackled, entertained as usual by the dynamic between Gray and Dru.

"I have cereal," Dru stated. "Or Pop-Tarts." She set the items on the table alongside bowls, spoons, and a carton of milk. "You can help yourselves."

"Cap'n Crunch and Apple Jacks?" Gray asked. "Where's the healthy cereal, Dru?"

"At your house," she answered. "This is my house, and I prefer cereal that actually tastes good."

"How do you stay so skinny?" Mack asked. "I look at a bowl of Cap'n Crunch and gain five pounds."

"I run every day. But mostly it's just genetics. I have a fast metabolism. I eat a lot, but it doesn't stick."

"Wish I had a fast metabolism," Mack muttered.

"I'd have thought that Revengeress would drink green smoothies and eat complex carbs," Gray said.

"Who's Revengeress?" Mack asked.

"A comic book character Dru and I know," Gray answered.

"Revengeress doesn't have to worry about green smoothies or complex carbs," Dru told Gray. "Superheroes can eat anything they want. We passed a law about it back in the seventies."

Gray laughed.

"I'll see you ladies later," Dru said, vanishing toward the back of the house.

Gray felt a pang of loss. "Where are you going?"

"Running," she called.

He made his way to the back door, where she was pulling on one of those headband/ear warmer things and a sweatshirt.

"Can I come with you? It'll be a good warm-up for me."

"Mack can't keep up, and I'd rather not run with a gun strapped to me."

"Come on," he coaxed. "We have to leave soon, so I'll just stay with you for ten minutes, then run back here for ten. I want to see what you've got."

"I've got speed."

"I'd be surprised if you didn't."

She studied him for a long moment, then went upstairs, he guessed, for her holster and pistol. He began stretching.

When she returned, they set out together at an easy jog, with Fi running alongside. A stream wound along the bottom of a small valley next to them. He could hear its trickling sound, water over rocks. Cold air blew against their faces.

His hip flexor started out tight but began to lengthen as it warmed. They increased the pace gradually. His hip was finally improving.

"That thing you said to me last night?" he said. "That thing about me living like I'm unforgiven?"

"Yes?"

"That's been bothering me."

"It's been bothering you"—her rhythmic breathing brought her words forward in bursts—"because it's true, and the Holy Spirit is—convicting you."

"It's not true. I believe that I'm forgiven."

She tossed him a skeptical look.

"I do. I believe that."

"I stand by my statement—from last night. I can't look into your psyche—or anything. I'm not shrink or a priest—"

"You can say that again."

"But I think there's some sort of—disconnect between you and God."

She was completely wrong. He wanted to convince her of her wrongness, but how could he? When she got to know him better, she'd see. He was a Christian. He drank and he had girlfriends, yes. But he behaved better than most of the guys he knew.

Dru increased the pace. He had the conditioning of a professional athlete on his side. He was faster than she was. But where he was heavy, she was light. She barely seemed to touch the ground as she ran, her long legs moving quickly and gracefully. She lengthened her pace and stride even more. He stayed beside her, highly amused, shooting glances at her.

He could easily imagine her as a young girl, trying with all her might to keep up with her brothers, her jaw set at exactly that determined angle. The tenderness he felt for her was like a hot drink on a cold day. He'd gone frighteningly soft over her. He liked her feistiness, her bravery, and her stubborn independence. Even her competitiveness he liked.

Later that morning, Dru left the shooting range and pulled into the parking lot at the grocery store. She reached across to her Yukon's glove box for the list of food items she bought most often. She always used it to jog her memory as she made her way up and down the aisles.

She took hold of the list that lay behind the car's registration and insurance papers. And just that suddenly she realized exactly what had been bothering her about Mildred Osbourne and her maroon Ford truck.

Meg was moving slowly these days. Sort of like a lumbering train over-packed with too much cargo.

She approached the paddock behind Whispering Creek's brood mare barn, half walking like a normal person, half waddling like a heavily pregnant lady. A mother and foal were inside the fenced enclosure, which was fortunate. December wasn't the season for baby racehorses.

Gently, she set a forearm on the top slat of the white-painted fence, then positioned her belly to the side so she had a good view of the two horses within.

Both were black. A white blaze ran down the mother's forehead, and white marked all four of her feet. Her baby was unbroken inky black and very young. Spindly legs comprised most of the foal's body. It had the horse equivalent of peach fuzz for a mane and tail.

Meg smiled, watching how the foal stayed within inches of its mother. Whenever the mare took a few steps to graze, her little one walked alongside, their ribs practically rubbing against each other.

It had been several months since she'd been out to this paddock. Almost a year, maybe? That long? Yes. That long. Once upon a time, she'd come here often. Then life and work and more urgent things had intruded.

She'd first stood at this fence eight years ago, shortly after she'd inherited the ranch. At the time, she'd been in mourning for her father. Panic attacks had been devouring her, and she hadn't wanted to take on the ownership of a Thoroughbred farm.

What she'd always loved about the ranch, however? The foals. From the very first time she'd set eyes on them, she'd adored them. They were beautiful and sweet and innocent and a tangible reminder that life goes on. Every year, a new beginning.

She'd become friends with Bo at this very spot. In fact, once she realized that he'd appear every time she visited this paddock, she'd started visiting *just* so she could hang out with him. He'd smiled his rugged smile at her. Those meltingly beautiful gray eyes of his had calmed, what had been back then, her very troubled and lonely heart. God had ministered to her through Bo.

They'd fallen in love.

And because of that, God had bent her destiny in a surprising way. She, the woman who liked art and museums far more than horses and racing, had decided to keep her father's horse farm running.

Thank God she had. This farm was Bo's calling. The ranch provided the vehicle for Jake and Lyndie's brilliance at training Thoroughbreds. The trail horses they kept brought delight to the families who lived at the main house. Without this farm, Silver Leaf never would have had the chance to inspire the world with his astonishing speed and valiant heart.

God had worked it out like it had been meant to work out.

She closed her eyes and turned her face toward the winter sun, asking God to bring her the same relaxation that He'd once brought her in this place.

Twenty minutes ago, she'd been sitting at her desk at Whispering Creek's main house, catching up on work for the Cole Foundation. She'd experienced a sharp, scraping sort of pain right at the lowest point of her uterus. Instantly, her heart had jolted, and she'd grown short of breath with fear. She'd called the direct line she'd been given to Dr. Peterson's nurse. The woman, well acquainted with Meg, had serenely explained that the sensation was commonplace and nothing to worry about.

Commonplace? She'd tried to return to work, but she'd ended up staring at the computer screen while her thoughts churned with sickening worry. On a whim, she'd decided to get out of the office and drive here.

She'd put on her wool coat to combat the day's coldness. Without wind, though, and with plenty of sunshine pouring down, it felt fine—better than fine—outdoors. The air carried the crisp bite of December. She could smell wood smoke and crackling dry leaves and a faint whiff of pine.

The sound of footfalls carried to her. She turned to see Bo walking toward her. Just like old times. A wave of nostalgia swept over her.

He still wore the same style of jacket that he'd always preferred. Dark brown corduroy with a sheepskin collar. She'd given him this particular jacket for his last birthday. His jeans were well worn, his boots scuffed, his dark hair shaved short.

"How in the world do you do that?" she asked.

"Do what?"

"Find out that I'm here?"

"I have a network of spies." He gave her a quick kiss of greeting. Slinging an arm over the fence, he faced her. "What brings you to the brood mare paddock, Mrs. Porter?"

She shrugged. "I just needed a break. I wanted to get outdoors."

His face held entirely too much wisdom. "Why'd you need a break?"

"I had a weird pain that scared me. Dr. Peterson's nurse assured me that everything's fine, but I needed to settle my nerves." She could tell Bo anything and everything. The fact that she could, without censoring herself, brought enormous comfort.

BECKY WADE   223

"'Kay." He took hold of her hand and kissed the top
of it before turning his attention to the mare and foal.
His hand remained interlaced with hers, warming her
chilled fingers. Quiet strength surged between them.
"This is only the second time these two have been outside," he said.

"How old's the foal?"

"Three days old. But he was born a month premature, so we kept them inside longer than we normally
would have."

"He looks great."

Bo studied her, waiting until she met his eyes. "He was
born early. But mother and baby are doing very well."
With those two sentences, Bo spoke an entire sermon of
reassurance to her. The foal had been born early, like their
babies very likely would be. But the mare and the foal
were flourishing, just like Bo was certain she and their
babies would flourish. God had taken care of these two
horses even when things didn't go according to plan or
schedule. He could be counted on to take care of them.

She wove her arm around his bicep and rested her
head on the outside of his shoulder. They stood like that,
watching the beauty of the example in front of them
without need of conversation. They had a long history.
Their communication didn't always require words.

When Meg looked back over the course of her life,
she could see the stamp of God's faithfulness on every
circumstance.

Her mother had died when Meg was two. God had
provided Sadie Jo as her nanny, cheerleader, caregiver,
and foster grandmother.

Her first husband had lied to her, stolen from her,

and abandoned her. God had sustained her through it. He'd given her a new start in a new place. New hope.

Her father had died when she'd been in her twenties. God had summoned her to Whispering Creek. He'd brought Bo into her life. He'd introduced her to her life's work.

The complications threatening this pregnancy had the power to terrify her right down to her marrow. The panic attacks she'd been so relieved to see the last of years ago were doing their best to mount a comeback.

She wanted to banish the fear and trust God instead. She'd prayed for Him to remove her worries. Daily, she'd been giving her family over to Him. But so far, He was choosing to go the route He had after her first marriage had disintegrated. He wasn't taking her concerns away. Rather, He was holding her up *through* them. At times, it felt like He was holding her up by a fraying thread.

She sighed and squeezed Bo's arm. "I don't want to keep you if you have work to do," she whispered.

"You're my priority, Countess. For you, I have all the time in the world."

"Did Dru tell you that I'm taking her out for dessert tonight?"

Corbin's words hit Gray like ice water. He blinked once. "Come again?" He was sitting in front of his locker at the Mustangs' practice facility.

His friend stood a few feet away. Looking smug, Corbin crossed his arms. "We set it up a couple days ago. We're going to get dessert tonight in that little town of hers. Holley? She didn't say anything to you about it?"

"No." Gray bent and tied his shoe as if his life depended on it.

"I smell victory."

Gray frowned, hard. Tied his other shoe, then slowly rose to standing. He was two full inches taller than Corbin. They'd both come through difficult childhoods. They were both completely committed to their team. They shared similar interests and a similar sense of humor.

Gray had always liked Corbin. But neither the anger circling within him nor this sudden urge to punch Corbin were very friendly.

Corbin took Gray in, brows lifting. "If you rip my head off, big man, remember that I won't be able to throw you passes." Gradually, Corbin smiled. "You're really starting to like her, aren't you? What happened to your belief that she was too hard? Too competitive? Remember that?"

"I changed my mind."

"You're not usually possessive."

"Not usually." In the past, that had been one hundred percent right. It was also one hundred percent wrong where Dru was concerned.

"What's different about Dru?"

"She's my . . . friend." He realized it was true. For the first time ever, a woman he wanted to date was also his friend.

"Well, good luck with the friendship thing. I'm going to see if I can convince Revengeress to be more than friends with me tonight." Corbin winked and moved to his locker.

Gray stood rock still, the bustling activity of his teammates and the equipment guys surrounding him.

He knew how things would go down tonight on their date. Everyone they came into contact with would fall over themselves idolizing Corbin.

There were a handful of famous names on every NFL team, but the starting quarterback was right at the top of that list. As tight end, Gray appreciated a skilled QB. Without one, no matter how good the rest of them were, the team was screwed. Corbin Stewart had been named MVP of the Super Bowl they'd won. He'd owned one of the best quarterback ratings in the league for the past five years straight. He was as calm as the surface of a lake under pressure, a natural leader, and he could throw a football through the eye of a needle.

On the other hand, quarterbacks were a little bit wussier than the rest of them, in Gray's opinion. If a QB got sacked, he'd throw a tantrum. Gray got hammered on every play.

The guy who got hammered on every play didn't want *his* Dru going out for dessert with Corbin. Everyone would be bowing to Corbin and women would be drooling and Corbin would be using his charm.

Jealousy sat square in the center of his torso, heavy and boiling hot.

THIRTEEN

Dru returned to her cabin that afternoon just before the start of her shift. When still a long way off, she caught sight of Gray's Denali and Mack's truck parked out front.

Even a glimpse of Gray's Denali, for pity's sake, had the power to send a little thrill of expectation through her. Pitiful.

After her errands this morning, she'd returned to Urban Country. With the help of a ladder, she'd scaled the back of the old-fashioned one-story building across the street from the restaurant. She'd found some fresh footprints in the roof's dirt, surrounded by an area completely trodden by feet. She assumed the undisturbed footprints were the shooter's. During their investigation the cops had carefully avoided them, walking only around their outskirts.

Dru had taken photos of the prints and measured their length and width. The prints appeared to have come from the grooved bottom of a man's athletic shoe. The sole was about ten inches long. Which meant approximately size nine feet.

The shooter hadn't been obliging enough to leave behind any other obvious clues, so she'd called Anthony Sutton, who'd informed her that he'd spoken with Detective Carlyle. In addition to processing the footprints, the police had dusted a few of the outside areas for prints and had asked local shop owners with video security to provide access to their video.

The bullets were 7mm Remingtons, which were widely available. The ammunition wouldn't help them locate the shooter. Dru believed that the shooter *was* Gray's stalker, so she didn't hold out hope of uncovering his or her identity through prints or video surveillance. The stalker was too careful for any of that.

All day, she'd been mulling uneasily over the aspects of last night's shooting that she didn't understand. Why hadn't the stalker corrected his aim after he'd seen that his (or her) first shot had landed too high? If he (or she) wanted to kill Gray, why had he ceased firing after just two bullets?

What Dru knew for sure? Sealing words into an envelope was a completely different thing than taking a gun into your hands and shooting at people. Gray's stalker had vaulted the line of that difference yesterday, and thus the danger Gray was in had heightened.

Dru had asked Sutton if she could keep Gray at her cabin one more night, and Sutton had said that she could, so long as Gray agreed. She didn't have actual, laid-out plans to ask for Gray's agreement. She'd secure his agreement simply by telling him he was staying.

The smell of popcorn greeted her when she entered

her cabin. Gray sat on one of her living room chairs, a foot crossed over the opposite knee, her newest issue of *Guns & Ammo* open on his lap and a bowl of popcorn on the side table next to him. He looked thoroughly comfortable, completely at home in her house. "Welcome home," he said.

"Thank you." It felt surreal to have him here, so settled in. She always came home to an empty house. Always. It was dangerously, temptingly . . . wonderful to come home to him. "What's up, Mack?"

"Nothing much, Dru."

She smiled at Big Mack, who'd settled his mass onto her sofa.

Inexorably, her attention tugged back to Gray. He had on a Mustangs ball cap and a black zip-front hoodie over athletic clothing. He looked freshly showered, and he probably smelled like a million dollars.

"You're going to be staying here one more night," she informed him.

"What?" He pretended outrage. "That thing you call a bed is about the size of a bar of soap."

"Yes. And your discomfort makes having you as a houseguest all the more fun for me."

Mack guffawed.

She went to her kitchen in search of a Coke and sanity. Having Gray in her cabin was causing the most humiliating and girly pleasure to bubble up through her like champagne bubbles. It pleased her domestic side to have Gray here.

Wait, domestic side? What? She didn't have a domestic side.

She washed her hands at the sink, trying to wash her

ridiculous response to him away as thoroughly. Fi sat beside her feet.

Word to the wise, Fi. Don't fall for cocky, womanizing football players. Every smart woman knows it would be dumb to do that.

Her retriever peered up at her with questioning eyes.

"How are you, Fi in the sky with diamonds? Hungry?" She tossed Fi two treats, then popped the top on her Coke can and drank back the sweet, carbonated caffeine.

When she had herself in hand again, she carried her Coke into the living room. Mack was on his feet and doing a dance move that looked like the snake. He snapped his fingers to the beat as Miley Cyrus sang out through the earbud he'd left dangling. "Bye, fools." He grinned and danced his way to the doorway. "I'm outta here. See you two tomorrow."

They called out their goodbyes.

The door shut behind Mack, leaving Dru and Gray alone in an environment that suddenly felt intimate.

"Mack's a lot more fun than you are," Gray said.

"But you like me more anyway."

"True." He chewed some kernels of popcorn. "Any new information on last night's shooting?"

She sat on the coffee table and told him what she'd learned.

"Basically," Gray said when she'd finished, "they haven't discovered anything yet that'll help us learn the identity of the shooter."

"Except his approximate shoe size." Dru took a sip of Coke.

"What are you not telling me?"

She gave him a blank expression.

"Out with it."

"It's probably nothing."

"Out with it anyway."

Dru scratched her jaw. She'd come to know him pretty well, but it surprised her each time he revealed that he'd gotten to know her pretty well, too. "Something occurred to me earlier, about Mildred Osbourne and her maroon truck."

"Which was . . ."

"I opened my car's glove box this morning and saw my car's registration papers inside. Which got me thinking. My car's registered in my name, no surprise. I'm single, and I'm in my twenties. But Mildred's married and in her eighties. Why would a woman of that generation have a car registered in her name only?"

"That mindset seems sort of . . . chauvinistic of you, Dru." His lips hitched up at one corner. He was throwing the accusation she liked to toss at him back onto her.

"Which might be why it took a while for Mildred's solo ownership of the truck to occur to me as something worth digging into. I'm an advocate of girl power."

"You don't say," he said dryly.

"We already researched Mildred's son Rich, because he's the one with possession of the truck. I've asked Julie, the tech person at Sutton, to take another look at Mildred."

"My stalker better not be a little old lady, Dru. I'm attached to my image as an intimidating NFL superstar."

"Huh."

"Having you for a bodyguard and Mildred as my stalker will ruin my street cred—"

"I'm not suggesting that Mildred *is* your stalker," Dru

said. "I'm just going to check into her history a little more. That's all."

From beneath the brim of his cap, he studied her. Instead of his eyes looking darker in shadow like one would expect, they smoldered like pale embers. As she watched, the teasing in those eyes began to wane. Something that looked like soberness took its place. More than soberness, really. Almost hurt. "I'm here for another night," he said.

"Yes."

"What're we going to do to pass the time?"

"This afternoon, we're going to visit my neighbor. Augustine will throw Precious Moments figurines at my head if she finds out you were here and I didn't bring you by to see her."

"What else are we going to do? Like, tonight, for example?"

Ah. He'd found out she had plans with Corbin tonight. That's what was bothering him. "Do you already know what I'm doing tonight?"

"I heard a rumor."

"I'm going to hang out with Corbin for a while. Weston will be here with you so you'll have company."

His chin set. His mouth settled into a hard line. "You're going on a date with my friend and teammate and you think I'm concerned about whether or not Weston's going to be here to keep me company? I told you last night that I wanted to date you."

"And I told you that it wasn't possible."

"Dru." He looked at her squarely. Serious. "I don't want you to date anybody but me."

Her passionate independent streak rasped against her

temper like a match against flint. "You're my client." She girded the words with steel. "You're not entitled to care about my personal life."

"Too late."

She stiffened.

"In order for you to keep your job," he said, "we can't date each other right now. I don't need for you to explain it to me again. I get it."

"Good."

"However, I'm not out there chasing other women. I'd rather wait for you."

"I never promised to become your girlfriend once you finish being my client."

"Are you open to becoming Corbin's girlfriend?"

"I'm not planning to elope with Corbin tonight, if that's what you're asking. He invited me out for dessert, and I said I'd go. No big deal."

"He asked you on a date, Dru. And you said yes to a date."

"Have you seen Corbin? He's handsome and nice and successful. I could do worse."

His body tensed with irritation. "*I'm* handsome and nice and successful."

"You're not all that nice." Honestly, *nice* wasn't that high on her list of desirable qualities. Nice was next to biddable.

A ligament arced down his neck. "What about the fact that you're supposed to be posing as my girlfriend?"

"We're going to a tiny restaurant in downtown Holley. No one there will recognize me as your girlfriend."

He pushed to standing. Six feet, four inches of powerful, glaring male. "You realize that Corbin's no altar boy, right? Has he gotten himself straight with God? Or does that standard only apply to me?"

Ouch. Fair question. She rose to her feet. "I believe my exact words were that you'd need to get straight with God before I could take you *seriously*. I'm not taking Corbin seriously. I've talked to him on the phone and we've gone to a restaurant. So far, we're developing a friendship."

Perhaps wrongly, she'd spent almost no time worrying about Corbin's spiritual life or confronting him regarding it. Gray was different. She was invested in Gray. She had insight into him. She cared, which was why she'd called him out. She did hold him to a different standard.

"You can be sure," he said, his voice low, "that Corbin is interested in developing more than a friendship with you."

"It's just dessert, Gray."

"I don't want you to go," he said bluntly.

Dru had a lifetime of practice at standing tall and keeping eye contact with brothers who loomed over her in size and age. Cowed she was not. "I'm going."

Taking a man you were angry with—and who was angry with you right back—to visit your neighbor did not make for a good time.

Dru, Gray, and Augustine, plus two bowls of English pea salad, sat at Augustine's dining room table, a table that had been polished to the sheen of a mahogany ice rink. Dru's neighbor spent the first twenty minutes gushing over Gray and recounting all the reasons for her deep fondness for football players. The whole time, tangible anger flowed back and forth between Dru and Gray, even though both worked to extend kindness to Augustine.

Poor Augustine fell, as defenselessly as an apple from a tree, for Gray's good looks, fame, and easy conversation. The fact that he ate every bite of her pea salad, then complimented her on it, didn't hurt his cause, either.

Cad.

A Precious Moments figure of a child holding a flower stared at Dru disapprovingly, as if the little porcelain girl had read Dru's testy thoughts.

"My ex-husband, Roy, was a huge football fan. He collected player signatures and memorabilia and such, and if football was on, then he was sitting in his recliner, watching."

Gray nodded.

"Roy left me twenty-some years ago." Augustine's arthritic hand smoothed a piece of fluff off her table. "I haven't seen him since. Until recently, I didn't want to see him again. But lately, I've had a change of heart. I'd like to lay eyes on Roy one more time. Just once. I don't think I'll be able to rest easy until I give him a piece of my mind. So my sons and I have been looking for him. No luck."

"I'm sorry to hear that," Gray said.

"Roy doesn't want to be found." Behind her glasses, Augustine's eyes slowly narrowed, then rounded. "I wonder if . . . well, my goodness. It just occurred to me to wonder if Roy would come out of hiding to attend an event if he knew you were going to be there."

"Augustine," Dru warned. She didn't want her neighbor hitting Gray up for anything. People hit him up for stuff constantly.

"It's fine." Gray didn't look at her.

"Are you going to be doing any sort of—of appearances in the next few months?" Augustine asked him.

"A charity called Grace Street puts on a Winter Family Fun Day every February. I'll be at that."

"You don't say!" Augustine looked on the verge of one of those I-died-and-went-to-heaven-then-came-back-to-tell-about-it moments people wrote books about. "Would you mind writing down the details for me?"

"Happy to."

"You'll only be at the Fun Day if we've found your stalker by then," Dru reminded Gray.

"If we haven't found my stalker by then, I'll have committed suicide."

Dru went to retrieve a pen and paper so Augustine wouldn't have to get up.

"How do you spend your off-seasons, Gray?" Augustine asked.

"Physical therapy. Training in the gym. Last spring I traveled to Australia."

"Australia! I've been scuba diving at the Great Barrier Reef."

Dru slid the pen and paper near Gray's elbow, then stood with her hip against the dining room's sideboard as he jotted down information about the Family Fun Day.

"We swam with jellyfish and the dangerous stonefish," Augustine continued. "Have you gone diving at the Great Barrier Reef?"

"I have."

"On that same trip, we went on an airboat safari and took a three-night horseback tour of the Snowy Mountains."

"Wow."

"What do you think, Dru?" The older lady turned her hopeful attention to Dru. "Should I plan a trip for the two of us Down Under? We can go bushwhacking with some of the world's deadliest animals."

"Sure, Augustine. Anytime." *All we'll need is to first go back in time and return you to the body you once had.*

"Did you know that Dru takes me to church every week?" Augustine asked Gray.

"No need to brag on me," Dru told her.

"And she comes by here to keep me company. And takes out my trash. Mmm! I just love Dru."

Gray looked into Augustine's eyes. Hostility rolled from him in Dru's direction. "Dru's the most interesting and the most frustrating woman I've ever met."

Dru sucked in a breath and pushed her tongue to one side of her mouth. Really? He was going to go there with Augustine?

Augustine blinked twice with owlish fascination. "Why do you say Dru's frustrating?"

"Because I want to date her and she knows it and she likes me. But tonight she's going out with my good friend instead."

Augustine whistled. "Well, that explains it! There's been enough sparks in the air in here to start a dead car battery." She looked back and forth between them with her wise, gentle face. "You know what I think?"

"That Gray's going to drive me to drink?" Dru asked.

"That you're perfect for each other," Augustine proclaimed.

Dru spent forty-five minutes getting ready for her date. Gray knew this because, while she was getting ready, he was sitting downstairs alone, staring at Mavericks basketball.

Weston had arrived a few minutes ago but had quickly ducked back outside, probably to dart from tree to tree conducting surveillance on a bunch of empty darkness.

Gray was leaving tomorrow for a game against the Patriots on Sunday. Competing on a national stage could get intense. He preferred to keep his mind relaxed in the days leading up to games. In fact, that was how he liked to keep his life off the field all the time: relaxed.

Yet here he was, sitting in a north Texas cabin in the middle of nowhere, ready to chew nails.

Football mattered most to him. It had owned the primary spot in his life since the tenth grade.

Why was he tying himself in a knot over a woman?

When he heard her footfalls on the stairs, his gaze cut to the stairwell. She came downstairs in a sweater, jeans, and boots. She slid into a leather coat, met his eyes for no more than a fraction of a second, then sailed through the door.

"He's half drunk," Weston told Dru when she returned to her cabin thirty minutes past midnight.

Drunk?

She considered Weston as if he'd spoken in a foreign language. Gray was ordinarily self-controlled enough not to want his drinking to interfere in any way with his performance on the field. The team would fly to Massachusetts in the morning and play on Sunday. The Mustangs administration and hundreds of thousands of fans were counting on him to be at his best.

Weston sat on her sofa, legs crossed. The twenty-nine-year-old's slicked-back blond hair was so pale that it nearly matched the color of his skin. At first glance, his wiry build and trendy clothing gave off a harmless impression. At second glance, you noticed how keenly observant he was, which made you think there was something going on behind his quiet demeanor. At third glance, you determined him to be absolutely deadly.

Tonight, Weston looked as unruffled as ever in his plaid shirt and brown skinny jeans. A book about the history of Constantine rested cover up on the upholstery next to him.

"Where is he?" Dru asked.

"Upstairs in the guest room."

"Where did he find alcohol?"

"In your pantry."

She winced. "I'd forgotten I had any." When she'd quit drinking, she'd stuck the liquor she'd owned onto the top corner shelf of her pantry to get it out of sight and out of mind. She should have poured it down the sink.

Shrugging from her coat, she lowered to a chair. Fi ambled over, and she turned her attention to rubbing her retriever's head and ears.

"About an hour ago," Weston said, "Gray wanted to get in his car and drive off. But he'd left his keys on the side table and I'd confiscated them as soon as he started drinking. He wasn't pleased."

"I bet he wasn't."

"Gray's usually easygoing." Weston sized her up. "Any idea what may have set him off tonight?"

She opted to sidestep his question. "You think he's easygoing because he sleeps during most of your shift, Weston." She rose with what she hoped looked like a relaxed smile. In truth, her conscience was whispering to her that she wasn't completely without fault. It could be that she should've rescheduled with Corbin. When Gray had told her he didn't want her to go tonight, her headstrong tendencies had lashed back. She'd dug in her heels. Discretion had never been the better part of her valor. "I'm going to head up. Good night."

"'Night."

On the second floor, the door to the spare bedroom yawned open. Fi clicked up behind Dru, then padded into Dru's bedroom, no doubt to wait to be lifted onto the mattress.

Dru paused in the doorway of Gray's room. The lamp had not been turned on within. Light from the short upstairs landing reached into the room, revealing the outline of Gray's broad, tall physique standing at the window in shadow, looking outward. He'd buried his hands in the pockets of his sweatshirt.

"Did you have a good time?" Gray asked without moving. His consonants were rounded. Instead of sharp squares, they were all sloping edges. But he wasn't slurring badly or weaving on his feet. It seemed that Weston's assessment had been right. Half drunk.

"I did have a good time." There'd been molten lava cake and cappuccino. How bad could it have been?

She pursed her lips and wondered how much alcohol he'd consumed. She hadn't had anything to drink in so long that she'd surely lost her ability to hold it. It would only take a shot glass full to get her tipsy. But Gray? He'd probably drunk enough to fill a pail.

She set her teeth against the temptation to lecture him. She couldn't lecture him for the same reason that Weston had been unable to prevent him from drinking.

Sutton's clients had vices. The agents weren't there to judge or control. They were simply there to protect.

"Did you fall for him?" he asked.

"Corbin and I are friends."

He still hadn't turned around, so she went and stood beside him. The two of them looked out at the scene beyond the windows. Illumination from the house painted strokes of gray over the reaching fingers of the treetops. A crescent moon hung in the cold sky like a conductor surrounded by an orchestra of stars.

Dru felt no sparks for Corbin. It was strange, really, that she didn't. He had all the qualifications that should result in sparks. But she didn't experience that mystical pull toward Corbin.

The man standing beside her, however? The most overwhelming pull drew her toward him. Emotionally. Physically. It grew stronger and thicker and more insistent with every slowly dragging second.

Dru was not a woman accustomed to losing control of her ability to rule herself. She did not want to want Gray Fowler. However, it couldn't be prevented. "I think you've done enough brooding, don't you?" she asked mildly. "You're not jealous so much as you're *competitive*. You don't really want me, you just don't want Corbin to have me."

"You're completely wrong." He shifted, and she knew he'd slanted his gaze down to her.

She looked up at him, and their eye contact resulted in a physical shock of power.

"I think . . ." he said with that sexy, sleepy, hazy tone.

"Yes?"

"That I love you."

Her lips plopped open. His words dove down through her, a surprise attack of hot, reverberating pleasure. "You're not allowed to tell a woman you love her when you're drunk."

"Loving you isn't going to be good for me. Is it?"

She took a few steps toward the door. "It's late, and you've got a plane to catch tomorrow. You need sleep, and you need sobriety. Get in bed, big football player."

"You gonna join me?"

"You already know I'm not."

He stretched out on the twin bed, which was comically undersized for his frame. He propped his back on the pillows. His hands returned to his sweatshirt's pockets. His bare feet crossed. He studied her with an odd mixture of animosity and vulnerability, and it terrified Dru—it *terrified* her—how tenderly she felt toward him.

"I got to where I am," he said, "by being determined."

"I've no doubt of that."

"I'm just as d—" His tongue slipped around the words, tripping on the sounds. ". . . as determined about you."

"Go to sleep, drunk tight end."

"You're going to love me," he said.

Dru closed the door on him, heart knocking. She clung to the scraps of her impartiality toward him because if she lost the last of those, she'd have to step down as his protection agent. Maybe she *should* step down—

No! She hadn't found his stalker yet.

"You're going to love me," he'd said.

Oh, God, she prayed, needing steadying. She was outright terrified that he might be right.

FOURTEEN

The Mustangs lost.

Gray blamed Dru.

No matter what was going on in his lousy home life when he'd been young, no matter his injuries and how much his body pained him, no matter the concerns in his personal life, he had always been able to focus solely on football while he was on the field.

Gray reclined his airplane seat. It was Sunday evening, and he and the rest of the team were flying home to Dallas while the sky darkened from the bright orange of sunset to the gray of night. Reggae played softly through his earbuds. Gray tried to let the music wash over him and calm him.

It wasn't working.

It had been ridiculously cold, of course, in Massachusetts. Snow had fallen on them during the game. It had created a field of slush and turned the ball slippery. Hits always hurt worse in subfreezing temperatures, and the Patriots defense had been a beast, relentlessly rushing Corbin.

Even so, none of that accounted for his average play today. He *hated* playing average. He'd played average because Dru had been on his mind. While he'd dressed in the locker room and listened to the coaches talk, he'd thought about how much he missed her. On the sidelines, he'd remembered every detail of what she'd looked like when she'd come to stand next to him at the window, tilted her face up, and met his eyes. On the field, jogging to the line of scrimmage, he'd recalled her smooth voice saying, *"You're not allowed to tell a woman you love her when you're drunk."*

The gorgeous brunette with the turquoise eyes had distracted him *during a game*. Which was bad. She'd also cracked his connection with Corbin, a connection that had been in place for eight years and had never before been challenged.

He and Corbin had hung out together on this trip as usual. They'd laughed and ribbed each other. But resentment toward his friend had been stirring deep inside Gray the entire time. It had put them out of sync with one another on the field.

Groaning silently, he brought up a hand and rubbed his scalp.

He *hated* to play average. And he *hated* to lose.

Dru's night out with Corbin had been one of the worst nights Gray'd had in a long, long time. He'd been restless and angry, and those two things had combined to make him desperate for alcohol.

The alcohol had only worsened his restlessness and anger. He'd been unable to stand the fact that he was cooped up in Dru's house with Weston and Fi while Dru was across town with Corbin.

His first boneheaded move had been to try to leave. His second boneheaded move had been telling Dru he thought he loved her. He regretted both.

He couldn't believe the thought of loving Dru had even crossed his mind, much less that he'd made the mistake of speaking it out loud to her.

What an idiot thing to have said. He didn't love her.

He dropped his wrists onto the armrests. Irritated with himself, he turned his face to the side, trying to find a comfortable position.

Love was not for him. He'd seen firsthand the kind of damage that love could do not just to one person, but also to all the people connected to that person.

"You're worthless, Gray!" The words snarled out of his past. The dirt bag had shoved him from behind. He stumbled forward, smacking his head on the edge of a cupboard. Dull pain cracked through his skull, and he instinctively pushed a hand to the spot, as if he could hold in the injury and the hurt. *"Get on your knees and apologize for being such an ungrateful, self-centered little jerk. Now."* A hand had clamped around his shoulder and shoved him onto his knees. *"I said now!"*

Every time he'd been to a wedding reception he'd toasted the couple while looking at the groom and inwardly thinking, *Congratulations, sucker. I can't believe you're smiling about the fact that you just handed over your freedom and half your money.*

He'd never wanted to fall in love. Never wanted a wife.

He still wanted what he'd always wanted. Another Super Bowl victory. This team of guys had a real shot. This thing with Dru was getting in the way. His affection for her had turned him into a fool who'd begged her to go out with him and gotten drunk when she wouldn't and who missed her with a physical ache in his chest even though he'd only been away from her since yesterday morning.

Who had he become? He didn't recognize himself.

Maybe because of all the time he'd spent with Dru, or maybe because of his bet with Corbin, he'd gotten way more involved with her than he'd ever planned to get.

It had to stop now.

He'd give Corbin his Rolex, and he'd let him have her.

Pain carved into him at the decision, but the pain didn't sway him.

Love was not for him.

Dru stood in the player lot of the Mustangs' practice facility alongside a small cluster of girlfriends, wives, and family members. Moody industrial lighting fought against the night's overcast gloom as the Mustangs' team bus pulled to a stop. Players began to file out.

Gray came into view wearing suit pants and a business shirt.

A dumb sense of joy towed upward within Dru like a kite on a windy day. She'd watched every down of his game, which had been a long exercise in torture. She'd *felt* the sharp, unrelenting cold just as clearly as she'd felt Gray's mounting frustration. He'd been slammed again and again into the ground. He'd given as good as he'd got. But when the cameras had focused on his face, he'd looked grim—eyes narrowed, his mouth a stern line.

He approached her carrying his duffel bag, weariness in the lines of his body.

"Hey," Dru said.

"Hey."

She had a foolish urge to hug him. She wasn't a hugger.

"Did you bring the Denali?" he asked.

"Yep." She nodded toward where she'd parked it, and they made their way over. Gray slid his things in, then extended his palm.

Without a word, she dropped his keys into his hand. See how agreeable she could be? How gracious?

Within moments, he'd steered them near the facility's fenced outer perimeter. A hundred or so fans waited near the gate. Some held poster-board signs; most were cheering, some were calling out. The gathering would have been a lot peppier, no doubt, had the Mustangs won.

Super-fan Kevin Lee rushed to the front of the pack wearing a Mustangs jacket and ski hat. He waved determinedly and shouted, "Gray! Gray! You're the best, buddy! Can you sign a picture and mail it to me?"

"Keep moving," Dru instructed. "Don't open your window."

Gray lifted a hand and acknowledged Kevin, but the SUV continued rolling.

"You'll get the Patriots next time!" Kevin called, running beside them. He did everything but jump onto the SUV's running board in order to get closer to Gray. "Can you send me a picture, buddy? Gray! Please? I'd really like one of your jerseys. . . ."

"Aww, Dru. Let me give him something. The guy's literally sprinting to keep up with us." The Denali slowed.

"I advise against it—"

"He's harmless."

Gray stopped the car and stretched to reach toward something on the floor of his backseat. Dru tensed, her attention on Kevin, gun hand ready.

Kevin stood outside the car, his head centered in the Denali's side window like a photo in a frame. He panted, smiling hopefully.

Gray came up with a football. He found a pen in his middle console, wrote *To Kevin* on the ball, then signed his name. After sliding down the window, he passed the ball over. "Here you go, man."

"Thank you! Wow! Thank you so much." Kevin's face glowed with elation. "This is awesome."

"Take care of yourself," Gray said as they pulled away.

"See you soon, buddy! Go Mustangs! I sure would like a signed jersey someday! And a picture . . ."

They turned onto the road, and Kevin's voice faded into the distance. The heating system did its best to pump warm air into the car's chilly interior. The headlights cut into the darkness.

Dru split her attention three ways. She paid attention to the obstacles on the road before them. To the road behind them in case they were being tailed. And to Gray himself. He seemed subdued tonight. Down. "You tired?" she asked.

"Yeah."

"In pain?"

"A medium amount." Several minutes passed in silence as they whirred north in the direction of Gray's neighborhood.

Almost two days had come and gone since Gray's *"I think that . . . I love you"* declaration. He'd followed it with the sucker punch of *"Loving you isn't going to be good for me. Is it?"* Then the annihilating *"You're going to love me."*

She'd been thinking about little else. She kept pulling out those sentences as if they were treasured newspaper clippings and going over them in detail. Remembering the timbre of his voice. Seeing again the way he'd looked, swathed in night shadows, as he'd said them.

His words . . . his words were strangely beautiful to her. It came as something of a surprise to her that she found them so appealing. But she did. The things he'd said to her had been glowing within her, melting away some of her emotions that had long been encrusted with ice. And, in response, she'd been coddling the memory of them the way one might coddle a butterscotch candy one didn't want to swallow.

But now, looking at him, the possibility that Gray Fowler had ever spoken those words to her seemed far-fetched. His demeanor broadcast a worn-out kind of remoteness.

"You hungry?" he asked.

"Not really."

"I'm starving."

"It's eight-thirty. You didn't eat on the plane?"

"I did, but that was hours ago." He turned into the parking lot at Hillstone, a restaurant located on the outer rim of his Preston Hollow neighborhood.

Every time he added an unscheduled stop to his itinerary, Gray made her job more difficult. She'd come with him to Hillstone before and had already performed an advance on the restaurant. However, her familiarity with the site didn't put her at ease. She hadn't seen anyone following them, but ascertaining that was more difficult at night. Plus, he'd been shot at inside a restaurant just three nights prior, and she had an edgy sense that his stalker had begun to grow impatient.

Pulling out her phone, she brought up the information she'd saved on Hillstone. Exit routes, the location of the chosen safe room, nearest hospitals, the restaurant's address and phone number and more.

They walked toward the establishment side-by-side, the *clack* of Dru's high-heeled boots underscoring the unusual lack of conversation between them.

Gray ran his fingers through his brown hair, which had been flattened slightly in the back by the plane's headrest. His efforts made his hair look sexily finger-combed, as if he'd just woken from a nap.

The hostess's young face went slack with shock when she recognized the man nearing her stand. She'd probably been standing there daydreaming about Nick Jonas when she'd caught sight of Gray.

"Two, please," Gray said to the girl.

Her face turned pink. "Yes, sir. Of course. Right this—" She gave herself a small shake. "Right this way." She led them to one of the low-slung leather booths while glancing around to see who else might be noticing this astonishing celebrity in their midst.

Dru hid a sigh and carefully ran her attention over the restaurant's patrons. Hillstone boasted subdued lighting, plates as big as platters, an abundance of chocolate-brown leather, and glossy wooden surfaces. The air smelled delectably of grilling ribs.

They'd barely been seated long enough for Gray to set aside his menu when two women around Gray's age approached their table. One was either hiding partially behind the other or pushing the other. They apologized profusely to Gray for interrupting, then asked if they could have his autograph and perhaps—maybe?—a picture with him.

Politely, Gray rose. Dru stood, too, both scanning the environment and keeping a careful eye on Gray as he interacted with the women.

Over her time with him, she'd begun to notice something subtle during these types of exchanges with fans. Very subtle. He was so excellent at dealing with people that it had taken her a long time to see that a degree of sadness stole over him whenever others covered him with praise. He hid it well.

Gray and Dru returned to their seats in the booth.

"You know," Dru said, "I assumed that the fact that other people idolize you must make you feel valued. But it doesn't, does it? It makes you feel the opposite."

His lips parted slightly. He didn't look surprised so much as arrested and also bemused, like he couldn't quite believe her nerve.

"Meaning isn't in money or success or fame," she continued. "God's made everything but Himself hollow, so that we all have to keep searching until we find Him. But you know that already, don't you? That everything else is hollow?"

"I have no idea what you're talking about," he answered, without heat.

"You do know what I'm talking about. I can tell. Just like I can tell that the compliments of strangers make you feel emptier."

"And you, Dru?" he asked, a hint of fondness or maybe

compassion in his expression. "Does striving and never finding contentment make you feel emptier?"

His words penetrated with cunning precision.

Continuing to stare at her, he shifted and casually extended an arm along the top of his seat.

She'd understood something key about him. But he understood something key about her, too. She *had* been striving all her life. Striving hard and earnestly. For freedom. For a rush. For domination at whatever pursuit she attempted. And even though she'd found God, there was still a part of her that had remained stubbornly unsettled.

"Yes," she admitted, "sometimes it does make me feel emptier."

"What are you striving so hard for?"

She thought it over. "Respect, I suppose."

"In case you haven't noticed, you've already got everybody's respect. How about you kick back and relax for a few minutes and eat a hamburger and French fries with me?"

She pushed her lips to the side, searching Hillstone's interior for the person who posed the highest threat. "I've already eaten, but I won't turn down the five-nut brownie à la mode."

Their server took their order without writing down a single detail. Dru supposed waiters and waitresses did this in hopes of impressing diners into leaving bigger tips. But the practice always made her dubious. She'd rather this guy get it right than bust his brain trying to remember everything.

"Do you want to spend your whole career in executive protection?" Gray asked when they were alone again.

"No. I don't see enough action in this role."

"Not enough action?"

"I'd like to do tactical support and crisis response for the FBI on their Dallas-based SWAT team."

"That ought to provide you with more action."

"It ought to." She held her chin at an unapologetic angle, ready to defend her career choice against his aspersions.

"You'd be good at that" was all he said.

Gray thought she'd be good on the FBI's SWAT team? His unexpected confidence in her felt like a gift.

Quiet drifted between them. He considered her with the same understated seriousness that had dogged him since he'd exited the bus while she doted over the fact that he thought she'd be good at SWAT—

"I missed you," he said.

Her heartbeat pattered, then began to pound. Mentally, she formulated a gentle scolding.

"You're starting to mess with my head, to be honest," he said. "I missed you, and I thought about you a lot while I was gone. Too much. This is the most important time in our season. I should be concentrating on football."

"I agree."

"So I'm going to do what you've been asking me to do and back off."

She hadn't really seen that coming. "Oh?"

"We're friends, and you're my bodyguard."

"Yes."

"And I'm going to be okay with that and quit pushing for more. I just wanted you to know."

"Excellent," she replied with far more positivity than she felt. Something that shouldn't be disappointment—

but mimicked it well—settled over her. She'd known better than to put any stock in something a half-drunk guy had said about loving her. She really had. Known better.

"It would be easier to quit pushing for more if I didn't like you so much." He brought his big hands together on the table's surface. Lazily, he motioned two fingers in her direction. "And if you weren't so beautiful."

"That last part didn't sound like the kind of thing a friend should say to his protection agent."

"I forget how beautiful you are when I'm apart from you," he went on, ignoring her comment. "And then I'm sort of amazed by it when I'm with you again."

"You're not terrible to look at yourself," she allowed. Large understatement. Those green eyes! The gladiator's face.

"I told you I thought I loved you the other night."

She was used to being blunt with people, but not as used to people being blunt with her. She hadn't expected Gray to address the I-love-you thing directly. It took her aback for a second. "I wasn't sure whether you'd remember."

"I remember. Do you hold it against me?"

"No."

"Good. Thank you."

He wasn't backpedaling on his statement of love, but neither was he sticking up for its validity. He nodded once, as if satisfied with the closure he'd brought to the topic of their relationship.

Their server slid a bowl of crispy homemade tortilla chips with big flecks of salt sprinkled over them onto their table. "This is on the house," he told them.

"We're . . . well, a lot of us are football fans, including the manager. So . . . go Mustangs." Next came a ramekin of steaming spinach artichoke dip and two tiny containers of sour cream and salsa.

"Thank you," Gray told him.

Their server nodded and slipped away, smiling.

Gray angled his chin toward the food questioningly.

"You first, hungry one," Dru said.

He loaded up a chip. "Any news on my case?"

"We received another letter from your stalker in the mail yesterday."

Gray polished off the chip. "Did he invite me to his country club for eighteen holes?"

Dru brought the scanned image of the letter up on her phone. "Shall I?"

"Be my guest." He went to work on another chip.

"'You,'" Dru read aloud, "um . . . expletive expletive . . . 'I can't stand you.'"

"That's friendly."

"'Do you think I'm an idiot?'" Dru continued reading, her voice pitched very low so that no one could overhear. "'Who sees their girlfriend five days a week during the same hours each day? She's your bodyguard. Not your girlfriend.'" She slanted her attention to Gray, who'd gone still. "'You coward,'" she read, "'You think that bodyguards can save you? Nothing can save you. I'm going to kill you both.'"

Gray leaned back. "So it *was* my stalker who fired into Urban Country."

Dru nodded.

"And he could tell based on how you acted in response to the gunfire that you're not my girlfriend."

"That's my conclusion. Apparently ordinary girl-friends don't tackle their boyfriends at the first crack of gunfire. Who knew?"

He frowned.

"I'm beginning to wonder whether he or she ever meant to hit you at Urban Country," Dru continued. "The shots were high. It could be that he'd grown suspicious of our relationship. . . ."

"So he shot into the restaurant to test you? To see how you'd react?"

"Right. He or she shot into the restaurant in order to see if I was your protection agent."

"That would explain why he didn't keep shooting. He'd seen how you'd reacted, which was what he'd come for."

"Yes."

He rapped his knuckles softly on the table a few times, thinking. "Why go to the trouble just for that information, though? If he was a good shot, he could have killed me then and there. Why didn't he?"

"I can only guess it's because he or she didn't want to take you out at Urban Country. Your stalker must have a plan. I think he or she has already decided to take you out a different way and in a different setting."

Forty-five minutes later, Dru situated Gray at Hill-stone's bar and exited the restaurant to run her customary safety check on his Denali. A slick of moisture gleamed on the surface of the sidewalk and parking lot, evidence of the light rain that had begun to fall while they'd been indoors. As she stepped down from the curb, she noticed a large dry patch of ground centered in the parking spot to her right. She paused.

Up until a few moments ago, a car must have been there. It had parked before the rain, thus the dry area beneath. It must have just left . . . almost as if the occupant had been watching Gray and pulled away when he or she had seen him get up from their table. The vehicle couldn't have been gone long. If it had, the rain would have saturated the parking space.

Squinting, Dru turned slowly, searching for red taillights that might belong to one of the vehicles she constantly watched for. The maroon truck. Kayla's Lexus. A beige Cherokee. The minivan belonging to Kevin Lee's family.

The night encircled her with the city's subdued Sunday-night hum. A couple walked across the far end of the parking lot, bundled against the cold. A BMW purred down the street. That was all.

Dru went back inside the restaurant and asked for a tape measure. They produced one from a toolbox. She returned to the parking space and took quick measurements of the dry area's length and width. It seemed longer and more rectangular to her than a sedan.

A truck?

The maroon truck?

Gray sat on a barstool inside Hillstone, his brow furrowing as he watched Dru through the windows, measuring something on the ground outside.

It had been a brutal day. The ibuprofen the trainers had given him earlier had worn off, and his back and neck ached with knotted pain. His physical issues were heavy, so it was saying something that his thoughts were bothering him even more.

Dru had clocked him when she'd told him she could tell that his interactions with fans left him emptier. His relationship with football fans was . . . complicated. On some level, he'd always enjoyed receiving their praise. In fact, a big part of him had been greedy for the attention during his time at A&M and his early years in the NFL. He'd tried to use the fans' adoration to fill the holes in his self-esteem his childhood had left.

It didn't ultimately work. He'd learned the hard way how quickly fans could turn on you when you screwed up an important play or went into a slump. They were in your business when you wanted privacy. They were always watching you and always judging. They'd write articles about your faults or criticize you on social media or suggest other players in the league who should take your place because they could do your job better. A player couldn't fully trust his fans. Gray protected himself by shrugging off the bad and enjoying—on a surface level— the good the fans brought to him.

In the end, he hadn't built his self-esteem through people who'd told him he was capable. He'd built it through countless days on the field and in the gym. When no one had been watching, he'd proven his capability to himself.

He liked people. And he usually didn't mind talking to people. But Dru had been right, in a way. His conversations with fans sometimes left him feeling like an object. A windup toy football player. He was well aware that the people who told him they loved and admired him didn't actually *know* him. And that awareness emphasized his aloneness.

He was a thirty-two-year-old man who'd built a life, partly on purpose, without many real or deep connections with other people. Hadn't he decided, just a few hours ago, to step back from Dru because his relationship with her was getting too real? Too deep?

He needed a drink. "Can I get a shot of Southern Comfort mixed with amaretto?"

"Sure thing."

He eyed Dru, who'd moved on now to his Denali and was doing whatever it was she did to make sure the SUV wouldn't explode into flames when she turned the ignition.

He'd decided to step back from Dru, but there was no denying that he *was* connected to her. When she'd told him that his stalker had discovered her role as his bodyguard, concern for her had gathered inside him like a clenched fist. It still hadn't loosened.

He'd been telling himself that it didn't change much. His stalker had threatened to kill Dru in the latest letter, but he'd also threatened to kill her back when he'd thought her his girlfriend.

But back then, he'd never fired shots. He hadn't shown himself willing to take action.

Since he'd first started receiving the letters, Gray had written his stalker off as a coward. He'd never worried much about his safety. But now the stalker had given him reason to worry about Dru. And he didn't like it. Didn't like the weight that worrying about someone else brought with it.

He tossed back his shot, taking it down in a single, determined swallow.

Later that night, long after Dru was officially off duty, she sat on her cabin's sofa with her computer on her lap. She searched for and finally found length and width specs for the 1988 Ford Ranger.

The dimensions jived closely with the measurements she'd recorded outside Hillstone. She gnawed the edge of her lip and stroked her fingers through Fi's fur while her mind turned the information over and over, hoping to shake loose a usable lead.

Come out of hiding, she willed Gray's stalker. *Show yourself. You can't have Gray, but me? Me, you can fight.*

I'm ready.

CHAPTER FIFTEEN

Have you recovered from the trauma of the other night?" Dru asked Ashley the next afternoon.

Dru was leaning against the island in Gray's luxurious kitchen while Ashley whipped potatoes with a hand mixer. The potatoes would be accompanying asparagus and stuffed chicken breast on Gray's dinner plate.

Since Dru had been here last, Gray's house had been professionally decorated for Christmas. Fresh greenery wove up the staircase handrail. A tree towered over his formal living room, and wreaths of cuttings hung on the outside of every window. "I'm Dreaming of a White Christmas" slid from the sound system.

A paid wife, Dru was beginning to conclude, was a nice thing to have.

"I've had nightmares every night since the shooting," Ashley confessed. "I've never been that close to an . . . emergency."

Dru made a sympathetic clucking noise, though she couldn't imagine having nightmares after what had happened at Urban Country. The bullets, after all, had come nowhere near them.

"Do you think Gray's doing okay?" Ashley gave her a look that dripped with stricken concern.

"Sure."

"I'm worried about him. This situation with his stalker is really scary." Ashley's blond hair skimmed against her slender throat. The bow at the back of her floral apron bobbed. "You guys are taking good care of him, right?"

"Right."

Ashley seasoned the mashed potatoes with salt and cream. "So . . . you're not a preschool teacher *at all*?"

Dru laughed. "No. Not at all."

"What about how Gray met you? How he came to your preschool and you were wearing a Thanksgiving headband and teaching the little ones how to use the potty?"

"Ashley." Dru indicated herself. "Look at me. Do I look like someone who would wear a Thanksgiving headband and teach little ones to use the potty?"

Ashley sighed. "I guess not. It's just that I thought it was so cute, you know, that you worked with little itty bitties." Her tone went into the high-pitched upper ranges of preciousness.

"Why don't you teach preschool, Ashley? You'd be good at it."

"Oh, no. Because then I wouldn't . . ."

Be near Gray. Dru could easily fill in the blanks.

It was impossible not to like Ashley in the way that it was impossible not to like a puppy. However, Ashley's devotion to Gray grated on Dru. Couldn't Ashley see

that he was never going to love her the way she dreamed
that he would?

Dru's phone rang. She pulled it from her inside jacket
pocket and saw that it was Julie, Sutton's tech guru.
"Excuse me." She made her way to the front formal living area. The Christmas tree's deliciously piney scent
wafted over her. "Hey, Julie."

"Hi, Dru. I have some news for you about Mildred
Osbourne."

Dru's concentration focused on the wide swath of
Gray's property beyond the windows. "I'm listening."

"Mildred has been married twice."

"Okay."

"First to a man named Eugene Osbourne. Rich Osbourne is their son."

"Got it." She'd spoken to Rich on the phone, gone
to his house, and seen the maroon truck parked on the
far side of his garage.

"It turns out that Mildred was only married to Eugene
Osbourne for a couple of years. He died young of a heart
defect. Two years after his death, Mildred married Walt
Wright. Didn't you tell me you met Walt when you went
out to speak with Mildred?"

"Yes, but I didn't know that Walt had a different last
name than Mildred. I thought his last name was Osbourne." She'd had no reason to suspect otherwise.

"No."

"So . . . even though she's been married to Walt
Wright for decades, Mildred kept her first husband's
last name?"

"She did. A year after she married Walt, they had a
son named Dennis Wright."

"Ah." Vaguely, she remembered Mildred saying something about "the boys" watching football together. She had more than one son.

Dru rubbed her thumb against the window's casing, thinking. Mildred's first husband had died tragically young. She hadn't been able to give him many years, which might explain why she'd been motivated to honor him by keeping his name. Also, Osbourne was her son Rich's surname. In keeping Osbourne as her own surname, Mildred had ensured that each of her sons would have one parent with their same last name.

Mildred had a more independent spirit than Dru had realized. Ladies who didn't change their last name when they married were the type of ladies who bought cars and registered them in their own names.

"What do you know about Dennis Wright?" Dru asked Julie.

"He's fifty-six and lives in Bonham. He married at twenty and worked for a long time at a plant that manufactures drain pipes. Then, nine years ago, he stopped working for the plant and divorced. As far as I can tell, his ex-wife moved back to the Midwest, where she was from."

"What kind of work does he do now?"

"He's a part-time custodian at an office building. His one child"—Dru could hear Julie's computer mouse moving around on its pad—"a son named Alex, died in a car accident ten years ago at the age of twenty-four."

"Just twenty-four?"

"Yeah."

Which might explain why Dennis's job and marriage fell apart. Tragedies fractured lives.

"Let me know what else I can do for you, all right, Dru?"

"Thanks, Julie."

They said their goodbyes and disconnected as Dru made her way to Gray's office. She knocked.

"Come in."

He sat behind his desk. Taking his time, he leaned away from his computer and swiveled his desk chair to face her. Exactly as he'd declared at Hillstone the night before, he'd quit pushing her verbally for anything more than professional friendship.

But his attraction to her was still there, fierce and bright, in his eyes. She'd been on duty with him for a few hours today already, and every time they'd been in a room together, she'd been able to feel his gaze.

After practice, he'd showered and donned an old pair of jeans and a pale gray sweater. He didn't usually wear shoes around his house, even now, in December. Which Dru found odd. Weren't his feet cold?

"Mildred Osbourne," she said, "owner of the maroon truck, has another son." She came to a stop directly across his desk. "His name is Dennis Wright. Do you know anyone by that name?"

Gray thought about it. "No."

"What about Alex Wright? Have you ever heard of him?"

His posture straightened. His head tipped up an additional inch, features alert. "Alex Wright, did you say?"

"Yes." Her intuition started buzzing. "Alex is Dennis's son. He was killed ten years ago in a car accident. He was—"

"Twenty-four," Gray finished.

Chills skimmed down Dru's arms. "You knew Alex."

Nodding, he lifted his hands to clasp his head. The muscles in his shoulders and huge upper arms arched. His body had a sculptured quality to it. Michelangelo would have jumped at the chance to carve Gray's physique into marble. Stunning lines, a fine balance of grace and power, of splendor and destructive potential.

She lowered onto the front of one of the chairs facing the desk.

He released his arms, his hands coming to rest on his thighs. "Alex was Mildred Osbourne's . . . ?"

"Grandson."

"I was Alex's replacement," he said, each word measured. "He played starting tight end for the Mustangs for two seasons. He was solid, but he wasn't great. He might have become great in time. He had trouble transitioning from college to the faster pace of the NFL. It happens. He was young." Gray's forehead lined, and he appeared to be looking back through time at memories.

She waited.

"The Mustangs drafted me. Then they hired a free agent to play the position, too, which meant that Alex was in danger of being cut. Alex worked hard to keep his spot on the roster."

"And?"

"The Mustangs kept him up until the deadline to submit the fifty-three-man roster. Then they cut him."

Dru could only imagine how that must have gutted Alex. "What do you know about the car accident?"

"After the Mustangs let him go, Alex spent days trying to drink away his disappointment." His chest expanded with his breath. "Some guys have a hard time letting go of football. For a lot of us, it's all we've known . . . all we've wanted since we were kids."

"I understand."

"About a week after the Mustangs released him, Alex got behind the wheel of his car after he'd been drinking. Just a mile or two later, he wrapped it around a tree. He was killed instantly."

Dru regarded him with level sorrow.

"Alex was a good guy," Gray said. "He had a lot of potential and a whole life to live. I've always felt lousy about what happened to him."

"His parents must have been devastated."

Gray dipped his chin. "One week their son was playing for the NFL. And the next week he was dead."

"Within a year of Alex's death, his parents divorced, and his mom moved away," Dru informed him. "His dad stopped working for the company he'd been with for a long time. It's possible that his dad's misery over his son's death turned into hatred toward you, Gray. You're the one who took over Alex's position."

"That was the coaching staff's decision. They'd made the choice to start me at tight end months before, when they drafted me."

"I realize that. But I'm not sure that grieving parents are always cool-headed enough to consider things logically."

He pushed from his chair as if he could no longer stand to sit in it. He paced down and back the room's length, coming to stand a few feet from her with his arms crossed.

Trying to meet his eyes was like looking up the face of the Empire State Building. Uncomfortable. She stood.

"You think Alex's dad—Dennis—is my stalker," he stated flatly.

Her heart twisted at the guilt and concern that had sharpened his features and paled his skin. "I think it's possible."

"You think he hates me that much?"

"Maybe. You spotted Dennis's mother's truck following you, and we don't have reason to suspect Mildred or Rich."

"Mildred told you that Rich is the one who drives the truck. You saw the truck yourself, parked at Rich's house."

"It could be that both brothers use the truck but that they keep it at Rich's house. Or it could be that Mildred told me that Rich is the one who drives the truck because she knows that Rich is the upstanding one. She knew we wouldn't find anything on Rich. It's possible that she called Dennis the moment I left her house and told him to drive the truck over to Rich's. He could have done so before I got there."

"But didn't Rich tell you that he takes the truck out on errands?"

"Yes. But if you knew your brother was struggling, would you cover for him when a nosy agent called to ask questions?"

He set his mouth grimly. "If Dennis is my stalker, I don't want him arrested. He and his family have suffered enough."

She let a few moments pass. "They've suffered," she said reasonably. "But that suffering doesn't justify the threats against you or the shots fired into Urban Country. If Dennis is your stalker, then we need to stop him.

That's the only way we can keep you safe and prevent him from doing something that will land him in jail for the rest of his life."

"What are you going to do next?"

"I'm going to call Detective Carlyle. We may finally have a suspect and a motive."

Dennis Wright could not be found.

After learning of Gray's connection to Alex Wright, Dru relayed the information to Detective Carlyle. The next day, her day off, she loaded Fi into her Yukon and drove to Bonham. Julie supplied Dru with an address for Dennis, which took her to a run-down condo. Dennis wasn't home. His unit's curtains were drawn, his mail slot overflowing. According to DMV records, he drove a '94 blue Camaro. It wasn't parked in the condo's lot.

She stopped by the office complex where Dennis worked. His boss told her that Dennis hadn't shown up for work for the past ten days.

The police pulled information on Dennis's credit cards. He only had two. Neither had been used since his disappearance.

Dennis had abandoned his job, left his condo, and switched from credit cards to cash. All of which seemed to Dru like the actions of a guilty man, a man who knew he was either being hunted or soon would be.

Dru guarded Gray hawkishly during her work hours. When she wasn't with him, she read and reread the stalker's letters. She pored over every online and print article that had ever been written about Alex Wright.

Alex had garnered his share of press. He'd been a

standout tight end at Alabama before signing with the Mustangs. He'd publicly thanked his father more than once. It seemed that Dennis had been a high school football player in his own right, then Alex's elementary school football coach, then Alex's most dedicated supporter.

There were plenty of pictures of Alex, who'd been a brawny, dark blond, easygoing, steak-fed-looking person.

She'd only been able to unearth a few pictures of Alex's parents. His mom was a mousy brunette. Dennis resembled the photos she'd seen of his brother Rich. Ruddy and stout. Thinning hair. It hurt Dru to view the photos of Alex's family of three, because in the grainy images, everyone in the Wright family had been smiling proudly, unaware of the heartache rushing toward them.

Every morning, she went running.

She spent time with Meg, who'd recently been restricted by her obstetrician to bedrest. Apparently, the medications weren't keeping Meg's blood pressure as low as the doctors wanted. So bedrest it was.

Dru brought Meg Sudoku books, packages of Oreos, and DVDs of the *Underworld* series. Because, really, when you were restricted to almost zero physical activity thanks to a doctor's orders and a big pregnant tummy, why wouldn't you want to live vicariously through an awesome female vampire slaying bad guys?

Meg was as kind as always during Dru's visits, but also a little ashen and somewhat distracted. More than once Dru had caught her twirling the back of her earring, something she did unconsciously when anxious. It was only when Bo entered the room that Meg's posture relaxed.

Dru had to admit that Meg had scored a very good Porter brother. Ty was an unruly blend of cocky charm and willfulness. Jake was overprotective of his wife and about as much fun as a funeral. Bo, though. The things about Bo that Dru had once considered dull, she now appreciated. He was a great combination of subtle humor and steady courage.

Dru took Augustine to biker church.

She babysat her nieces and nephews.

Gray received two more letters from his stalker.

Dru had become good at compartmentalizing during her time with the Marines. But Gray's case had seeped over its borders, the same way her feelings for him had. She cared about him personally and professionally, which must be why a sense of menace concerning him wouldn't quit slanting over her like a long shadow.

Christmas fervor rose to a silver-bells pitch all around Dru. She put up a few decorations inside her cabin and bought a gift for everyone in her large family. That was about it. She wasn't a homemaking mom of five. She was a single girl who liked guns and martial arts. Christmas wasn't a beat-down for her like it was for some women.

Corbin continued to call Dru, continued to ask her out. She met him once for barbecue at Holley's Taste of Texas restaurant. But despite his obvious eligibility, eating barbecue with Corbin made her feel disloyal to Gray. Disloyal to a client? Who she wasn't even dating? Go figure. She told Corbin she was glad they were friends but she wasn't interested in anything more at present. She didn't permanently close the door on the future either, either to Corbin verbally or in her own mind.

It's just that, for right now, Gray had taken up all the

space in her life that a relationship with Corbin would require. Until she found the stalker, she didn't have the heart or the patience for dating. Not even for dating likeable NFL quarterbacks.

Ever since the dinner at Hillstone, her relationship with Gray had been locked in a stalemate. So much so that she was beginning to think she preferred it the old way, when they'd talked about things in a forthright manner. When he'd told her he wanted to date her and she'd rebuffed him. He no longer told her he wanted to date her. Yet the unspoken sea of desire and emotion between them rose a little higher and a little higher and a little higher every single day. Soon it would overflow. Their mutual silence in the face of it was making her edgy.

The Mustangs played in San Francisco on the twelfth of December. Another win.

One week after they'd discovered Alex and Dennis Wright's connection to Gray, on a cloudy Monday, Dru received a text from Big Mack. *Something's the matter with Gray's mom. He's going to drive down to Mullins to see her today. My shift ends right after his PT sessions. You up for a trip?*

Yes, she texted back. Mullins lay deep in the heart of Texas, to the west of Austin. It would take them about three hours to drive there.

Is his mom okay?

I think so. Meet us at the practice facility?

Dru had a security pass, so she parked her motorcycle in the players' lot of the Mustangs complex and waited, half leaning, half sitting against her bike.

The sky hunkered above her, a tapestry of dove gray and pewter. She flicked the collar of her jacket around her neck to combat the chill and buried her gloved hands in her pockets just as Gray and Mack emerged from the building.

Gray's hair was wet from his shower. Stubble marked the lower half of his face. He wore a black pullover sweatshirt with a short zipper at the neck. Jeans. The simple, casual clothes looked effortlessly handsome on him.

Attraction to him thrummed to life within Dru. Instantly, she went on the defensive against it, countering with a block.

"How about I drive?" she said by way of greeting.

"You wish," he answered and opened the passenger's-side door of the Denali for her.

Within minutes, they'd reached the freeway.

"So." Dru took in his profile. "What happened with your mom?"

"She's not . . . doing well. My sister, Morgan, is in Arkansas with a friend for a couple of days. She left her two kids with my mom."

"And?"

"Morgan tried reaching my mom first thing this morning, but the phone just rang and rang."

Worry stabbed Dru.

"Morgan called Mom's neighbor in Mullins, a young mom who has little kids around the same age as Morgan's, and asked her to go by my mom's house. The neighbor found my mom in bed. The baby was crying in the crib, and the three-year-old was playing by herself in the kitchen."

"Where are the kids now?"

"The neighbor took them with her to her house."

"And your sister?"

"On her way back from Arkansas. But she's still several hours behind us. She asked me to go check on Mom."

"How come your mom didn't get out of bed this morning?"

His green gaze flicked to her. In the past, he'd always been very close-lipped about his family and his childhood. He didn't need to say out loud how much he hated talking about this. She already knew.

He faced the road, features grim. "It's a long story, Dru."

"We have hours, Gray."

"I don't want to lay my family's mess on you."

Translation: he didn't want to trust her with his family's mess. "You don't really have a choice since I'm not planning to let you out of my sight."

Muscles tensed along the area where his jaw met his neck. He punched the button on his car's sound system. Lilting reggae filled the space, closing the topic.

"How long will we be staying in Mullins?" Dru had to raise her voice to be heard above the beat.

"Not long. We'll drive home tonight."

Dru kept an eye on the side mirror, watching for cars that might be tailing them. The deeper they drove into the country, the more sure she became that they weren't being followed. Rural roads left stalkers no place to hide.

She glanced over at Gray and found him looking at her, his expression hooded. A pulse went through her before he broke the connection.

Strange man. Secretive. Shuttered. Frustrating. And more than a little hunky despite all that.

She pulled free the backpack she'd brought, which contained her laptop, a weighty literary tome of a novel that she'd been reading for about six months, and her phone.

They made just one stop, at a 7-11. The customers and staff within gawked at Gray as if Elvis Presley himself had just entered their middle-of-nowhere establishment. Gray bought bottled water, a granola bar, and spearmint-flavored Trident. "What can I get you?" he asked Dru.

"I buy my own snacks, big football player." Dru purchased a Coke and a package of Sour Patch Kids.

They'd been back on the road for less than ten minutes when his phone started chiming to signal incoming texts. It chimed thirteen times in twenty minutes.

"What in the world?" Dru finally asked him.

Pushing his finger up the face of his smartphone's screen so that the messages rolled, Gray handed the phone to Dru. All thirteen messages were from ex-girlfriend Kayla Bell.

"Shall I communicate these to you?" Dru asked.

He inclined his head.

"Kayla wants you to know that she loves you. That you guys were perfect for each other. That she was the best thing to ever happen to you and that she's the best thing that has possibly happened anywhere in the world, ever. That she's furious with you. Let's see here. The second-to-last one states that she never wants to see you again. And the last one says that she expects that you'll die alone and miserable."

"Happy thought."

"Kayla's always so full of joy."

"Sounds to me like she might be full of Cosmopolitans this afternoon."

Dru reread each message carefully, attempting to pair Kayla's wording with the wording in any of the stalker's letters.

"She's not my stalker," Gray said.

"She might be."

"She's not."

"Why haven't you blocked Kayla's number on your phone?"

He shrugged. "I hadn't really thought about it. It doesn't take a lot of effort to ignore someone's calls and text messages."

"How about I block her for you?"

"Be my guest."

Dru hit buttons on his phone. "Have you ever considered reporting Kayla to the police? It's not okay how she parks outside your house."

"She's a mom, Dru. Reporting her to the police would just stir up trouble for her and her little girl."

"What about the trouble she causes you?"

"What trouble? She doesn't park in front of my house very often. It's not difficult to walk out my front gate and chat with her for a few minutes now and then."

"You're not stringing her along in any way, are you?"

"Nope. Whenever I talk with her, I tell her as nicely as I can that we're done and that I wish her all the best. I keep expecting her to find a boyfriend who she likes better than me."

Little chance of that, Dru thought.

"Maybe I'll introduce her to Corbin," Gray said.

Mile after mile of Texas land passed by. The clouds muted the color of the scenery today, casting the fields and hills and shallow valleys in irritable light that seemed to echo Gray's mood as they approached Mullins.

They passed a rodeo arena on the outskirts of the town. Then a placard announcing the population of Mullins to be 5,883. Then they zipped toward a massive wooden sign that read *Mullins, Texas, The Hometown of NFL Player Gray Fowler!* The sign listed his Pro Bowl appearances and his Super Bowl victory. The newer the addition, the less faded the green paint. Gray's accomplishments were so numerous that they'd just about consumed all the available space.

Dru pointed at the sign as it swept past. "You have a sign."

"I have a sign. Every time something happens in my

career I drive down here with a paintbrush and a can
of green paint."

Dru grinned, and Gray went back to bumping the side
of his thumb against the steering wheel in time to the
reggae. The carefree Caribbean music and the thumb-
bumping didn't fool Dru. She'd become attuned to Gray.
She could sense his inner resistance to this place.

Mullins didn't have an old town square like Holley. This community revolved around its main street.
They passed a Walmart. Ace Hardware. An imposing
old courthouse and county jail. An establishment called
The Beer Barn that offered drive-thru alcohol. A Sonic.
McDonald's, of course. Then several shops inside some
thickly constructed historical buildings.

Gray parked in a curbside space.

"Your mom lives at"—Dru took in the store next to
them— "Cindy's Cinnamon Rolls?"

"Cindy's cinnamon rolls are the best thing about Mullins. I'm starving."

"Gray—"

But he'd already let himself out and closed the door
behind him with a sturdy, expensive *shlick*.

Gray held open the door that led into Cindy's for
her. The interior smelled like a Cinnabon at the mall. A
chain of fake holly framed a case displaying three types
of cinnamon roll: original, with nuts, and small, which
were each about the size of a spool of thread.

They ordered two originals. Dru waited, holding her
paper plate with the cinnamon roll centered on top while
Cindy conversed with Gray. The store's owner alternated
between treating him like a fan-girl and treating him like
a Cub Scout den mother. On their way out the door,

Cindy admonished Gray to visit Mullins more often and to try his best to return for the town's public school auction night fundraiser.

Gray led Dru across the street to a low-slung building built of yellow brick. "This is the old train station," he said. Massive crescent-topped windows marked its sides, and the town's name had been carved into a smooth rectangular stone set high into the masonry. "A few years ago, someone bought it and turned it into a breakfast and lunch restaurant."

Which explained the station's deserted status at five in the evening. They sat on a bench at the back of the restaurant, on what had once been the train platform. Empty space bristling with brown winter grass spread out below and before them where the tracks had once lain.

Dru uncoiled her cinnamon roll and pulled free a bite. She savored the soft, warm cinnamon-y dough and cream cheese frosting.

Gray set his plate between them on the bench but didn't make a move toward it. It had been hours since practice, and she hadn't seen him eat anything except a granola bar and gum. Even though he'd claimed to be starving, he'd set his mouth the way people set their mouths when they have no appetite.

She ate a few more sections of her cinnamon roll, waiting for him to say what was on his mind. It seemed he'd turned to stone.

"You didn't stop at Cindy's and bring me out here for the cinnamon rolls," she finally said.

"I wish this trip would have fallen during Mack or Weston's shift." He spoke in a flat, controlled tone. "I don't like bringing you here."

"Quit blowing sunshine at me, Fowler. You'll give me a big head." This was hard for him, both this trip and having to tell her things he never shared. Talking smack would make things better for him than sympathy could.

He looked across his shoulder at her.

She arched an eyebrow challengingly. "You've decided to fill me in on your mom before taking me over there. Right?"

"Yeah."

"Because . . ."

"Because what we find at my mom's might not be . . . pretty. I want to explain. Before we go." He'd probably been arguing with himself up until now about whether or not to tell her.

Gray might wish this trip had fallen during another agent's shift, but she did not. She wanted to be here. She wanted to be the one. Using one of the napkins she'd brought, she wiped frosting from her fingertips.

"My mom grew up here." He sat back against the bench, crossing his arms in the protective pose she'd seen him take countless times. The black fabric of his sweatshirt tautened over his shoulders. His vision trained on the empty space before them. "When she was seventeen, she fell in love with a guy named Jeff Crawford. They dated for a year or so, and then they broke up. To say she was upset is an understatement. She dated a few other guys, then got pregnant after her freshman year in college." He didn't speak for a long moment.

"With you," she guessed.

"With me. She dropped out of school and got licensed to cut hair. Jeff went to a university out of state, but he came home often. He and my mom started their relationship up again. Then they fought and broke up. Then they

started dating again. Then they broke up. And so on."
He said it all coldly and impersonally, not giving Dru a
shortcut into him any more than he'd already been forced
to. "When I was five, my mom married a guy named Dan.
Nice guy. Me and my mom moved out of my grandparents' house where we'd been living and into Dan's
trailer. My brother, Colton, was born. I started school."

"How'd that go?"

"Fine, except that the whole town knew me as Sandy
Fowler's bastard."

She held her tongue because she knew he wouldn't appreciate her compassion toward him or her anger toward
the prejudices people directed at children. It was too late
now to stick up for the five-year-old he'd been so long ago.

"My mom's marriage didn't stop her from continuing
to see Jeff on the side."

"No."

"Her marriage to Dan lasted a couple of years. When
it ended, she moved us into a junky little rental house.
It was right around that time that Jeff got married. My
mom didn't take it well. She started drinking heavily,
and things came apart."

"Were you and your brother ever removed from the
home?"

"No."

Distantly, she could hear a mother calling to her child
and the sound of a siren.

"My mom's second husband was a good-looking
guy who turned out to be as mean as a snake. He had
a temper. I was ten when they married." Anger lined
Gray's forehead, hollowed his cheeks, formed brackets
around his mouth.

Dru's heart thumped in her ears. She could read what had happened in the bitterness of his expression. "He took out his temper on your mom, and you, and your brother?"

"He'd yell at my mom and Colton."

"And you?"

"Me he'd both yell at and hit."

"That's horrible, Gray." She tried to keep her fury out of her voice but didn't fully succeed.

He met her eyes just long enough for her to see shame there. Shame, when he hadn't been the one who'd done anything wrong. He turned to look toward the coming sunset.

"How long did it go on?" she asked.

"Three years." His voice remained emotionless.

Dru's mind reeled at the thought of Gray at the ages of ten, eleven, and twelve being beaten by his stepdad. Those were the awkward adolescent years when kids were already so unsure of themselves. "How did your mom respond to the abuse?"

"We all tried hard to keep the peace."

"Okay."

"None of us confronted the dirt bag. We just tried not to make him mad."

"And when he got mad anyway? Then what would your mom do?"

"When she'd come home and see me with bruises or a split lip or whatever, she'd pretend not to notice. If she was there when it happened, she'd look the other way. She stayed away from home a lot and drank hard when she was home. Pretty soon, she and Jeff started back up their cycle of sex and fighting. They just had to work harder to make it happen now that they were both married."

The scent of cinnamon roll carried to her, causing her stomach to twist and harden.

"The dirt bag finally stormed out one night. My mom divorced him a few months later. By then she was pregnant again. We moved into an apartment. I was in bad shape. My brother was almost as bad. My mom did her best to stay off alcohol while she was pregnant, but shortly after she had Morgan she went back to it. It was around then that I found football."

The sport must have seemed to him like a life preserver. "Did your mom ever marry again?"

"One more time when I was in high school. Another good guy she screwed over. It lasted a year and a half. I've never been so glad to leave a place as I was to leave Mullins. This isn't my . . . favorite place to come back to."

"So your mom never got sober?"

"She's gotten sober so many times I've lost count. Staying sober is the problem."

"Please tell me that she came to her senses and finally kicked Jeff to the curb for good."

He regarded her evenly. "No. She's still on-again-off-again with Jeff. Still. More than thirty years later."

"Gray" was all Dru managed.

"Jeff had three kids with his wife. They stayed married up until a couple of years ago when she died of cancer. I didn't know Jeff's wife well. But from what I've heard, she was a great person. Everyone in town liked her."

"What happened to Colton and Morgan?"

"Colton's in jail. Morgan's never been married, but she already has two kids with two different guys." Gray released a cynical laugh. "It's bad, isn't it? Like a tragic country-western song."

"Right up until the part where you rose above it all and made a big success of yourself. What happened to the dirt bag?"

"He got into a bar fight. The other guy hit him in the head with a pool stick and killed him. He did me a favor because I'd gone after him myself eventually."

A pause of quiet. "Do you know who your biological father is?"

Gray leaned forward, setting his elbows on his knees. "No. My mom called me once when I was in college. She was three sheets to the wind, and she kept saying, 'You know, right, Gray? You know who your father is. Don't you?' I kept hanging up, and she kept calling back. She finally told me that Jeff's my father."

He flipped his palms up and studied the lifelines and creases running through them. Those palms were famously brilliant at catching footballs, protecting them, and running them across infield lines. "I don't think she knows who my father is. And if she does, I don't want her to tell me because I don't want to run the risk of finding out that it is Jeff."

The sun dipped below the line of trees and homes on the western horizon, leaving a blazing coral-colored halo.

"If you asked my mom about her choices in life, she'd tell you that they were all because of love. Because of the great, amazing, unstoppable love that she and Jeff share."

No wonder Gray had kept his relationships as superficial as a puddle. Who could blame him for wanting no part of his mom's version of love?

"Enough." He pushed to standing. "Let's go to my mom's."

CHAPTER
SEVENTEEN

His mom's house didn't look like the house of a drunk homewrecker, Gray knew. He'd bought this place for her after signing his first NFL contract. The four-bedroom house with the Austin-stone facade sat on a lot in Mullins' wealthiest part of town.

He and Dru stood on the porch in the dark, waiting for his mom to answer his knock. She didn't.

He texted her. *I'm at the front door. Open up or I'll let myself in.*

Still nothing.

The porch light hadn't been turned on when darkness had fallen. Neither had the lights in the living areas on the other side of the front windows.

He pulled his keys from his pocket. "When we get inside, I'll go talk to her. Alone."

"All right." Dru's two simple words said much more. They said that she understood and that she'd respect his privacy. "I'll just walk through the house to make sure

I have a handle on the layout. Then I'll wait for you in the foyer."

"Good."

He'd meant what he'd said earlier about regretting the fact that she'd been the one on duty when he'd needed to make this trip. He didn't talk to anyone about his childhood. It embarrassed him that, of all people on earth, he'd been forced to talk about it with Dru, the person he most wanted to impress. The last person he wanted to show this side of himself.

He wouldn't have been able to stand it if she'd tried to cover him with pity. She hadn't. She'd mostly just heard him out. Now she was standing beside him, quietly on his side, with her shoulders back and her chin up, as unflinching as ever.

Gray wished he felt the same. He'd rather get knocked out cold on the football field than do this. He unlocked the door. Inside, weak light fell from the hallway, revealing a house that looked as tidy as always. His mom liked to decorate. Especially with animal prints and leather and rhinestones and shots of the color red.

The heated indoor air smelled like peppermint. For every holiday, she filled a bowl with scented stuff—he couldn't remember what you called that. And then she set the bowl on the coffee table in her den. This December she must have gone for peppermint.

Dru started closing all the curtains, no doubt trying to hide him from a sniper.

Flicking on lights, Gray went into the kitchen. He filled a glass with ice water. From the pantry he grabbed a box of Triscuits—her favorite—then made his way down the hallway to her room. Her door stood open.

Through it he could see her lying in bed in the dark, motionless, her back to him.

His heart sank.

Slowly, arming himself, he went around the bed so that he could see her face. She'd closed her eyes, but he knew she was awake.

His mom was only fifty-two. She looked even younger than her years because she kept her brown hair long and her body slim. On good days, she put a lot of effort into her makeup and clothing. Today was not a good day. Even so, she looked deceptively . . . beautiful on the outside.

She had on a pink sweatsuit. She'd removed her makeup at some point. Last night? Which meant that the tears easing from her eyes were leaving shiny tracks on her skin but not dragging mascara with them.

He set the water and crackers on her bedside table, next to where she'd left her cell phone. He lit the lamp, then lowered to sit on the edge of her bed near her knees. Without a word, he picked up her hand and held it. Her fingers were small and fragile and cold.

Crushing heaviness settled onto Gray's shoulders. He felt exhausted and battered, like a one-hundred-year-old man.

He had nothing to say to her. Over the years, it had all been said. He'd tried reasoning her into a life without Jeff and drinking. He'd tried charming her into it. Arguing her into it. Once, he'd checked her into a mental health clinic. There'd been a time when he'd thought that the financial security he'd given her would fix her.

None of it had worked long-term. None of it would or could. There were no more words. He was out of energy for this—and almost out of emotion, too. Almost, but not quite. There was still sadness inside of him for her. And duty.

A light whiff of her perfume reached him. She'd worn the same perfume, called Paris, for as long as he could remember. It was floral, fresh, hopeful. Her room should smell the opposite way. Like darkness and hopelessness and alcohol. But no. She drank vodka, and vodka was odorless. She was lying hopeless in a room that smelled like hope.

When he'd been young and he and his mom had been living with his grandparents, the two of them had shared a room. He slept in a small bed against the wall, and she had a double bed. Every weekend morning, she threw back the covers of her bed for him. He jumped in, and she flipped the sheets and covers over their heads. They scooted down as far as they could go, lying side-by-side on their backs. She extended her arm straight up, creating a miniature circus tent for the two of them. It was dim and warm under there, and it smelled like her perfume. The light underneath the blanket was golden-colored.

"Once," she said.

"Upon," he said.

"A."

"Time." Their laughter filled their little tent as they made up a story together, alternating turns adding the next word.

He could remember as clearly as if he were looking straight at a film reel that had tinged yellow with age turning his face toward her under that tent. She turned her young face toward him, and the two of them smiled.

"Love you," she said to him.

"Love you, Mommy."

He'd felt safe. He'd loved her and trusted her.

The memory dimmed, and another one rushed forward from the past. Details of the crappy rental house they'd lived in after her first marriage came into focus. He'd been about eight, and Colton had been three. He'd been playing in the backyard and had come inside late one afternoon to the desperate sound of her crying.

Panicked, he'd followed the sound and found her on the hallway floor, her knees bent up, her back against the wall. It was as if her grief had stopped her from going another step and she'd collapsed right where it had overwhelmed her.

He dropped onto the ground beside her and patted her back. She smelled like Mom—like her perfume. Her heartbroken sobbing was the saddest sound he'd ever heard.

"He . . . got . . . married," she rasped.

Who? Why could anyone's marriage make her so sad?

"I *love* . . . him! And . . ." More awful sobbing. "And now Jeff's married to someone else. Today. Today's . . . their wedding day. He's married."

Colton walked out from the bedroom where he'd been napping, carrying his blanket. He took one look at their mom and burst into frightened tears.

She opened her arms to Colton, who went into them. She held Colton to her and rocked back and forth like he was about to die. Or she was about to die. Neither of them stopped crying.

Gray kept on patting her shoulder. Even though he was too big to cry, he cried, too, because he was so miserable and terrified and helpless.

He'd known that day, sitting on the hallway floor next to her, that the future held much to fear.

"I was a terrible mother," she said now.

Her words brought him back to the present. She'd opened her green eyes, but she wasn't looking at him. She was looking straight ahead. Moisture continued to run over her eyelashes, wetting them and making them pointy.

"You did what you could," he said.

"I wanted to be a good mother. I loved all of you. I . . . tried . . ." Her voice broke. "But I was a terrible mother. And now Colton . . . and Morgan . . . and you."

"What about me?" Last time he'd looked, he was a contributing member of society.

"You almost never come home."

He didn't bother to answer. There'd never been a time when he hadn't lived with some level of guilt concerning her. She wanted to see him more, but he couldn't handle dealing with her any more than he already had to. He spoke with her on the phone every couple of weeks. They texted back and forth in between calls. He supported her, Morgan, and Morgan's kids financially. He visited his brother in prison and had Ash send Colton the allowed books and magazines.

That was the balance Gray had struck between his sanity and his relatives. It was the best he had to offer. Should he do more? Maybe. Could he? No.

"What brought this on, Mom?" he asked, his words controlled. God help him, he knew what she was going to say. He braced for it.

Time pulled, and her silent tears began to flow harder. For the first time, she turned her head on the pillow to look at him. Right at him. He saw despair in her eyes. Brokenness. "It's over. Between Jeff and me."

Right, he thought cynically.

"We've been so happy together this past year. But we got in a fight last night, and we broke up." Her tone had gone thin and tight. "What . . . what's the point, Grayson? I'm no good to anyone. My life isn't worth anything."

She'd often taken him and Colton and Morgan to church when they'd been young, but she'd never gone in with them. Why hadn't she? Would things have been different if she'd had God in her life? If anybody was living like they were unforgiven, it was her.

"Sit up," he said tiredly. "You need to eat and drink something."

She protested, so he pulled her into a seated position beside him. He handed her the water and frowned at her until she drank it. Then he passed her two Triscuits at a time until she'd eaten ten.

"Is there food in the house?" he asked. "I'll make you some dinner."

"There's leftover spaghetti that I made the kids . . . last night." She let out a quiet sob and pressed a trembling hand to her forehead. "The kids! I'm an awful grandma. I just . . . I just couldn't get out of bed this morning. I heard them, and I wanted to . . . I just couldn't. I couldn't cope with everything. Morgan's going to be so upset with me—"

"Let's go to the den. I'll heat up the spaghetti, and we'll put on a movie"—*and I'll pour your vodka out like I always do*—"and we'll just chill for a while."

"Gray?" Dru called from the front of the house.

His mom's eyes widened, and she looked at him questioningly, almost accusingly. She'd been so wrapped up in her misery, she hadn't been aware that anyone else had entered the house.

"Yeah?" he called back.

"A Mercedes just pulled into the driveway. It's black. A C-class that's maybe three or four years old. Do you know who it belongs to?"

"It's Jeff," his mom said.

"Yes," he called to Dru. "I know who it belongs to."

His mom grabbed his wrist hard. Bitterness and demand glowed in her eyes. "Go out there, Grayson, and tell Jeff for me that I never want to see him again as long as I live."

Anger had been burning like coals within him since he'd received Morgan's call this morning. Now the coals reddened, overpowering his sense of sadness and responsibility. She wanted him to defend her? In this war *she'd* created?

He rose, and her grip fell away. He *hated* Jeff, who'd been jerking her around for decades, disrespecting her, never once acting with honor. But was she any better? She'd let Jeff do it. And now she'd neglected Morgan's kids because of her endless self-destructiveness.

"You can tell him yourself," Gray said in a low voice. "I don't want anything to do with this thing between you." He strode toward the front of the house. "I'm leaving."

Dru was looking through the front door's peephole. She stepped back from it as he neared. "A man and a teenager are coming up the walk. Who are they?"

He reached for the door, intending to yank it open—

Dru stepped between him and the door, stilling him by planting a palm against his chest. "You seem pretty, ah, irritated there, Gray. Care to tell me your plans?"

"We're leaving."

"Not before you tell me who's outside."

A knock sounded.

"It's Jeff."

"Who's with him?"

Gray glanced through the peephole. "His youngest son Daniel."

"How old is Daniel?"

He thought it through, mentally calculating. "Nineteen."

Dru considered him, her turquoise eyes serious. Another knock filled the silence. Despite it, she seemed in no hurry.

Personally, he couldn't wait to get out.

"Is there any reason why Jeff or Daniel would want to do you harm?" she asked.

"No."

"We can decide to not answer the door and wait until they leave. Or we can let them in."

"Jeff has a key. They'll come in regardless."

"I'll let them in, then."

"I'm ready to take off."

"Before you and I can take off, I'll have to run a check on the Denali."

"Why? We know my stalker didn't follow us here."

"Your stalker knows where your mom lives, remember? He or she has sent letters here in the past. I'll have to run a check on the Denali."

"Then now's a good time to get started on that."

"I'll take a minute to assess Jeff and Daniel, then I'll do it." She pulled open the door.

"Oh . . ." Jeff stuttered at the sight of her. "I . . ." Clearly, he hadn't been expecting a stranger to open the door.

"I'm Dru, a friend of Gray's."

Jeff recovered quickly. He introduced himself and his son, and Dru exchanged handshakes with them.

Jeff had been born into the richest family in Mullins. He looked like the president of a fraternity—the slick kind, the kind you automatically disliked. Even now, in his early fifties and wearing a business suit, he looked the part.

Daniel was shorter than his father, more introverted, and on the skinny side. He had close-cut sandy brown hair and big eyes set into pointy features. The kid was hunching into his camo jacket like he didn't want to be here.

That makes two of us.

"Gray." Jeff came forward with his hand outstretched. He wore the hovering expression of a funeral director.

If Daniel hadn't been nearby, Gray would have shoved Jeff in the chest and told him to get out of his mother's house. But the kid didn't deserve that. The kid was uncomfortable enough already. Gray set his jaw and shook Jeff's hand.

"How's your mom doing?" Jeff asked. He clapped his free hand around Gray's upper arm as if the two of them were close.

Gray stepped back, breaking the contact. "Not that well."

"I'm sorry to hear that." Jeff's lips pursed with concern. "I've been trying to get in touch with her."

Gray angled his gaze to Dru, asking her without words if they could leave.

"Daniel and I always eat dinner together at the country club on Monday nights," Jeff was saying, "and watch Monday Night Football on their big screen. We were driving by just now on our way there and saw your car out front."

"Yeah."

"Just a few weeks back, it was *you* we were watching up there on the big screen at the club." He smiled his fraternity smile. "Great playing. Really great playing. When we saw your car, Daniel and I just had to come in and tell you how good it is to see you back in Mullins." He went on, reminiscing about the highlights from the Mustangs' recent Monday night game.

Jeff might have wanted to stop when he'd seen Gray's car, but it was clear that Daniel hadn't. He'd nailed the classic teenager, my-parent-is-a-moron demeanor.

Jeff's kids were all much younger than Gray, so he'd never known any of them well. But he'd seen them around town plenty. It was hard to like the kids of someone you couldn't stand, yet part of Gray could relate to Daniel. He was stuck with Jeff for a father. He'd been affected by his parents' poor decisions, too.

If Gray was one side of the coin that made up his mom's relationship with Jeff, then Daniel was the other side. Daniel was more than a decade younger and much smaller than he was. But he could see some of himself in the kid. The resistance he sensed in Daniel mirrored his own.

Was Daniel in college? He was pretty sure his mom had told him that Daniel lived at home and went to classes at the local podunk community college.

"Anyway . . ." Jeff's conversation drifted off.

Gray felt no need to speak. Dru didn't, either. She pushed her hands into the pockets of her leather jacket and watched Jeff with distrust.

"So." Jeff chuckled. "I'm getting a team together for a golf tournament in March."

Dru narrowed her eyes.

Jeff was about to ask Gray for a favor. Gray's annoyance level, already at its limit, rose.

"It's one of those best ball events," Jeff continued, "to raise money for the high school booster club. What do you think about coming down for it, Gray? A lot of the guys would really like to meet you. Hey, maybe we could set up a photo op with you—"

"Jeff." His mom walked into the foyer carefully, as if putting one foot in front of the other required her full concentration. She set a hand against the wall to steady herself. "Hello, Daniel."

"Hello."

Then, to Dru. "I'm Sandy, Gray's mom."

"I'm Dru, Gray's friend."

His mom had told him that she never wanted to see Jeff for as long as she lived, but he could tell right away that she'd combed her hair and put on some makeup before coming out to see the man she never wanted to see again.

Jeff crossed to her. "You doing okay, honey?"

Depends on your definition of okay, Jeff. She's been comatose all day.

His mom gave a nod that said, *My feelings have been terribly hurt, but here I am, being very brave in spite of it.*

"Dru?" Gray asked. He wasn't willing to wait any longer. Two more minutes of this and he was going to say something ugly.

Dru walked backward toward the door. "Gray and I were just leaving."

"No," his mom said. "Already?"

"Already. I'll go start the car," Dru told him. Then she was gone.

Thank God for Dru. Thank God he had an ally. Dru was honorable and stable, and he believed that she had his best interests at heart, which couldn't be said of any of the people left in the house.

Jeff remained next to Gray's mom, holding her elbow. "What do you think about the golf tournament, Gray?" Jeff asked. "Maybe you could sell jerseys or photos or signed footballs? You know . . . collector-type items? The profits would go to the booster club, of course."

"I already work with a few charities," Gray said. "Beyond those commitments, my schedule is full."

"Okay. Sure. I understand."

"Bye, Mom."

"Grayson." Her eyes tipped downward at the corners with pleading. "Stay and eat spaghetti with me like you suggested—"

"Thanks, but I can't. Good night." He exited the house and walked toward his SUV, feeling like he'd just escaped a dungeon, taking his first full breath since passing the *Mullins, Texas, The Hometown of NFL Player Gray Fowler!* sign.

For a full thirty minutes, Gray didn't speak. He just drove.

Dru sat in the passenger's seat, considering him. He looked dazed by what he'd just endured.

When Jeff had entered Sandy's house and Dru had gotten her first good look at him, her stomach had dipped. Jeff was clearly Gray's father. Gray had plenty of reasons to live in denial over it, but Jeff looked too much like Gray not to be his father.

Gray had probably stumbled upon genes that made him the biggest and tallest of all his relations. But Jeff was over six feet himself, and in very good shape. He had the same chin as Gray, the same mouth.

Then Sandy had made an appearance. After hearing her life story, Dru had expected her to look wasted. Instead, she'd been painfully delicate, but also surprisingly pretty, with her strong cheekbones and her green eyes.

Between Jeff and Sandy, Dru had been able to see exactly where Gray's physical traits had come from. His internal traits, though? Gray's internal traits were sterling. His parents' were ash. So she was at a loss as to where his internal traits had come from. The football field? His coaches? Had they been stamped into him by the necessity of caring for his younger siblings?

It blew her mind to think that Jeff had never come forward as Gray's father.

He hadn't provided for Gray when Gray was young and Sandy had had so little money. He hadn't played ball with Gray in the front yard, or taught him to drive, or taken him hunting. He hadn't given him his name or his heritage. Worst—indefensibly worst—Jeff hadn't stepped in to protect Gray when Sandy had started drinking and when her second husband had been *beating* Gray.

Beating him. She was still trying to wrap her mind around that . . . and what that must have been like for Gray. How had that period of his life affected him over the long haul?

She'd thought she'd known Gray. She had known large parts. She'd known his hard work. His charitable spirit. His toughness in the face of physical injury. She'd been very, very attached to him before today. But today had changed things. Now she knew his hidden parts, and that knowing had deepened her feelings for him, made them even more personal, and filled her with ferocious protectiveness.

"That," Dru said at last, gesturing in the direction of the people they'd left behind, "was messed up."

"It was," he said after a moment. "Right?" As if he needed confirmation that he wasn't the crazy one.

"Yes." She answered with assurance. "None of that had any overlap with how functional families act. Definitely not the part when your mom staggered out looking like a martyr, or when Jeff tried to get you to participate in his golf tournament."

"Like a tragic . . ." Gray said, inviting her to finish the sentence.

". . . country-western song." Her lips tipped up ever so slightly and ever so sadly. She wanted to lighten the mood for him. Wished she could.

Instead, she lost him back to his dark thoughts. Sitting next to him, she could *feel* him battling his anger and frustration and tiredness.

"I'm sorry about your mom," she said. He'd no doubt prefer that she not address what had happened today. She was his protection agent, after all. But she couldn't *not* say something and let his past suck him under. "I'm sorry about Jeff and about your childhood. It's not fair, what you've gone through. And it's not your fault. You should be proud of what you've accomplished and who you are. You have plenty of goodness in you."

He didn't react for so long she thought he wasn't going to react at all.

Then he looked across at her, and she could see a sharp light of futility in his eyes. Their gazes locked before he returned his attention to the road. He set one hand on the armrest between their seats and turned it palm up. She hesitated no longer than a split second before placing her hand in his. In so doing, she stepped across the client/agent line.

Understanding and comfort and delicious sparks rushed through the contact. Holding his hand felt like the most right thing that had ever been. Like coming home.

Gray had chipped away at her protective exterior. All her life, she'd been unable to tolerate it when others viewed her as inferior. She hadn't liked being left out by her older brothers. She'd been raised on rough Texas land, and she'd become sturdy inside and out. She didn't enjoy being . . . vulnerable. She didn't need a man to feel complete.

But she had come to a point, driving down a nighttime ribbon of road, where she needed to face the fact that her feelings for Gray had grown big enough to jeopardize her ability to execute her job. She was involved with him. Too much so to remain impartial.

She'd have to call her boss, explain herself, and resign from Gray's detail. A howling denial rose in her mind. She clamped it down. She loathed the idea of stepping back and entrusting others with Gray's case. She'd viewed this case as *hers*. And she dearly wanted to continue working it. She wanted to be the one to uncover the identity of his stalker.

But she owed the truth to Anthony Sutton, who'd set out rules for his agents for good reasons. And she owed it to Gray, because he deserved the best protection possible.

Tomorrow, she'd call Anthony.

And she'd take herself off Gray's case.

CHAPTER EIGHTEEN

W hat do you think?" Bo asked Meg the next afternoon. "Cowboy hat or no cowboy hat?" They were standing beside his truck on one of Whispering Creek's back lanes.

Meg studied her husband. "You know I like the cowboy hat, but I vote for no cowboy hat for the photo. I'm already worried that we're going to look like J.R. and Sue Ellen Ewing as it is."

He tossed his straw hat into the truck and took hold of her hand. They began the fifty-yard walk to where the photographer and the photographer's assistant were completing the setup for the shoot. Silver Leaf, flanked by one of his grooms, stood motionless and regal at the site.

For the third year running, Meg had agreed to allow Grace Street to hold their Winter Family Fun Day on Whispering Creek's grounds. Her own charity, the Cole Foundation, had partnered with Grace Street several times over the years. A few of the needy families that had lived at Whispering Creek's main house had been referred to Meg through Grace Street, which provided shelter to abused women and children.

Meg offered up the land for the Family Fun Day, and Grace Street handled most everything else. The charity brought in ice sculptures and a sledding hill, regardless of the weather. There'd be roasted chestnuts, hot apple cider, cocoa, fudge, taffy, vendors, games, rides, bands, and celebrity appearances. The entire event had an old-timey Texas wintertime feel to it. Rustic and charming.

Months ago, Meg's contact at Grace Street had asked if they could take a photo of her, Bo, and Silver Leaf to include in their press kit for the event. She'd agreed. So here they were. Bo looked fit and gorgeous. And she looked as big as a hot air balloon.

Nonetheless, she wanted to have this picture made for Grace Street's sake and also because it would be the final "before" photo of her and Bo. Everything about their family of two was about to change forever. She wanted to be able to look at this picture years from now and remember this pregnancy.

Whew. The gentle incline was making her breathless. She paused.

Bo stopped, slanting a look of concern down at her.

"I'm okay," she told him before he could ask. Her blood pressure had turned unruly again recently, so Dr. Peterson had placed her on bedrest. But not complete and total bedrest. Dr. Peterson had encouraged her to get up and move around for short periods every day. Within their house, she walked from room to room. If the weather was halfway decent, she liked to venture outside and park herself on her back patio. Daily, she made her way into their home office to concentrate, reclining with her feet up, on Cole Foundation work for a few hours.

Admittedly though, her world had become small since the bedrest prescription. She'd been glad for the chance to drive here this afternoon and take a break from her usual surroundings and her usual worries.

The photographer had chosen this location from among the many available at Whispering Creek because of the way the land fell away in a sweeping vista.

Meg smoothed the front of the pale blue coat she had on. It was fitted down the arms and bust, before darts loosened it outward. She wished she could do *pregnant chic* as effortlessly as Duchess Kate. That was what she'd been shooting for when she'd selected this coat. But alas, no.

"You look beautiful," Bo said.

She smiled at him. The man was literally heaven-sent. "Thank you."

"Ready?"

She moved her focus to the chair the photographer had waiting for her and gathered herself.

"You don't have to do the picture if you don't want to, you know," Bo said suddenly, holding her back from motion.

She blinked at him.

"I can take you home and get Jake to come out here and take it with me," he continued. "He'll be an ugly substitute for you, but he'll do in a pinch."

"No. I want to do the picture."

"Do you want me to ask the photographer to bring the chair here? We can take the picture here, if you'd rather."

"Nope. It's fine."

Bo didn't move. He continued to stare at her. Solemnity marked the set of his mouth. She could tell that he wanted to say more, so she waited.

There'd been a time in her life when she'd had difficulty trusting men, trusting *him*. Looking at Bo now, it almost seemed hard to believe, like the mistrust she'd had in him had belonged to a different woman entirely.

"We're fortunate," he said.

"Very."

"These two babies will be more than enough for me."

She heard in his words much more than what he'd spoken. He was acknowledging that this road had been long. Not the literal walk from the truck to the photographer, but the multi-year road they'd taken in order to have a family. He was telling her that when they got to the end of it, to the delivery of their twins, that he would be fully satisfied. No future children necessary.

With one sentence, her husband had raised the topic of family planning. Here, on a grassy slope, with three people and a stallion watching.

Thing was, if Bo had wanted to talk to her about something important while they'd been balancing on a high wire in hundred-mile-per-hour winds, she'd have stopped and listened.

She hoped that she'd been a loving influence in his life. She'd wanted to be. It was certainly true that she'd loved him as best she could. With every cell of her body, every hope, every corner of her soul, she'd loved Bo Porter. But when it came down to it, it seemed to her that he'd loved her even more. He'd been a cornerstone. He'd never complained, and he'd unfailingly believed in the best and most positive outcome.

Even so, infertility and the concerns of this pregnancy

had weathered him. She could see the evidence of it in the grooves beside his eyes, the faint lines across his forehead. She remembered thinking when she'd first met him that his face would have suited a Texas Ranger from the Old West. Masculine and no-nonsense. She still thought so.

"All these years," she said, working to overcome the sentimental tightening of her throat, "I've been asking God for a baby. Just one. But out of His generosity, He's sent us two. If—" She stopped herself from saying *if all goes well and the babies are healthy* because it would only upset him and force him to reassure her. "Our son and daughter will be more than enough for me, too. That's for sure."

Relief smoothed across his features.

And it *was* for sure. If God would only bring her and these babies through this in good health, she'd be light-years past content. She might never ask God for so much as a cracker for the rest of her life. "Now come on. I just got a little out of breath, that's all. Let's take this photo."

Together they walked the rest of the way and greeted the photographer and his assistant. Bo made small talk with them while Meg lowered onto the chair she'd be seated in for the picture. "Hi, Mike," she said to Silver Leaf's groom. "How's Silver Leaf today?"

"He's as happy as any horse can be, Mrs. Porter." The groom led Silver Leaf to her. Wind rustled through her stallion's snow-hued mane and tail. His dapple-grey body glistened with cleanliness. He'd put on weight since his running days, but the bulk suited him. It filled him out and only increased his stature.

Silver Leaf lowered his head to her like a king greeting a subject. She rested her hand on his silky nose. "Hello,

Silver Leaf." It had been too long since she'd had an up-close visit with her most famous and beloved horse.

Greetings, wee human, Silver Leaf seemed to say.

"You're as fabulous as always," she whispered.

He gave her a look that said, *I am indeed,* then took a step back, tossing his head.

"I'm looking forward to bringing the babies out to see Silver Leaf one day soon," she said to Mike.

He nodded, his face creasing with pleasure. "Won't that be something."

Silver Leaf lifted his chin even higher. *You may bring your offspring to pay homage to me when next I'm holding court and allowing plebeians to call,* his posture seemed to say. *Consult my secretary.*

Bo gave the horse a scratch under his cheeks. Then the photographer handed Silver Leaf's lead rope to Bo and positioned them all. Man. Wife. Horse. Silver Leaf, of course, was by far the best subject. He did exactly as asked, angling his neck loftily.

"One, two, three," the photographer said. "Smile."

And the camera clicked.

More than two days had passed since he'd seen Dru.

Gray was sitting on a barstool at his kitchen island at home, trying to read the news on his iPad but mostly watching the clock mounted on the wall as it counted down to the start of Dru's shift.

Big Mack sat three barstools down. Both of them were working on the buffet of snacks that had been waiting for them when Gray had returned from practice, thanks to Ash.

When he and Dru had arrived back at the Mustangs' facility from their trip to Mullins on Monday night, Weston had been waiting. Dru had been officially off duty, so she'd parted from him with a mocking salute, climbed on her motorcycle, and sped off. She hadn't left in any way that was different.

But Gray knew that things were different, and he'd been thinking about what had changed—driving himself crazy, actually, because he couldn't seem to think about anything else—all across Tuesday and Wednesday, her regular days off.

Days ago, he'd decided to back off his pursuit of Dru. It had been a struggle to follow through on that ever since, but he'd done his best. He'd behaved himself with her, even though his awareness had focused on her as if she were his doggone sun. It was pitiful. Uncontrollable, too. He'd tried.

When they'd left his mom's house, he'd had a knot in his stomach. His past wasn't pretty. Neither was his family. Neither was he. A lot of people looked at him and thought he was, but Dru had seen his reality. He'd been horrified by the thought that she was sitting beside him feeling sorry for him or disgusted by him.

Then she'd blindsided him by handing him something worth more than gold. *"It's not fair, what you've gone through. And it's not your fault. You should be proud of what you've accomplished and who you are. You have plenty of goodness in you."*

She didn't sugarcoat things. She spoke the truth. So he trusted that she'd meant every word. She knew him better than anyone had known him in a long time, and she'd . . . meant every word.

Tenderness and gratitude had wrenched through him. He'd put out his hand. And she'd taken it.

A few months ago, he'd have laughed at the idea that he could get mentally worked up over holding a girl's hand. What was he? Twelve? But the fact that *Dru Porter* had held his hand was a huge deal. Hard-earned. His heart—his bored, worn-out heart—had actually pounded over it. His brain had spun.

He thought that moment might have meant to her what it had meant to him. That she liked him. Not Corbin. Him.

She worked for him, so nothing more could come of it now. But he was willing to wait. And now that he knew she liked him—not Corbin—all his jealousy and doubt could calm. If he knew for sure that she liked him, then he could manage his feelings for her *and* give football what football needed. Things could settle.

All that could happen *if* she liked him. He was only guessing that she did. It was possible that she'd just held his hand out of normal human kindness. He didn't think so. But it was possible. Today, he aimed to find out where she stood.

His vision returned to the clock. He'd missed her. He was itching for her to arrive. So much so that he'd come home and changed into a white dress shirt that he'd worn a couple of time to clubs and one of his better pairs of jeans. Mack had given him a questioning look when he'd come downstairs. Gray had pretended not to notice.

Still five more minutes before two?

"Gray?" Ash's voice drifted down from upstairs. "I'm going to hang up your dry cleaning. Is that okay?"

"Fine."

"I have a wife," Big Mack grumbled. "But I sure could use a . . . What's Ashley's official title again?"

"Woman who gets everything done."

"Yeah. I sure could use one of them."

Gray quirked a brow teasingly. "Your wife doesn't get everything done?"

"No. That whole women's lib thing happened a while ago. You might have noticed?"

"What women's lib thing?" Gray asked dryly.

Mack threw back his head with one of his rumbling laughs. "My wife and I both have jobs, man. We split the housework and taking care of the kids and all. We're ti-red. I'd like to spend more time kicking back, you know? Resting it up. I could do that if we had an Ashley around the house."

"I recommend it." Gray scrolled through a few more articles. The next time he glanced at the clock, it showed two minutes past two. A thread of unease wove through him. Dru was never late. He set aside his iPad. Turning on his barstool, he frowned toward the front of his property as if he had the power to see through the walls.

His security unit buzzed.

Thank goodness. She was here. Mack went to the tech panel in Gray's office to check the video screens and let her through the gate.

Gray exited through the garage and waited on his driveway in the cold winter wind. Dru's familiar Kawasaki didn't appear. Instead, a silver truck approached.

Confusion churned inside him. Something was wrong.

Mack came to stand beside him.

"Where's Dru?" Gray asked tightly.

"I don't know. I expected to see her at the gate just

like always." He scratched the side of his neck. "The guy who's driving up is Rod Campbell, another of the agents that Dru and I work with at Sutton."

A man with graying hair and military posture climbed down from the truck and came forward.

Mack introduced them.

"Where's Dru?" Gray asked Rod, wasting no time with small talk.

"I'll be taking over Dru's shift, starting today."

"For how long?"

"Permanently."

The word hit Gray in the chest. "Why?"

"I don't know why," Rod answered calmly. "I just know that Dru met with Sutton, and one or both of them decided it would be better for her to step down."

"Better?" Gray scowled at Mack.

Mack's usual cheerful expression had disappeared. "I don't know anything about it, Gray."

Dru wasn't his agent anymore? Why? Because . . . of the trip to Mullins? The hand-holding? That had been so innocent! Or did this have to do with something else? Had Sutton removed her because he'd found fault with her job performance?

After what had happened in Mexico, Dru had been extremely determined to do a good job on his case. And she had. Of all his bodyguards, she was the best.

Gray looked between the two men, anger throbbing within his skull. Why hadn't Sutton notified him about this change? Rod was a complete stranger, but Rod had known about Dru's departure before Gray had known.

He refused to accept that Dru wasn't coming back.

"You okay, man?" Mack asked.

Gray returned to his kitchen and swept up his car keys. "Ash?"

She dashed down the staircase, her feet making no sound. "Yes?"

"I need you to cancel my afternoon appointments."

"One of them is an interview with a sports blogger."

"Ask if we can reschedule." He strode for his Denali.

Mack and Rod stood together in the garage, talking. Their conversation cut off when they saw him. "Where are you going?" Mack asked.

"To Dru's house."

"Let's think this through a little bit more," Mack suggested.

"No need to."

The new agent barely had time to rush around the Denali and lower himself into the passenger's seat before Gray reversed from his parking space. He needed answers, and he wanted those answers from Dru in person. What had happened with Sutton Security? And if he wasn't her client, then what was he to her now?

From the time she'd woken, a strange and lonely sadness had been pulling at Dru. It had intensified as the time of day when she usually left for work had approached, then passed. She'd taken up a spot on her sofa with Fi curled next to her. She'd clasped her literary tome in her hands like a shield and determined to read.

When two o'clock had come, she'd waited, full of selfish, foolish hope. She'd expected Gray to be upset when she didn't arrive for her shift. She'd daydreamed about him throwing a gratifyingly big fit. Telling Sutton that it was her or no one. Calling her immediately to demand an explanation. All these scenarios had been . . . charming . . . to imagine. They'd have meant that he cared.

Two o'clock had come and gone without even a text from him.

Now it was two-fifteen, and an infuriating mix of depression and confusion had her in knots.

Good grief, Dru! You're acting like such a . . . such a girl.

She'd been certain on Monday night that she needed to step down from her post as Gray's executive protection agent. She was still certain of that, despite that she'd spent every minute since her meeting with Sutton mourning the loss of her role in Gray's case. She'd valued her role. It had made her feel alive to return to the field again and to be responsible for Gray's safety. The puzzle of his stalker had captured her to such a degree that she'd worked on and researched the case even when off duty.

Also, her shot at Gray's protection detail had been her chance to prove herself. So stepping down from his detail had meant stepping down from her valued chance to prove herself, too.

When she'd met with Anthony Sutton about Gray, he hadn't chastised her. He relied too heavily on his agents' candor to chastise them for it. Even so, she knew it didn't reflect well on her that her last client had been killed and that she'd failed to maintain objectivity for the client who had come after.

Anthony had firmly and respectfully informed her that he'd be assigning another of his agents to her shift. Likely in an effort to diffuse a romance between her and Gray, he'd offered her a post protecting an executive who was about to depart on a month-long trip to London.

She'd turned down his offer. She preferred to ride a desk at the Dallas office because at least from there she'd be able to continue contributing to Gray's case.

Sutton had told her to take a few days off to clear her head, then to report for work at the office Friday— tomorrow—morning.

Suddenly, her primary reason for resisting Gray had been removed. The future seemed as wide open as the Texas sky, but also disturbingly uncertain.

Her concerns about Gray's disconnectedness from God remained. Something *was* the matter there, between him and God, exactly as she'd told him to his face the night shots had been fired into Urban Country. But was it enough to stop her from dating him—if he wanted to date her?

No. If he wanted to date her, those concerns weren't enough to stop her. It wasn't as if she was going to sleep with him. It wasn't as if dating him had to mean she'd be forced to compromise her own actions. Maybe she could even help bring Gray around? Maybe Gray's mistakes were behind him?

Now that she knew about his childhood, she couldn't help but want to give him the benefit of the doubt because of what he'd been through. Considering the abuse he'd taken, he was a shining example of success. Very dateable.

It sounded like rationalizing. Even to her.

Closing her eyes, Dru groaned and laid her head against the sofa's top. She wasn't used to wanting someone as much as she wanted Gray. The sensation didn't coexist well with her independent personality. Nor her ruthless self-honesty. Caring about Gray this much was humbling.

It was instructive to remember that this soul-searching might be moot anyway. Gray had told her that he'd decided to back off pursuing a romance between them. He'd been following through on that since, and she didn't know whether the hand-holding in the car the other night or the removal of the client/agent dynamic between them would change his stance or not. He might not want to date her.

Irritated with herself, she stormed from the sofa and strode into the kitchen. She'd had a long, full life before Gray Fowler!

One would think that time to herself would come as a Godsend. Problem was, she liked action, activity, work. Filling even two days a week with leisure was stretching it for her. She'd slept late this morning, gone on an extra-long run with Fi, hung out with Augustine, cleaned her house, and done as many errands as she could think to do.

From the freezer, she lifted the tub of frozen chocolate chip cookie dough she'd bought from Addie for a school fundraiser. She set about scooping dough onto a cookie sheet. She was just straightening up after sliding the cookies into the oven and flicking on the timer when motion beyond the over-sink window drew her attention.

Gray's Denali was coming up her drive. He was far away yet, but she could make out his car clearly.

He's coming up the drive!

Her disappearance from his detail *had* mattered to him. That he'd driven here was a very promising sign. It suggested that something more might be possible. Elation sent eddies of goosebumps over her skin.

She dashed upstairs to her bathroom. *This is stupid, Dru. You don't act like this over men*, she told herself even as she brushed her hair and then, very quickly, her teeth. After her shower earlier, she'd put on a black, boat-neck shirt and a pair of snug faded jeans she'd had for years. The outfit would have to do.

As she hurried downstairs, he bellowed her name from outside her front door. He hadn't bothered to knock. He was just standing on her porch, hollering.

She threw open her door and was greeted by six feet, four inches of rock-hard, angry athlete.

Longing for him broke over her, through her, like a wave crashing. Oh boy. She had it for him bad. Her feelings were drowning her caution.

She stepped past Gray to address Rod, who stood several feet from the cabin, looking unsure. "You're certain you weren't followed?" she called.

"Certain," Rod assured her.

"Go ahead and check the perimeter," Dru said. "He's safe with me."

"Sure thing, Dru."

Gray had moved inside her cabin. He waited for her in the foyer.

She walked purposefully toward him, kicking the door closed as she passed it. At the same time, he walked toward her, the tension between them snapping, his eyebrows drawn down.

Her body met the unstoppable force of his, and she kissed him. No sweet words. No tentativeness. No slow caresses. Just a millisecond of difference between the two of them standing feet apart and the two of them kissing in complete and total and hungry accord.

She rose onto her tiptoes and locked her arms behind his neck. He took her face in his hands. The sensations of their kiss poured into her, an overload. Heat. The feel of his lips on hers. The crisp freshness of his soap. The heated swirl of desire in her lower abdomen, insistent.

She was kissing Gray. For so long, she hadn't even allowed herself to entertain the idea of kissing him. She didn't know if this was a good idea. She only knew that it felt like a glorious storm—lightning and soft rain and sweet wind—caught in a bottle.

She leaned back to catch her breath and looked into his intense sea-glass green eyes.

"It's about time." He spoke the words gravely, as if making a promise to her. He took a few blistering seconds to study her before his mouth curved with lazy challenge. "What else you got, Dru? Surely that kiss wasn't all? It only lasted thirty seconds."

"Bull. It had to have lasted at least five minutes."

"It just seemed like that to you because you're out of practice."

"Wrong." She decided to steer him to the wall next to the opening that led to the kitchen. Planting her palms on his broad chest, she exerted pressure. He'd have something to lean against there, and they could kiss more—

He chuckled wickedly. He didn't—wouldn't budge.

With his legendary speed, he reached for her waist. She stepped back and used a simple karate block to knock his hand away. He wasn't the only one who was fast.

Grinning, he changed tactics, extending a hand at a leisurely pace toward her temple, as if intending to sweep a piece of hair to the side. She raised her palm with equal slowness and used it to stop his fingers. In the next instant, he bent and came toward her and upward simultaneously, sweeping her against him and off her feet with one arm. "Kiss me?" he asked.

She found herself above him, her profile tilted down an inch from his. She kissed him, and he carefully lowered her until her feet balanced on the tops of his shoes.

She reached for his free hand, interlacing her fingers with his. The moment she had a good grip, she darted to the side and behind him, efficiently bending his arm up behind his back.

"Ouch," he said mildly.

She wasn't hurting him, of course. She had no plan to strain any part of his million-dollar body. She drew him to the wall where she'd originally tried to push him and scooted around in front of him. "There," she said, pleased to have emerged victorious.

He stood obediently, shoulder blades against the smooth plane of the wall, humor on his face.

"Quite docile," she remarked. "No more tricks?"

He jabbed a hand toward her, and she reacted instantly, springing into her karate stance and blocking.

He laughed. He'd only jabbed the hand toward her for the pleasure of seeing her reaction, she realized. He hadn't intended to grab her.

Gray wrapped his hand around the wrist of the arm she'd extended and tugged gently, tipping her against the length of his muscled frame. "No more tricks," he whispered, and then they were kissing again.

Kissing him, touching him, feeling the pounding of her heart and the answering pounding of his beneath her hand sent joy flowing through her. The tough-girl loner had fallen for him.

A timer sounded from her kitchen. Dru jerked back. "Cookies."

Before he could respond, a knock sounded at the door. "I'll get the cookies," Gray offered.

"I'll get the door." Rod stood on the threshold. With obvious curiosity, he looked from her to where Gray was moving around in the kitchen.

"Everything all right?" Dru asked, trying to appear cool and competent. She probably looked like she'd just been kissed. Her lips felt slightly puffy, her skin feverish. Her hair was probably laughably messy.

"Everything's good," Rod answered. "I'll be alternating surveillance from the Denali and counter-surveillance from a post to the rear of the house in the woods."

"Sounds great."

Before Rod had so much as stepped off the front porch to go about his duties, Gray started jerking all the downstairs curtains closed. "Prying eyes," he said.

Her kitchen smelled strongly of chocolate chip cookie. She lit a flame under her kettle, pulled down two mugs, and emptied hot chocolate packets into each. Gray took up a position a few feet away, leaning his hip against the lip of the counter. He resembled a cat that had just eaten a canary.

"Yes?" she prompted.

"You like me."

"I like you some."

"You like me enough to kiss me."

"True." She went about moving some of the cookies onto plates and setting out napkins. "You like me enough to kiss me, too."

"True," he agreed.

All her wonderings about whether or not he liked her and how he might react to the news that she was no longer his agent had been emphatically answered by his actions. *Gray liked her.*

"You like me better than Corbin," he clarified.

"I can always count on your competitive streak."

"Admit that you like me better."

"Mmm . . ." She pushed her lips to the side. "I might like him as a person more. But for some reason, I'm more interested in kissing you."

He nodded smugly. She rolled her eyes.

The kettle began to whistle. She poured steaming water into their mugs and stirred them both until the mini-marshmallows bobbed on top of pale brown hot chocolate swirled with white.

"Would you mind spiking mine with whiskey?" Gray asked.

She chuckled. "I poured it out after you overindulged the last time." They settled into seats at her kitchen table. "So tell me. To what do I owe the pleasure of this visit today, Gray?" She took a bite of warm, gooey cookie.

"I waited all Tuesday and Wednesday for you to come back to work today. At two, Rod showed up instead." He hadn't touched his food yet. He rested his forearms on the table. "You're not . . . replaceable, Dru."

Pleasure sunbursted within her. "Rod's male. He fits the stereotype of the bodyguard you wanted right from the start. With him, you won't run the risk of having your ego insulted."

"You've won me over," he said. "Rod told me that you met with your boss. What happened?"

She gave a subtle shrug. Ate more cookie. "After the trip to Mullins, I didn't feel that I could remain unbiased toward you. I'd become biased and I knew it, so I told

Anthony Sutton where I stood. He took me off your detail immediately. It was the right thing for me to do, to tell Anthony. I'm mad, though, that I haven't found your stalker. I wanted to be the one to get him. Plus, I don't like having to give my shift to Rod." She took a sip of cocoa. Sweet and silky, it curled its way into her stomach.

He bit into his cookie, chewed, then popped in the rest.

"I'll do what I can from Sutton's headquarters to hunt down your stalker. I'm planning to dig through everything I can on Dennis and Alex Wright again. If I can turn up something new, then that might give us a clue as to Dennis's whereabouts."

"Okay." He smiled. His face was better to her than "classically handsome" could be. His was the face of a man, no trace of youth clinging to it. Now that she'd experienced the bliss of being in his arms, she was slightly embarrassed to admit how much she wanted more of *that* again.

"I want to date you," he said. "Only you. And I want you to date me and only me."

She laughed. "We've kissed three times. It's too early to negotiate an exclusivity clause."

"I feel like I've been dating you for weeks already. I won't date anyone else if you won't." Gray appeared extraordinarily comfortable with the change their relationship had just undergone. Of course, she reminded herself, he was a pro at this. He'd navigated the beginnings, middles, and endings of relationships many times before. "Deal?" he asked.

"It's too soon to have a define-the-relationship conversation. Much too soon."

"Fine." He stood and held out a hand for her. "Is it too soon to slow dance with me?"

She took his hand, and he drew her against him. They slow danced in her kitchen without music. Smiling, she laid her cheek against his chest and memorized the feel of her hand in his, his other arm holding her to him. "Spend the rest of the day with me?" he asked.

"What about your schedule?"

"I had Ash cancel everything."

He had? "We could do some shooting. It would be fun to humiliate you with my superiority."

"I'd like to see you try. Then can I take you to dinner?"

"Take me and Rod to dinner, you mean?"

"Whatever."

"Sure."

They swayed some more, then he dipped her backward. Obligingly, she kicked out a foot. He brought her up, into a twirl, and then safely back against his chest. He'd been raised in a small town in Texas, which meant he had country dance skills. He didn't need music to have rhythm.

He's smooth, Dru. Her inner warning bells began to clang. You can't take him—this—too seriously. *"Who said you need to take me seriously, anyway?"* Gray had once asked her. *"You don't have to be serious about me to go out on a date or two."* He'd had numerous not-serious relationships. Which might define his desires for this relationship with her. Easy come, easy go.

But even as she issued advice to herself, she slipped a little more under his spell.

CHAPTER NINETEEN

Ordinarily when Gray's alarm clock sounded to wake him for practice, he responded with a growl. His first conscious thought was usually for his pain and injuries. His second was for the responsibilities that lay before him for the day, which, in turn, filled him with duty and determination.

But this morning, the morning after Dru had stopped being his bodyguard and started being his girlfriend, he reacted to his alarm clock with none of that.

Instead, a feeling of lightness stole over him.

He hit the snooze button, then lay back on his California king in his huge master bedroom, eyes closed, smiling as memories of Dru from the day before came back to him, one by one. She had literally *kicked* the front door of her cabin closed with a bang. Then she'd walked straight up to him and kissed him. It had been pure Dru. Direct and to the point.

No other kiss of his life, not even the first kisses he'd had back in junior high, had affected him as powerfully.

He'd been rocked by it, stupidly overcome. Him. The poor kid, the veteran football player. It wasn't like he was new at kissing. Or naïve. He considered himself to have been aged beyond his years by the life he'd led. There wasn't much he didn't have or hadn't tried.

He opened his eyes and ran a hand through his hair, studying the heavy metal lines of his chandelier.

Dru wasn't fun-loving or agreeable. He'd dated women even more beautiful than she was. But he'd never been this . . . *hooked* on anyone before. It turned out that he liked feisty and confident better than fun-loving and agreeable. Dru's personality made her prettier to him than anyone else's outward beauty could make them.

He and Dru, they just clicked. They got along. Well, sometimes they argued. But either way, it was real, genuine. They understood each other.

His alarm clock buzzed again. He punched it off, climbed from bed, then walked to the windows and opened the blinds. Dim morning light and mist covered his pool and backyard like a blanket.

He and Dru definitely clicked. So much so that he needed to watch himself. He was happy as a clam at high tide—to use one of the sayings he'd grown up hearing—to have her as his girlfriend. But that didn't mean he wanted to wake up weeks or months from now and find himself madly in love with her.

Love. Just the word gave him a cold chill.

The muscles running from his neck into his shoulders tensed. He didn't want any part of—

He cut off the line of thought by drawing in a breath, then slowly blowing it out. There was no reason why he and Dru couldn't continue liking each other, dating, laughing, talking, hanging out. It didn't have to end with him falling in love with her.

Their dating relationship had just started yesterday. He was getting way ahead of himself with his worry.

An hour later, Gray spotted Corbin's Escalade on the freeway. They were both on their way to practice. Ordinarily, Gray would pull up next to his friend, wait for him to look over and see him, then do his best to gun it and leave Corbin in the dust.

This morning, he had a bet to collect on, so he settled in behind Corbin and tailed him the rest of the way to the facility. Smoothly, he slid into the parking spot next to the quarterback's.

"She kissed you, didn't she?" Corbin asked the second he exited his car. "That's why you've been following me with that stupid smile on your face."

"That's why. How's this smile, Corbin? Big enough?"

Corbin shook his head, doing a good job of pretending disgust. "You jerk!" They set off side-by-side across the parking lot. "I put in a lot of effort with Dru. She must have a screw loose. That's the only reason why she'd have picked you over me."

"No screw loose there. You and I both know she's stone-cold sane. What this proves is very simple. The ladies love me better."

"One particular lady loves you better. And only for the moment." They entered the building and took the hallway leading to their locker room. "I've lost the bet, but it's possible that at some point down the road I'll be able to convince her to give me another try."

"Actually, I'd appreciate it if you'd back off."

"Back off?"

"I like her," Gray said simply.

Corbin came to a stop. Two defensive backs greeted them as they walked past.

"You *like her* like her?" Corbin asked.

Gray understood his friend's surprise. He'd never admitted to feeling even this much for any woman in the past. "I like her."

"I like her, too, Gray."

"No. I *really* like her." He held Corbin's gaze.

"Well, doggone."

"Stranger things have happened."

"Like what?"

"You being named Super Bowl MVP."

Corbin released a bark of laughter. They started into motion again. "Seeing as how this bet of ours ended so well for you, Gray, I'm guessing you're not going to want my flat screen. Revengeress is reward enough."

"Revengeress is reward enough. Definitely. Which is why it'll be pretty amazing to have your TV, too." He clapped Corbin on the shoulder as they entered the locker room. "Have it delivered anytime this week." Gray parted from his friend and made his way toward his locker.

He didn't care about the TV. But he planned to enjoy rubbing Corbin's nose in his defeat. Bragging rights were ninety percent of the fun of winning a bet.

Later that afternoon, Dru sat at her desk at Sutton, reading the scanned image of the letter from Gray's stalker that had arrived today. She typed notes into a document she had open on her computer, determined to uncover something that might lead her, like Hansel and Gretel's bread crumbs, to Dennis Wright.

Her phone chimed to signal an incoming text. From Gray. A thrill shimmered through her—no less of a thrill than a high school girl might feel when the boy she had a crush on smiled at her.

What was with these out-of-proportion reactions to him? This was Gray's fifth text message of the day. Was she blushing? She was definitely smiling.

Will you come over and hang out at my house after work? he asked.

No.

Please?

Nope. She saw no reason to let *him* know about the blushing and the smiling. Or to make things easy for him.

Ashley's roasting chicken and vegetables, he texted.

Suddenly I'm more interested.

And I'll be here to hang out with.

Huh.

And I'll be here to kiss. You know. Should you want to.

I might swing by, she typed. *Some of us have work to do, you know.*

See you at six.

"Anything else you need before I go?" Ash asked Gray that evening.

"I don't think so." He was sitting in his den next to the kitchen, waiting for Dru to arrive.

Ash paused at the mouth of the short mudroom that

led to the garage and began putting on her winter clothing. Jacket, scarf, gloves, and a knit cap.

"Not sure why you're dressing for Alaska, Ash. It's
only in the forties out there."

"You're warm-natured, but I'm always freezing.
Haven't you noticed that I've had on a sweater over my
outfit every day this week?"

"No." He viewed Ash as a cross between an employee,
a younger sister, and a friend who was too innocent for
her own good. Ask him about Dru and he could tell you
about her down to the tiniest detail. He could tell you,
for example, about the pattern marked into the top of
the silver ring she sometimes wore. Ask him about Ash
and it was like he had amnesia.

A buzz sounded from the security system.

"Dru's here," Rod called from the front office.

Finally. He went to wait for her on his driveway.

She parked her Kawasaki and stalked toward him.
When she tugged free her helmet, she revealed eyes sparkling with irritation. Planting her palms against his bi-
ceps she guided him backward until they were both deep
inside the covering of the garage.

His pulse kicked with desire. "Are you planning on
attacking me the way you did yesterday at your cabin?"
he asked hopefully.

"No. And I didn't attack you."

"If you're not going to attack me, then why'd you
push me in here?"

"Because I'd prefer that you not stand outside under
the lights where any idiot with a sniper scope can take
you out."

"Hello to you, too. Welcome."

After a moment, she gave a grudging smile. "Hello."

"You're not my bodyguard anymore," he reminded her. "It's not your job to worry about idiots with sniper scopes."

"Just the same," she removed her hands from his arms, "I'd rather not see you get shot in front of me this evening. It might spoil my appetite for dinner." Punching the button to close the garage as she passed, she led him into his kitchen as if she were the one who owned the place.

Ash and Dru exchanged greetings while Gray went to the oven and pulled out the chicken. It was golden brown and crispy-looking. Carrots, onions, and potatoes surrounded its base, and the whole thing smelled like rosemary and pepper. He was starving.

"Does the dish look okay?" Ash asked.

"You're kidding, right?" Dru said to her.

Ash shook her head, which she'd covered in a snow hat.

"Your dish looks like something that should be on the cover of a cooking magazine," Dru stated. "Just own the fact that it's awesome. Seriously. Stick your chin up like this." Dru demonstrated.

Ash imitated.

"Shoulders back. Now try to look ultra cocky and superior."

Ash broke into a self-conscious giggle.

"Your food is the reason I came tonight," Dru told Ash.

"Your visit had nothing to do with me?" Gray asked.

"Nothing." Ash might not be able to pull off ultra cocky and superior, but Dru had it down.

"Then I'm glad I have Ash as a secret weapon." He

caught and held Dru's eye contact. Their chemistry grew heavy.

Ash cleared her throat. When neither of them moved, she cleared it again. "Um . . . so, you guys are really good at pretending to be a couple."

"We're not pretending to be a couple anymore," Gray said. "Now we *are* a couple."

Ash spent a moment looking back and forth between them. "Hmm?"

"When I started work as Gray's protection agent, I was pretending to be his girlfriend," Dru explained. "Now that I'm no longer his agent, I've decided to give dating him a try."

"Oh?"

"He kept hounding me about going out with him," Dru continued, "until I finally told him I'd date him just to get him off my back. It's not serious between us. I give this relationship two months, tops."

Gray grinned. He could do better than two months. It was never wise to give an athlete a challenge.

"Well, I'm happy for you guys. Very!" Ash gave a little clap with her gloves. "I wish you two the best. You're both so sweet."

Sweet? Neither he nor Dru was sweet.

Ash smiled a big smile that didn't look all that genuine. "Does this mean that you are a preschool teacher, after all?"

Gray laughed.

Dru put her hands on her hips. "I was not, am not, and will never be a preschool teacher, Ashley." She spoke calmly. Had it been anyone else, Dru would have zinged a comeback. But she didn't treat Ash that way. It would have been unfair. Like pitting a heavyweight against a two-year-old.

"You should consider it, Dru. You'd be good at it."

She'd be terrible.

"I'd be terrible," Dru said.

"Well, I think you'd be wonderful." Dimples showed in Ash's cheeks. "'Kay. See you all later. Have a nice evening."

"See ya," Gray called. Ash let herself out.

"Who raised Ashley?" Dru asked. "I'm beginning to think it was happy, singing animals in a forest some-where."

"Yeah. Pretty much."

"I felt bad for her when you told her that we're a real couple."

"Since when do you feel bad for people?"

"Me?" Her face filled with fake confusion. "I'm full of sensitivity."

He snorted.

"She looked at you for a long moment just now, before walking out," Dru said.

"What long moment?"

"The long moment when you weren't paying attention and she was staring at you with tragic, doomed longing."

"Ash has never said one thing about having tragic, doomed longing for me."

"That's why it's tragic and doomed. I recommend that you marry her. I mean, is this bread *homemade*?" Dru peered at the bread Ash had set out as if it was the Mona Lisa.

"It's homemade."

"Ashley's a dinosaur. Maybe the last of her kind." She

pulled off a bite of bread and sampled it. "I'm surprised that you were so quick to announce us as a couple."

"Why hide it?"

"Have you said anything about it to Corbin?"

"Of course I have. He has tragic, doomed longing for *you*, Dru."

"He wouldn't be the first."

Gray had the uneasy sense that he should tell her about his bet with Corbin. Dru valued honesty. A lot.

On the other hand, the fact that they'd bet on kissing her would probably make her mad. She wouldn't be happy to learn that she hadn't been pursued at the same time by him and Corbin purely because they'd liked her. He and Dru had just managed to break down the walls that had kept them from dating. He didn't want to rock the boat tonight.

They filled their plates with chicken and vegetables, spinach salad, and thick slices of sourdough bread. After some argument over where they should eat, Dru convinced him to take their meal into the front living room because she wanted to sit by his Christmas tree. They set their plates on the small rectangular table positioned in front of a group of windows. Rod had shut the blinds of those windows at nightfall. The table already had two chairs at either end, so all Gray had to do was move aside the antique checker set that rested on top.

They talked about their day while they ate. His huge fir tree stood beside them, and the goofy Christmas music Ash liked hummed through the sound system.

Several times, Dru glanced over at the tree to admire it. Each time she did, he stopped eating and stared at her. Ash or the decorators Ash had hired had wrapped the branches of the tree in white lights. The illumination from the tree lit Dru's features the way a candle might. Her straight nose. Thick, dark eyelashes. Graceful cheekbones. Small, firm chin.

It was no longer his stomach that was starving. It was all of him. He needed Sutton Security to find his stalker because he didn't want bodyguards under his feet when he was trying to focus on Dru. Even now, in his own house, Rod, who was currently in Gray's office, could walk in on them at any minute.

More than that, though, he wanted her safe from danger. The stalker had threatened Dru specifically when he'd thought she was Gray's girlfriend, and again when he'd determined she was his bodyguard. Until yesterday, she'd been on duty whenever Gray had spent time with her. She'd always been armed and defensive and prepared for an assault.

But she wasn't armed any longer. He was still getting used to the sight of her without one of the jackets she'd always worn before. Tonight she had on a tank top with thin straps under a slightly see-through, loose gray blouse that she'd opened at the neck and rolled up at the sleeves.

She was quick and tough and she could fend for herself, but she also seemed more vulnerable to him than she had before.

Fear spidered across his heart, cold and dark. Full of warning.

Until now, she'd shouldered the burden that came with one person's duty to protect another. Now, he felt that burden shifting to him. "When you leave here tonight, make sure you're not followed," he said. "The guy who's after me wants you, too."

She turned her face from the tree to him. "Big football player?"

"Yes?"

"You don't have to worry about me. I can take care of myself."

Her words didn't comfort him. She lived in a remote, unprotected cabin in the woods.

After they'd finished their meal, he talked her into playing Xbox against him, because his upstairs media room was closed off and private. He put in his favorite racing game and hauled out steering wheel controllers for them both.

"If I win, then we kiss," he stated.

"You have no desire to kiss me, it appears." She sent him a challenging glance out of the corner of her eye.

"How wrong you are. I'm a bad loser."

"So am I."

"I want to win, Dru. And I want to kiss you. Bad."

"Then grab the steering wheel, Ricky Bobby." She floored the gas pedal on her virtual car and zoomed off the starting line. He'd been too busy looking at her to realize that the starter had been counting down.

To his incredible frustration, she slipped by him at the last possible second to win. She'd beaten him. He was awesome at this game. And she'd beaten him.

The grin she sent him held pure triumph. It said, *Never underestimate me, you donkey* more clearly than words.

"Again," he growled.

The next time, he won. The instant his car crossed the finish line, he shoved aside his steering wheel so hard it fell to the side. He moved onto the floor that separated their positions. From his knees, he grasped her wrist and pulled her onto the floor with him. She laughed and straightened to face him. They were both on their knees, just inches apart, him still twice as wide and much taller than she was. "I thought you said you were a bad loser." He intertwined the fingers of both his hands with hers. She did not look angry. Her face had softened, her lips had parted slightly.

His heart drummed with desire.

"Only when I get beaten fair and square," she said. "I let you win."

"Liar." His breath began to come unevenly. What was happening to him? Just having her this close to him was pulling him apart piece by piece.

Dru's attention traveled down his face, taking in every detail. He wasn't handsome. With women, he'd always counted more on his career than on his looks. Without football, he didn't have much game.

"There's only one fair way to settle this," she said.

"Mmm?"

"We're going to have to have a lot more races tonight. A lot more." Teasing him, she moved away as if to return to her seat.

"No way." He brought her back. "First I want my kiss." He slipped his big hands carefully behind her neck, taking a lot of time with it, feeling the silk of her hair whispering against his skin as he gently supported the back of her head. A shiver went through his body.

She smiled slightly at him. Then their lips met and all thoughts fell away.

CHAPTER TWENTY

The next day, Gray checked into the team's Dallas hotel. The day after that, the Mustangs played the Dolphins at the Mustangs' stadium. Gray had invited Dru to attend the game. As had become her habit, she'd declined and opted instead to watch the game on TV in private where she could stress, gasp, and literally live out the term nail-biter in private. The Mustangs won, thanks to a last-second field goal.

Gray called her after the game. "Well?" he asked.

"That was a little too close for comfort," Dru replied.

He chuckled. "You must not have gotten the memo. You're supposed to be very, very complimentary to me after games."

"If I ever receive that memo, I'll spit on it."

"Have dinner with me."

She wanted to see him. She wanted to have dinner with him. But this thing between them was stirring up emotions and responses within her that were . . . scary strong. "Some other time. Christmas is just six days away, and I've got a bunch of stuff to do." *A bunch of thinking about you and taking deep breaths, mostly.*

"When can I see you, then?"

"Wednesday night?"

They texted often and talked over the phone across the next few days. Dru stayed busy at work and, in the evenings, with her family. Gray stayed busy at practice and, in the evenings, with his closest friends on the team: Corbin, Duayne, and Rashid.

What're you hungry for? he asked via text message Wednesday afternoon.

Italian?

I'll get us a table at Morelli's at seven. You're going to show, right? He'd been ribbing her for making him wait a few days to see her again.

Even if I don't show, Dru answered, *you won't be alone. You'll have Rod.*

Rod can sit where he wants. I'm getting a table for you and me and don't even think about leaving me there alone looking like an idiot.

What an enticing thought! Don't give me such good ideas. . . .

You better show, he texted. *I miss you.*

Dru closed her eyes after reading the words. I miss you. One sentence, but one sentence so piquant that it elicited swirls of delight. One sentence so powerful that it frightened her. He'd missed her even though he'd had plenty of activities and people to fill his time.

She'd wisely stepped back from Gray for a few days.

But she wasn't sure whether she'd succeeded at either cooling down or letting her head catch up.

Dru showed at Morelli's promptly at seven.

She and Gray ate antipasto followed by the most delicious baked lasagna Dru had ever tasted in her life.

It wasn't terrible to be taken on a date by someone who appreciated good food, who ordered things off the menu she wouldn't have because they were too expensive, who could cause her skin to heat just by meeting her eyes.

Rod sat at a table three over from theirs. He was keenly observant and, apparently, a fan of linguine.

Gray's admirers interrupted them a handful of times. Twice, Dru obligingly took photos of Gray with women who looked like they were hovering on the edge of excitement-induced hyperventilation.

After their meal, Dru and Gray waited just inside the restaurant's doors while Rod went to get the Denali.

Dru had seen Gray wince when he'd risen from the table, and she could read strain on his face. "What's hurting?" she asked.

"My back."

"Lower back or upper?"

"Lower."

Dru subscribed to the tough-love school much more than the coddling-love school. But she had a feeling Gray dealt with pain much more often than he let on. He hadn't said anything about his back during their long dinner, and she didn't know whether to chock up his silence to dumb machismo or admirable toughness or simple survival.

Simple survival, probably. Pain was part of his job description. Since she'd met him, she'd watched him move through it, go on about life despite it. She placed her hand on his lower spine. Thick slabs of muscle arched away from the vertebrae. "Here?"

"Just to the left of there."

Using her knuckles, she kneaded the area.

He glanced over his shoulder at her, his green eyes glinting with amusement and softness. The softness, she tried to steel herself against. The amusement might have been directed at her or at himself. She hoped the latter, seeing as how he was the one with the career that involved getting body-slammed on a weekly basis.

Rod pulled the Denali to a stop at the curb.

"Hold on a second." Dru exited the building before Gray had a chance to reach for the door. Some habits were hard to break. She didn't want him out in the open between the restaurant and the SUV until she'd had a chance to scan the street in both directions.

Morelli's occupied space at Mockingbird Station, a modern mini-community made up of a few streets of shops and restaurants on the bottom level and several stories of apartments and lofts above. At nine-thirty on a Wednesday night three days before Christmas, just a smattering of people ambled along the sidewalk. The surroundings had taken on a work-night-time-to-wind-down feel.

She looked toward Mockingbird Lane. Saw nothing out of place. Then she looked toward the distant steps leading to the movie theater that anchored the development's north end. Her gaze crossed over a blue vehicle slotted into a long row full of parked cars.

She moved her vision back to the blue car and squinted. Why had this particular car tripped her radar? This car looked like a . . .

Comprehension flared like a match lighting. This car looked like an older model Camaro. Dennis Wright drove an older-model blue Camaro. There were thousands of Camaros on the road, and from this distance she couldn't tell if the one she'd spotted was the right year. Nonetheless, the hair at the back of her neck lifted.

She opened the passenger's side of the Denali. "I may have spotted Dennis Wright's vehicle," she told Rod. "Gray's inside the restaurant. I'd like for you to get him as far away from here as possible."

He nodded, and Dru set off in the direction of the Camaro, using her senses to scour her surroundings for details.

The high-end clothing shop next to Morelli's lay dark, except for the Christmas lights swagged along its exterior. College girls were ordering dessert at the counter of the next establishment, a gelato store. After that came a coffee shop. Just as she passed, a man flipped over the sign on the door so that it read *Closed* and turned away. Dru continued past . . . paused. A few people remained within the coffee shop. Its mellow lights glowed. She located the store hours, marked on a pane of glass next to the entry. *Daily: 6:00 A.M. to 10:00 P.M.*

It wasn't yet ten. Whoever had flipped over the sign had likely not been an employee.

Could that have been Dennis? She hadn't seen the man's face, but he'd had the right sort of build. It was possible that he'd followed them to Morelli's and been watching and waiting within the coffee shop for their departure. If so, he'd likely recognized her and turned over the sign to dissuade her from coming in and finding him inside.

She entered the shop, which smelled of coffee grounds and leather chairs. None of the patrons were Dennis. She'd spent hours poring over photographs. She'd know his face when she saw it.

The door at the end of the hall that led to the bathrooms made a clicking sound as it closed. No one remained in the hall. If it had been Dennis who'd turned over the sign as she'd walked by, he'd just left.

She needed to get him—now. To her knowledge, she'd never before been this close to him and might never be again.

She rushed past the bathrooms and through the exit door, which spilled her into a long, wide industrial corridor. Empty. Windows and glass doors issuing into a parking garage lined one side of the corridor. Doors to the retail establishments ran along the other side, as well as banks of mailboxes and stairwells that likely led to the apartments above. Several yards away, a woman disappeared out of sight up a set of stairs. The dimly lit garage beyond the hallway lay motionless. She couldn't see Dennis. Couldn't hear him.

Scowling with frustration, she began moving down the corridor in the direction of where he'd parked the Camaro. No matter what, she had to reach his car before he did. Her feet moved swiftly over concrete floor. Her ears strained.

Where are you?

She hadn't forgotten Dennis's history. The loss of his only child. Or the fact that Gray didn't want Dennis to endure more hardship than he had already. Nor had she forgotten the venom that filled the letters Gray had received, the shots that had been fired into Urban Country, or the relentless way that Gray had been pursued.

Her right hand tingled with the urge to grip her pistol. Her fingers curled inward, then flexed. She hadn't been on the job tonight, so she didn't have her pistol with her.

From far behind her, a door crashed open. She spun in time to see Gray barrel through the coffee shop's exit and come to a stop in the corridor, Rod on his heels. Gray stood with his feet apart in a fighting stance. Color stained his cheeks. He looked wild-eyed and furious.

Her heart plunged. She motioned angrily with both arms for them to retreat, because if she called out she'd give away her position to Dennis if he was nearby. What was Rod thinking? She'd wanted Gray far away from here, safe.

"Dru!" Gray yelled, starting toward her. "What are you doing? You're not my bodyguard. Come back—"

A man burst from a door located between Dru and Gray. He turned immediately toward Gray, never giving Dru a view of his face. The body, though. The body was right, as was his general age. For a split second, both the man and Gray stilled as their eyes met.

"Dennis," Gray said, calm and authoritative.

At that one word—the only confirmation she needed—adrenaline kicked through Dru and she broke into a run.

Dennis, too, started into motion toward Gray.

Rod shouldered in front of Gray and pulled free a weapon. "Stop," he demanded.

Dennis didn't stop.

"No!" Gray pushed Rod's gun arm down.

Dennis moved fast, and Dru had to exert herself to catch him. When she did, she gripped the shoulder of his flannel shirt and used all her might to pull his upper body around and toward her.

Dennis spun, one hand extended and swinging toward her face. Dru lunged out of the way.

Finally, she was confronted with him. Dennis. Unmistakably him, despite that his features were twisted by grief and rage. His ruddy skin had mottled red.

He rolled a hand into a fist and threw a punch at her. Again, she feinted out of reach. Dimly, she was aware of the sound of Gray and Rod running toward them—but they were still a good distance away. Dru went on the attack, striking at Dennis's stomach with a side kick. She connected. Dennis grunted and stumbled back but only seemed goaded by it as he returned, both hands extended to push her into the wall. She threw her momentum forward, blocking his hands to the sides by hitting the insides of both his wrists, then burying a punch into his midsection. He was huge and heavy. The blow she'd landed, while true, failed to slow his forward progress. He continued into her, taking them both down. Pain crashed through Dru as she hit the ground. She lay on the floor, partially trapped beneath Dennis's bulk, trying to suck in air.

He reared over her, pressing a meaty palm into her sternum to trap her against the floor. Dru countered by driving the heel of her hand into his throat. He howled, his hold on her lessening—

He was suddenly jerked back and away. Off of her.

Gray, with his great strength, had grabbed ahold

of Dennis from behind and yanked him to his feet. As she watched, Gray moved into position behind Dennis, locking one arm around Dennis's neck. Dennis fought against him, fueled by desperate heartbreak. The older man had been able to use his brute, bullish size against Dru, but it was no match for Gray, who was younger than Dennis, fitter, stronger, bigger. And irate. She'd seen Gray's face harden with concentration numerous times during games. But this was different. This was icy, terrifying anger.

Wheezing for breath, Dru braced an arm under her and pushed herself to sitting.

Dennis thrashed and attempted to ram his elbows back into Gray's torso. Gray's hold on him didn't budge.

Dru got herself into a kneeling position. She was unsteady, still trying to shake off the effects of the jolt she'd taken when Dennis's body had driven her into the concrete.

Rod moved near Dennis's back, a plastic restraint jutting from between his teeth. After a brief struggle, Rod fastened the restraint around Dennis's joined wrists. "I've got him."

Gray let go, pushing Dennis away from him with a huff of disgust. Rod went into motion, using a move that leveraged Dennis's own bodyweight to bring Dennis into a sitting position on the floor. Rod clamped a hand on his shoulder and exerted downward force to keep him there.

Gray reached for Dru, carefully bringing her the rest of the way to her feet. His face had been a ruthless mask a moment ago, but now it looked shaken. "Are you all right?"

"Yes."

He pulled her against him in a bear hug. "Even your head?" His hand covered the spot where she'd knocked it. He rubbed gently.

"Even my head." She could hear Rod on the phone with the police, explaining what had occurred and giving the details of their location.

"Is this hug meant to reassure me or you?" she whispered against Gray's shirt.

He kissed her hair. "Me."

If so, then his hug was doing double duty because his warm, solid hold was reassuring her, too. It was addictive, this feeling of comfort seeping into her like warm honey. It relaxed her tension and quieted the quaking of her limbs. She'd been an island her whole life. It stole her words, this embrace. Emotion burned against the back of her throat.

"I was worried that he'd hurt you," Gray said.

She shook herself out of her uncharacteristic sentiment and leaned back enough to look at him. "Ye of little faith. I did an excellent job of intercepting him before he could jump you."

"You were fierce."

"I kicked his butt."

"You *were* kicking his butt," he corrected. "Right up until I stepped in and stopped him from kicking yours."

Before she could get her hackles up and insist that she would have subdued Dennis without his intervention, he gave her a small, uneven smile.

"You already know that I could've handled him myself," she said because she could see that it was true.

"Yeah. But just for the record, the next time a big,

angry guy comes at me, I'd prefer to deal with him my-self."

"I'll take it under consideration. Just for the record, the next time I'm pursuing an assailant, I'd prefer to deal with the situation myself. You followed me and then yelled out when I motioned for you to retreat."

He tilted his head. "You didn't really think I'd let Rod drive me off once he told me what was going on, did you?"

"Yes."

"Wrong. Anyway, you should be thanking me for Dennis's capture. He only came out of hiding because he heard my voice."

"To my way of thinking, I don't have you to thank. I have you to chastise."

"Shhh." He settled her back against the expanse of his chest. "I liked it better when I was hugging you, and you were being quiet."

Dennis began to mumble. Then he stopped. Then more of the agitated mumbling. Gray and Dru separated and faced him.

Dennis raised a face that had been shattered by the loss of everything he'd valued. He fastened his seething gaze on Gray. "I *hate* you," he rasped, low. He strained against Rod's hold, trying his best to rise and come at Gray. Rod held him fast.

"Look at you," Dennis hissed. "Full of yourself with your money and cars, like you don't have a care in the world when you're responsible."

Dru stiffened with protectiveness.

"Alex is dead," Dennis said to Gray. "Because of you."

Gray's expression remained impassive. Even so, Dru

could tell that Dennis had scored a direct hit. Gray was tough, but he was also, at his core, incredibly decent.

"He'd dead," Dennis continued. "And it's your fault."

"No," Dru answered. Gray was a big enough person not to need to silence Dennis in this moment of Dennis's defeat. But she wasn't. "Alex's death isn't the fault of anyone here. Not you. And definitely not Gray. The only one at fault for Alex's death . . . is Alex."

Overwrought, Dennis railed against the handcuffs and tried again to stand, without success.

"Alex is the one who got drunk and climbed behind the wheel of a car." Dru spoke in a voice that didn't invite argument. "I'm sorry he did. Very sorry. But Gray wasn't responsible."

Dennis struggled for a long, painful stretch before his shoulders finally slumped. His head sagged forward. "Oh, God," he breathed. "Alex."

Gray and Dru glanced at each other. Sadness passed between them.

Sobs racked the older man's body. "My son," he kept whispering. "My son. My Alex is dead. My only child. My son."

Gray knelt a few feet from Dennis. "I'm sorry about what happened to Alex. I liked him. He was a good football player and a good man."

Dennis didn't respond.

Dru felt for Dennis, she did. Her feelings were, in fact, a stew of empathy, satisfaction at having apprehended him, animosity toward him, and relief because the threat that had been hovering over Gray had now been removed.

She'd met Dennis's mother, Mildred, and she was glad for Mildred's sake and the rest of Dennis's family that they'd found Dennis before he'd had the opportunity to do worse. There was still time for Dennis to make something good out of the rest of his life. Dru had firsthand experience with God's ability to redeem.

They'd gotten Gray's stalker.

It was done.

Gray felt sick to his stomach for the rest of the night.

Every time he attempted sleep, his mind played the sight of Dennis tackling Dru over and over again, as if it was on a constant rewind-play setting. He'd been running toward her at top speed to help, but it had taken him too long, and Dennis had tackled her before he'd been able to stop him. What actual good were his size and speed if he couldn't use them when it mattered most?

Gray had left his bed some time ago and now stood in his bathroom, staring at his reflection. Why had she done what she'd done? She should have let him handle Dennis. He could have taken care of the situation. Instead she'd chased Dennis down.

It scared him—what she'd done. And left him confused and worried.

Anthony Sutton had met him and Dru at the police station after Dennis's capture. Even Brian Morris, GM of the Mustangs, had come. Detective Carlyle had informed their group that Dennis had lawyered up and confessed only to having followed Gray. Wisely, for his sake, Dennis had not confessed to writing the letters or to the shooting at Urban Country. He'd also refused to tell them where he'd been staying. Until the detectives could determine that piece, they'd have no access to evidence that could tie Dennis to the letters or the shooting.

They needed to find Dennis's rifle, the shoes that had made the prints on the rooftop across from Urban Country, or, for example, drafts of the threatening letters saved on his computer.

Still, Dennis's appearance tonight at Mockingbird Station proved that he'd been following Gray. His son's tragedy gave him motive. And his attempted assault on Gray showed that he'd wanted to do him harm.

It was highly likely that they had their man. Their man was in custody.

Gray, Anthony Sutton, and Brian Morris had agreed that removing Gray's twenty-four-hour protection was appropriate.

So why? Why this confusion and worry?

Part of it had to do with Dru.

Twice now, she'd risked herself to protect him. The first time, at Urban Country, she'd been on duty. But today she hadn't been on duty, and he felt like his legs had been knocked out from under him because her behavior challenged something he'd long held to be true.

When he was young, he'd learned that he couldn't fully trust his mom to take care of him or protect him. Since he couldn't trust her, he hadn't felt confident about placing his trust in anyone. He'd counted on himself to get by, believing that was the way it would always need to be.

But Dru had proven she was willing to do what his mom hadn't been willing to do. She'd put herself between him and someone who wanted to hurt him.

She was trustworthy.

He rolled the idea around in his mind, trying to get used to it, to test his own response to it. Dru was trustworthy. He could trust her. *Trust her?*

Could he? Defensiveness sprang up in him at the question. So did need. He wanted to trust her. To let someone in. Yet it was going to take a leap . . . a big leap for him to get there.

He wasn't ready. He was still trying to get used to the depth of his feelings for her.

Gray sat on the lip of the big, modern bathtub he never used. Hunching forward, he rested his elbows on his knees and stared at the clean tiles of his master bathroom floor.

He'd seen something else tonight. More than what Dru had done. He'd seen Dennis collapsed on the floor, shaking with sorrow. Dennis had been unable to move past what had happened to his son, Alex. The hardship Dennis had faced had derailed his life.

Gray's mom had faced hardship, and it had derailed her, too.

Gray had faced hardship. Like Dennis and his mom, he'd been unable to move past it in some ways. To admit to himself—to admit he was anything like Dennis or his mom—required brutal truth.

"You're living like you're unforgiven," Dru had said to him.

He'd denied it to her and to himself at the time, but Dru was observant. She'd hit very close to the truth. It wasn't that he was unforgiven so much as that he was *unforgiving.* Which explained why his past still had the power to hold him back in relationships. And also explained the problem between him and God that Dru had accused him of. God forgave. But He also demanded that His people forgive. Forgiveness was challenging for Gray.

He hadn't ever truly forgiven the dirt bag for beating him—

No. As soon as his mind went in that direction, he knew it was wrong, empty. He had forgiven the dirt bag. The minute he'd learned of the man's death, all his fury toward him had drained out. Even though Gray hadn't been the one holding the pool stick that had killed his stepfather, Gray had still felt as if his revenge had been satisfied. The dirt bag had gotten what was coming to him, end of story.

No, his unforgiveness wasn't directed at the dirt bag, the most logical choice. He pushed his fingers into his hair and rubbed them back and forth, messing up the strands. His unforgiveness was directed at his mom.

He'd loved her once. She claimed to love him still. He'd always feel a responsibility to her, and on some level he did pity her. But on another level he blamed her. When he thought of the grief she'd caused him and Colton and Morgan and herself, bitterness choked him.

He made himself go completely still, cleared his mind, then prayed. He wasn't a stranger to praying. When he'd told Dru that he was a Christian, he'd meant it. Had he gone to Christian camp and read Christian books and done Young Life and worn t-shirts with Christian slogans on them when he'd been a kid? No. But he believed. He prayed. He often led the prayers among his teammates—

"You mow through women and throw back liquor."

It was true. He did. A lot like the way his mom mowed through men and threw back liquor. Except he did those things to a lesser degree.

Self-hatred washed over him. To a lesser degree? That didn't make him innocent, did it? That didn't make it okay.

After what he'd seen happen to his mom, he shouldn't be messing around with those things at all. He'd known it, but he'd gone ahead and done what he wanted to anyway and ignored the low-level guilt. For years he'd told himself it was all right because he was better than most of the single men his age he knew. He hadn't been breaking the law. He'd been careful not to hurt anyone—

An image of Kayla slipped into his mind.

Forgive me.

He needed to change the way he lived. Change the way he thought. Change his old habit of keeping himself apart, and thus safe, from other people. And he needed to forgive.

I forgive my mother. He tried to make it honest. He visualized opening both palms and letting go of all the useless stuff from his past that he'd been hanging on to.

The time had come to drop it. To drop it and move forward.

I t was a Porter family Christmas Eve for the ages.

The celebrations began with a kid-friendly church service at 3:00 p.m., which was attended by everyone in their large family. They required two pews. Then they caravanned to Ty and Celia's house and nibbled on Dru's mom's legendary Christmas Eve cheese ball while the rest of the food was assembled.

They'd just finished dinner and were awaiting dessert and coffee. After which, Dru's dad would read the Christmas story from the Bible. After which, Dru's mom would insist against everyone's protests that they go caroling.

These people and these traditions were what made Christmas *Christmas* for Dru. She leaned against the opening between the dining room and living room, baby Ellerie on her hip, taking in the details of the activity surrounding her.

Every year, Dru's parents invited town newcomers to their Christmas Eve get-together. Two exchange students from China were sitting on Celia's blue-checked sofa, blinking at Lyndie as Lyndie's spaniels made themselves at home in their laps. A family that had moved to Holley from Idaho was listening to a monologue from Dru's mom about the cheese-ball recipe and how it had been passed down through the generations of her family for forty-eight years.

Ellerie's older sister, Addie, sat next to Jake on a love-seat, talking to him about the art she'd created and placed in the portfolio she had open.

Hudson, in the corner, was double-fisting the home-made Christmas cookies they were supposed to be saving until later to leave on a plate for Santa. Hudson might have inherited his defiance of authority from her, which made Dru misty with pride. An aunt could hope, couldn't she?

Bo was holding Connor upside down against his chest and talking to Meg as if everything was completely normal, as if he wasn't wearing a giggling toddler like a necktie.

It was almost hard to remember now how this house had looked when it had been Ty's bare, neutral-colored bachelor pad. After marrying Celia, both Ty's life and his home had undergone a renovation. Celia liked color. Lots of bright, bursting color. She'd painted the walls of the downstairs rooms a cheerful shade of yellow. Folk art hung everywhere. Happy patterns in primary colors graced the rugs, curtains, throw pillows, furniture upholstery.

Ellerie stretched a hand toward the nativity set arranged on top of a nearby buffet table. "Gah."

"Want to check that out?" Since the set wasn't fancy

or breakable, Dru handed the miniature Mary to Ellerie to examine. "What do you think, sweetheart?"

"Gah. La."

"Yep." Dru smiled at the baby. "You said it, sister."

Celia had dressed Ellerie in a red-and-green plaid dress and a stretchy headband that supported a huge bow. One loop of the bow had begun to dip over Ellerie's eye. Dru scooted it back into place.

So . . . yeah. Everything about this Christmas Eve was fairly awesome. Ellerie's warm weight was cozy and comforting. Someone had put on Jewel's Christmas album. She had Celia's cheesecake with the hardened layer of chocolate and crushed peppermints on top to look forward to. If only she could get Gray out of her mind and concentrate fully on the people around her, things would be Hallmark-card ideal.

If only.

Dennis Wright had been charged with stalking and assault. Gray's attorneys had filed a restraining order against him. He'd been arraigned, posted bail, and been released under the condition that he have no contact with Gray or with her, that he not possess weapons, and that he not travel outside Texas. If evidence could be found connecting Dennis to the shooting at Urban Country or to the letters, then the prosecutor would beef up the charges. Detective Carlyle remained confident. He'd told Dru yesterday that he simply needed more time.

The minute Dru had learned of Dennis's release, she'd gone to Anthony Sutton and asked him to urge Brian Morris to reinstate Gray's round-the-clock protection. Sutton had listened with his usual patient calm. Nevertheless, Dru had quickly realized that Sutton now viewed her opinions regarding Gray as those of a worried girl-friend. Not as a well-informed agent.

Dennis didn't have much of a police record to speak of. He'd not actually hurt anyone. The stalker they'd all once feared to be dangerous had turned out to be a heartsick dad, and now no one except Dru was extraordinarily concerned about him. It might be months and months until the trial. The rest of them had judged the prospect of saddling Gray with protection for such a long and uncertain stretch of time to be overkill. Gray had a good home security system, Sutton had said. And Gray had assured Sutton and Brian Morris that he'd be vigilant about his surroundings and about watching for trailing cars when on the road.

So that was it.

Dru didn't like it. She liked finality. She wouldn't feel peace about it until they'd linked Dennis to the shooting and the letters. She might not feel peace about it until they'd secured a conviction.

Dru made her way to the tree so that Ellerie could study its retro, big-bulbed, multicolored lights. A mish-mash of store-bought ornaments and kid-made ornaments covered the branches.

There likely wouldn't be any kid-made ornaments on the tree at the party Gray was attending tonight at the home of one of his teammates. Which brought her to her other reason for thinking about Gray incessantly tonight. His agents had protected him, but they'd also acted as somewhat of a moral conscience. He didn't have agents with him anymore, and she really hoped he stayed reasonably sober tonight and resisted the temptations of the many, many women who would be throwing themselves at him.

She hadn't let herself set up fairy tales in her mind about the two of them dating long-term, getting serious. She preferred to keep things real. They liked each other. They'd recently started going out. That's what was real and founded. It was just that—that she wanted him to behave well at the party so they could keep on dating because . . . Drat. She didn't want to have to let him go just yet.

If she'd invited him to come here tonight, Dru suspected that he would have said yes. She hadn't invited him because bringing a boyfriend to Christmas Eve was too strong a play. It was the type of thing a woman would do if she were about to get engaged or something.

"Want to look outside, sweetheart?" Dru strolled to the front windows. The lawn and walkway sparkled with white twinkle lights.

She'd see Gray tomorrow. She'd invited him to stop by her cabin for an hour or two in the morning before he had to check in at the team hotel for Sunday's final regular season game and before she was expected at her parents'. When he'd taken her up on her offer, she'd been quick to warn him not to bring a gift. No sense in anyone going all mushy about anyone else just because it was Christmas or feeling obligated to buy a present—

"I heard you started dating that traitor Gray Fowler," Ty said, sauntering up to her. He stuck a tiny hot dog into his mouth and pulled its toothpick free.

A couple of days ago, she'd told her mom about Gray because she'd known she could count on her mom to break the news gently to Bo, Ty, and Jake. "Yes," Dru answered. "I'm dating him."

"Even though he caught that touchdown pass against the Cowboys in September?"

"I'm pretty busy here, taking care of your youngest child and all. Would you mind grabbing me a few of those mini hot dogs?"

"Nice try. How long have you been dating him?"

"Not long."

"On the day they dedicated Silver Leaf's statue at Lone Star Park"—he made circles in the air with the toothpick—"I seem to remember you saying that you had no intention of dating him."

Dru slitted her eyes. "That was true at the time. I didn't want to date him right up until suddenly . . . I did. I don't see why my love life is your concern, Ty—"

"You're my sister. Plus, it's fun to ask you about your love life because you get all frustrated and spiky."

"Spiky? I'm not getting spiky."

Bo and Jake approached. Dru stifled a groan. A full brother offensive. Ty must have sent the other two a top-secret telepathic alert.

"Remember how Dru acted that day at Lone Star?" Ty asked the others. "When she told us she was guarding Gray Fowler and we warned her not to fall for him?"

"I remember it exactly," Bo replied. "Dru said, 'I don't fall for men. I prefer to let them fall for me.'"

"I wouldn't go so far as to say I've *fallen* for Gray," Dru lied.

"Bull," Jake said quietly, his expression grave.

Lecturing others came more naturally to her than being lectured. "Anyway. Gentlemen! I have a baby here."

She held up Ellerie like a shield. "Isn't there a rule against brothers grilling their sisters about their social life when there's a baby present?"

"There should be a rule against sisters having a social life. Ever." Ty stuck the toothpick in his mouth and grinned. He was diabolical enough to enjoy her discomfort.

"Gray seems like a decent guy," Bo said, the voice of reason among them.

"He is decent," Dru agreed.

"For a lousy Mustang, he's not *terrible*," Ty allowed.

"I don't like him," Jake said.

"Jake!"

"Speaking for myself, I'm most concerned about the fact that Gray Fowler is known to be a womanizer," Bo said.

"I wouldn't call Gray a womanizer, exactly," Dru said. "He's had a lot of relationships, and many of them were not very long. But at least they weren't one-night stands. At least they *were* relationships." Even to her own ears, that sounded colossally stupid.

None of her brothers were buying it.

"You wouldn't dream of letting him use you, right?" Bo asked.

She bristled. "Of course not." In order to keep her cool, she had to remind herself that Gray had a reputation that would give a lot of older brothers pause. He hadn't exactly been a preacher's kid. "We're just dating. I'm not planning on having some big love story with him like you guys have with your wives."

Ty's eyebrows rose. "Why does that statement feel like it's begging to be proved untrue?"

"Fellas. For the sake of all that is good and right, there's a baby present." She lay a sheltering hand over one of Ellerie's ears. "She shouldn't be subjected to all this sibling disapproval. Can't be good for her reflux."

"What's the status with Gray's stalker?" Jake asked. "Bo saw something on the news this morning about a man being charged."

So the close-knit band of three had been talking to one another about Gray. She explained the status of the investigation.

They all frowned.

"You're not bringing Gray around tomorrow." Jake spoke the question like a statement.

"No."

"I don't think it's a good idea for him to be going to your house, either," Jake said. "At least not without making sure he's not followed."

They were starting to chap her hide. "I'll ask Gray to ensure he's not followed. And with that, this conversation is done. *Seriously*. If any of you say one more word, I'm going to have to perform a judo flip on you."

"Can I ask why my child is gumming Mary from Celia's nativity set?" Ty nodded to Ellerie.

Dru had forgotten all about handing the statue to the baby. Sure enough, Ellerie was working Mary's feet steadily around her mouth. Dru gently popped Mary from Ellerie's drooly lips.

"Granddad is about to read the Christmas story," their mom called in a loud voice.

The Chinese students were still blinking. The family from Idaho was murmuring about the cheese ball. Dru's

dad settled into a wingback chair with two of his grandkids on his lap and read the familiar words from Luke 2.

When he finished, the family prayed, then Dru's mom
clapped to gain the room's attention. "Joyeux Noel to
everyone! To you, Lin and Changchang. And to you,
Myer family. Now let's do some caroling!"

"Pardon me, Mom," Ty said. He stood next to Celia,
an arm around her shoulders. "We haven't eaten any
cheesecake yet. I've been waiting for the Christmas
cheesecake for twelve months, and I'd pretty much rather
die than go caroling before I've eaten it."

"You're right!" Nancy exclaimed, slapping her hands
together and laughing. "I'm getting ahead of myself.
Land sakes! We're fixin' to eat dessert. And right after
that we'll go caroling."

"I'd rather stick a poker in my eye than go caroling,"
Dru stated.

"I'd rather walk on hot coals," Bo added.

"I'd rather be shut into an iron maiden," Jake said,
then ruined his dire tone by cracking a ghost of a smile.
His wife, Lyndie, chuckled.

"They give me a hard time about caroling every year,"
Dru's mom told the Myers. "But I don't let it bother me."

"We can't hold a tune," Bo said to the exchange students. "We've actually had people turn their porch light
off when we come up their walkway singing."

"We manage to spread anti-Christmas spirit." Ty
grinned.

And so it went. As Christmas Eves go, it was pretty
perfect.

Gray's Christmas Eve should have been perfect. Duayne, the host of the party, lived in a mansion. The band and the food were excellent. Many of his close friends from the team surrounded him, and a tipsy blonde in a sexy Santa outfit clearly wanted to get busy doing sexy Santa things to him.

Since he'd received his first NFL paycheck, he'd spent big chunks of his money to buy himself a good time. *A good time* had been something worth chasing. If you asked a hundred guys his age, they'd all agree that this Christmas Eve party was a good time. Like on *Family Feud*.

Survey says?

Good time.

Yet Gray felt as though he were standing outside himself, looking at all the things around him that should have been fun, but weren't.

He'd heard people say that they'd been "born again" through their faith in God or made into a new person. He'd been praying, thinking, and reevaluating. Most of it had been painful, and none of it had made him feel born again or like a whole new person. So far, he'd mostly been trying to let go of the old. Any change had been subtle.

Until now. Because here, at this party, he was experiencing the first change that wasn't subtle at all. It was as if God was shining a bright light on things that had looked a lot prettier to him in the dark.

For example, he understood that Sexy Santa could only offer him the sort of physical satisfaction that would pass very quickly. This crowd of people didn't have the power to make him feel any less alone. The music was so loud it was giving him a headache. And he couldn't *believe* how much he wanted a drink.

He'd thought his drinking was an optional thing he did because he enjoyed it. Yet he was craving a Southern Comfort on the rocks. Craving it. Not because he had any chemical addiction—at least he didn't think he did—but because he knew the whiskey would loosen him up and take away these disturbing thoughts and dim the light that God was shining.

He'd been using his drinking as a crutch without realizing it, which was pathetic.

He was thirty-two years old. He'd been applauded and complimented and called great. He'd given himself anything and anyone he'd wanted. He'd traveled a million miles across the world. He'd trained and practiced and gone to war on football fields too many times to count.

And all of it had left him, in this moment, drained and empty.

He ached for Dru. He missed her with actual physical pain.

"Want to dance?" Sexy Santa asked him.

"No thanks. I'm dating someone."

She reacted with a split second's disappointment before her optimism returned. "Is she here tonight?"

"No."

"Then let's dance."

"I'm good where I am."

"She won't mind. And since she's not here, she definitely doesn't have to know." She lifted both hands above her head, one of them holding her drink, and started dancing. "C'mon," she prodded. "It's just a dance." Her eyes met his, and he could read all the things she was willing to give to him.

If you asked a hundred guys his age, they'd all say this woman was hot.

Survey says?

Hot.

Her red shirt outlined her cleavage with white fur. Three inches of her abdomen showed beneath the shirt's hem. Her skin was toned and tan. Her navel piercing sparkled.

"How about I get you a drink?" she suggested.

"I'm good. Excuse me." He nodded to her, moving past, making his way through the bodies. He fielded one greeting after another. Politely, he acknowledged those who called out to him. But firmly, he kept on moving.

The forecasters had suggested a chance of snow tomorrow. Tonight, no snow. Outdoors, the black sky stretched above him, cold and hard and dry. He'd driven one of his motorcycles, so he didn't have to wait for the valets. He went to where his bike was parked, pulled on his helmet, and revved the engine. Within moments, he was flying toward home.

His past life was behind him. His future life waited ahead.

Tomorrow, thank God, he'd get to see Dru.

CHAPTER TWENTY-TWO

M erry Christmas." Dru opened her cabin's door, smiling.

Gray swept her against him in a hug that smelled like clean, crisp linen. "Merry Christmas."

He held on. And on. Dru sensed a thread of need stitching through his embrace. She snaked her arms behind his back and rested her head against his chest. Fi, not wanting to be left out, did her best to wedge her body in between their knees.

The clock had reached midmorning on Christmas Day. People—journalists and pastors and the like—often said that Christmas could be one of the hardest days of the year for some. Maybe Gray was one of those. He'd opted out of traveling to Mullins and celebrating with his family, so he had to be feeling lonely.

Either that or he'd done something very bad last night and was wracked with guilt.

"How was the party last night?" she asked lightly.

He looked down at her, only slightly loosening the

clasp of his arms. "It was everything anyone could ask for from a Christmas Eve party. In other words, it was terrible."

"Why was it terrible?"

"Because you weren't there."

Delight blossomed within her. "I'm guessing there were plenty of available women."

"Plenty. But like I said . . . *you* weren't there."

The blossom continued to expand, as if bathed with sunlight. "You know, right, that I've become friends with several of the guys on your team?"

"Just as a public service announcement, that's a bad idea. They'll all try to hit on you."

"Tell Corbin that he's welcome to hit on me anytime."

"Dru," he growled in a mock threatening voice.

"As I was saying, I've become friends with your team-mates, so I'll find out if you messed around with anyone at the party. Thus, you might as well be honest with me." She spoke cheerfully. "The truth will come out."

Understanding stole over his features. "Have you been worried that I messed around with someone last night?"

"The possibility crossed my mind."

"Should I be offended because you think I'm unfaith-ful or complimented because you like me enough to have been worried?"

"Both, I guess."

He smiled crookedly. Ah, that smile! That gladiator's half-wicked, half-enamored smile. It caused her tummy to lift and tingle with butterflies.

"I'm really glad to see you," he said.

"I'm really glad to see you, too." She placed her palms on the sides of his face and kissed him. She'd meant the kiss to be sweet, but the attraction between them leapt to life. Her breath turned shallow. Her heart began to thump—

She needed to be careful. Restrained. "Come into the living room, big football player."

They'd only made it a few steps when Gray stopped and scanned the space. "Where's your Christmas tree?"

"Here." She flicked the top of the ten-inch-tall fake tree sitting on a side table. Every year, she unpacked it from the one plastic box that contained her entire collection of Christmas decorations.

"That's not a tree. That's a weed."

"I'm not Mrs. Claus, Gray."

"We're going to need to go and get a tree, Dru."

She gaped at him. "Everything's closed."

"Then we'll have to go get one from out there." He hooked a thumb toward the trees beyond her cabin.

"You want to go out on my property and cut down a tree?"

"It shouldn't be any problem for you, Revengeress. Just send a laser through your fingertips and chop it down with that."

"You realize that there are no pine or fir trees out there. All I've got on my property are Texas trees."

"We'll find something that'll work."

Twenty-five minutes later, they'd located a Yaupon holly tree, about twenty feet high and fifteen wide. They stood side-by-side, eying it.

A cold front had brought Arctic air rushing across north Texas, so over his brown sweater and jeans, Gray had pulled on a black insulated jacket that made him look like a SWAT team member. Dru had covered her plum-colored blouse and gray skinny jeans with her silver jacket, black cap, and black gloves.

"What's our plan of attack?" Gray asked, his breath misting the air.

While not a traditional Christmas tree, the holly was clearly the best choice available to them. Its leaves stayed green all winter, and the clusters of bright, translucent red berries looked festive. Five main narrow trunks grew upward from the ground to form the tree. "I say we cut off the littlest section."

"Done." He raised the handsaw they'd dug out of her yard shed. She held the trunk steady for him while he worked. It didn't take long. Soon, they were walking back toward her cabin, Gray dragging the six-foot-tall branch behind him and Fi jogging happily alongside.

When the first fleck of moisture hit Dru's cheek, she automatically assumed it was rain. Looking up, she saw instead a host of tiny white snowflakes. She stopped. Extending her hands with palms up, she tilted her face to the sky.

She wasn't often overcome with a sense of wonder. In some ways, she'd been jaded and hard-bitten as a teenager, even before encountering danger and death firsthand on her tours with the Marines and, later, in that ambush in Mexico.

But here, on Christmas Day, with snow dancing down as if she and Gray were at the center of their own personal snow globe, an awed sense of wonder lifted inside her. Around them, the woods echoed with magical quiet. It was as if God's creation had hushed in order to more fully absorb the beauty blanketing them.

"Snow is rare around here at Christmastime," Dru

murmured. It usually snowed once or twice each winter. The snow never stuck around for long. Across her entire lifetime, snow had come to Holley on Christmas maybe three times. "Very rare."

"You're rare," he said. "Come kiss me."

"You come and kiss me," she challenged.

"I'm the one dragging a tree," he grumbled, but he came anyway and kissed her, their mouths a point of warmth in a landscape of cold.

Fi interrupted them with a nervous bark. "Fi doesn't like precipitation," Dru explained. "She's going to hold a grudge about this for days."

"Then let's get back to the house. I won't be able to sleep at night if I know your dog's holding a grudge against me."

They started off again, through nature tingling with white. Small accumulations of snow began to grace branches, the leaf-covered ground, Gray's wide shoulders.

Once home, Dru dried Fi with a towel, then wrapped her in a green, red, and white plaid throw blanket. Gray lifted the retriever onto the room's coziest chair, where she curled into a ring. With just her eyes and nose peeking out from the blanket, she looked like a Christmas-themed dog burrito. Dru gave her two dog treats. One as an apology for subjecting her to snow. One for off-the-charts adorableness.

Before bringing the holly branch inside, Gray used a pair of shears to snip it into a roughly triangular shape. Since Dru had no Christmas-tree stand, they put the tree stump in a vase and rested the tree against the bank of windows on the far side of her living room.

"Do you think it needs any decoration?" Dru asked. "Maybe the berries are enough?"

"It needs decoration."

"You're turning out to be quite a bossy Christmas tree man."

She found white satin ribbon with her stash of wrapping paper. After searching the house, she came up with only one other prospective ornament idea.

"Matchbox cars?" Gray asked doubtfully.

"They're small and colorful."

"How come you have a set of Matchbox cars?"

She quirked a brow. "You're not going to treat me to more male chauvinism and say I should have played with Barbies when I was little, are you?"

"Wouldn't dream of it."

Gray balanced the mini cars on the tree. Dru tied white satin bows. When they'd finished, they stepped back and appreciated their strange, quaint, surprisingly likable creation.

"Hot chocolate?" she asked him, making no move toward the kitchen.

"Please."

"Before you ask, the answer's no. You can't have yours spiked with whiskey."

"I've given it up."

"Drinking? You've given up drinking?"

"Yes."

She began to smile. "That's very good news, Gray." For him. For them as a couple.

"Maybe."

"Why'd you give it up?"

He paused, uncomfortable. "The things you said

to me a while ago about the women and the drinking bothered me."

"And?"

"Ah . . . there's not much to say."

Rather, there wasn't much he wanted to say, Dru suspected.

Gray rubbed the back of his head. "There may have been some things that were . . . off between God and me. I've been working on that."

Like dew in daylight, the most central of her concerns about his faith began to melt away.

"Anyway," he continued, "it's possible you weren't completely wrong about me."

"Just so you know, I'm *always* right."

"You were wrong not to have purchased a real Christmas tree."

She was the one who'd suggested hot chocolate, but now found herself suddenly reluctant to move. If she moved, she'd break the spell.

Peace and joy were here. Here on this Christmas Day. Here in her cabin and also twining within her. It was easy to choose the words *peace and joy* for your Christmas card template. Far harder to attain them.

Snow drifted from the sky beyond the windows. Fi was snoring softly. The candle on Dru's entry table smelled of oranges and cloves.

Gray looked over at her, then reached down and linked his two little fingers with her two little fingers. He did it as seriously as if he were brokering world disarmament.

Something happened inside her then, a fervent softening. She might . . .

No! She couldn't love him.

She might love him. Just a little.

No.

Yes.

Oh my word. *Love?!* "I'll be right back." She scaled the stairs. Once out of his line of sight, she darted into her bedroom and leaned against the inside of the closed door. She needed a moment.

She didn't want to let herself love a man who wasn't capable of loving her back. She'd always understood Gray's romance m.o. He'd never led her on. Until this moment, his m.o. had been fine with her, because she wasn't an I-have-a-burning-love-for-you kind of person herself.

At least, she never had been before.

Shoot! This whole thing was supposed to have stayed within her control. She'd managed herself all her life. She didn't want to harbor feelings that couldn't be managed.

Troubled, needing something to do with her hands, she moved to her bed and smoothed each of the quilt's wrinkles. Fluffed the pillows. Adjusted the fleece blanket she'd folded along the end.

December 25th was the calendar equivalent of a hot fudge sundae. She should simply enjoy today. And him. Over the next week or two, she'd have plenty of time to consider what to do about Gray. She could pull back from him later, if needed.

After more quilt smoothing, pillow fluffing, and self-talking, she had herself in hand.

Halfway down the stairs, she heard her front door close quietly. Had Gray left? Or had someone else just entered? Dennis? Fear flashed in her like lightning, and she hurried down the next few steps. She saw that Gray hadn't left. Nor had Dennis found them. The sound she'd heard had come from Gray closing the door behind him as he'd come back inside.

His powerful physique took up her entire foyer. In his big hands, he gently held a Christmas gift. He must have slipped out to his car to retrieve it.

"For you," he said, his grin both sheepish and defiant.

Looking down at him, emotions gusting, she saw two things very clearly. One, she *did* love him.

Och.

Two, she was afraid for him. She was very afraid that she'd done everything possible to keep him safe, and it might yet not be enough. She'd been so fast to jump to Dennis when she'd heard the harmless click of her door against the frame because of her insistent sense of foreboding.

"Well?" he asked.

She'd ruin some of his fun if she didn't give him at least a little flak for having brought a gift after she'd admonished him more than once not to. Dru straightened her spine and blasted him with a ferocious glare. "You!" she accused, making her way to him. She wasn't pulling off the glare as well as usual. She could feel a wisp of a smile on her lips. It's just that he looked very cute standing there, holding the present. And how angry could a person really be at another person for buying them a gift? "I told you not to bring a gift. In very plain English."

"So? What're you going to do about it?" he drawled, looking pleased with himself. "Accost me? . . . Please?"

Lumpy, wrinkled paper covered the rectangular mystery item. The ends were wadded more than folded, and big chunks of tape had been stuck on to hold the wads in place. No ribbon. No gift tag.

Ashley had definitely not wrapped this gift. Gray had wrapped it himself, and the charm of that tugged at her. *Yeeps.* All this goofy sentimentality was a bit sickening.

She reached into the middle drawer of the small chest in her entryway and brought out a Christmas present of her own. Dru took her gift from Gray and passed over the gift she'd bought for him.

His face went slack. "You got me something?"

"I did."

"But . . . you told me not to bring a gift."

"I had a sneaking suspicion that you might disobey me. You're not very good at following my orders."

He chuckled. "I like you."

"I'm learning to tolerate you."

He studied the gift he held. "I didn't expect this. Thank you."

His family had given him gifts this Christmas, right? His friends? Surely. He'd opened gifts from someone this morning. Hadn't he?

Suddenly she didn't feel so sure. She imagined the kid he'd been, stuck in dumpy houses with his younger brother and sister. Had there been Christmas presents then?

"You first." He motioned to her gift.

"You first."

"What're you going to do if I refuse to go first? Accost me? . . . Please?"

She rolled her eyes and pulled free her gift's hideous wrapping. She uncovered a gorgeously framed print. The image appeared to have come from an old magazine.

The black-and-white artwork showed a woman lying on the back of a sleek and galloping horse while aiming her rifle upward. The caption read, *Amateur Circus Folk Rehearsing. Miss Annie Oakley, the Star Rifle Shot.*

"I love it," she said honestly. She could remember Gray telling her once that she reminded him of a modern-day Annie Oakley. She couldn't imagine where he'd found this antique magazine image. It couldn't have been easy, which was incredibly touching. "Thank you."

"You're welcome."

She went up on tiptoes to kiss him. This was all very domestic. Next, she'd be tying on an Ashley-like apron and murmuring about cooking a Christmas goose. "Now open yours."

He tore off the wrapping with one swipe. Inside, a small box holding a single piece of paper waited. Picking up the paper, he read aloud, "A day of racecar driving. Come out to Texas Motor Speedway and test your driving prowess on our 1.5-mile oval behind the wheel of a racecar."

"I found a way for you to drive fast and not get scolded by me afterward."

His eyes met hers. "Unlike when I did over a hundred on the tollway."

"Precisely."

"Thank you," he said. "This is awesome."

"You're welcome."

"Will you come with me to the track the day I go? You won't be able to beat my time, but it would be fun to watch you try."

"I'll consider it." Which was a cover for the answer

that had leapt to her mind: *We might not still be together, Gray, by the time you visit the track.*

"Will you consider making me some hot chocolate?" he asked. "You offered me some, then didn't follow through."

"Yes, big football player. I'll make you hot chocolate."

Four days after Christmas, Gray stood at the mouth of Augustine's open garage eating a bowl of pea salad and watching Dru and Augustine prepare to leave for Wednesday night biker church. Dru had on Dr. Martens, jeans, and a black leather motorcycle jacket. Augustine wore a purple shirt that read *RIDE OR DIE* under a vest covered with insignias and patches. The older lady's earrings dangled skulls and crossbones.

Dru was planning to drive Augustine's Harley to church with Augustine tucked into the sidecar, which sounded to Gray like a harebrained idea. I mean, they were going to stick poor Augustine in a *sidecar*? But since both women were taking themselves so seriously, Gray was making an effort not to bust out laughing.

Dru sank to her knees near the bike's rear tire to check its pressure. Augustine limped over to Gray, beaming at him from behind her glasses. "Since they've found your stalker, are you going to participate in the Winter Family Fun Day?"

"Yep. I've already told Grace Street I'll be there." He finished the last bite of salad and clasped both the bowl and spoon in one hand near his thigh. "Dru's brother and sister-in-law are hosting the Fun Day at Whispering Creek Ranch."

"Dru told me that, and I'm so, so pleased. They raise Thoroughbreds at Whispering Creek. I once raced an Arabian Thoroughbred across the desert of Qatar with one of the princes of Dubai."

"Impressive."

"Dru?" Augustine called. "We should organize a trip to Qatar. *Mm-hmm!* The falafel there is amazing."

"It's a plan," Dru answered.

"Anyway." From her hunched position, Augustine had to twist her head and look up at him from the corner of her eye. "My sons have finally located an address for Roy. He's in Decatur, which isn't all that far away. We decided that Marvin should write to him, because Marvin's the most levelheaded of us. So Marvin wrote. But Roy hasn't answered either of the two letters he sent. So I asked my sister to drive me out there last week. He didn't answer his door."

"I'm sorry."

"The trip took a lot out of me, you know? There's no way for me to guess when Roy will be at home. Even if he is home, I have no guarantee that he'll answer once he sees that it's me."

She resettled her vest with her crooked fingers. "A few days back, when Dru told me that it looked like you might attend the Fun Day, my boys and I put our heads together. We think we ought to send Roy a postcard, anonymously of course, so he won't know it's from us. On the postcard, we'll advertise your appearance at the Fun Day. He'll see that postcard. And he'll come."

"Are you sure you want to see him, Augustine?" He didn't want to burst her bubble, but he didn't want her to put herself through useless pain, either. "In my experience, lousy people usually stay lousy. I wouldn't want you to regret seeing him."

"I won't. I want this meeting for me. I don't care how he acts."

"In that case, I hope your plan works."

"It will. He'll come." She extended a hand. "Here, let me take that bowl inside for you."

"I'll take it in." The last thing he wanted was to cause Augustine more steps. "It was delicious, by the way." The woman made a great pea salad.

When he returned from the house, Dru had finished padding the Harley's sidecar seat with a blanket.

Gray put a hand under Augustine's elbow and helped her into the small sidecar. Dru settled two more blankets around the older lady, then straddled the Harley. Both women fastened their helmets under their chins.

"Are you guys really going to do this?" he asked. The sight of them, sitting on the motorcycle and sidecar in their biker clothes and shiny black helmets, was tempting him to laugh again.

"We're absolutely going to do this." Dru pushed a pair of Ray-Bans onto her face and smiled.

She had the smile of a supermodel. It could freeze him with its power.

"My sons bought me this sidecar attachment a few years back," Augustine said to him. "I don't know why. I *told* them that I can still drive the Harley." Augustine couldn't drive a riding lawn mower. "But my sons insisted, so here we are."

"This is always how we get to and from biker church," Dru added.

Augustine snapped down a set of shades that she'd

clipped to the top rim of her glasses. "Let's burn some rubber!"

Gray laughed. It wasn't physically possible not to.

Dru rumbled up to him.

"I'll follow you there in my car," he said.

"Good luck keeping up."

"I don't need luck. I have a Ferrari."

He stayed close behind them on the way to biker church. If nothing else, his car served as a shield between Dru and whatever semi-truck might otherwise roar up and flatten her and Augustine.

About ten minutes into the drive, Gray realized he hadn't thought about football since he'd pulled up to Augustine's house and found Dru waiting for him on the front lawn with a bowl of pea salad extended toward him.

Had—had he missed something about football he should have remembered? Concern bolted through him. Was he supposed to study film tonight? Had he told one of the PTs he'd come in for therapy on his back? His team had lost on Sunday, but they'd put together such an excellent season that it hadn't mattered. Their twelve and four record had earned them a berth in the divisional round of the playoffs. Which meant they'd have a break this weekend while the wildcard teams battled it out. They'd play at home the weekend after.

He ran through his calendar mentally. What had he forgotten?

Nothing. He'd taken care of his football responsibilities.

He supposed this was what people who had a life outside of football did. They thought about other things for long periods of time. They lived. They had girlfriends.

Maybe, like him, they had a hard time thinking about anything *except* their girlfriends. Maybe they didn't want to do anything other than hang out with their girlfriends. Maybe they even did ridiculous things like attend biker church to be near their girlfriends.

He glanced into his rearview mirror and noticed a car two back that looked like a beige Cherokee. Squinting, he eyed the car more closely.

The stoplight at the intersection ahead turned red. Before he reached the light, the Cherokee put on its blinker and turned off. Gray slowed, continuing to keep an eye on the road behind him.

It had most likely been a coincidence that the Cherokee he and Dru had spotted weeks ago in the rain had taken a few of the same turns that they had. Because of the stalker situation, he'd become very aware of beige Cherokees and maroon trucks and blue Camaros. So much so that he noticed those makes and colors everywhere.

If that had been a beige Cherokee behind him just now, it was definitely gone.

CHAPTER
TWENTY-THREE

The entire Dallas/Fort Worth metroplex came down with a huge case of Mustangs fever in the days leading up to the team's playoff game. For the most part, Dru was too wrapped up in one particular Mustang to notice. With every passing day, Dru's affection for Gray sent roots deeper and became more intractable.

She and Gray met every evening when she got off work. At her house. At his. Or at her favorite restaurants. Or his. Twice in the week and a half between their outing with Augustine to biker church and the Mustangs' playoff showdown, they snuck in before-work restaurant breakfasts, during which they laughed and talked over Belgian waffles and crispy bacon and steaming cups of coffee. More than just the day seemed new to Dru during those breakfasts. The whole world felt fresh, bright with possibilities for her and Gray. Sunnier.

They attended a New Year's Eve party thrown by Gray's agent. With the exception of Ashley and Corbin, all of Gray's friends had believed her to be Gray's girlfriend from the beginning, so it was seamlessly easy to continue on as his girlfriend in public. At midnight, they welcomed the new year with a kiss so memorably long that "Auld Lang Syne" echoed into applause and confetti dotted their hair and shoulders by the time they pulled apart.

She recognized—it would have been impossible *not* to recognize, for anyone who'd seen their New Year's Eve kiss from yards away would have recognized—that her desire for him, and his for her, was powerful. Dangerously tempting. So much so that there were times when hormones fogged Dru's brain to the point that she began to wonder dazedly whether *that* sin with *this* man might almost be . . . worth every second. But the pro football player who could go to any bar in the city and bring home the most beautiful woman present did not overstep. As worldly as he was, he never once tried to cross the boundaries Dru had established in order to keep their physical chemistry in check.

Things were going so well, in fact, that her romance with Gray *might* have made Dru wonderfully happy except . . .

They never spoke openly about matters of the heart.

And her concerns for his safety continued to plague her. She didn't take him to see her family. She used the Montana surname when in Gray's circles in order to protect her true identity and her connection to her parents, Bo, Ty, Jake, and their families. When behind the wheel, she constantly searched her rearview mirror for evidence that she was being tailed. Whenever Gray visited her house, she insisted he go through maneuvers designed to ensure he wasn't followed. When they were out together, she evaluated and reevaluated every stranger to determine who posed the greatest threat.

She kept an eye out for ex-girlfriend Kayla Bell and crazy fan Kevin Lee because she hadn't written off either of them completely. But far more compulsively, she watched for Dennis. For his face, for the cars he was known to drive, his hair color, his body shape.

Part of her wanted to spot him. If she did, Dennis would be in violation of his restraining order and in contempt of court. He might be taken into custody outright. Even if he wasn't, she'd have ammunition she could take to Anthony Sutton and Brian Morris when she lobbied to have Gray's protection reestablished.

As hard as she tried, though, she could find no trace of Dennis. Even the letters had stopped coming. Gray hadn't received a single one since the day Dennis had been arrested.

Whenever Gray teased her about her vigilance, she either said that she was merely being intelligently careful or shrugged and made some flippant comment along the lines of *So long as we're dating, I'd prefer for you to have a heartbeat. When we break up, do as you like, big football player.* Then she'd stick up her chin and smile.

But inside, she didn't feel flippant about the subject. Not in the least.

The final seconds of the Mustangs' playoff game ticked downward. Dru watched the inevitable unfold, her stomach a stone fist. They were going to lose.

Gray had asked Dru to attend this game in a way that had made it impossible to say no. There'd been kissing involved in his request and a few whispered *pleases* thrown in. So Dru had broken her own habit of watching his games on TV and taken the seat he'd offered her in the stands. She sat surrounded yet again by friends and family of Mustangs players. Last time, they'd all been jubilant. This time they were all bereft.

When Dru had been five, she'd played on the Fighting Unicorns soccer team for a season. She'd occasionally bumped other little girls to the ground, she'd often hogged the ball, and after every loss she'd gone into a funk for hours.

Her mom hadn't registered her to play soccer again.

After Fighting Unicorns games, Dru could remember sitting in the old minivan they'd had that had smelled like dust. Her mom had talked to her in patient tones about why it wasn't good to be too competitive and how it didn't matter if you won or lost, it was how you played the game.

She'd thought her mom was nuts. Of course it mattered if you won! That was why Dru played for the Fighting Unicorns. To win.

That same mindset was responsible for the misery churning within her now. Gray had been a warrior today. No one could call into question his genius or his determination or toughness. Just like the cliché went, he'd left it all on the field. The Mustangs' offense had racked up a masterful thirty-four points. The loss could be set squarely on the shoulders of the Mustangs' defense, which had been unable to hold the Colts back.

Dru's attention flicked to the Jumbotron. An image of Gray standing on the sidelines filled the big screen.

He'd taken off his helmet. His cheeks were flushed, his hair drenched with sweat, his features grave.

Five seconds left. Two. The game was over. And with it, the Mustangs' season.

The head coaches made their way forward to shake hands. Players from both teams flooded the field.

Dru pulled in a painful breath. *You don't even like the Mustangs, Dru. They're not your team. Remember? You're not a fan.*

Gray caught sight of Dru's motorcycle parked next to his garage as he drove his Denali up the driveway.

It was ten at night. After the game, he and a few of his close friends on the team had met up at Corbin's. Sometimes it helped to talk through a game with the guys who knew the pressure, the strategy, their opponents, their coaching staff, and just how devastated their fans would be. His fellow players understood how rotten it felt to pour everything you had into a season. To earn a record as good as the one they'd earned. And to come as close as they had to the Super Bowl, then fail.

Stupid helplessness had been turning within Gray ever since the game had ended. Regret. Frustration. Disappointment.

The other guys had made a dent in Corbin's well-stocked bar, and if ever there had been a time to throw back a few glasses of Southern Comfort, tonight had been the time. God was a football fan, surely. Even He'd agree that Gray deserved liquor after tonight's playoff defeat.

Gray had wanted Corbin's alcohol so badly that his

wanting had scared him into refusing. When had he become so weak that he'd started turning to drinking to dull his feelings? He needed to be better than that.

When he'd shaken his head at the offered alcohol, his buddies had heckled him and called him a choirboy.

If so, he was a darkly depressed one.

Dru hadn't contacted him since the game, and he hadn't contacted her. It was dumb, but he felt like he'd let her down. She'd been at the game. Every time he'd looked up and seen her in the stands, motivation had surged through him. He'd wanted to win. In part, he'd wanted to win *for her*. It shamed him that he'd been unable to give her something that meant so much to him, so he hadn't texted her because he hadn't been sure he could take seeing her tonight.

The sight of her familiar motorcycle shattered his doubt. He *did* want to see her, desperately. A storm of emotion gathered.

The day they'd first kissed, after she'd resigned as his bodyguard, she'd tried to give him back his gate opener and garage door opener. He'd told her to keep them. She'd been his brand-new girlfriend at the time, a girlfriend he'd had to wait for and work hard at getting. He'd wanted her to feel welcome at his place. This was the first time she'd used the access he'd given her.

He couldn't park his car and get inside his house fast enough. On his way through the mudroom, he glanced down at himself. The business shirt he'd bought, intending to wear it after the win, was wrinkled and hanging open over his undershirt and black suit pants. His fingers scrubbed through his hair, trying to put it in order.

His kitchen smelled like vanilla. It had been left the

way Ash always left it when she took off for the day: spotless, with a few lamps lit.

Where was Dru? He swung toward the small den that opened off the kitchen—

She straightened to standing and tossed the remote control onto a chair. She met his eyes in that direct way of hers—no shyness or pity at all.

His pulse responded with fast, pounding beats. He walked straight up to her, cupped her face in his hands, and kissed her deeply.

He wasn't alone. Dru was here.

He loved her in that moment, kissing her in his den after a devastating defeat. Of all the women he'd dated, she was the only one he'd ever loved. Perhaps she was the first person he'd truly loved since he was a child. She understood him better than anyone had in all that time.

Dru *knew* him, the real him. And not only did she know him, but she accepted and liked him exactly as he was. Before her, he'd had no idea how much he needed that in his life.

She kissed him in return, her hands pressing up the back of his neck, tunneling into his hair.

She tasted like heaven. She smelled like hope. And her body was warm against his.

His need for her had been eating at the edges of him, like a flame, for days now. It tightened his nerves. Caused his muscles to brace. He heard himself groan. He wanted to—

He wanted to do things with her that she'd told him outright he couldn't do. He'd agreed to her terms because he'd sacrifice whatever she wanted to be with her. And because, like with the drinking, he wanted to be better than he'd been in the past.

That didn't mean he found it easy to keep himself under control. Kissing her was like going to war with his own body.

He ran kisses down the slim line of her throat, then back up. He caught her ear gently in his teeth. She gave a gasp of laughter, and he smiled at the sound, wolfishly, before wrapping a hand behind her head and pressing a kiss to her forehead as if he were sealing a promise he hadn't spoken out loud.

Gray hugged her to him, and they stood there, interlinked and wordless for long moments. He rested his chin on her head. Kissed her hair. Rested his chin on her head again and simply held her, soaking in the comfort of her nearness.

She'd been hired to protect him, but he'd come to a place where he'd do anything, give anything, risk anything to protect her. He'd rip apart anyone who tried to separate them. She made the things he used to value above everything—football, income, achievements— seem like less than the most important things in his life.

His rough childhood, his difficult family, his string of surface relationships had brought him to a soul-deep understanding of just what Dru was worth.

"I'm glad you're here," he finally said. His voice was scratchy, and his words were such an understatement that they were almost a joke. "That game . . ."

"I know," she said.

"I feel . . ."

"Lousy?"

"Yeah."

"I know." She leaned back to look at him. "*You* were great, though. You understand that, right? You played brilliantly."

He kissed her cheekbone, her temple, her lips.

She wrapped her fists into his shirt and pulled him closer. Kissed him back. The flame between them leapt higher. His breath grew short—

Playfully, she shoved him back a step. "I need popcorn. You?"

Popcorn? Amusement pulled at his mouth. "Yes."

"And I need a movie."

"Whatever you say."

"You get the movie going. I'll handle the popcorn." She moved toward the kitchen.

He lowered his battered and bruised body onto the sofa. Propping his feet on his ottoman, he flicked through one of his subscription movie channels. "The newest Transformer movie?" he called.

"Perfect."

Before the opening credits had finished, Dru arrived with the popcorn. He opened an arm for her, and she fit in beside him perfectly, the back of her head resting on his shoulder. The dark-haired, blue-eyed beauty had a powerful effect on him. Because of her, the tight places within him had begun to unwind.

He loved her.

He didn't know what to do with that. He'd been so determined not to let himself walk off that cliff. However, it turned out that love didn't behave the way you told it to. It wasn't very practical or careful. He might be opening himself up to a world of hurt—

Don't go there, Gray.

He definitely wasn't ready to say anything to Dru about where he was at. What he felt. He'd just keep on doing the inner work he'd been doing—forgiving, letting his past roll off him like rain, allowing God to change him.

He had no practice at trusting women. He wasn't good at it yet.

Yet.

But in time, with Dru, he hoped he could be.

Dru had always cringed when she'd heard women say that they loved to cuddle with their boyfriends or husbands. *Cuddle?* Yick. The word brought to mind an image of a child with a Care Bear.

How the mighty have fallen, Dru thought, sitting next to Gray, eating popcorn, and watching Transformers. They were cuddling. There was a lot to recommend it, turned out. Since her feet couldn't reach the ottoman, she crossed them at the ankles and set them on top of Gray's nearest shin.

Here, with him, she felt as if she belonged. Here, she wasn't excluded. Here, she was integral. Necessary and appreciated.

For weeks, she'd been arguing with herself, without resolution, over her attachment to Gray. Her love for him was her weak spot, yes. But so was this yearning of hers to belong, she knew. The idea of finding a place to belong with Gray, in his heart, in his life, seduced her totally and turned her judgment murky. It was a loophole in the armor that made up her steely personality.

She had no hard evidence to support the idea that she belonged with Gray. The truth: he cared about her as a person and wanted her as a woman. Also the truth: he kept her at arm's length in subtle ways. He hated talking about his childhood. He didn't often mention the future, either. And every time he noticed their conversation veering toward a topic that might lead to a discussion about their relationship, he used humor to steer it another way.

There was no getting around the fact that Gray's upbringing had damaged him. She'd gone online and researched the effects that childhood abuse could have on adults. Lack of trust and difficulties with relationships came with the territory. She wasn't a psychologist skilled in understanding how to handle Gray, but it seemed clear that he required time and plenty of space and patience.

Here was the rub. The woman who wanted to belong couldn't belong until the man who couldn't trust could trust.

And Dru didn't know how long she could stand to wait. For starters, her heart was becoming more invested in him by the hour. Also, she was a forthright person. It went against her grain not to talk about the issues that were on her mind.

How do you feel about me, Gray? What's our plan here? Where are we headed?

One of these days, they'd have to talk.

It wasn't an *if*. It was a *when*.

CHAPTER
TWENTY-FOUR

Two weeks later, Dru and Gray still hadn't had The Talk.

Dru was thinking about exactly that as she stepped up to the coffee shop's register to place her order. Just as she did so, the shop's door whooshed open. She turned, anticipation catching within her. Gray was a few minutes early—

Corbin strode into the coffee shop. His steps faltered with surprise when he caught sight of Dru. Then a grin overtook his face. "Dru. My favorite girl."

"Your favorite *woman*," she corrected without malice. She doubted that any female could muster a good case of malice against Corbin. He had on jeans and a navy quilted jacket. Ordinary enough, except that on him the clothes looked drool-worthy.

Everyone in the establishment hushed with reverence as Corbin crossed to Dru, as if the Apostle Paul were entering their midst. Corbin had one of the most recognizable faces in the Dallas/Fort Worth metroplex.

Wherever he went, worshipful attention focused on him like spotlights, seeming to cast him in a wash of gold.

"What can I get you?" he asked, pulling free his wallet.

"Nothing, seeing as how I can afford to pay for myself."

"Spunky as usual, I see."

She ordered plain coffee. He ordered plain coffee. They moved to the far end of the counter.

This particular coffee shop was located nearer to the Mustangs' training facility than any other, which explained why players frequented it and why Dru and Gray had chosen it as a meeting spot on this late-January Saturday. Gray was going to redeem the gift Dru had given him for Christmas this afternoon. They'd booked racecar-driving sessions at Texas Motor Speedway and planned to make the lengthy drive over in just one car.

"Did you come from the training facility?" she asked Corbin.

"Yeah. Just finished a conditioning session. Gray was there doing the same thing. Are you meeting him?"

"In a little bit."

"One of the PT guys was still working on him when I left."

The barista slid their coffees to them. Corbin followed Dru to a table, then helped himself to the chair across from hers.

She hadn't seen him in a while. He'd shaved his hair short at some point, which accentuated his handsome features even more. He appeared better rested, his brown eyes brighter, his whole demeanor more relaxed now that he'd had time to downshift into his team's off-season. The NFL's walking wounded were slowly recuperating.

Several of the coffee shop's patrons approached Corbin, just as Dru had known they would. She'd grown used to spending time with famous athletes and accustomed to occupying herself with her own thoughts while they did their thing with their fans. She crossed her legs and took long sips of the hot, delicious coffee.

"Sorry about that," Corbin said when his fans had gone. "I have an adoring public." A mocking dimple flashed in his cheek.

"What're you going to do when the day comes that you no longer have an adoring public, Corbin?"

He made a sound of disbelief. "Like that'll ever happen. There're lots of eight-year-olds who adore me. When I'm ninety, they'll only be sixty-eight."

"You've given this some thought, I see."

"It's good to plan ahead." He studied her while taking a drink of coffee. "You and Gray still together?"

She nodded. Other than the fact that they hung out and kissed, she wasn't sure what *together* meant for her and Gray. Still! She'd never imagined that she could attain this level of patience. This level of patience might be wise or it might be idiotic.

"I'm waiting for you guys to break up so I can make my move," Corbin said.

"As I recall, you already made your move. Your move wasn't successful."

He winced as if she'd caused him pain and rested a hand on his chiseled chest.

Mercilessly, she smiled.

"You can cut me up with your words all you want. Go ahead. Just know that when your relationship with Gray ends, I'd like another chance."

"*If* my relationship with Gray ends, I'll think about it."

"In the meantime, I'll try to be cool with the fact that Gray ended up with you *and* my new flat screen."

Her brows drew together. "How did Gray end up with your new flat screen?"

Corbin's expression slackened slightly. "Gray told you about our bet, right?"

Worry slid into her then, an awful feeling, like the slither of a snake. "What bet?"

"Never mind."

"No, really. I'd like to know."

"Dru." He spoke in the direct way of a man accustomed to leadership. "It's nothing that you need to stress over."

"I'm not stressed," she said with deadly calm. "I'd like to know about the bet."

He paused. Looking away from her, he sipped from his to-go cup.

"I'm waiting," she said.

"It's not a big deal."

"Then go ahead and tell me."

"It's just that"—he shrugged—"Gray won a bet against me, and I had to give him my flat screen. I was sure that he would have bragged to you about it. He deserved to brag. But since he didn't, I'm sorry I mentioned it."

"Explain the bet, Corbin."

"Thanks, but I'd rather not stick my foot in my mouth more than I already have. I don't know if you've noticed, but I have big feet."

Dru's gaze panned across the coffee shop—

And collided with Gray.

He was standing just inside the door, his attention on her and Corbin, his face cold.

The jealousy swamping Gray was too big a reaction to the sight of Dru and Corbin together. He knew it was too big. Irrational. Yet telling himself he was in the wrong wasn't doing much to stop this sickening, gut-twisting feeling.

He'd been missing Dru all day. He'd walked into the coffee shop eager to see her. Then he'd spotted her and Corbin having some sort of intense conversation and his optimistic mood had turned instantly to ashes.

They were sitting at a table for two. Had they planned this meeting behind his back?

Of course not. Neither one of them would do that to him. He was thinking like someone who didn't trust his girlfriend or his longtime friend.

He walked up to them.

"Hey, man," Corbin said easily. "Look who I found when I came in for coffee."

"I see that," Gray said, trying to act normal.

Corbin stood, coffee cup in his hand. "I'm outta here. Before you got here, Gray, I was doing my best to charm Dru. She still refuses to fall for me."

Hilarious.

"See you guys later." Corbin dipped his chin and made his way out.

Gray's eyes met Dru's. She set her mouth in an angry line. What was that about? He didn't trust himself to ask. He didn't want to say something he'd regret and, like a bull in a china shop, end up breaking things that were very important to him.

Avoiding Corbin's chair, he brought up another one. He angled his body so that it shielded them from the stares of their spectators.

"What bet did you make with Corbin?" she asked. Each word came out clear and sharp.

His stomach dropped. He stared at her, mentally scrambling for balance.

"Well?" she asked.

"What . . . ?" His voice sounded rusty. He was going to kill Corbin. Even as he had the thought, his conscience turned an accusing finger on himself. All along, he'd known he should have said something to her about the bet. "What did Corbin say to you?"

"He said he was trying to be cool with the fact that you have me *and* his new flat screen." She leaned back a degree, distancing herself from him. "What do I have to do with Corbin's flat screen?"

"We made a bet the night you first met Corbin. At the steakhouse."

"What was the bet, exactly?"

He didn't want to say. But it was too late for that. She knew about the bet. He could tell her the truth. Or he could lie, which might make everything ten times worse. "We bet on . . ." He ran a hand down his face. "This is going to sound worse than it was."

"How about you just tell me?"

"We bet on a kiss, that's all. We bet on which one of us could get you to kiss us first."

Time pulled. "And what did you wager?"

"If Corbin won, he'd get my watch. If I won, I'd get his TV."

Her eyes looked like chips of ice. "You bet on me like I was a sporting event?"

"In the past, Corbin and I have bet on a lot of things."

Slowly, she tipped her finger back and forth between them. "How much of this has been about winning a bet?"

"During the first few weeks that you were assigned to me? Maybe thirty percent," he admitted, dead honest. "Since then—since long before our first kiss—none of this has been about the bet."

She said nothing. He watched her run her vision slowly over the coffee shop. She was doing that thing she did whenever they were out somewhere together. She was sizing everyone up, looking for signs of danger. Even now, she was protecting him.

"He gave me the TV weeks ago," Gray said. "If I'd been interested only in the bet and not you, I wouldn't have had any reason to keep dating you after I got the TV."

"Is that supposed to warm my heart?" Her tone had a flatness to it that he'd never heard in her voice before, and she was acting way too controlled. She was hurt and she was mad, and he'd rather she come at him yelling like she had that day in the church parking lot.

"I'm sorry about the bet."

"Are you willing to return the flat screen to Corbin?" she asked.

"Done. I couldn't care less about the flat screen."

"You're competitive, though. You do care about winning bets."

"You are the only thing I care about in this conversation. I'll lose a hundred bets to Corbin. I'll give him my watch. I'll give him my car. It's you I want to keep."

She seemed to weigh his words. "Why didn't you tell me about the bet?"

"Because I didn't think you'd like it."

"Are you planning to keep everything from me that you think I won't like? Because that's not going to work."

He bit down on his back molars.

"I'd rather we communicate openly. About the hard things, and the good things, and the ordinary day-to-day things." She looked at him, seeming to wait for something. He didn't know what. He'd already said he was sorry. She slid her purse strap over her shoulder. "I'm going to cancel my reservation at the speedway."

"Then I'm going to cancel mine. Look, Dru . . ." Again, he was at a loss. Unsure what to say.

"We'll talk later, Gray." The sound of her footsteps grew softer until he could no longer hear them.

What had just happened?

This morning, they'd talked on the phone before he'd left home. He'd told her that Ash was making him homemade blueberry pancakes, and she'd told him she was eating a homemade blueberry Pop-Tart.

He was having a hard time comprehending that, since entering the coffee shop, he'd messed up everything.

No, he'd messed up everything a long time ago by agreeing to a boneheaded bet and then following that up with the bad decision not to tell Dru about it.

His thoughts swam with fury directed at both Corbin and himself. Mostly himself.

He might have lost her. No, he couldn't lose her. Fear chilled him. It would be okay. He'd make things right.

When he called Dru that night, she answered.

She asked him how he'd spent the rest of his day and responded to his questions about how she'd spent the rest of hers.

He stood in his media room, cell phone to his ear, looking out at his dark front lawn and the professional lighting that illuminated the trees. "Will you come over?" he asked. He'd thought he'd be better at this, at convincing her to make up with him in person. He hadn't expected to be great at it. Just better.

"Not tonight."

"I'll let you beat me at Xbox, and you can eat the rest of the double chocolate brownies Ash made."

"Her double chocolate brownies are delicious."

"So you'll come."

"No."

Inwardly, he swore. He had no experience at bringing women around to forgiveness. In the past, if things had gotten rocky with a girlfriend, he'd simply moved on.

"Dru, I shouldn't have made the bet with Corbin in the first place. And I . . . I regret that I didn't tell you about it. You believed me earlier when I said that our relationship has nothing to do with the bet. Right?"

"I think I do believe you."

An *I think I do* meant she was still working through it. He rested his forehead on the glass of the windowpane and closed his eyes. His day, since the coffee shop, had been awful. He'd spent the hours at home, mostly watching TV. He hadn't bothered to turn on the lights when night came. He'd been too busy thinking about her and calling himself an idiot.

"Dru," he said unevenly. The bet was such a small

thing. How had it tripped up something as big and important to him as his relationship with Dru?

"I need time to think about us," she said.

"What's to think about? We're having fun."

Silence met his statement. Then "Good night, Gray."

The line went dead.

TWENTY-FIVE

Romance could be hazardous to your mental health. Like the thousands of other women across America currently sniffling into tissues over their boyfriends, Dru was in a depressed and grumpy funk. Over a man!

It was all very degrading.

She thumped her knuckles on Julie's desk as she passed by, then exchanged goodbyes with Anthony Sutton's personal assistant and the firm's receptionist before leaving the office for the evening. When she reached the hallway elevator bank, she slung her backpack over one shoulder and zipped up her jacket.

It had been more than two days since she'd seen Gray at the coffee shop. He'd called her the first night and then again last night. Last night, she'd said again that she needed more time. All in all, he'd been respectful of her request.

One minute she appreciated that he'd responded so respectfully, the next she wondered why he wasn't banging on her door and screaming along the lines of the *"Stella!"* scene from *A Streetcar Named Desire*.

The elevator arrived, and she punched the button for her floor of the high-rise's parking garage.

She didn't like it, not at all, that Gray and Corbin had bet on her affections. It was as if she were an inanimate object that they'd both seen, liked, and bartered over. Two extraordinarily rich men, entertaining themselves through pointless competition.

But the bet was not her main problem. She believed Gray when he'd said that the bet had spurred his pursuit of her at the beginning but hadn't been a factor in a long time.

Her main problem was exactly what she'd always known to be the main problem. Gray did not tell her things. She was not his confidante and not someone he trusted. Her discovery of the bet had simply shoved that fact to the fore.

So? What should she do about Gray?

Half of her thought that she should pick up their dating relationship where they'd left off and continue on the way they had been. Wait and see. Give him more time. Hold on to him as long as possible in hopes that he'd eventually trust her and love her. Put off The Talk, since it was guaranteed to push him up against a wall and make him declare his emotions. Forcing him to declare his emotions at this point might ruin them. The plus side of this option: she might end up with a gem of a man at the end.

The other half of her insisted that Gray declare his emotions now. For the love of self-respect! Yes, The Talk might ruin them. But if their relationship ended in heartbreak now, that would be easier than having it end in heartbreak a month or a year from now. The plus side of this option: she might save herself a tremendous amount of pain.

She exited the elevator and walked through the garage in the direction of her motorcycle. The air hung chilly here. She could hear the distant give and take of conversations between co-workers walking to their cars and the hum of heating units working to warm the offices above.

She pulled free her key and abruptly froze. Gray was leaning against the concrete wall on the far side of her bike. His hands were stuffed into the pockets of his jeans. The black insulated jacket he'd worn on Christmas Day when they'd gone tree-hunting hung open, revealing a simple white shirt beneath. He wore a Mustangs ball cap, pulled low.

He looked big, foreboding, sexy, and steadfastly patient.

Her heart began to thud in a gulping, winded way merely at the sight of him. Perhaps it was best that he hadn't gone the *"Stella!"* route. It was very betraying of her body to react so powerfully when all he was doing was leaning against a wall, staring at her.

"Have you been waiting long?" She made a stab at sounding debonair.

He pushed upright and took a step toward her. "Forty-five minutes."

She stashed her key in her backpack, then set it on the ground near her bike.

"I don't like this . . . whatever it is . . . this . . . separation between us," he said. "I don't know how the past few days have been for you, but they've been rotten for me. I don't think I'll be able to focus or breathe or smile until you and I are good again."

It was quite a speech. A very good speech. Dru felt herself weakening in the face of it and of him. He was painfully appealing to her, and she'd have liked to throw herself into his arms, feel his strength band around her, set her hands on his face, and kiss him.

But she assumed that grown-up people in grown-up relationships didn't operate purely on whims.

"I said I was sorry, but that didn't work." His green eyes were grave and beautiful. "If you'll tell me how to fix it, that's what I'll do. I want us to go back to how we were."

"I liked how we were, too." For a moment she wavered over the two options before her. Wait and see? Or make him declare himself? "I liked how we were," she repeated, "but I don't want to continue that way because it wasn't as deep as I wanted it to be."

"What do you mean, deep?" he asked calmly. "We haven't been going out that long."

"We were in each other's presence for countless hours across five weeks before we started dating. Since we started dating, five more weeks have passed."

"True."

"I feel as though you've put up a shield against me that I haven't been able to get past. It's kept me where you're comfortable with me being. But . . ." She knit her forehead. *Be brave, Dru.* "I'm not content there anymore. I want more from you than that."

She'd flown bareback across wide-open Texas land. She'd once shot a charging boar and never flinched. She'd put her life at risk for her country without a complaint. She was not a weakling, and she was not willing to walk on eggshells to make Gray comfortable.

She *longed* for a place in his life. But she was strong enough and sure enough in herself and in God's plan for her to want Gray wholly, or not at all. The time for making excuses for him had passed.

"I'll give you more," he said.

"Good." She stood tall. "Then tell me how you feel

about me and tell me what you want out of this relationship."

He whitened. "I . . ."

She waited, her hopes twisting.

"You know how much I like you, Dru."

"No." She shook her head. "I don't."

No response.

Gray wasn't ready or wasn't able to move forward. He wanted to. She knew that to be true. When it came down to it, though, he couldn't make himself vulnerable.

In her way, Dru couldn't make herself vulnerable, either. She'd spent her childhood feeling left out, and she refused to accept being made to feel left out by her own boyfriend.

"Why . . . ?" He scowled, and she could tell that the offensive ace was about to go on the defensive. "Why does everything have to be so serious?" His tone indicated that she was the one out of line. "Let's just keep dating each other and see what happens."

"I didn't say things had to be serious. I merely said that I needed you to tell me how you feel about me."

"Dru . . ."

The elevator made a muted *bing*. Out of the corner of her eye, she watched a businessman stride toward his car. He shot them a questioning look, then continued on.

One painful second rolled into the next while Gray Fowler's silence destroyed their future.

"Look," he said, the soul of logic, "let me buy you dinner. You can tell me about all my faults, and I'll try to convince you of all my assets. We'll . . ."

Frustration elbowed its way into her crushing disappointment. Charm? He was attempting to use charm on

her in this moment? "Since you've started seeing me,"
Dru said, "you've had one foot planted in my camp and
one foot in freedom's camp. If you're ever going to have
an intimate relationship, then you're going to have to
step into it with both feet." Shaking inside, she pulled
out her key, thrust her arms through her backpack's
straps, arced a leg over the seat of her motorcycle, and
awoke her bike's engine with a satisfying roar. She met
his eyes. "Go ahead and plant both feet in freedom's
camp, Gray, because I'm no longer available. I wish you
the best. I really do."

Then she swung the bike around and drove in the
direction of Holley. When she hit the freeway, she realized she'd been so upset that she'd forgotten to pull her
helmet from its compartment.

The wind whipped away the tears of the woman who
prided herself on the fact that she never cried.

Gray stood alone in the cold parking garage, his feet
rooted to the floor long after her motorcycle had disappeared from view.

You want to know how I feel about you, Dru? *I love
you.*

You want to know what I want out of this relationship? *You. I want you. I want you to love me back.
That's all.*

You are what I want.

His fingers curled into fists.

He knew these things in his head. So why hadn't he
been able to say them to her? She'd handed him an opportunity to save their relationship. He'd wanted desperately

to save it. Yet the words that would have saved it hadn't come. His doubts and slithering fears had silenced them.

A dark voice deep in his own mind had asked, *What makes you think you have the right to be happy? If you open yourself up to her, you'll end up wrecked and heart-broken. Useless to others and to yourself. You always knew this thing with Dru couldn't end well, didn't you?*

Brain spinning, stomach aching, he walked to his car. Devastation seemed to be caving him in from the inside like buildings falling into a sinkhole. He sat behind the wheel.

Why had Dru put him on the spot like that? She'd asked too much, and she hadn't held herself to the same standard. She hadn't said anything to him—not once since they'd started dating—about how she felt about him or what she wanted out of their relationship. But she'd expected him to spill his guts in the middle of a garage.

He wanted to blame her. It would be easier to blame her.

Only he couldn't pull it off because he knew why she'd put him on the spot. She'd done it because it was important to her to know where he stood. Good boy-friends and good husbands honored the things that were important to their girlfriends and wives. They answered honest questions with honest answers. That was how people in good relationships acted.

Good relationships had never been a Fowler specialty.

He drove home and walked directly to the built-in bar located in the wide hallway between the kitchen and the formal dining room he never used.

He stared at bottle after bottle of expensive alcohol while the words he hadn't said to Dru filled his mind over and over, haunting him. By keeping them inside, he'd doubled, or even tripled, their power.

I love you. I love you.

A week later, Gray was once again standing in front of his built-in bar.

January was almost gone. February would come tomorrow. He'd stood in front of this bar every day for the past seven days. Sometimes he'd stood here several times a day. Even when he hadn't been standing here, he'd been thinking about drinking what the bottles on these glass shelves offered. So far, he hadn't had even a sip of Southern Comfort or any of the other choices stored here.

His good behavior made him feel no better.

Late-afternoon light slanted from the tall dining room windows, slicing across the carpet but not reaching him.

The only time in his life when he'd been more miserable than he'd been this past week was when he'd been living under the same roof as the dirt bag.

He'd hardly slept. Even when surrounded by his friends, he'd felt embarrassingly lonely without Dru. He'd kept himself busy, yet nothing he'd spent his time doing had meaning.

And what bothered him most?

How controlled she'd been that day in the parking garage.

He'd seen women throw tantrums. He'd seen them cry and try to hit him and shout. Kayla Bell had thrown a few fits. In those situations, he'd remained even-keeled.

In the garage, when Dru had been breaking up with

him, she'd been the even-keeled one. He'd been the one who'd wanted to cry and hit something and shout.

It got to him, her control.

The words she'd said to him also got to him. He couldn't make them go away no matter how loud he turned up the music or how hard he tried to focus on the television or the person talking to him or the road while he was driving.

"I thought you might be hungry." Ash filled the doorway that led to the kitchen. She held a tray loaded with salad, soup, and a roast beef sandwich. She regarded him with gentle concern.

"Thanks." He wasn't heartless enough to tell her he wasn't hungry.

"You didn't eat much for lunch. So . . ." She moved her weight from foot to foot. For the past week, she'd been doing her best to feed his depression away. "I'll just set this on the dining room table?"

"Good."

Ash edged past him. Gray regarded the bottles longingly, furiously as the memory of his mom's tears from long ago drifted back to him.

"I love . . . him! And . . ." That awful sobbing. "And now Jeff's married to someone else. Today. Today . . . was their wedding day. He's married."

How had his mom handled her misery and her relationship difficulties? With alcohol. He understood his mother in a new and humbling way now. That didn't mean he wanted to be like her. Just the possibility of being like her turned his soul to ice.

Viciously, he yanked up a bottle, unscrewed its cap, and poured it down the bar sink. *Glug glug glug.*

"Um . . . what are you doing?" Ashley now stood framed by the other doorway, the one on the dining room side. He hadn't realized she was still around.

"Pouring this out," he answered. "I don't want it in the house."

A gap of silence. "Do you . . . ? Can I help?"

"I've got it." He grabbed another bottle. "Thanks, though."

Glug glug glug.

"Gray? Have you . . . heard from Dru?"

He angled a look at his housekeeper. Her eyes had gone round, and she was clearly afraid for his sanity. She must have had to work up a lot of courage to ask him about Dru. She knew they'd broken up, and she'd seen firsthand the effect it had had on him since. "No. I haven't heard from Dru."

Ash bit the edge of her lip but held her ground. "I remember all your past girlfriends. Each of them had great qualities, but none of them were right for you, I didn't think. Just like I'm not right for you—" A nervous laugh. Her hand fluttered to her chest. "Of course, *I'm* not right for you." She rolled her eyes. "I'm your employee. We work together. But I do . . . I want you to be happy."

He nodded.

"So I feel like I need to tell you that Dru was it, in my opinion. She was the right one for you. In my eyes, you two were a perfect match." She gave a wobbly smile. "Have you thought about going to see her and telling her that you're sorry you broke up with her? If you are . . . sorry, that is."

"I didn't break up with Dru. She broke up with me."

"She did?" Ash gasped, as if she couldn't imagine a world in which such a thing was possible.

"Yes. She did." He dumped another bottle.

Ash rushed to fill the ominous quiet with updates. She talked about the food she'd left in his fridge. His dry cleaning. The emails she'd sent at his request. Tomorrow's schedule and the fact that Grace Street had called about the Winter Family Fun Day.

Finally, Ash bundled up in her cold-weather gear. With one final worried look, she left for the day.

When he'd drained the hard liquor, he poured out all the wine and all the beer, then carried the empty glass bottles to the recycling and let them fall into the bin with a crashing explosion.

Unbearably restless, he walked circles around his enormous backyard while the sky lost its light.

He hadn't wanted to love Dru. From the start, he hadn't wanted that.

Love.

He thought through all the arguments between his mom and her husbands and boyfriends. The times when she'd stayed away from home for long stretches. Or been unable to get out of bed. Or walked through life like a ghost who looked like his mother.

He thought about the dirt bag and the way his stepfather's face had always tightened with fury right before he'd slammed Gray up against the wall or tossed him onto the ground.

An old memory came into sharp focus.

"You worthless idiot. You're nothing, you no-good, spineless kid." Gray's shoulder, the outside of his thin arm, and his cheek had throbbed from the punches he'd already taken.

The beating was over, though. It was over, thank goodness. The dirt bag was settling down. Gray hung his head and backed away. He could feel tears stinging his eyes, and he was desperate for the privacy of his room.

"You're pathetic."

Gray looked up just in time to see a hand slashing through the air toward him. The sight brought a bolt of sickening realization. The beating wasn't over.

Those moments of dread when he'd understood what was about to happen had almost been worse than the impact.

Dru had told him that he'd put up a shield to keep her where he was comfortable with her being.

It was true. He couldn't imagine himself as part of a healthy, normal relationship that could actually go the distance. He had difficulty believing that love wouldn't end up ruining him, because he believed he had the capacity to love like his mother loved. He'd always felt it there, that ability. If he really let himself love Dru, then she'd have power over him. To defeat him.

You're not your mother, he told himself. *And Dru is nothing like Jeff. You coward. You're not your mother—*

But he could be. He could be like her.

He was supposed to be forgiving his mother and leaving his past behind him. He knew that was what God wanted him to do. For pity's sake, that's what *he* wanted to do. He'd been working at that the best way he knew. Through prayer and through giving up the stuff in his life that had only messed him up more.

But what he was doing didn't seem to be working.

Why hadn't God fixed things inside him? Why was he still screwed up?

Maybe God wasn't as powerful as Dru and people

at that strange biker church seemed to think He was. Or maybe Gray wasn't doing Christianity right. If he wasn't, he didn't know how to do it better.

Returning to his house, he walked through each room and looked at all the expensive things he'd accumulated. None of them comforted him.

Exhaustion weighed his limbs. His brain was dazed. His emotions raw. He was spent. He couldn't walk any farther.

He made his way into his master bathroom, ran hot water in his shiny, modern shower, and sat on the bench inside, too tired to stand. He washed his hair, his body. Got out. Brushed his teeth.

He clicked off most of the lights and stretched out in his big bed in his perfectly clean, organized, decorated bedroom.

Sleep wouldn't come.

He could only see Dru, standing in the forest outside her house on Christmas Day. Her gloves were outstretched to catch the snowflakes. She glanced at him, a charmed smile on her lips, her turquoise eyes bright with affection.

He'd lost her.

He stacked his hands on top of his head and worked to take deep breaths, to fight off the panic that was threatening.

He couldn't go back to the good *enough* that his life had been before Dru. And he didn't want to go forward into the *definitely* not good enough that his life would be in the future without her.

He was an unforgiving man, outwardly tough and inwardly terrified of trusting. He had so many flaws and scars. He could see himself as he really was. If other people could see him that way, they'd see a man covered in black.

Anxiety and despair rose.

Gray.

He froze, listening.

And into that place he heard mercy call to him.

It called him by name, and it sounded like peace.

He was forgiven. It didn't matter that he was a man covered in black. He was forgiven. God had the ability, through grace, to take his darkness and exchange it for white. Forgiven.

Did he believe it? Yes.

Calm moved over him, the first real calm he'd experienced since he'd walked into the coffee shop that day and found Dru and Corbin together. It relaxed tense muscles, settled his mind, and opened doors around his heart that had been locked tight for a long, long time.

Maybe faith and prayer didn't change everyone in one miraculous instant. For him, forgiving and letting go might be things he'd have to work at continuously. If he didn't work at them, though, the alternative was to end up like Dennis Wright, a man trapped by grief because he'd been unable to overcome the things that had happened to him.

Gray visualized again, like he had the night Dru had apprehended Dennis, opening his hands and letting it all—his grudges, his fear, his childhood—fall away.

The following Saturday, the Winter Family Fun Day dawned blessedly clear. Meg was not responsible for the Fun Day. She merely offered up her property. Even so, she couldn't help feeling maternal about Grace Street's event. She wanted the best for them and had been checking the weather forecasts more avidly than Al Roker. The temperatures wouldn't climb out of the low fifties this afternoon. But it wouldn't rain. And wind wouldn't blow the booths away.

Meg sat on the padded stool in her master bathroom in front of her mirror. She'd just finished showering, dressing, and putting on makeup. Those things would merely kick off a normal person's day. But these days, getting ready for the day was sometimes the sum total of her entire day's accomplishments.

She slid closed the drawer containing her makeup just as one of the babies, the one on her right, which meant her girl—unless they'd done some flip-flopping lately—gave her a good jab with a little foot. Pausing, Meg set her hand on the spot. Two more kicks. Then some shuffling and stretching.

Carefully, Meg rose and made her way into the room they'd prepared as the nursery. They'd painted half of it blue and half of it pink. Back when she'd been put on bedrest, the nursery had been unfinished. The walls had been painted, the rug had been unrolled, and the furniture had been ordered. But that was about it.

Since then, everyone in their close circle of family and friends had put in time working on this room. She eased herself into the blue-patterned glider rocker. She'd sat right here, in this exact spot, many, many times in recent weeks while Bo, his siblings, their wives, his parents, her girlfriends, and even her own eighty-eight-year-old former nanny, Sadie Jo, had put together this room for the twins.

Two cribs. Two glider rockers, each covered with the

same beautiful fabric, except one was shades of pink and the other shades of blue.

A wall decal of a graceful white tree began on the pink side near the windows at the room's end and arched over the crib toward the door. On the blue side, the tree began near the door and reached toward the windows. Mobiles hung from the ceiling above both cribs. The delicate white birds on the mobiles swished in the warm air wafting from a vent.

Across the way, a bookcase held a collection of board books, stuffed animals, and silver-framed pictures of all the babies' relatives. Meg had asked Bo to unearth some of the things that had been packed away from her childhood and from his. They'd sprinkled the worn, retro items in between the frames.

Bouncy seats waited for their occupants. Swings. Boppy pillows. Diapers. Wipes. A sound machine.

A changing table/dresser held drawer after drawer of washed and neatly folded items. Tiny, downy gowns. Blankets. Burp cloths. Miniature socks.

The nursery surrounded Meg with a serene sense of expectation. It was organized and pretty and industrious. It was everything she'd ever hoped this room could be when it had been an ordinary guest bedroom, when she'd dreamed about how she would decorate it should she ever have the opportunity to turn it into a nursery. Looking at it now was like looking at a dream come true.

I'm ready, the room seemed to whisper. She clicked on the lamp on the side table next to her and imagined what it would be like to hold their little boy, her *son*, in her arms and look over to see Bo in the pink glider holding their little girl, her *daughter*, in his arms. It would be joy immeasurable. It would stamp everything that had come before with one word: WORTHWHILE.

Her eye caught on the two blankets and two outfits sitting on the floor near the inside of the nursery door. They'd come in the mail yesterday from cousins on her mother's side of the family. She'd just pop them in the wash with the special dye-free, scent-free, whatever-might-possibly-be-harmful-to-newborns-free detergent on her way to her usual reclining spot on the living room sofa.

Bo would be picking her up in a few hours to take her by the Fun Day. They wouldn't stay long. She'd heard that Gray Fowler, Dru's Gray, would be speaking to the crowd in between bands and then, afterward, signing autographs. She wanted to sit in the audience to hear him speak.

With a groan of effort, she rose and made her way in the direction of the blankets and outfits—

Her vision warbled. A wave of dizziness rolled through her, and she had to shoot out a hand and brace it against the bookcase to steady herself. Her—her blood pressure must be soaring.

She dipped her head and concentrated on staring at the rug. Blurry. Fear wanted to swoop in and devour her, but she held it at bay. With all her might, she willed her eyesight to focus. Instead, it became spottier, then began to narrow, as if she were looking down a tunnel. The room started to sway.

She reached for her cell phone, which she'd kept close since the last incident. She was wearing her softest, stretchiest pair of maternity sweatpants, the same ones she wore every third day at this point because very few things still fit and very few things were still comfortable. Trembling, her fingers strained into the pocket of her sweatpants and found only emptiness.

Her mind reeled. What? But it had just been there. It . . . *think!* It must be in the glider. Through her graying vision, she could just make out her cell phone. There. On the edge of the glider's cushion. She walked in that direction, growing more light-headed with every step. She was about to pass out.

With a mother's determination, she continued forward, her hands grasping in front of her. She would not faint. She had to call Bo. Her shin struck something with a painful, blunt whack. She lowered unsteadily onto her knees. The glider was right in front of her. When her palms met the front edge of the upholstery, she released a gasp of relief.

She yanked up her phone. It was barely visible to her, but her hands and brain knew what to do. She only needed to push a couple of buttons to call Bo. Another swell of nausea and dizziness came for her.

She punched his number.

Then darkness pulled her under.

"Meg." Bo's voice.

She felt heavy and very sleepy. It was the kind of liquid-limbed feeling that made you want to turn your head and relax back into it. Goodness, she was tired. Every bit of her was weary. She'd just go back to sleep for a little bit—

"Can you hear me? Open your eyes."

He sounded tense.

"Meg. I love you. Can you open your eyes for me? You passed out, but I'm here now, and I need you to look at me and talk to me if you can."

Memory rushed in. She'd been in the nursery. She'd been groping to call him. On a jagged breath, she cracked open her eyes. He was next to her, kneeling. She was still in the nursery, on the floor near the blue rocker. He must have propped up her head and back with pillows.

"Thank God." He had ahold of her hand, she realized. He squeezed. She squeezed back. "The ambulance should be here any minute," he told her.

"So the . . . the call I tried to make to you must have gone through."

"It did, but I could only hear silence on your end. I was at one of the barns."

Meg's eyesight still wasn't right. Yet a strange sense of God's presence slipped in and around her. The Holy Spirit glowed like a warm light in the center of her, spreading up through her neck, head, outward along her arms and legs. She was still afraid. But her confidence in God began to outpace the fear.

She'd experienced this sensation another time, long ago, at one of the most terrifying moments of her life. She'd understood then that God was with her, and if He was with her, then she could face whatever came. She understood it afresh now. "Bo?"

"Yes." He was shaking, she could see. His gray eyes were bright, his lashes spiky with moisture. He slid her hair back from her face and kissed her forehead.

"Our twins don't belong to us. They're God's babies." It was something she'd prayed over and over during her pregnancy. *These babies are yours, Lord. You've given them to me, and I entrust them back to You.* "He loves them more than we do."

Bo nodded.

"His will for them is trust . . ." Her head ached, and her breath had grown short so it wasn't easy for her to speak, which only increased her urgency to communicate this to him. "His will. For them. Is trustworthy."

"It is," he agreed.

She had a totally inappropriate urge to laugh. Because had she said anything at all just now—*"I'd like to shave my hair as short as yours, Bo"*—she had a feeling he'd have agreed with her.

"If anything happens to me," she said, "I want you to know that it's all right."

He stiffened. "It wouldn't be all right with me."

Ah. Well, apparently he wasn't ready to agree with her about *everything*.

Meg had lost her mother when she was very young, but God had been there to shepherd her through her childhood. And in time, He'd given her Bo and the entire Porter family. Their marriage had blessed her beyond counting. "I'm thankful. For you. If something happens to me, you'll be a wonderful father."

"Nothing is going to happen to you," he said firmly. "You and the babies are all going to be fine."

The wail of sirens reached them.

She rested her free hand on his cheek. "I love you."

"I love you, Meg. It's going to be fine," he said again, his voice filled with the force of his determination.

CHAPTER TWENTY-SIX

H ow're you feeling?" Dru asked Augustine.

"Hopeful. That postcard we made for Roy, advertising Gray's appearance here, looked very professional. You should have seen it, Dru. *Mm-hmm!* I have a feeling, down deep in my bones, that Roy will come."

Augustine had a walker and two wheelchairs. One wheelchair for smooth surfaces, the other with thick wheels similar to those of a mountain bike for "off road" terrain. Despite that Augustine had tried to assure Dru she could navigate the grounds of the Winter Family Fun Day without a wheelchair, Dru had insisted on the "off road" chair.

The walk from their parking place to the Fun Day site alone would have done Augustine in. Dru wanted the older lady to save her strength. Confronting the husband who'd abandoned her and her children twenty-five years prior would be exhausting enough.

Dru had been power-walking behind the chair, but she slowed as they reached the first booths, in deference to the people of all ages strolling the grounds.

A wooden sign labeled this lane of booths *The General Store*. Stalls on either side offered monogrammed children's clothing, art, jewelry, jars of preserves and more. A white stake introduced each stop, the vendor's name written down the length of it vertically. Greenery had been tied to the top of the stakes with fluttering pale blue and white ribbons.

Meg and Bo had told her about previous Fun Days, but she hadn't attended in the past. Single twenty-something women who ate Doritos and wore black leather motorcycle jackets with gray jeans (her current outfit) probably weren't the primary demographic for open-air fairs that sold things like handmade organic soap and offered ice sculptures for viewing.

The Fun Day was a bigger deal than Dru had envisioned, highly organized, and unexpectedly charming. She was obnoxiously pro-Texan, and this event definitely had a "God Bless Texas" feel.

"Isn't this nice?" Augustine asked.

"It is."

"Reminds me of the open-air market in Marrakesh." Augustine chuckled fondly. "We got terribly lost in that market. So lost that we eventually embraced it and enjoyed a cup of Moroccan coffee. Delicious! They used spices in it like cinnamon, black peppercorns, and cardamom."

They reached an intersection. According to the signs, The General Store continued forward. The sledding hill, skating, ice sculptures, and Arcade Road were to the left. The Chuck Wagon and The Town Square were to the right.

"There, I think." Augustine pointed right, and Dru

rolled her in that direction. She'd studied the event map online this morning. Gray would be speaking in—she checked her watch—twenty minutes from the stage in The Town Square.

"On that Morocco trip," Augustine continued, "we rode camels into the sunset." She went on to suggest adventures to Morocco that the two of them could pursue.

Earlier, when Dru had arrived at Augustine's to pick her up, she'd been expecting her neighbor to be in grim, it's-go-time mode. Instead, the older lady had been as relaxed and quick to laugh as ever.

Her neighbor hadn't wanted her sons to accompany her here today. She'd told Dru numerous times that should Roy show up, her own feelings would not be hurt if the meeting didn't go well. Her sons, though? There was no telling how they'd react. Augustine was the one who wanted the meeting with Roy, not them. She'd seen no point in stirring up her sons' resentment toward their father, so she'd asked Dru to bring her.

Back when Augustine had asked her, Dru had still been dating Gray. She'd immediately told Augustine that she'd be glad to bring her. An opportunity to help a friend and watch Gray give his talk? Sure. Two birds with one stone.

But now that she and Gray had broken up, she was somewhat dreading having to see him. He did very well in front of a crowd. He'd be gorgeous and direct and funny, and he'd look as if he were flourishing without her, which he probably was. Everyone present would be hero-worshipping him. He might even have brought a date along to hero-worship him one-on-one, a possibility that ran through Dru's heart like a spear.

The days since their breakup had been . . . What was

the best word to describe them? Abysmal? She was someone who was very slow to make an attachment. But once
she had, she had tremendous difficulty moving on from
it. Her feelings about Gray were still reeling. This was
not the time to watch him being fabulous in public. She
wanted to stand fiercely behind the decision she'd made
concerning him. She didn't want to regret the loss of him
or second-guess herself.

They emptied into a large area filled with tables. Almost every seat was already occupied, many by people
wearing Mustangs jerseys, jackets, and hats. A band
playing country music filled the stage directly across
from their position. The temporary establishments arranged in a huge square around the tables were serving
everything from cider to bratwurst to funnel cake. The
distinctive funnel cake smell carried to Dru on the breeze.

"I'd like to stand." Augustine's twisted hands gripped
the armrests of the chair.

Dru came around and helped her friend up. So many
things had been taken from Augustine. But the woman
still had a great deal of dignity, the heart of an explorer,
and courage. Plenty of courage. The older lady stood as
tall as she was able and took her time studying the crowd.

"I see him," she said at last, her tone ringing with
victory.

"Really?" Dru came fully alert. For ages, she'd listened
to Augustine talk about her desire to find Roy. Dru had
hoped for a meeting between them for Augustine's sake,
but she hadn't had a ton of optimism in Augustine's plan
to draw Roy out via postcard.

"Yes." Augustine squinted through her glasses and
began hobbling toward one of the tables near the center.

Dru parked the wheelchair. "Do you want me to come with you?"

"Come with me, but stand a few feet back, if you don't mind. If I shake my head, that means not to come farther, to leave us alone together. If I scratch my ear like this"—her large peacock-feather earring jiggled—"that means I need reinforcements."

"Got it."

Augustine approached an African-American man sitting with several pieces of Mustangs paraphernalia on the table in front of him. Presumably, he'd brought the paraphernalia for Gray to sign. He was bald and dressed the way a high school teacher might dress. Preppy and plain.

The family sitting on the far side of Roy's table was eating corn dogs, and all four of their kids seemed to be talking at once. For the best, maybe, since the kids' voices masked sound and would give Augustine's speech privacy.

Roy looked over at Augustine, then away, before his head swung back again. His features loosened with shock. Not guilt or annoyance—just simple, abject surprise. He rose to his feet.

Roy was fit and appeared to be years younger than Augustine, though Dru knew that he was the older of the two. Life wasn't always fair. Augustine was the one who'd been left behind by him. She was the one who'd spent the subsequent decades pouring herself into her children and grandchildren. She was as good-hearted as any Christian Dru knew. Yet Roy was the one flush with health.

Dru hung back, just barely within hearing distance, not wanting to intrude.

"Hello, Roy." Augustine spoke smoothly, confidently, and Dru experienced a burst of pride.

"Hello, Augustine."

"I'm glad you're here. I've been wanting to see you again."

His face registered confusion.

Augustine was about to let him have it, Dru knew. Real fire and brimstone stuff. Dru might need to defend Augustine if her neighbor started shouting or clawing.

"I've been wanting to see you," Augustine said, "because I want you to know that I forgive you."

Dru's jaw sagged. *What?*

Augustine's face beamed, her cheeks glowed rosy. She looked like an angel. "We had some good times together, and the hard memories can't take those away. I'm grateful to you for giving me our boys. And I wanted to tell you that I wish you the best."

Roy looked even more stunned than he had at her arrival.

"Thank you," he cobbled together.

"You're welcome."

Augustine had said that Roy's response was not her primary concern, and Dru could finally see why. Her neighbor had been able to do what she'd long felt led to do—she'd delivered her speech of forgiveness. Augustine had accomplished the final step in making peace with her history. Next to the enormity of that, Roy's reaction was secondary.

Augustine gave a small shake of her head, Dru's signal to leave them alone together.

Dru made her way into the crowd at the perimeter of the tables. The band wound down, the final notes of their song hovering. Dru had just placed an order for hot chocolate at a booth near the stage when her cell phone rang.

"Hi, Jake." She handed the saleswoman cash.

"Lyndie spotted you. We're here at the Fun Day, too, sitting at a table diagonal from you, near the back."

She accepted her change and swiveled to see her brother stand, phone to his ear, and wave. She bobbed her chin in response, then turned back to wait for her drink.

"What're you doing here?" Jake asked. Always so full of charm, Jake.

"I brought Augustine."

"Ah."

"What are you and Lyndie doing here?"

"Meg told Lyndie that she and Bo are planning to come by to hear your boyfriend talk. Lyndie wanted to get here early and save Meg a seat because . . . well, you know. She can't really stand or walk. I'm not sure why Meg and Bo aren't here yet."

"He's no longer my boyfriend."

A pause. The woman behind the counter handed a lidded to-go cup to Dru.

"You guys broke up?" Jake asked.

"Yes."

"Would it be rude of me to say I'm glad?" He gave a half-laughing grunt. "Lyndie just punched me in the arm and gave me an offended face. Clearly, she thinks it's rude of me to say that I'm glad you broke up."

"I'm used to your rudeness," Dru pointed out. Though, foolishly, Jake's words did goad a part of her into wanting to defend Gray. To tell Jake about Gray's childhood. To explain that her relationship with Gray had felt like a place to call home. Or to confide that he'd given her a framed drawing of Annie Oakley, and any man who would give her such a ridiculously perfect gift couldn't be all bad.

"Do you want to come sit with us?" Jake asked.

"Once Gray's done, I'll come by and say hi."

"You're not avoiding him, are you?"

"Me?" she asked in a scandalized tone. "I'd be more likely to take up knitting." She disconnected and slid into a hollow area between the hot chocolate stall and a candy apple stall. In fact, she was sort of, not really, kinda, whatever . . . somewhat inclined to avoid a situation in which Gray would notice her in the crowd. From the stage, Gray would have a direct line of sight to Jake and Lyndie's table, and she didn't want him to see her there and think she'd come to hear him because she was lovesick.

A friendly woman with a clipboard had stepped up to the microphone onstage. She was going on and on about how honored Grace Street was to have Gray Fowler as a benefactor and how thrilled they were that he'd agreed to make an appearance at Winter Family Fun Day. He'd be meeting with fans and signing autographs at the end of The General Store alley. She went into a detailed explanation about how the line for autographs would form. Then she launched into Gray's long and exemplary bio.

From her concealed position, Dru observed the now-packed square. Uneasily, she noted that the rent-a-cop security personnel hadn't funneled everyone through a central entrance, which would have allowed them to assess each individual. Nor were they situated at regular intervals in front of the audience, looking outward into their assigned segments, which would have been the most effective tactic with this sort of gathering. She counted only three guards. One or two booths down from her position who was checking his phone. One directly across, talking to a child holding a stuffed lion. One at the far end who appeared to be about fifteen years old.

Dru sipped her hot chocolate. Incredibly delicious.

"Eight-time Pro Bowl selection," the woman with the microphone announced grandly, "Super Bowl winner, and veteran tight end for the Dallas Mustangs—Gray Fowler!"

A few die-hard Cowboys fans grumbled good-naturedly. But far more people had come to the Fun Day at this time specifically *because* they were Mustangs fans. That group went wild as Gray climbed onto the stage via stairs at the rear. He wore a dark gray suit that looked like it had cost a fortune, a white business shirt, and an understated pale-blue patterned tie. The white of his shirt made his skin look tanner and his eyes lighter. He lifted a hand to acknowledge the raucous delight of his fans.

Physical longing wrenched through Dru.

Seeing him was even harder than she'd expected. He looked healthy and handsome. Like a man who didn't have a care in the world—and certainly didn't mourn the latest of his short-term girlfriends. The thought was instantly painful but, like a sore tooth, she couldn't seem to quit nudging it.

The mass of people took a long time to quiet.

"Thank you for coming out," Gray said into the microphone. "Doesn't Grace Street do a great job putting on these Winter Family Fun Days?" More hooting and enthusiastic clapping. "As many of you know, Grace Street reaches out to women and children in our community who've suffered domestic violence. It takes a team to offer women and kids the support they need, so the organizers of this event asked me if I'd talk for a few minutes about my experience with teamwork and what can be accomplished when we all work together."

He began recounting the story of how the Mustangs had gone from a struggling team heavy on rookies to Super Bowl champs just three years later. The crowd hung on every word, silent except for a few coughs, the tones of murmuring kids, and distant noise from other areas of the fair.

As was her custom, Dru searched across the sea of faces, looking to identify the person who posed the greatest threat.

This is foolish, Dru. You're not his bodyguard—

There. A teenager had just emerged from the rear corner of the square, straight back. Her forehead lined as she studied him. He radiated edgy tension. He hadn't faced her, which was also off, because had he been watching Gray like everyone else in the area, he'd have been looking directly toward her.

The sharp lines of the teen's profile stirred her memory. Did she know him? From where?

People moved between Dru and the teen, stealing him from view. She set aside her cup and moved out from her position until she spotted him again.

She knew him from the day they'd visited Mullins! This was the sullen boy, the son of Gray's mom's boyfriend, Jeff. What was the kid's name? She worked to pull it up. Daniel. What was he doing here so far from home? Could he have come with Jeff and Sandy? To support Gray?

She began weaving through people in his direction, panning the area around him for Jeff or Sandy. She didn't

see either one. Focusing again on Daniel, she noticed
that he'd buried his hands in the pockets of his oversized
camo jacket. The pockets on both sides looked heavy.
The fabric at the base of the pockets dipped downward.

Guns were heavy. They'd do that to fabric.

Instinctively, she shifted into a jog, staying low and
keeping people in between her and Daniel so he wouldn't
notice her approach. Daniel could have filled his pockets
with harmless things. He could be here for a harmless
reason. But Dru's intuition—that foreboding intuition of
hers that had never once allowed her peace concerning
Gray's stalker—was warning her of danger.

Daniel moved away from the corner across the back
row of food stalls.

Danger. Danger.

She didn't have her gun. All these people. Not enough
security. Gray. She needed a gun.

She neared the security guard who still had his attention on his cell phone. His gun was strapped into the
holster on his belt.

Dru's gaze cut back to Daniel just in time to watch
him lift two pistols, one in each hand, from his jacket
pockets and point them at the stage.

Dru dashed forward, stripped the gun from the security guard's holster, and broke into a run as she clicked
off the weapon's safety. Vaguely, she heard the guard's
shout from behind her. There were other sounds now,
too. Gasping and a woman's frightened scream.

She was twenty yards out from the teen's location,
closing fast. She'd done her best to protect Mark and
she'd failed. Her good friend had lost his life, and his
family had lost their husband, father, grandfather.

She wasn't about to let the same happen to Gray.

"Daniel!" she yelled.

He didn't respond.

Dru lifted her handgun, leveling it at him as she rushed forward through the crowd. The realization that she'd been outsmarted washed over her with sickening certainty. Gray was unprotected. Daniel had pistols in both hands, both barrels aimed at Gray. Had she been next to Gray, she'd have shoved him down, been able to dodge in front of him to keep him safe. But she was much too far away from him for that. Despair arced through her mind and heart. She was too far. He was unprotected.

"Lower your weapons," she demanded, shouldering past bystanders.

Daniel's face turned sharply in her direction, giving her a direct line of sight into facial features that were drawn and blank. Viciously cold.

He kept one of the guns trained on Gray. The other pistol moved, with chilling deliberation, until its barrel aimed squarely at Dru.

"No!" Gray yelled.

Daniel's attention returned to Gray, fingers whitening on the triggers.

Dru fired.

Her bullet met its mark.

But so did his. *So did his.*

Ammunition tore into tender flesh, destroying the muscle and bone and organs in its path. A screaming denial the color of red obliterated Dru's thoughts.

Furious, she fired again.

Again, she struck her mark. Daniel's body flailed like a puppet's, one arm out to the side, one flung over his head. Before he could regain his footing, Jake rammed into Daniel's side, taking him to the ground.

Dru faltered, then haltingly came to a stop. She looked to the stage, terrified of what she'd see. Gray was running toward her, pushing people out of the way to clear a path to her. No wounds. No holes in his beautiful suit. Thank God. Thank God. Uninjured. It was all right. She'd protected him. Thank God.

She faced Daniel again. She could no longer see him now that Jake had tackled him. But she could make out her brother's face, which was merciless. A teenaged boy, no matter how angry or vengeful, had no chance against Jake. It was good that Jake had been here. She was glad of that. Knew she could trust him.

She sank onto her knees, then stared down and to the left at her own jacket. One jagged tear there. Blood.

Interesting, she thought with odd detachment. *It's almost hard to see the blood against the black leather.* Her right hand hung down at her side, still clutching the gun.

Scared faces were peering at her. So many faces, all of them swimming together in her vision.

She wanted to reassure them. She wanted to organize an orderly exit for these people. Those were the things she had the will to do. Just not the ability.

Already, her breath had turned fast and shallow. She managed to get herself onto the ground and to prop her back against an empty chair.

Gray shoved his way into the space directly in front of her. Their eyes met, and she released a thin huff of relief. He was here, and his arrival was an unexpected gift. Gray was here.

He knelt, his focus stalling on her jacket. "We need a doctor!" he yelled.

Voices were answering.

"I've already called 911!"

"I'll make sure the onsite ambulance is on its way."

Buzzing activity around and behind him.

Gray's chest was heaving. He took hold of her hand and his warm grip enclosed her fingers. His eyes were so pretty, like pastel emeralds, but full, at the moment, of distress.

She was the one who'd been hurt. She didn't want him to be the one broken by the outcome. "I hit exactly where . . . I was aiming . . . to hit," she said proudly, wanting him to know that she was satisfied with how things had played out. Unlike in Mexico, she'd protected her client. This time, the one she cared about had come through healthy and safe. This moment was the answer to all the guilt and doubt and suspicion that had plagued her after Mark's death. "I'm a . . . very good . . . shot." Her words were strangely raspy.

"I love you," he said, raw truth and a world of anguish in the statement.

She could see his love for her in his face, feel it in the pressure of his hand. She tried to smile. "Well . . . a girl sure has to go . . . to extreme measures . . . to get you to tell her . . . you love her."

She was having the last laugh, because here in this peculiar vacuum of sound, with a slice of sky looking down on them and wind whispering against her face, Gray was very clear and real, and *he loved her*.

"I knew . . . you were trouble . . ." She sucked oxygen into her laboring lungs. "The moment . . . I . . . saw you."

TWENTY-SEVEN

Panic pounded through Gray's body.

His chest was lead. His brain chaos. His arms useless weight. Dru was dying. He couldn't let her die. She could not die. Where was help? He refused to wait. He needed to find help.

He lifted her in his arms, and she raised an eyebrow at him as if amused.

Around him, people were hurtling in every direction, trying to find their way out. On the outskirts of the square, he caught sight of two male EMTs making their way against the crowd toward him. He ran in their direction.

Several yards in front of him stood Jake, like a statue in a flood, with Lyndie, his blond wife, next to him. They were searching the scene. The moment they saw him, they went into action, helping to make a way through. He passed the place where Daniel had fallen. The teenager lay facedown on the ground, restrained by two security guards. Gray spared him no more than a glance.

With Jake and Lyndie moving ahead of him, they reached the EMTs. Gray carefully laid Dru on their gurney. They all hurried to the waiting ambulance. A firetruck rolled up to the scene, and a fireman paramedic jumped down to lend a hand as they slid Dru into the ambulance. One of the EMTs jogged around to drive. The other EMT and the fireman hopped into the back.

Gray made to climb inside after them—

"I'm sorry, sir," the EMT told him. "You're not allowed to ride in here."

They were already strapping Dru to monitors. The doors shut in his face, and the ambulance started off.

No, he thought, his heart hammering with terror. They were taking her away. She was alone inside the ambulance, without family or friends.

Three firemen remained. Two of them went toward where Daniel had gone down. One stayed back. He was middle-aged and carried himself with authority. "Do you know the victim?" he asked Gray, Jake, and Lyndie.

"The victim is my sister," Jake answered. "This is my wife and we—we need to get to the hospital."

"Is your car parked in the visitors' lot?" the fireman asked.

"Yes."

The visitors' lot was far away. Too far. "Mine's parked nearby," Gray said.

The fireman considered Gray for a moment. "Even so, I'm afraid you folks will get caught in a traffic jam. There'll be a huge number of people trying to leave right now, and police trying to enter."

Desperation stole Gray's voice.

"If you'd like, we can take you to the hospital in the

truck," the fireman said. "We're authorized to use the ranch's back entrance."

"Thank you," Jake said, immediately taking him up on his offer.

"This isn't the first time we've driven family to the hospital. We take care of our own here in Holley." Briefly, he clasped Jake on the shoulder. Another ambulance arrived, and the fireman separated from them. "I need to make sure that the other victim is squared away. Pardon me for a minute."

When he'd gone, Jake turned and faced Gray. "Lyndie and I will ride in the truck."

"I'm going, too."

"No."

"Yes," Gray growled.

Jake didn't give an inch. His chin set, his facial scar turned whiter. "Dru told me that you're not her boyfriend any longer."

"Not because I don't want to be. *I'm going.*"

Lyndie rested a hand on her husband's forearm. "Jake." A communication passed between them, and Jake's body language eased slightly. "Didn't you say that Dru told you she was here because she'd brought her friend Augustine?" Lyndie asked.

"I'd forgotten about Augustine."

"We need to make sure she's okay and has a way to get home."

"I'll find her and be right back." He loped off.

Gray watched Lyndie wrap her arms across her middle. She gave him a look of sympathy, then turned her focus toward Daniel, who was still on the ground with EMTs and firemen kneeling around him.

They'd taken Dru away. She was dying, and they'd taken her away.

Tremors began deep within him, right at the center of his torso. Everything had happened with tremendous speed. Daniel's appearance. His exchange with Dru. Gray's charge to reach her. The run to the ambulance.

It had all taken just a handful of minutes, but those minutes had been tragic minutes. A person could live a million ordinary minutes that changed nothing. Then a few tragic minutes could change everything. They could divide a life into *before* and *after*.

The firemen and Jake returned simultaneously. They all piled into the truck. Gray sat on one side of the small interior, Jake and Lyndie on the other. The vehicle slid into motion.

"Did you find Augustine?" Lyndie asked Jake.

"Yeah. She has her phone with her. She said she'd call her sister to come and get her. She's worried about . . . Dru." Saying Dru's name seemed almost too painful for Jake.

The truck took Whispering Creek Ranch's back lanes. Soon they'd exited the property and were flying down country roads.

Gray hunched forward and gripped his head in his hands. *God. Dru. Oh, God.* He couldn't seem to form sentences or thoughts that made any sense. It was all just an urgent mess of words begging God to save Dru's life.

After a time, he got himself upright and saw that Jake was staring at him. Lyndie leaned against Jake, holding his hand. Both of them looked pale. Dru had told Gray about the IED that had injured Jake and taken the lives of three of his Marines. Jake knew firsthand how life could be separated into *before* and *after*.

"Was that your stalker back there?" Jake asked him.

"I don't know. Maybe. We thought we'd gotten my stalker. We thought my stalker was a man named Dennis."

"Who's the kid who shot Dru? Do you know?"

Gray wished he didn't know. "He's my mom's boyfriend's son."

Tense quiet met his words. "I didn't think Dru was your bodyguard anymore," Jake said.

"She's not. I had no idea she was going to be at the event today." He hadn't forgotten Augustine's plan to use his appearance at the Fun Day to bring her ex-husband out of hiding, but he'd never known that Dru planned to bring Augustine.

He raked his hands through his hair. If not for his scheduled appearance, Augustine and Dru wouldn't have come. If not for his mom's screwed-up relationship with Jeff and Jeff's messed-up son, Dru would not be injured.

"How did Dru get ahold of a gun?" Jake asked.

"I don't know."

Deep concern lined Jake's face. "Why didn't she just take the gunman out? She could have easily shot him in the head, but she didn't. Instead, she shot the gun he had pointed at you out of his hand just as he was firing at her."

She'd . . . shot the gun that had been pointed at him out of Daniel's hand? He hadn't seen where her shots had landed. The moment he'd caught sight of Daniel and Dru, he'd started into motion.

Why would Dru have shot the gun pointed at him

first? He wasn't her client. She hadn't been on duty. Had she done it out of some sort of misguided professional obligation to him?

No. He didn't think so. She'd protected him fiercely from Dennis that day in the hallway. She hadn't been on duty that day, either. His gut was telling him that she'd protected him then, and again today, for one very simple reason. Because she cared. She didn't want him hurt.

"After she'd been shot, she fired again and hit the kid in the arm that held the second gun," Jake said. "She protected everybody but herself. I would have expected her to kill him as soon as she saw him draw his weapons. Why didn't she?"

"She's met Daniel." His throat was raw. "She knows his story and . . . maybe she was trying to protect him, too."

Jake looked like he was on the verge of crossing the space that separated them and strangling him. He didn't blame him. His sister was fighting for her life while Daniel would recover.

They'd never been able to connect Dennis to the letters or the shooting at Urban Country. Could Gray possibly have two enemies? Dennis had been stalking him, that much they knew. But could Daniel have been the one sending the letters?

Daniel had come to the event today ready to kill Gray and potentially a lot of innocent people, too. He'd chosen a public place, which meant he'd either been content to be caught or had planned to die.

Gray remembered how the author of the letters had promised to kill Dru first and then him. However, Gray hadn't been seen with Dru for some time now. If Daniel had been stalking him during that time, he'd have noticed her absence, and he might have reasonably expected that he wouldn't have to deal with her today. Not even Gray had known that Dru would be at the Fun Day. There was no way Daniel could have known or planned for her.

Gray couldn't stand to think about how many by-standers might have been shot if Dru hadn't stopped Daniel. He couldn't stand to think of what *had* happened, either. He longed for Dru to be the one sitting here, her body unmarked.

He wanted to tell her again that he loved her. To apologize. But he didn't know if he'd get another chance. He might have overcome his fears too late. Nausea churned his stomach.

Two cell phones dinged to signal a text message at the same time. Lyndie's. Jake's.

Lyndie glanced at her husband.

"It could be that my family has heard about Dru," Jake said.

Lyndie pulled free her phone. "No. It's from Bo, about Meg." She read silently for a few seconds. "They're about to take Meg into the OR and deliver the twins through an emergency C-section."

The term *emergency* made Meg think of hysteria and confusion and noise. None of those things were present in her operating room in the Labor and Delivery wing. Dr. Peterson spoke authoritatively, but with composure. The nurses moved fast, but in a businesslike manner. No one was shrieking, or looking overwrought, or running around waving their arms in the air.

The room was somewhat quiet, actually.

Meg wanted a safe delivery for the twins as much as she'd ever wanted anything in her life. However, back in the nursery at home, she'd surrendered everything to the One who held their future and hers. He was the God who was able. Who was good. Whose grace was sufficient for her family.

God's presence had not forsaken her. It had remained, and even her fears were not strong enough for it.

She found this all a bit surreal. After the years of infertility. The anxious first trimester of this pregnancy, when she'd dreaded miscarriage. The wonderful weeks after making it through the first trimester. The preeclampsia diagnosis, which had tinged everything with possible heartbreak.

After all that, here she was. She'd made it to thirty-five weeks gestation. The twins would be five weeks early. Premature, but not devastatingly so, she hoped.

She was about to deliver their twins. Today. Right now.

Their birthday will be February fifth. What a nice day to be born. I'll have to make sure to get a newspaper from today. Two newspapers. For their baby books.

I think the doctor has her hands in my body and is about to pull the babies out. Glad I can't see any of that. Whoever thought to put up a sheet between the mother and whatever is happening with the C-section was a genius.

In a few seconds, I won't be pregnant anymore. This is the last time I'll ever be pregnant. I'm about to see our babies. I'm about to look into the faces of our little boy and girl for the very first time. Maybe I should memorize this moment—

I really can't forget to ask someone to get those newspapers. It won't be any good to get them tomorrow. They have to have February fifth on their fronts.

Bo was sitting beside her, holding her hand, wearing a hospital gown, hat, and mask. She gave him a small smile, and she thought he might have smiled back, because his gray eyes crinkled. He looked handsome, like an actor on a hospital drama that women all across America would go crazy for.

"Today's the twins' birthday," she said.

"Yes."

And then, suddenly, a puny cry broke through the room.

"Meg and Bo," Dr. Peterson said, "you have a beautiful son."

Meg gasped at the miracle of it.

The doctor went on to note the time of birth.

A nurse brought a small, red infant partially covered in white goo around the edge of the curtain. Meg had just enough time to drink in the sight of thrashing arms tipped with outstretched fingers, a little round belly, and a screaming O of a mouth before the baby was whisked away.

Our son. She gaped at the place where her baby had just been. She wanted more time to look at him. She wanted to hold him. But Dr. Peterson had told her ahead of time that, because of the babies' prematurity, a NICU nurse would be present in the OR and the babies would need to receive evaluation and treatment directly after birth.

She rolled her head in Bo's direction. He was crying.

Just a little. Happy tears, she could see, even though his face was mostly covered.

She laughed softly. "I'm the one who always cries."

"I have enough tissues for us both, Countess."

He had a heart as soft and valuable as melted gold. A heart as strong and dependable as tempered steel.

"I love you," he said.

"I love you, too."

"Meg and Bo, you have a beautiful daughter," Dr. Peterson announced. A second mewling newborn cry rent the air. "Congratulations."

Another nurse appeared, holding a tiny baby girl forward. This one wasn't quite so red but had a startling crown of brown hair. All that hair!

Our daughter, Meg thought with shimmering wonder.

And then their little girl was whisked away, too.

The staff in the OR had spent a good long while, after the delivery of the twins, making sure that Meg's blood pressure stabilized properly. Then they'd wheeled her into this private hospital room on the maternity floor. A new room, modern, furnished in shades of pale green and brown. A very nice room—perfectly nice—except that there were no babies here.

Bo paced by the window.

So far today, Meg had been through a fainting spell, a C-section, and the birth of her children. A strange combination of exhaustion, physical pain from surgery, and buzzing adrenaline filled her. She was dressed in a hospital gown, lying in bed, twirling her earring back around and around, watching the door, and pretty much *dying* for news on the twins' condition.

When at last a knock sounded, she nearly jumped out of her skin.

Dr. Peterson stuck her head into the room. "Are you ready to go see your twins?"

"Yes!" Meg answered instantly.

"They're in the neonatal intensive care unit, so we'll have to take a short walk."

"How are they doing?" Meg asked.

"They'll both need to stay in the NICU for a bit, but they're both going to be fine."

Meg's spirits lifted so piquantly that tears piled onto her bottom lashes. *They're both going to be fine.*

Bo and the doctor helped Meg into a wheelchair. Then they made their way along the corridor, Bo pushing Meg's chair, Dr. Peterson leading the way.

A diminutive lady with a white doctor's coat, sweetly wrinkled face, and gray hair ushered them inside the NICU. Incubators and open-air cribs lined the perimeter of the large space. A nurse's station dominated its center. Dr. Peterson introduced the older lady as Dr. Field, the lead pediatrician on call.

"You have two very, very pretty babies, Mr. and Mrs. Porter," Dr. Field told them, a kind sparkle in her eyes. "Come right this way."

They reached two incubators on the room's far side. The twins were both asleep and dressed in nothing but diapers. Both had a few patches stuck on their chests that hooked up to monitors. Both had another monitor on their tiny toes. And both had tubes running beneath their noses.

It was glorious to see them, and at the same time very sobering to see them like this—with so many wires attached to their small bodies.

"Babies born five weeks early," Dr. Field told them, "often have lungs that aren't quite mature and a tendency toward high levels of something called bilirubin in their blood that causes jaundice. Both of those conditions apply to your twins, but I'm very happy to tell you that the jaundice is mild and their lungs are almost there."

"Are they receiving oxygen through the nose tubes?" Bo asked.

"Exactly. Those tubes function like a CPAP machine, delivering a constant flow of oxygen. That flow makes things easier on their developing lungs."

"How much do they weigh?" Meg asked.

"Your daughter weighs four pounds and ten ounces, and your son weighs five pounds even."

So little!

"How long will they need to stay in the hospital?" Bo asked.

"I can't predict exactly, of course," Dr. Field answered. "Perhaps seventy-two hours? With any luck, they'll be able to leave the hospital with mom."

They all might be able to go home together? It was the best news Meg could have hoped for.

"Ready to hold them?" Dr. Field asked.

"Please," Bo said, the word deep with emotion.

A rocking chair was brought over for Bo, and one of the nurses arrived. The nurse and Dr. Field opened the incubators and carefully passed the babies over to Meg and Bo. Meg was *cradling* her little girl.

Half laughing, half crying, she dashed away tears

with her free hand. "Thank you," she said to the doctors. "Thank you so much."

Dr. Peterson and Dr. Field both looked extraordinarily pleased with Meg and Bo, the babies, their miraculous jobs, and the world in general.

"What are their names?" Dr. Field asked.

"This is—" Bo had to gruffly clear his throat before he could continue. He looked as overcome as Meg felt. "This is John William Porter. We named him after my father and Meg's."

"And this is Mollie Patricia Porter." This was the first time they'd said the names they'd chosen to someone outside their marriage. They'd wanted to keep them a surprise and share them after the babies were born. It felt new and wonderful to speak their names out loud. "We named her in memory of my sister-in-law's sister and my mother."

"Congratulations." Dr. Peterson patted Meg's forearm fondly. "I'll be back to check on you soon."

"Enjoy!" Dr. Field encouraged. "I'll be right over there, and I'm happy to answer as many questions as you have." She moved away. "Take as long as you'd like."

"My gosh," Bo whispered, looking at the retreating backs of the doctors. "Are they really just going to . . . leave them here? With us?"

"I guess so." Meg laughed, and he grinned as if they'd pulled off an outrageously unlikely scheme.

They spent long minutes marveling over their babies. They were small, but absolutely perfect. Their tiny noses! Little chins. Pristine, miniature mouths. Occasionally, either Mollie or John would pull a funny face as he or she slept and send Bo and Meg into a fresh round of *oohs* and *ahhs*.

They snapped numerous pictures. When they traded babies, both John and Mollie roused long enough to peer at their parents. Meg cozied little John against her, her face tilted down to his, their gazes interlocking. "Hello, sweetheart," she murmured. "I'm your mommy."

Their struggle to have these children had been a mighty one. God answered prayers in many types of ways. He could have written their family's story with dozens of different outcomes. In this moment, Meg was so glad and thankful and amazed that He'd chosen to write their story with this *particular* outcome. With these miraculous twins.

Praise God! Their babies were going to gain in size and strength. They were going to grow up healthy and as loved as any babies had ever been.

Praise God.

D ru came awake to the sounds of hushed voices and beeping machines. She squinted.

A hospital room. A nurse. Her parents hovering at the side of her bed. "I feel like crap," she said.

"Honey!" her mom gushed, wreathed in a relieved smile. "You're awake."

"Hi, sweetheart," her dad said.

She must be in bad shape if her dad was calling her sweetheart. He only used *sweetheart* in his most affectionate moments. Growing up, she'd far more often heard him say *Dru* in a long, low-pitched rumble that meant she was in serious trouble.

"I'm not paralyzed, am I?" she asked.

"No, no," her mom assured her. "You were shot in the side." She pointed to the general area. "Do you remember?"

Recollections trickled in hazily. Winter Family Fun Day. Daniel. The ambulance ride here. Then nothing but darkness.

"I remember. Did they operate on me?"

"Yes," her dad answered. "You're going to be fine."

"Where did the bullet hit?" She remembered that it had gone in on the left side. A few inches higher and toward the middle and it would have ripped through her heart.

"It went between two of your ribs and ruptured your spleen," her dad answered. "They had to remove your spleen and dig out the bullet."

Breathing hurt. Her head felt like a swamp. Her body seemed to be floating in a sea of narcotics. If she had to guess, she'd guess she looked like a corpse. "Where's Gray?"

"He's downstairs," her mom said. "He's been here since you arrived at the hospital."

"What time is it?"

"Two in the morning."

She groaned and tried to corral strength and sense. "Did you tell him that I'm going to be okay?"

"He was with us," her dad said, "when the surgeon came into the waiting area to give us the news. We didn't know . . ." He and Mom looked at each other and then back at her uncomfortably. "We weren't sure about how things are . . . between you and Gray. We didn't know if you two were . . . good."

What was she, fifteen? How come it had never gotten any less awkward to discuss her dating life with her mom and dad?

"Gray and I are good. I think. Maybe." She closed her eyes again and left them closed. Her lips bowed as she remembered his words when he'd crouched before her after the shooting. *I love you.*

She hugged the words to her like a blanket as she exhaled. "I'm tired. I'm really, really tired," she murmured, then let herself tumble back into sleep.

Gray did not go home when Dru's family went home. He stayed in the waiting room, in case she woke up alone and needed someone familiar nearby. In case there was an update on her condition. In case she asked for him.

She didn't ask for him.

He was standing at the ICU waiting room windows on the second floor, overlooking the front entrance, when John and Nancy Porter returned to the hospital. He watched them make their way inside, walking quickly and holding hands. Only then did he feel free to drive home for a shower, food, and a change of clothes. He looked at his watch. 5:55 a.m.

An hour later, he'd accomplished everything he'd needed to at home and was waiting on his driveway for his gates to open so that he could exit. As he pulled onto his street, he caught sight of a car parked in front of his house. The sun hadn't yet risen, but there was enough light on the horizon for him to recognize the car.

Kayla's.

He paused.

During the hours since Dru had been shot, worry and regret and guilt had been eating him alive.

The doctors had said Dru would recover, but he was desperate to see her for himself. He needed to reassure himself that she was okay and tell her how sorry he was, that he loved her, and that he'd been a fool. The only thing in the world he cared about this morning was getting back to the hospital. Kayla was the last person he wanted to deal with.

Thing was, he'd never been in love with anyone until now. Before, he'd been unable to understand Kayla's inability to let him go. Now he could sympathize with her. She was waiting outside his house just like he was about to go wait outside Dru's hospital room. He couldn't *not* go to the hospital. Maybe Kayla hadn't been able to *not* come to his house.

He parked behind her. They both stepped into the freezing air and met between their vehicles.

Gray stuffed his hands into the pockets of his insulated jacket. He'd been trying to let God change him. Here was a chance to show the inward changes through outward actions. "How've you been, Kayla?"

"I've been fine. I . . ."

He waited.

"I watched the news last night. I heard about the shooting at that fair. Out in Holley?"

He nodded.

"The woman who was shot is the same one I met here that day. Right?"

"Yes."

"Your girlfriend."

"Yes." *I hope.*

"I thought so. At first when I saw the story, I sort of felt like I'd gotten my revenge, you know? Finding out that my ex-boyfriend's new girlfriend—who I don't like, by the way—got hurt was . . . like a dream come true." She gave an unapologetic shrug. "Just keeping it real."

He set his jaw. He'd known for a long time how self-centered and cold-blooded Kayla could be.

"But the more I thought about the story," Kayla continued, "the sadder it made me, because you guys must have a pretty good thing going if she was willing to put herself between you and a shooter."

"She's brave."

"She must love you."

"I'm not sure about that, but I do know that I love her."

Kayla flinched as if he'd physically slapped her, then looked away from him toward his house.

He'd wanted this conversation to help Kayla, not injure her more. He could execute the hurry-up offense perfectly, but he wasn't very skilled at this.

After a long moment, Kayla met his eyes. "I want someone to love me like that. So much that they'd put themselves between me and a shooter."

"It will happen for you, Kayla. With the right guy, it will happen."

"I wanted that guy to be you."

"I know." Painful wind whipped across them. "I'm sorry it wasn't me. I'm sorry about a lot of things. If I led you on, I'm sorry. If I broke your heart, I'm sorry. I know I disappointed you, and I know I hurt you, and I'm sorry. Can you forgive me?"

She pursed her lips.

Gray waited.

Still nothing.

"I'm sorry," he said again.

And finally, her posture relaxed. It was as if she'd at last received what she'd needed from him all along. Now that she'd received it, maybe she'd be able to let the past—and him—go. "Okay."

"You forgive me?"

"Fine. Whatever," she grumbled, but a bittersweet smile had overtaken her mouth.

"Come here." He hugged her.

Kayla whispered three words against his shoulder so quietly that he almost couldn't hear them. "She's not yours."

He knew exactly what she was saying to him. For the first time, she was acknowledging that her daughter wasn't his child.

"I hope God blesses you, Kayla. You and your daughter both."

At Dru's second awakening, she felt more like herself.

This time, she opened her eyes to sunlight bursting through a bank of windows. She was in a different room than she had been in the last time. This room looked more normal, in part because her brother Ty sat in the corner reading an investment magazine, one boot crossed over the opposite knee.

Dru slid her attention across the room's interior, looking for Gray. No Gray. Only Ty. She wanted to see Gray but was glad he hadn't been in here peering at her while she'd been unconscious with machines strapped to her. Just the thought of that was mortifying for a woman who liked to be in control of herself. And in control of others, too, come to think of it. She adjusted her position slightly.

Ty's face lifted. He set aside the magazine and approached. "Trust you, Dru, to run into a bullet with your chest."

"You're not supposed to talk that way to people who are recovering from a near-death injury. You're supposed to dote on them and give them understanding smiles."

"No older brother is supposed to act that way with his younger sister. If I did, you'd boo me out of here. So . . . what happened yesterday?"

"I was very noble and brave, that's what happened. I'm a heroine."

"Mm-hmm," he murmured doubtfully, but she could see grudging respect in his face. "The whole family's here. Since we didn't think you'd appreciate all of us stuffing into your room while you were sleeping, the rest of them are waiting in the cafeteria. I'm supposed to call them now that you're awake so they can come up."

"Don't even think about calling them until I've had time to get cleaned up." Since she'd woken and found her parents at her bedside, she could recall nothing but nurses drifting in and out and the recurring tightening of a blood pressure cuff around her upper arm. "What time is it?"

"Lunchtime."

"The day after the shooting?" She hadn't been drifting in oblivion for days, had she?

"Yep."

She tried to sit up—stopped when pain stabbed her side.

"Where you going in such a hurry?" Ty asked. "Out for your daily run?"

"Is any of my stuff from home here? Toothbrush? Hair—"

"Brush? Toothpaste? Makeup? Toiletries?" He went

to a suitcase lying against the wall and pulled free her overnight kit. "That kind of thing?"

"Yes. Exactly."

He set it beside her. "I went by and got it for you."

"No, you didn't. One of my sisters-in-law did." She unzipped it and rooted around within. "Was it Celia?"

"Yeah."

"I love Celia."

"Me, too," he said with feeling.

"Did someone get Fi?"

"Lyndie's parents have been dog-sitting Fi and Lyndie's dogs since yesterday. No worries there."

It was lame how dizzy and weak her body was. By the time she'd brushed her teeth with the help of some cups of water Ty ferried back and forth to the sink for her, combed out her hair, and used a washcloth to scrub her hands and face, she was embarrassingly relieved to relax back into the mattress.

She needed protein. "How 'bout you make yourself useful and get me a Big Mac, fries, and a chocolate shake?"

Ty put his hands on his hips. "You realize that you saved the life of a Mustang yesterday, right? And that every Cowboys fan is mad at you? Including me?"

"He might be a Mustang, but I'm a heroine either way. And this heroine is starving."

"Fine." He crossed to the door. "Just so you know, I'll be calling the family now." Then he disappeared from sight.

Within minutes, the Porters began filing into her room. Celia and the four kids. Jake and Lyndie. Her parents.

"Where are Bo and Meg?" Dru asked.

"Well . . ." Celia said. Every person—every single one—smiled enormously. "As it turns out, we have a surprise for you."

"A surprise?"

Dru's dad held open the door, and Meg entered the room in a wheelchair, Bo behind her.

"No way!" Dru exclaimed.

Bo came over and showed her a picture on his cell phone of two newborns. They had a lot of stuff strapped to them, though she wasn't one to talk since she had stuff strapped to her, too. With or without the cords, the twins were absolutely, undeniably gorgeous.

"Babies!" little Hudson announced proudly. Then everyone started talking and clapping and laughing at once.

Bo and Meg took turns detailing the events that had led up to and followed the C-section, as well as the condition of the babies. Both of their faces were lit from within with excitement.

"It's taken Meg and me a while to work out the timeline of everything that happened yesterday," Bo said. "But I think you were in surgery right around the time the twins were born. The Porters were taking up two of the operating rooms here simultaneously."

"I'd planned to be conscious for the twins' birth," Dru said wryly. "I can't believe I missed my big moment of auntie glory."

"You were a little busy at the time."

"I want to see them as soon as possible."

"You bet," Bo said.

"How are you feeling?" Lyndie asked.

Dru took a moment to consider her answer. "Grateful." The weight of concern she'd carried for so long regarding Gray had finally lifted from her. He was safe. And she'd recover.

"You look really good," Meg told her.

"So do you," Dru answered, meaning it. Meg had dressed in pink pajamas and a matching robe with satin piping. Motherhood suited her in every way.

For the next twenty-nine minutes, Dru managed to visit with her family without once asking anyone about Gray. It took Herculean effort. When the twenty-ninth minute ticked into the thirtieth, she could wait no longer. "Is Gray here?" she asked Celia and her mom, who happened to be standing closest.

"Yes," Celia answered. "I went to get something out of my car a little while ago and saw him sitting in the lobby."

"Will one of you go tell him that I'd like to see him?"

"I will," her mom volunteered. Then louder, to include the room at large, she said, "The nurse in charge of Dru told me it would be all right for us to chat with her for a little while, but our time is up. Let's head out and let her rest."

Dru accepted hugs from her nieces and nephews. Each hug from each little pair of arms brought a dose of healing magic.

"Love you." Dru waved as her family left.

Jake brought up the rear of the line. He'd almost made it out when Lyndie steered him back in Dru's direction. "See you later, Dru," Lyndie called.

"See ya, Lyndie."

Jake made his way to her bedside.

"I remember you tackling Daniel yesterday," Dru said. "Thank you for the help."

"You're welcome. I'm glad you're all right."

Coming from Jake, that statement was as flowery as a Shakespearean love sonnet.

"As for"—he coughed—"Gray . . ."

She lifted an eyebrow.

"Lyndie and I were here at the hospital until late last night. We came back early this morning. Gray was here when we left, and he was here when we got back."

"And?"

"Based on his actions yesterday and today, I no longer think he's completely terrible." Again, if you could translate Jake-speak into English, then you knew that *not completely terrible* meant *acceptable boyfriend material*.

Dru had to work to keep from grinning. "Glad to hear it."

Jake nodded and made his way out. "He's still a Mustang," she heard him mutter.

She turned her face toward the windows and let the quiet of her sudden solitude sink over her. The sky beyond the glass stretched out in a band of azure. Not a cloud in sight.

Methodically, she went back over all that had happened after Gray had taken the stage yesterday. Most of all, she lingered on the moments when Gray had gone to his knees before her. She remembered his *I love you* in startling detail. There'd been no shield between them. He'd spoken to her with unadulterated honesty, exactly as she'd asked him to that day in the parking garage.

She'd gotten what she'd wanted and needed and hoped for from him.

On the other hand, he'd been under duress at the time. Last night, during her blip of consciousness, she'd been too woozy to consider the context of Gray's words. But now she was thinking clearly, and her clear thoughts were coated with uncertainty.

Gray had told her he loved her right after she'd been shot defending him. He might have felt honor-bound or rattled. He might have thought it necessary to say what she wanted to hear in case she died.

His face, though, Dru. His face had been so blunt when he'd said the words. His gaze had burned with green intensity.

Groaning, she screwed her eyes shut. Caring about him was sweet torture. But perhaps . . . There was a decent chance . . . It seemed possible that he might, after all . . .

Love her. And not only love her, but be ready to let her in.

"Gray." It was Dru's mom, Nancy.

Quickly, he rose from the uncomfortable lobby chair he'd been sitting in for what felt like a week.

Nancy had tied a band of fabric around her short, dark hair. Her cheeks were pink, her expression affectionate as she took him in. "Dru would like to see you."

Relief poured through him. Thank God. "How is she doing?"

"According to her doctors, very well. Much like her usual self, I should warn you." She chuckled.

Emotion squeezed his throat, and he almost felt like he might cry. "That's very good news."

"This is a good news kind of day for my family, Gray. Dru's in room 484."

"Okay. Thank you."

"Dru's my favorite child, you know."

It surprised him that Nancy would confide in him, but it didn't surprise him in the least to learn that Dru was her favorite.

"I had three sons," Nancy said. "I'd given up hope of ever having a girl. And then, when the boys were getting up in age, I found out we were having another baby. I was ninety percent sure it would be another boy." She smiled. "Instead, I had Dru. *Whoooeee*, I could *not* believe my luck. A little girl! After all that time, the Lord saw fit to give me a daughter. And one so full of . . . spunk. She'll always be my baby so, land sakes, how could she not be my favorite?"

"I don't see how she couldn't be," he answered truthfully.

"You're not allowed to tell my other kids, mind you. It's our secret."

"It's our secret."

"Bye, hon."

He rode the elevator to the fourth floor. He was walking down the hall, reading the numbers on the doors, when he caught sight of Ty coming toward him from the other direction, holding a white sack from McDonald's. "Her Highness asked for food," Ty told him when they were within hearing distance. "Will you give this to her for me?"

"Yeah."

Ty passed over the sack and gestured to the door next

to them. "She's in there. Good luck with her, man." He walked on until Gray could no longer hear his footsteps.

Gray's heart began to beat like a drum. This meeting between him and Dru meant everything to him. His future rested on it.

He pushed into the room.

She was looking straight at him when he entered, as if she'd been waiting. Blankets covered her from the waist down. Her skin was pale, and he could see bandages climbing over her shoulder beneath the neck of her hospital gown. A few machines stood at her far side, monitoring her.

Despite everything, her blue eyes glittered with feisty challenge. Her dark hair was achingly familiar, and the lines of her face were crisp and clean and so . . . her . . . that he could finally take a deep breath. She'd lived. She was still completely herself. Completely Dru. The events of the past day hadn't changed her in any tragic way. One day soon she'd probably even be well enough to execute karate blocks when he tried to hug her.

He couldn't move. He just stood there with the McDonald's bag, his eyes filling with tears because he was so blasted grateful and because he'd been so incredibly scared.

You are not given many chances at great loves in this life. In Gray's life, he'd only been given *one* chance. Just one. When you are given that chance, you have to reach for it with all your strength. Your worries don't matter. All the reasons you had for failing to trust don't matter. Your history doesn't matter. You simply have to do it. To risk everything and love the person. Because life is fragile, and it could be taken from you in an instant.

God had showed him that over these twenty-four hours. God had said to him, **love.**

Love her.

Gray looked harshly gorgeous to Dru. He had on an austere black sweater. Jeans. He hadn't worn a hat, so he couldn't hide the exhaustion that marked his masculine face.

It was better than the most amazing dessert she'd ever eaten—simply to look at him. "You're the handsomest McDonald's delivery man ever," Dru stated.

"Oh." He started as if he'd forgotten about the sack of food, then brought it to her.

Dru peeked inside the white paper bag. "God bless Ty. He supersized it." She set it on her side tray, then grinned at Gray. It was impossibly good to see him. Impossibly good. He loved her, right? He did. Didn't he?

"You're okay," Gray said raggedly. It was a statement—but a statement that seemed hungry for confirmation.

"Yes." In actuality her body felt lousy, but he was here, so at this present moment she was more than okay. Everything was right with the world.

"You're okay," he said again.

"In no time at all, I'll be back on my motorcycle. What about you? Are you all right?" He was big and powerful, yet it appeared that her injury and his long vigil had just about wrecked him. She extended a hand, and he took it. Sitting on the edge of her bed, he interlaced her fingers with his, then pressed her hand against his chest as if he had no intention of letting go, ever.

Home, the connection between their hands murmured to her. Home and belonging.

He pressed his wrist against one eye and then the other as if he was fighting back tears.

"Gray?"

He looked at her. "I'm sorry about yesterday. If it hadn't been for me, this wouldn't have happened to you."

"Don't ever think that." She squeezed his hand. "I made my own choice. No one, including you, forced me." A gap of quiet widened between them. "What have you learned about Daniel since yesterday?" she asked.

"Daniel told Detective Carlyle that he was the one who mailed the letters and the one who fired the shots into Urban Country."

"Ah." She considered the facets of what Gray's statement meant. "Daniel and Dennis Wright were both stalking you."

"Yes."

"Two stalkers," Dru said.

"Two stalkers."

"I'm guessing that Daniel drives a beige Cherokee."

"He does."

"So Dennis was following you around, at least some of the time, in his family's maroon truck. But Daniel was the dangerous one all along."

Gray nodded.

"And . . ." She thought it through. "When Dennis was arrested, Daniel must have seen the coverage of it and decided to use Dennis to his advantage. He stopped sending the letters to make it look like we had our man."

"The bodyguards were pulled off my case."

"Which made things easier for Daniel. Your appearance at the Winter Family Fun Day was publicized well in advance. Daniel probably planned all along to try for you there. He must have liked the idea of an audience."

"Maybe."

"How is Daniel?"

"He sustained injuries to both hands, but neither one is very serious. Your bullets hit the guns, not his hands, with amazing accuracy."

"Huh." If she did say so herself, she'd nailed both of those shots. "Is he in the hospital?"

"My mom texted me earlier to say that he was released and taken into police custody a few hours ago." Gray dipped his head and kissed each of Dru's knuckles.

Dru watched him, attraction thrumming within her. If he kept that up, she might have to share some of her fries with him. He . . . loved her. Right? As outspoken as she was, she refused to go fishing for an *I love you* by reminding him of what he'd said to her yesterday.

"Where did you get the gun?" Gray asked, lifting his head.

It took her a moment to reorient herself and figure out what he was asking. "I yanked it out of one of the security guard's holsters."

"You're kidding."

"Nope."

"A woman who can strip a security guard of his gun and shoot pistols out of someone's hands could have easily killed Daniel. If she'd wanted to."

"I could have, but he's—" *your half brother.* She remembered Gray's insistence that he didn't want to know who his father was. She believed, though, that he did know. He might have known ever since childhood, but he'd certainly known since his mom had called him years ago and made her drunken confession. If the barriers between them had come down, they should be able to talk about it. "I could have killed Daniel, but I didn't because he's Jeff's son. And you know what Jeff is to you, right?"

Gray stood. Crossing his arms, he walked the length of the small room. Back. Down again. Over to face the window. Finally, he nodded.

She stacked her hands on top of the blankets covering her middle. "I'm not excusing Daniel. Let's be clear on that. But he's obviously completely screwed up. His mother died, and he was left with only Jeff."

"Why would he have wanted to kill me, though? I've never done anything to him."

"He must know about his dad's long affair with your mom. And he must know that you're also Jeff's son. Except you're the son of a woman he hates and a woman who probably caused his own mom a lot of grief. You've never done anything to Daniel because he's a nonentity in your life. But there's no way you can be a nonentity in his life. You're a huge success. His entire town celebrates you, and even his dad sucks up to you."

For a long stretch, he moved not at all, except for the rise and fall of his chest. He seemed to be wrestling with his feelings, his family, the things that had happened yesterday. When he turned to her, he released his arms to his sides. "I've been working to leave my past behind. But in the end, it found me."

"Yeah." Her lips curled up at one edge. She gave him a look that asked him to see the bright side. "But in the *very* end, you got away."

"Thanks to you."

"We all need a little help sometimes, Gray."

He was huge and rugged. His body and heart had been battle-hardened. His eyes were chaotic and grave and beautiful.

"I love you," he said. Just like that. No preamble.

Sparks, like the kind that shoot from Fourth of July sparklers in snapping, bright curlicues, cascaded through her. She pushed herself more upright. "Say it again."

"I love you."

More sparkling curlicues. Goose bumps streaked along her body. She'd been hoping . . . and he'd just answered all her hopes outright. Without wavering. No bones about it. Gray loved her! "I love you, too."

He blinked. "Say it again."

"I. Love. You. Big football player."

"You do?" he asked.

"Of course I do."

Trust flowed between them, intertwining, locking into place. She'd spent her lifetime dogged by restlessness, aware of her isolation and beset by a wayward desire for someone to see her and love her. She'd responded by defiantly telling herself that she needed no one. God had seen, though. God had understood her complex heart, and He'd kept her restless until He'd been ready to bring Gray to her.

Gray neared. He planted one palm against the wall above her head, the other on the mattress, and pressed her back into her pillow as he kissed her.

She ran her hands into his hair and held on possessively, swamped by bliss. He loved her! The thundering exultation of it soared through her, her body too small to contain it.

He pulled back perhaps five inches. She stopped him from going farther by fisting a hand into his sweater. "More." She brought him back in, this time for a kiss as light as silk.

Then he rested his forehead on hers, their breathing uneven, mingling. Without words, they communicated wanting and love and the realization of what they were to each other.

"I love you, Dru."

"I love you, Gray."

He clasped her face in his hands. Kissed her. Rubbed a thumb reverently along her cheek. "You got shot because of me. I'm so sorry—"

"Shh. Don't take it so hard. I'd have thrown myself in front of a bullet for any of my clients."

"Yeah, but you threw yourself in front of a bullet for me when you weren't on the clock."

"True." She couldn't quit smiling. He loved her. She was hardly feeling any pain at all. Who cared about a gunshot wound? Gray Fowler loved her! "Love rescues," she said. "That's what love does. Love rescues. And if I had it all to do over again, Gray, I'd do it the exact same way."

EPILOGUE

D ru Porter was not what you would call a traditional bride. In fact, on her wedding day, the bride wore black.

Dru gave her appearance a final once-over in the full-length mirror. She'd chosen to wear the black dress that Gray had bought for her one day last winter at Nordstrom. Back then, he'd been her client and she'd been ogling his tattoo. This dress, that she hadn't tried on, that he'd bought without even looking at the price tag, seemed to have been made for her body and for her personality. Knobby, sharp-edged golden studs lined the crest of the shoulders. Scoop neck. Lithe, sleek lines. It was both tough and chic.

The strappy, very-high-heeled shoes she'd chosen to pair with the dress were nothing to sneeze at, either.

She grabbed up her bouquet, which consisted of calla lilies pieced together in such a way that they ended up looking like sculptural modern art. Some of the lilies were pale orange. Some a somber, dusky pink. And some an awesome purple so dark it was just a few shades shy of black. She held the bouquet in front of her and burst out laughing.

She, Dru Porter, was a bride.

Better yet, Gray Fowler was her groom.

She opened the door of the room she'd been given and found him waiting precisely where he'd said he'd be waiting when it came time for their ceremony. He was leaning against the opposite wall, hands in the pockets of a stunning charcoal suit. A mini calla lily had been pinned to his lapel. His silver tie caught the light.

Though thousands of women wanted him, he was hers. Her one and only.

He came away from the wall with an appropriately admiring look of awe at the sight of her.

She did a twirl. She'd been saving this dress for today and hadn't told him she'd be wearing it. She'd only told him not to expect, even for an instant, anything white or anything puffy.

"You're wearing the black dress I bought for you," he said.

"You'll find I can be agreeable when I want to be."

"You're the most gorgeous woman I've ever seen," he vowed.

"That's just your wedding day sentiment talking."

"Nah, it's that I . . . have a thing for superheroes." He caught her wrist and tugged her firmly toward his bulk. Dru rescued her bouquet from getting crushed between them at the last second, holding it aloft while they kissed. Seriousness came over them both as their chemistry snapped to life, mightily.

She stepped away. Oh, who cared if they were half a minute late for their ceremony? It wasn't like it could start without them. She stepped back against him, setting one hand on his jaw as she kissed him. "You ready to do this thing?" she asked breathlessly against his lips.

"Very, very ready."

"Then take me to the altar already."

Holding hands, they walked down the central, second-floor hallway of the remote hunting lodge on the shore of Lake Holley they'd rented for the occasion. She paused at a mirror along the way to make sure her hair, which she'd worn down and let Meg flat-iron, hadn't been too crazily mussed by the kisses. It hadn't.

The staircase ran down one side of the lodge's towering and rustic great room. Below, tables bearing appetizers and drinks waited at the ready. More arrangements of lilies. Flickering votive candles in circular glass holders. Creamy linens.

She and Gray hadn't wanted a stuffy service. So they weren't doing a wedding party or a unity candle or solos or poetry or programs or any of that. They simply wanted, so much they could hardly stand it, to get married.

Husband. And wife. Before God. And to share the day with their closest friends and family.

They passed through the lodge's enormous oak doors. The people standing on the wooded stretch of shoreline below broke into applause at the sight of them. There were a whole lot of Porters present. And Gray's mom and sister and his sister's kids. And a large number of jarringly oversized men who played football.

The one musician, a violinist, coaxed "Amazing Grace" from her instrument with notes unbelievably sweet and clear. An October breeze whisked through

Dru's hair, lifting some of the strands. It was that hour of the late afternoon when rays heavily tipped with bronze stretched down through the tree cover to dot the earth with sun.

The guests opened a path for them as they walked toward the waiting minister.

They passed Bo and Meg, who were each holding a baby and beaming. Bo made a gesture as if he was tipping his hat to her, and in his smile she could see the particular affection of an oldest brother for his youngest sibling.

Celia and Ty stood arm in arm, their four children around them. "You clean up good," Ty silently mouthed to her as she passed, then gave her a roguish wink.

They came even with Jake and Lyndie, who were holding hands. The face of the scarred and intimidating Porter brother lost its harsh cast as he nodded tenderly at Dru.

This was the end of an era for the Porters, Dru supposed, because after today they'd all be married.

They reached the minister, who stood with his back to the lake. The water's surface looked as though it had been painted with light by an Impressionist master. The last strains of "Amazing Grace" soared through the air. The trees sheltered them. Even though they weren't in a church, Dru could feel God's nearness. He was here. And His blessing was rich.

She turned to face Gray, still linked by the hands they'd joined back in the hallway. This was finally happening. They were getting married!

They smiled at each other, then he stepped forward for a kiss as if she'd called him to her with the force of her happiness. It was a very good kiss, a kiss that would be remembered for years to come.

"I love you," they whispered in unison when they stepped apart.

"I haven't even started the ceremony yet," the minister said, laughing.

Yes, today brought an end to something. But as Dru looked into Gray's face, all she could feel was uncontainable, joyous expectancy. Because this was the beginning of something, too, for both her and Gray.

The beginning of something beautiful.

See, I am doing a new thing!

Now it springs up; do you not perceive it?
I am making a way in the wilderness
and streams in the wasteland.

Isaiah 43:19